BAYSIDE
Romance

Bayside Summers
Love in Bloom Series

Melissa Foster

ISBN: 978-1948868358

BAYSIDE ROMANCE

Cover Design: Elizabeth Mackey Designs
Cover Photography: Sara Eirew Photography

PRINTED IN THE UNITED STATES OF AMERICA

A Note from Melissa

I've been waiting for the perfect hero for Harper Garner to speak to me since writing my Seaside Summers series. Harper is smart, careful, and family oriented. When I met Gavin Wheeler, I knew he was her man. Gavin is a brilliant designer, a loyal brother, and he's never forgotten the woman who touched his heart last summer. He also happens to be seriously sexy and knows how to have fun. I hope you enjoy their sexy love story as much as I do.

If you're an avid reader of my Love in Bloom series, you'll enjoy catching up with Harper's family, who are featured in the Seaside Summers series, and Gavin's brother, Beckett, who is featured in the Bradens & Montgomerys (Pleasant Hill – Oak Falls) series. If this is your first Love in Bloom novel, dive right in! All Love in Bloom stories are written to be enjoyed as stand-alone novels or as part of the larger series. For more information on Love in Bloom titles, visit www.MelissaFoster.com

I have more fun, sexy romances coming soon. Be sure to sign up for my newsletter so you don't miss them. www.MelissaFoster.com/Newsletter

FREE Love in Bloom Reader Goodies

If you love funny, sexy, and deeply emotional love stories, be sure to check out the rest of the Love in Bloom big-family romance collection and download your free reader goodies, including publication schedules, series checklists, family trees, and more!

www.MelissaFoster.com/RG

Remember to check my freebies page for periodic first-in-series free ebooks and other great offers!

www.MelissaFoster.com/LIBFree

Happy reading!

Melissa Foster

Chapter One

HARPER GARNER STARED at the blank page on her laptop screen, waiting for inspiration to hit. She'd thought she would be able to focus once she left Los Angeles, but if this flight home was any indication of her mental abilities, she was never going to write again. If only the guy sitting next to her would shut up. They were an hour into an almost-six-hour flight, and if he hit on her the whole way, she might end up stabbing him with her pen. Sure, *Trey* was hot, articulate, and well dressed in a dark designer suit, but if she'd learned one thing while working in Hollywood to help bring the pilot she'd written and sold to life, it was that guys could not be trusted. Neither could she apparently, but not trusting one's instincts was different from not being trustworthy.

"Are you heading to Boston for business or pleasure?" he asked.

He'd already told her he was on the tail end of a *round* of business trips, which she assumed was supposed to mean he was *important*. She was so sick of egotistical people, she could scream.

"You blocked?" He glanced at her laptop and said, "You know what I do when I hit a bump in the road?"

Her fingers curled around her laptop. Everything she'd written since her show was canceled a few weeks ago was crap. She had a month's work of rambling pages that weren't funny, sexy, or interesting. She tried not to snap, but months of pent-up frustrations poured out in sarcastic sass. "Let me guess. Make another notch in your Mile High Club belt? Or maybe you have a friend back home and you want to invite me to be the middle of your *manwich*? Listen, I'm sure many other women on this flight might take you up on a no-strings-attached fling, but I'm *not* that kind of girl." She couldn't stop the words from flying. "I've tried flings. *One* fling, exactly, and it was amazing, but then it was over, and *over* sucks. I think that's what left me vulnerable to the pretty-boy LA vultures, of which you are obviously one. And trust me, the others have already shown me that my taste in men sucks. I don't need to test that theory." She huffed out a breath, feeling immensely better.

His face went from confused to amused, and he belted out a laugh. "I'm not a talent agent, but if I were, that would have sold me."

Her jaw dropped open.

"Oh…" His eyes turned serious, and he rubbed his jaw. "You weren't acting? Well, shit. That sucks."

"I am *not* an actress. I'm a screenwriter. Or at least I was, before Los Angeles chewed me up and spit me out. Now I have to go home with my tail between my legs and tell everyone how much of a loser I am. So can we please *not* talk? I obviously can't be trusted not to sound like a bitch. I'm sorry. You didn't deserve to get the brunt of my bad mood."

He shrugged and said, "Or maybe I did." He flashed a warm smile. "I'll leave you to your staring."

He gazed out the window like her riot hadn't even ruffled

his feathers.

Harper spent the rest of the flight feeling like an idiot, writing exactly three words—*I am done*—and trying to figure out how to apologize to Trey. It wasn't his fault her life had fallen apart.

But by the time she figured out how to apologize, they were touching down and he was chatting on his phone. As she stepped into the aisle to leave, he tapped her shoulder, lowered his phone from his ear, and said, "Hey, Heartbreak, take this. I ran out of business cards." He shoved a piece of paper in her hand. "For when you get your mojo back. Not all people in the entertainment industry are assholes."

Before she could reply, he started talking into his phone again, and then she was swept into the line of people exiting the plane like rats from a sinking ship.

Harper rushed to the Cape Air gate so she wouldn't miss her connecting flight. When she was safely settled on the puddle jumper to Provincetown, she looked at the paper he'd given her, on which he'd written his phone number and *I run a TV streaming service. Call me when you turn all that energy into a screenplay. Trey*

She scoffed and shoved the paper into her purse. Being turned down by a guy she'd chewed out was one more level of embarrassment she didn't need to experience.

As the plane took off, she closed her eyes, wondering how she was going to face her friends.

THE HEAT OF the bonfire took away the sting of the cool bay breeze sweeping over Gavin Wheeler's skin as he sat with his feet in the sand and a cold beer in his hand, listening to his friend Drake Savage play the guitar. A few weeks ago Drake married Gavin's business partner and friend, Serena, in a small evening ceremony on the same beach where he had proposed. Gavin looked at Serena, who was chatting with their friends Chloe and Justin a few feet away. A year ago he never would have imagined giving up his high-powered interior design job at one of the nation's leading firms in Boston for a small partnership on Cape Cod, but it was the best move he'd ever made. He and Serena were both business-minded and put clients above greed for a bigger bottom line, which was just one thing that made them perfect partners. They were also down-to-earth and at the point in their lives where work simply wasn't enough for either of them. When Gavin had lived in Boston, he'd missed the camaraderie of close-knit friends like the ones he'd grown up with in Oak Falls, Virginia. Since he'd partnered with Serena and moved to the slower-paced Cape, the friends he'd made had already become like family, only better. No one here knew about all the crazy shit he'd done when he was younger.

"You guys should have seen the wife of one of our clients hitting on Gavin earlier today," Serena said as she tried to wrangle her long hair into a ponytail to keep it from blowing across her face. "I swear, the voluptuous Mrs. Cachelle had brass ones, didn't she, Gav?"

"What can I say? Babes dig me." Gavin took a swig of his beer.

Serena and Chloe rolled their eyes.

"Always the *woman whisperer*," Chloe said, sarcasm dripping from her every word. She was a blond smart-ass and a close friend.

"Thank God," Justin said with a laugh. "Best wingman

ever."

Gavin high-fived him.

He'd met Justin Wicked last fall, and they'd immediately hit it off. Justin was a leather-wearing, tattooed, bearded biker and a member of the Dark Knights motorcycle club. At face value, he was the complete opposite of Gavin's clean-cut athletic self. Justin was a sculptor, and they'd recently celebrated the opening of his show at a local gallery. In addition to being a successful artist, he and one of his brothers owned Cape Stone, a masonry and stone distribution company. Beneath that rough exterior, Justin was a smart, business-minded man who worked hard and played harder, just like Gavin. Gavin trusted Justin as much as he trusted his own brother. In fact, Justin was the only person who knew about Parker, the gorgeous, intelligent, down-to-earth blonde he'd hooked up with for one incredible night at a music festival in Romance, Virginia, last summer and couldn't get out of his mind. Like a teenager, he'd kept the matchbook from the inn where they'd stayed and had looked at it a million times over the past ten months, remembering the way they'd explored each other's bodies and how right she'd felt in his arms. Gavin had been a bit more careful with what he'd told Serena, leaving out Parker's name and where they'd met. She didn't need to know the sordid details of their incredible night together. When Serena had given him grief for not dating more often, he'd simply told her that there had been a woman he'd had a brief affair with and would have liked to have gotten to know better.

The one who got away.

Chloe looked at Gavin and said, "I've seen you in action, and I admit you can connect with most women, so *why* are you still single? I mean, I get why Justin is such a player. He has a rep to live up to."

"Damn right." Justin winked.

"Zip it, biker," Chloe said with a hint of a smile.

Justin held her gaze, leaning in so close it looked like he might kiss her as he said, "I'm happy to *unzip* it if you want to see what all the ladies are talking about."

Chloe rolled her eyes. "Pig. It's a wonder you get any women at all with lines like that. Maybe Gavin can give you lessons in being a gentleman."

Drake strummed his guitar louder and sang, "*Chloe has a crush on Gavin.*"

In addition to owning a chain of music stores, Drake co-owned Bayside Resort with his brother, Rick, and their buddy Dean Masters. The resort sat atop the dunes behind them, overlooking Cape Cod Bay.

"Get in the crush line, darlin'," Gavin said arrogantly. He got hit on by plenty of women, but in the ten months since he'd been with Parker, he hadn't met a single woman who could hold a candle to her.

Serena giggled.

Chloe sat back and crossed her arms, annoyance written all over her face. "Y'all are ridiculous. I'm being serious."

"Serious or *curious?*" Gavin waggled his brows.

Justin and Drake chuckled.

"*Ugh.* Never mind." Chloe grabbed Justin's beer and sucked it down.

Justin yanked on the ends of Chloe's hair. She'd grown her hair out from the pixie cut she'd had last summer, and Justin seemed to dig it.

"Babe, who else are we expecting?" Drake said to Serena, motioning toward the dunes, where a woman was coming off the path from Bayside Resort, heading in their direction. The breeze lifted her long hair from her shoulders, and her dress billowed around her legs.

"It's Harper!" Serena hollered. "I told you she'd come! Come on, Chloe."

Chloe sprang to her feet, and they sprinted toward the dunes.

Serena had been raving about her friend Harper, a screenwriter who had recently gotten her big break and had been in Los Angeles for the past several months. The way Serena went on about her, Gavin thought she had to be too good to be true.

"The fictional *wonder babe* has finally arrived?" Gavin scoffed. "We'll see if she lives up to the hype."

Justin stood up and said, "Oh *man*. She will. Harper's got it all going on."

"Care to wager on that? Fifty bucks says I won't think she's all that." Gavin took another drink of his beer.

"I'll take that bet," Drake said as he rose to his feet. He raked a hand through his dark hair and said, "Harper's cool."

"You're on." Gavin heard the girls giggling and stood to greet the infamous Harper.

The three girls were hugging as they stumbled through the sand, their hands moving animatedly, their voices carrying in the wind. His heart nearly stopped as the willowy blonde came into focus, the one who had haunted his dreams since last summer. Heat seared through his body, just as it had the first time he'd seen her, and that rainy afternoon came rushing back to him. It felt like only yesterday that he was standing on the slick, muddy ground, his heart hammering against his ribs, his eyes locked on Parker. She stood out from the crowd, looking a little lost and insanely beautiful in a bohemian-style cream dress with lace accents and an uneven hem, shorter in the front and back and longer on the sides, giving her an ethereal look, as if she'd been dropped from the heavens above just for him. Her hair had been tangled and damp from the rain. She'd worn about a dozen necklaces and just as many bangles on her wrists. Her brown boots had colorful dragonflies and stars all over them. She'd looked so freaking hot, he hadn't been able to look away then, just as he was unable to now.

"*Parker*," Gavin said absently as she embraced Drake.

"*Harper*," Serena corrected him. "Geez, Gavin, what's wrong with you?"

Harper? Unless the woman whose body he remembered more intimately than any other had a twin, his Parker was Serena's Harper. She'd left to catch a flight before the sun had risen the morning after they'd been together, and she hadn't woken him up to say goodbye. He'd been so into her, into *them*, he'd never gotten around to asking for her phone number, or even her last name. Hell, he didn't even know what she did for a living.

Now he did. She was a screenwriter, and apparently a good one, a beloved friend to the people he'd gotten close to, and best of all, she lived on the Cape, and hopefully she was back to stay.

Harper spotted him. Their eyes connected, and for a moment he was thrown back to that night, his hands and mouth traveling over her hot flesh, her sinful noises filling the room.

Her brows knitted, and a smile stretched across her beautiful face, and just as quickly, that stunning smile faded. "*Gavin?* What are *you* doing here?"

"I live here," he said.

Shock rose in her eyes, as tangible as the surprise gripping his chest.

Chloe's eyes moved between him and Harper. "You two know each other? But you said you didn't think Harper was real."

Gavin couldn't take his eyes off her. "Because she's Parker, not Harper."

"Dude, *she's* your *Parker*?" Justin said with shock.

Gavin nodded.

"Parker? Who's Parker?" Chloe asked. "I'm so confused."

"I think *I* am," Harper said.

"You told me your name was *Parker*." *Sweet Jesus*, she was even more gorgeous than he'd remembered, but her powder-blue eyes narrowed angrily, and she stepped back, holding her hands up between them. *What the hell?*

"No. You misheard me, and I didn't correct you." She looked accusatorily at him. "You said you were from Virginia."

"I *am*."

She swallowed hard, worry suddenly shadowing her eyes. His mind raced through the night they'd spent together, looking for a reason she'd be short with him, and as the things she'd said came rushing back, his gut clenched. She'd said a one-night stand was totally out of character for her. He hadn't believed her at first, but the longer they'd talked, the clearer it had become that she was telling the truth. Was that why she was worried?

Her gaze shot nervously toward the girls. "*How* do you know him?"

"He's my business partner," Serena said. "I told you I opened my own business. Gavin was a senior designer at the firm in Boston where I went to work."

Harper stole glances at him as Serena reminded her about how their partnership came to be. He wanted to pull her aside and tell her they didn't know about their night together, but Serena and Chloe were peppering her with questions.

"How do you know Gavin?" Chloe asked. "Did you know him before you went to LA?"

"We met at a music festival," Harper said, eyeing him nervously.

"Where? When?" Serena shot a confused look at Gavin. "You've been in LA and Gavin has been here except over the holidays."

"It was before I moved to the Cape," Gavin explained. "Now, how about you guys give Harper room to breathe. She looks like she could use a beer."

"Yes!" Chloe exclaimed, and they headed for the cooler.

Gavin grabbed Harper's arm and lowered his voice as he said, "Don't worry. Your friends don't know about our night together. Justin knows we hooked up, but he won't say anything."

Her jaw clenched, her eyes trained on the others as they pulled drinks from the cooler. She didn't look at him as she said, "There's nothing to tell, *right*?"

"Don't be like that," he said, shocked at her coldness. Had he fabricated their connection? Turned it into something that wasn't real? "It's good to see you again."

She turned those stunning eyes on him and wrenched her arm free. "You never even called, so it's not *that* good."

Harper stalked across the beach to the girls, leaving Gavin to wonder how the hell he was supposed to have called a woman whose real name he hadn't even known.

"You okay, man?" Justin asked as Gavin sat beside him. "You look shell-shocked, which I totally get now that I know Harper's the girl you've been comparing all others to. But, man, she doesn't appear happy to see you."

No, she didn't, and Gavin was going to find out why if it was the last thing he did.

Chapter Two

"LA WAS AMAZING," Harper gushed. She sat on a blanket between Chloe and Serena, showing off pictures on her phone, while her friends hung on her every word. "The weather is unbelievable, and the men and women are all gorgeous. It's a whole different world from here. The people there are *refined*. Even when they're dressed down, they possess an air of elegance that makes you want to *be* them. And there was *always* a party to go to or a movie premiere being planned…"

Gavin noticed Harper's laugh wasn't as carefree as it had been at the festival, and she was purposely avoiding eye contact with him. Her blond hair whipped around her shoulders, and she continually tucked it behind her ear, a nervous habit he remembered fondly. As familiar as she seemed, something about her was different. He couldn't put his finger on exactly what it was, but the woman who was raving about parties and luncheons was not the same woman he'd met that rainy afternoon. That woman had been more interested in walking through a small town, learning the history of the area, and exploring the shops than partying at a festival with rock stars.

Could she have changed that much in ten months?

"What are the studios like?" Chloe asked. "Are they as they

appear in movies, with famous people riding around on golf carts? Did you meet a lot of actors?"

"They're just like that. But actors have handlers, so it wasn't like I could walk up and ask for an autograph or anything." Harper's eyes flicked in Gavin's direction, and the space between them sizzled.

He hadn't imagined their connection after all.

Her cheeks pinked up, and she quickly looked away to answer more questions. She flashed her pearly whites, talking animatedly, but she was trying too hard. There was something fake about her actions and even her voice inflection. Was she trying to impress her friends? Impress *him*? Why would she do either? And why was it bugging him so much?

He ground his teeth together, knowing exactly why. Gavin didn't like fake people, and the night they'd spent together, there hadn't been an ounce of fakeness about her. She'd been heartbreakingly honest, so why did it feel like she was hiding something now? Was the stress of keeping the secret about their night together causing her to act like this? Or was there something more? He hated seeing her like this. Why weren't her girlfriends questioning her behavior? Did they even *notice* that she was acting strangely?

Damn it. He needed to know what was going on.

"What happens now?" Serena asked. "When do you go back?"

Harper lowered her gaze to the blanket, focusing on her index finger tracing a pattern as she said, "Gosh, I'm not sure. I never realized how much red tape there was in Hollywood. It could be a while."

In that instant, he knew something was definitely wrong. The Harper he knew wasn't a *gosh, I'm not sure* kind of woman.

She was confident, direct, and when he'd met her, she was *overly* knowledgeable about the festival's history and the background of the artists who were performing. She'd done her homework, despite having decided to attend only a few days before her spur-of-the-moment adventure.

"Now that we have the scoop on your trip, I want to know what's happening *here*." Chloe pointed between Gavin and Harper. "Between you and Gavin."

If anything, having their affair scrutinized would only make Harper more uncomfortable.

"I'd like to find that out myself," Gavin said as he pushed to his feet, heading for Harper, unwilling to allow anyone to make her more uncomfortable or let her play more games. They'd shared an incredible night, and he wasn't about to let her forget how great it was. "What do you say, Harp? Let's catch up." He took Harper's arm and lifted her to her feet.

Serena eyed them curiously, and Gavin wondered if she'd figured out that Harper was the woman he'd told her about.

"What are you doing?" Harper whispered harshly.

Gavin turned his face away from the others and said, "Getting some answers. You might be able to fool everyone else, but I'm not buying those fake smiles you're doling out." He grabbed her purse and said, "We're going for a walk. Don't wait around. This might take a while."

Harper's jaw dropped open.

Drake began strumming the tune to "Wrecking Ball." Their friend's curious comments carried in the air as Gavin led Harper away from the group.

"I DON'T KNOW what you think you're doing, but a guy who doesn't call after everything we did together doesn't deserve my attention." Harper tried to sound annoyed, but she couldn't hide how breathless she felt, and she hoped Gavin didn't notice. She might be taking a hiatus from men at the moment, but that didn't mean she was immune to Gavin Wheeler's good looks, his charm, or the memories of how all her inhibitions had fallen away when she was in his arms. Dragging her along a beach wasn't exactly *charming*, but the fact that he'd seen through her smoke and mirrors when the friends who had known her for years hadn't noticed was definitely...*something*.

He looked at her out of the corner of his wily green eyes and said, "Do I look like Houdini to you? How the hell would I have gotten your number when I didn't even have your *name* right? Which, by the way, you could have clued me in on. I've been fantasizing about Parker when it should have been Harper."

"Like that would have made a difference? I can't imagine you name your spank-bank inspirations."

He released her arm, slowing his pace without saying another word. She glanced over her shoulder, surprised to see how far they'd walked. The bonfire was merely a blur in the distance. After a long silence, Gavin stopped walking and moved in front of her, so she had no choice but to look at him.

All her womanly parts sparked to life, remembering the hungry touches, the thoughtful whispers, and the steamy, toe-curling kisses from the tall, handsome man before her. His brown hair was tousled from the wind, standing up in sexy little spikes, just as it had the morning she'd snuck out of their room at the bed-and-breakfast where they'd spent the night together. The other festivalgoers slept in tents and vans on the festival grounds. But not Gavin. He had a room at the Wysteria Inn, a cute B and B walking distance from the festival. He'd said he liked creature comforts and that had made Harper even more attracted to him. While she was an earthy gal who enjoyed being outside, she'd gone to the festival with her younger brother, Colton, and the idea of sleeping in his van hadn't appealed to her. But they'd both thought she'd needed to cut loose for once in her life, and the festival was her foray into doing just that. She was going to LA, after all, and as Colton had pointed out, *Little Miss Straitlaced needed a little experience before heading to the other side of the country.* She hadn't expected Colton to abandon her so quickly. But he was a huge fan of Axsel Montgomery, the lead singer in the band Inferno, and shortly after they'd arrived, Colton had gone *Axsel stalking.* Harper had been ready to head into town and do some shopping when she'd met Gavin.

What had followed was her first and only one-night stand.

It was the best night of her life.

Until it was over.

"So, I'm sorry for dragging you off like that, but…" Gavin said, jarring her from her thoughts.

Crap. She'd totally zoned out and had no idea what he'd said.

"Are you okay?" he asked.

"What? Fine. Why? I was just thinking."

He slipped his hands into the pockets of his black zip-up sweatshirt, studying her face. "Look, Harper, I don't know what's going on with you right now, or what that was all about back there, but it feels like something is off."

She sure hadn't had trouble talking the night they'd met. Or doing anything else, including dirty things she'd never thought she'd do with a man.

"I'm sure you think I'm crazy," he said, "because I don't know you that well, but you can talk to me. Whether you're over what we had or not, you have to admit that we had an intense connection, and it stuck with me."

She stood up a little straighter, as touched by his thoughtfulness as she was annoyed with herself for liking it. She crossed her arms, needing a barrier between the warm and enticing memories swirling inside her head and the man who'd caused them.

"If that's true, then why didn't you call me? I left you my number."

"You did? Where? I never saw it."

"Come on, Gavin. Can't you be more original than that? Just say you weren't interested in anything more than that night. It's what we agreed on anyway. But if you're looking for another, I told you I'm not a one-night-stand girl."

"You want original? How's this?" He stepped closer, his expression serious. "You blew me away that night, and not just because the sex was out of this world. But *you*, Harper. The woman I met that night was unlike any other person I know. If there had been a chance in hell that I could have seen you again, I'd have sold my fucking soul to do it. But *Parker* left before I even woke up. *Parker*, the woman who didn't really exist, never gave me a chance to take her to breakfast and ask for her number."

Her heart slammed against her ribs. The honesty in his eyes and his voice made her heart take notice, just as it had the first night. She swallowed hard, unable to think fast enough to respond before he spoke again.

"Tell me you didn't feel it, too," he challenged.

I did feel it! I tried not to, but I did.

After everything she'd been through in Los Angeles, she didn't want to put herself out there again. She'd already lied to her friends, which she'd never done before, and she was avoiding her family because her life was such a mess. She didn't need to get tangled up in something that would probably end badly, no matter how hot, manly, and earnest Gavin was. Instead of responding to his challenge, she said, "I wrote down my number and put it in the front zipper pocket of your suitcase."

His jaw tightened, and his gaze drifted out over the water as a small smile lifted his lips. He met her gaze and said, "I don't suppose you'd believe me if I told you I never looked there. Does anyone even use those pockets? You can't fit anything in them."

A laugh came out before she had time to process her thoughts, and that laugh earned one of his, which was deep and rumbly and so real she wanted to capture the happy sound to replay it later. He was right; those pockets were awful. She didn't even know why they made them or why she thought that was the one place it wouldn't get overlooked.

"That's the trouble. I *do* believe you," she confessed. "You would have known my real name if you'd seen it. I put my real name on the paper with my phone number. Sorry about the whole *Parker* thing, by the way. When you mistook my name, I figured I should go along with it to remain in a mysterious one-night-stand persona. And then, when I wanted to correct you, so many hours had passed, I just let it go. But it doesn't matter now. You have no idea what I've been through. I am not someone you want to get involved with."

"How about you tell me what you've been through and let

me decide for myself?" He touched her arm, his green eyes turning softer, urging her to let down her walls.

The wind carried his aftershave. It was a scent she'd never forgotten in all the months since she'd seen him. He smelled as *honest* as he spoke, which was odd in regard to a scent, but deeply reassuring. His aftershave smelled like him—potent yet understated, stable and trustworthy. He didn't need the pomp and circumstance that many men did, or to put on a facade to toughen him up in the eyes of others. He was confident in his own skin, the way Harper used to be in hers.

"You're kidding, right? Nobody wants to hear someone else's troubles."

"I want to hear yours, Harper. You left your entire life behind the weekend we met, and you moved across the country for an impressive adventure. I've heard all about that from your friends. Now I know our night together was the springboard to all those changes, and you managed to keep all those life changes and how you felt about them under wraps that whole night. Do you realize how brave you are? You're impressive as hell. You didn't seem like a woman who rattled easily, but something got to you, and I want to hear what it was."

"I don't feel very brave or impressive at the moment. I'm actually feeling pretty inadequate."

"All the more reason to talk it out."

She summoned the bravery he saw in her and said, "Can we walk while we talk?"

As they started to stroll along the shore again, he put his hand on her lower back and said, "You're shivering."

It was May, which meant comfortable breezy days and chilly nights, but she was more nervous than cold. Gavin shrugged off his sweatshirt and put it around her shoulders, leaving him in a snug gray Henley. Her mind went straight to what the muscles outlined by the fabric felt like.

"Thanks," she said, trying to change the direction of her thoughts. "You sure you want to hear this?"

He nodded with the playful smile that had first won her over. "Yes, I do."

"It's crazy, you'll never believe it, and you can't tell anyone."

"You sure do like your privacy."

"Is that a problem?"

He shook his head, holding her gaze. "No, sweetheart. I like mine, too."

"Okay." She inhaled a calming breath and said, "It started when I met you. Remember how I told you that I'd never had a one-night stand before?" She didn't wait for an answer. "That was true. I'm not a fling girl, but my younger brother suggested a no-strings-attached night would make me less uptight, more open to new experiences. And I know brothers don't usually suggest those things. My older brother would kill us both if he knew. But since my sister, Jana, used to *only* have flings and she fell in love and married one of them, I figured I'd give it a shot. Jana and Hunter are *so* happy together, it's like they were made for each other."

"Whoa, I know a Hunter and a Jana. How many Hunter and Jana's can there be? Hunter owns Grunter's Ironworks. Is that them?"

She should have figured he knew them since he knew the rest of her friends. "Yes."

"I met them one night when I was with Justin at Undercover. It really is a small world. I had no idea Jana was your sister. Hell, I didn't even think you—*Harper*—really existed. Your friends think the world of you, by the way. And now I know why, *Parker*," he said with a lift of his brows. "Wait, that means I know your older brother, Brock, too, right?"

"Yes. He owns the boxing club in Eastham." Eastham was a neighboring town.

"Ah, the pieces of the *Parker aka Harper* puzzle are all coming together. And Colton, the one who owns Undercover?"

"Colton's my younger brother. He's the one who took me to the festival and convinced me to do the whole no-strings thing."

Gavin's face turned serious again. "The one who left you *alone*? Selfishly, I'm glad he took off because I got to have you all to myself that night, but you could have ended up with a dirtbag. I've got to have a talk with him."

"No, please don't," she said, feeling *way* too good about his protectiveness. "That was my fault. I told him I'd be fine if he went off to stalk the guy he was there to see."

"The lead singer of Inferno. I remember you telling me that."

"How do you remember? You were pretty drunk."

"Nah," he said coyly. "I'd had a few, but I acted drunker than I was."

"Why would you do that?" She wasn't a big drinker, and she'd probably dumped more beer on the ground as they danced than she'd actually drank. She was glad they were walking, because she couldn't stop smiling and she probably looked like a fool. That was how it had been that first day, too. He'd instantly eased her discomfort with his candor and kindness. And those eyes. *God, his eyes.* They said *trust me*, and she had, just as she was now.

"Because you were all, 'This is a one-time thing,' and I didn't want to get weird about it and scare you off. Clingy guys suck."

"Somehow I don't think you're a clingy guy. So why did you really do it?"

He flashed that boyish smile again. "It was easier to pretend I was drunk and concentrate on that than to let you see how much I liked being with you. I hadn't expected to have feelings for you that were bigger than a one-time thing."

His arm slipped around her waist. The sounds of the waves crashing against the shore competed with the rush of blood through her ears and his deep voice as he said, "Or how incredibly hot and sexy you were when we were tangled up in the sheets. I've got to tell you, Harp, I'm not hearing about much trouble in your life."

Lordy, this man…

He was warm and strong and pulled off being a gentleman *and* a sexual god, which she knew firsthand he excelled at. She wiggled out from his grasp before she could forget the reason she *wasn't* supposed to want to jump his bones.

"I have a feeling I'm walking down the beach with trouble. Let's get back to all the reasons I can't do this with you." *I need the reminder.*

"Do what?"

"Fall back into your arms."

A cocky grin appeared, and he said, "But we fit so well to-gether. It's not every day that you find someone whose favorite muffin is the exact same as yours."

"Ah, I see. This is about our mutual love of chocolate-banana muffins." They'd discovered their shared love of the muffins when they were checking out a bakery in Virginia.

"It's *all* about the muffins. What's a little closeness between friends? We're not sleeping together. I'm just offering you comfort."

He reached for her hand, and damn her traitorous fingers, she took it.

"Now you may continue with your story."

He made it sound so easy, when just being close to him again brought back all the things he'd done and said that made her want to go right back to that night and experience it all over again.

She struggled to push those thoughts away and said, "After our night together—which didn't end like a *fling* since I left you my number, whether or not you found it. That just proves that I suck at flings—I went to LA to work on my script, which was being turned into a television show. I was in a new place where I didn't know anyone and totally out of my comfort zone. But I dug in my heels, and eventually I made a few friends and started dating someone. I thought things were pretty good. Thank goodness I didn't sleep with him, though."

"I know I'm thanking whoever *goodness* is for that."

"Right? It turned out that he was bisexual and he was looking for another person he and his partner could share. Um, no thank you. Not that I have anything against bisexuals. My brother Colton is gay, by the way."

"I know. He hit on me a few weeks ago at Undercover."

"Sounds like Colton. Well, I thought a fling was out of my comfort zone, but a threesome wasn't even on my radar."

"Seriously? *Damn.*" He stopped walking and huffed out a breath. "Guess we're done." He started walking back the way they'd come.

"Oh my God! See? My radar with guys is so messed up." She closed her eyes, and in the split second it took for her to sigh, he barreled into her, lifting her off the ground. She shrieked as he spun her around. "Gavin! Stop!"

He laughed as he set her on her feet, but he didn't let go. He held her close, laughing with her.

"You're crazy!" she said happily. He knew just how to cheer her up.

"Maybe a little. Sit with me." He took her hand, pulling her down to the sand beside him. "I just needed to get you out of your own head for a minute. So you got picked up for a potential *thruple* expedition. That just means you're hot and you seemed open to new experiences, which I happen to know you are, seeing as how we did our own *exploring*." He waggled his brows.

Heat rushed up her chest and neck. She'd been uncharacter-istically, shockingly uninhibited and free with him. They'd explored each other's bodies, playing out fantasies and trying new things like they'd been lovers forever. She'd felt so connected, so in sync with him, she'd let him do things no man ever had, and she'd loved every second of it. It wasn't until later, on the long flight to LA the next morning, that she'd wondered if he'd believed her when she'd said she'd never been that wild before. But even then, she hadn't felt embarrassed. She'd wanted to be with him again, just as she did now.

And that was a problem.

She tried again to push those desires aside and said, "But it also means I'm not catching the clues I should be."

"Maybe, maybe not." He leaned back casually, as if he'd heard it all before.

"Okay, well, that's just the start of my nightmare. After that guy, I met a man in a café on the studio lot, and we dated for a few weeks. We really hit it off, and things were great—"

"I'm not hearing the *thanking goodness* part I'm hoping to

hear…"

She laughed softly. "Yeah, well, I can't imagine you haven't been with a number of women since I last saw you."

"A couple," he admitted. "But they weren't you, so they didn't count."

"Oh, is that the rule?" She dug her toes into the sand and quickly said, "Don't answer that."

He sat up, gently taking her chin between his finger and thumb and drawing her face toward his. The intimacy of that touch made her heart race.

"Yes, that's the rule," he said with a gently authoritative tone. "They weren't you, and I never thought about them again, so they didn't count. Whereas you count very, very much."

The look in his eyes was so intense, she looked away before she could follow her thundering heart and do something she couldn't take back. "Anyway," she said a little breathlessly, "it turned out he was *engaged*. His fiancée caught us together at his place. I have never been so mortified or felt so awful." She looked at Gavin to try to read his expression and was glad to see concern rather than judgment. "That poor woman called me horrible names, and I couldn't even defend myself because I had no idea who she was or what was going on. I'd never intentionally be with a guy who was involved with someone else. She must have told everyone she knew, because rumors spread through the set, and my reputation was ruined. Then my show wasn't picked up, and my agent dropped me, and I just lied to my friends about all of it. I've *never* lied to my friends. I'm not a liar. I *despise* liars. But I managed to look them in the eyes and tell them tales of a fabulous life I never led."

"Technically speaking, you didn't look them in the eyes when you lied."

"That doesn't make it okay."

"Maybe not," he said carefully. "But it's how I knew you were hiding something."

She looked out at the moonlight reflecting off the water. It was so easy to be honest with Gavin. "I went to LA thinking I was making a name for myself. I was starry-eyed and proud. *Beyond* proud. Most producers and directors have their own writers for script modifications and that sort of thing. But they'd hired *me* to not only help tweak the scripts, but also to give my input during production. That's huge, and I know the producer I worked with wasn't a big-time guy or anything, but I'm just a small-town nobody. So to me it was huge."

"I doubt you've ever been a *nobody*, Harper."

"Thank you." She felt a little better having shared her burden. "A couple summers ago I was hired to write a racy sitcom for cable. I worked from home or in coffee shops and only went to New York for meetings. That experience was so different from this last one. I went to LA thinking I was making it big, making my parents and my friends proud." She shrugged as if it were easy to admit, but the pain in her chest was excruciating. "I was the girl who obeyed all the rules and did *everything* right. I studied hard through college, didn't party too much, have had exactly *one* fling, thank you very much, and still I managed to ruin my life."

"You've only ruined your life if you give those experiences that much power. And if it counts for anything, we had one hell of a fling. Not a day has passed that I haven't thought about you."

Her heart squeezed, realizing he'd thought about her as much as she'd thought about him. "Really? You're not just saying that?"

He nodded. "I've got no reason to lie, and I'd like to pick up where we left off."

"Gavin, I can't. I don't trust myself with guys right now."

"I hear that. It's okay. Eventually you'll be able to, and I'm a patient guy."

"*Confident* is probably a better word," she said, feeling happier than she had in a long time. "I'm sorry my life is so messed up. I haven't been able to write anything good since they canceled the show, and now here I am, lying to my friends and avoiding my family. I haven't even told my family I'm back in town."

"Why not?"

"Because I already lied to them, too. My brothers and sister called and texted all the time just to make sure I was okay. I didn't want them to worry, so I let them believe things were great, even when it looked like the show was falling apart. I was at the high point of my career, and I swear being out there, away from the people who know me best, made me feel like I was drifting. I don't know how to recover from it. I'm ashamed of everything that went on. Even though my family doesn't need to know about all of the personal stuff, *I* know it. The thing is, they knew I wasn't an LA type of girl, and they were there for me, holding my hand from thousands of miles away. Just last week I told them things were going well." She shook her head. "*Ugh.* I'm such a loser. Jana would have done great out there, but I'm not her any more than I am the fling girl I pretended to be with you."

"I've got news for you, Harp. You didn't do a very good job of pretending with me, either."

"But you just said you thought about me every day since we were together."

He held her gaze and said, "Exactly."

He didn't say anything more. She'd forgotten how good a listener he was and how the long pauses between them hadn't felt uncomfortable or like they needed to be filled. They felt natural. He was a careful thinker, and now she remembered how he'd taken his time before speaking, like he was now, and how much she liked that about him.

After a while he said, "Have you forgotten how we opened up to each other? You told me I was your first one-night stand, and I told you I wasn't a sleeping-around kind of guy. You tried to come across like you were cool with the one-night-stand idea, but I don't think either of us really was."

He paused again, as if he knew she was remembering each and every detail he'd just mentioned.

"When you have a meaningless one-night stand, the person you choose to have it with is usually forgettable." He moved his hand closer to hers, brushing his fingers over the back of her hand as he said, "I knew before we went back to my room that you were special, but I never imagined just how impossible it would be to stop thinking about you."

"Now you're embarrassing me, *and* my broken guy radar is telling me that you might be really good at picking up girls and not to fall for all your best lines."

He smiled. "Your guy radar *is* off, because these aren't my best lines, Harp."

"I'm *so* not ready for this. I need practice before I'm ready for a guy like you. I might never be ready for a guy like you, because you seem open and honest, but my instincts suck right now."

"Then let's fix that." His expression turned serious and he said, "I'll set you up on practice dates."

"Oh, no." She waved her hand. "I've practiced and failed enough." She yawned. "Sorry. It's been a long day. I chewed out this guy on the plane, lied to my friends, and now you're making me wish I trusted my instincts."

"Because you should." He stood, reaching for her hand. "Come on, I'll walk you back to your car and tell you about this friend of mine."

"No friends," she said as she pushed to her feet.

He draped an arm over her shoulder, keeping her close. "I said I was a patient guy, but I'm no fool. If you need to rebuild your man-confidence, there's no way you're doing it with just any old guy."

"I'm not doing it at all," she grumbled.

"You're too incredible to be off the market forever, and you're not getting any younger." He tickled her ribs with the tease.

"Hey!"

"Just sayin'. I'm not getting any younger either, so we have to move on this before age takes its toll and I get a beer gut and lose this amazing body."

She laughed.

"Anyway, I've got this friend, and I can vouch for him. He's handsome, smart, and funny. He'll treat you like a lady."

A breeze swept off the water, and she leaned into him, stealing his warmth. "You don't seriously want to set me up with a guy."

"Not just any guy. Like I said, he's almost as good as me, but not quite as handsome."

"Then why would I go out with him?" she teased as a wave crashed, sending water rushing toward them. Gavin lifted her off her feet, carrying her quickly away from the water.

"Because you need the practice, and I trust him." He set her toes in the sand, pulling her close again as they walked down the beach.

With the wind at their backs, the scents of the sea and *Gavin* filled her with happiness. "I missed being here more than I realized."

"Aren't California beaches supposed to be better?"

"They're not. I'm not sure any place is better than here. I love the cold Cape wind at night and the way people dress comfortably instead of impressively. There's a sense of comfort living where I grew up."

They must have been gone a long time, because their friends were no longer on the beach and they'd put out the bonfire. Bayside Resort came into view on the dunes, alongside the Summer House Inn, which her friends Desiree and Violet owned. She missed them, too, and she missed seeing everyone at the breakfasts Desiree and Violet hosted for all their friends. Drake and the guys from Bayside jogged together in the mornings and then joined the girls at the inn for breakfast.

As they headed up the path toward the parking lot of the resort, Gavin said, "We're going to work on your writing, too."

"*Too* implies we're working on something else."

He pulled her closer and said, "Don't fight it, Harp. We're going to make sure your instincts work, your writing gets back on track, *and* you stop lying to the people who love you."

His low, confident voice sent a shiver of heat down her spine. It had been a long time since that had happened. Since they were last together, to be exact.

"What makes you think you can help me fix any of that?" she asked as they reached the top of the dunes and headed across the lawn to the parking lot.

"Because I'm an excellent *guide*. Think about it. We nailed your first one-night stand, didn't we? This should be a piece of cake."

"We did not nail it as far as no-strings goes, though." She dug in her purse for her keys.

"We did too damn good of a job. If you'd just slipped up and given me your real name, or said you were a screenwriter or that you'd just moved to LA, maybe I could have connected the dots and found you sooner. We've wasted a lot of time."

He took the keys from her hand and opened her car door. He dangled the keys with a cocky grin that made her insides hot. She wished she had told him those things, but she'd listened to Colton and kept her personal information to herself. Well, other than the note in his suitcase, which hadn't done her any good anyway.

"We've got this, Harp. Now, what's your address?"

She reached for the keys, and he lifted them out of her reach. "Gavin…"

"I told you I'm a patient guy. I can stand here all night long, or you can give me your address."

"Has anyone ever told you that you're kind of a pain?"

"I can't think of anyone who hasn't."

"I need *time* to figure out my life, not *dates* with men I don't care about," she said, not having any idea what she really needed. But having a friend like Gavin seemed like a good start.

He set the keys in her hand and settled his hand on her hip. Her body flamed as he leaned in, as if to kiss her. Somewhere in her head warning bells were going off, but she closed her eyes. Her lips parted in anticipation of the kiss she'd thought about for too long.

"Your address, Harper?" he whispered over her lips.

As if he'd unblocked a damn, her address rushed out.

"He'll be there at seven." He pressed a kiss to her cheek. His hand slipped off her hip, and the air around her chilled as he stepped back and said, "Have fun tomorrow night."

She stood with her mouth agape for the third time that night, which was three times too many. Gavin waved and headed for his car.

"I'm *not* going!" she called after him.

"That's your prerogative, beautiful." He pushed a button on his key fob and his headlights flashed. "But I'm a kick-ass friend, so I'm still setting it up."

Chapter Three

"THAT SOUNDS PERFECT," Gavin said into the phone Friday afternoon when Serena came through the doors of Mallery and Wheeler Interior Design.

She plunked her messenger bag down on her desk, her high heels clicking on the hardwood floors. Gavin pointed to the samples he'd laid out earlier for a new boutique they were designing for Ocean Edge Resort, the largest luxury resort on the Cape. Serena gave him a thumbs-up and went to review them as he finished his call and confirmed his appointment for the following week.

When he ended the call, he said, "How'd the pitch go?"

Serena had pitched their services to the owners of the Wharf, a restaurant in Orleans. They had been referred through Jared Stone, who was one of their most prominent clients. They'd handled the interior design of a restaurant in Province-town for Jared over the winter.

"Do you even have to ask?" She carried over a ring of fabric samples and sat on the edge of his desk. "I'll put the contract together next week and get it over to their legal team. Once it's signed, we'll figure out the best time for our initial design meeting. I'll check your online calendar before I schedule anything."

"Sounds good. I just confirmed the Ocean Edge meeting for Tuesday with Mia. I'll get it on the calendar." Mia Stone was Jared's sister, though Gavin had only recently learned they were related. Mia was the assistant to world-renowned fashion designers Josh and Riley Braden, whose main offices were in Manhattan. They were opening a new boutique at the resort, which was owned by Josh's brother, real-estate mogul Treat Braden. Treat was making changes to the property to appeal to families of varying economic statuses rather than only the upper class. The new boutique, Coastal Enchantments, was one of those changes.

"Great. These are gorgeous, by the way." She ran her hand over the fabric samples and said, "Almost as gorgeous as *Harper*."

"Real subtle, Serena."

"Almost as subtle as doodling her name on your notebook. What are you, twelve?"

He glanced at his notes from a call he'd had earlier with a woman who'd rambled incessantly, and he was shocked to see he had in fact doodled Harper's name. He closed the notebook, cursing under his breath. The first thing he'd done when he'd gotten home last night was check the front pocket of his suitcase for Harper's number. He'd found it just where she'd said it was. He could have kicked himself for not checking there last summer, when he'd scoured the surface of every piece of furniture in their room at the inn, hoping she'd left a note.

"I want all the details!" Serena set down the fabrics, her eyes wide with curiosity. "The way you hauled her down the beach made it look like you two were a lot more than friends at that music festival."

"We had a connection," he said more casually than he felt.

"So are you two an item now? You'd be really great together."

"I'd love to be dating her, but no. She's not ready for that." He hoped to change that sooner rather than later.

"Why not? Unless she isn't into you, which I can't imagine would be the case." She glanced out the window, her brow wrinkled in concentration. "Or maybe you weren't that good when you hooked up…"

Gavin pushed to his feet and said, "This conversation is over, but just for the record, you couldn't be more wrong. *Unforgettable* is more like it."

Serena hopped to her feet with a loud, "Aha! You did hook up! I knew it. Chloe said she didn't think you had because Harper never hooks up with guys, or at least she never used to. This is so exciting! Two of my best friends together." She grabbed Gavin's hand and dragged him toward the couch. "You have to tell me *everything*."

He yanked his hand away and said, "Forget it, Serena. I'm not sharing all the dirty details of our night with you."

"Okay…so it was *one* night. Got it. Did you talk afterward, while she was in California?"

He sat on the edge of his desk and crossed his arms. "No. You heard me last night. I thought her name was *Parker*. I didn't even know her last name—"

"You know what? The more I think about this, the more I'm not buying it. That's not who Harper is. There's something you're not telling me."

He shrugged. "Have you ever known me to lie?"

"No, which makes this even more curious." She sat down on the couch, drumming her fingers on the cushions, her mouth twisting in concentration.

"You can stop wondering, because that's all there is. We met, we connected for a night, and then we had no contact until she appeared at the bonfire."

"But you didn't look like that was all there was last night." Her eyes widened. "Oh my gosh. She's *the one*, isn't she?" She pushed to her feet, not waiting for an answer as she paced the floor of their cozy office, talking a mile a minute. "The one you told me about? The woman you had a brief affair with and hadn't been able to stop thinking about? A *night* is a brief affair. And I've never seen you go after a woman like you did last night with Harper."

She looked at him, and he shrugged.

"Oh no, Gavin. You are not getting away with being coy. You said you'd like to be dating her but she's not ready, so what are you doing about it? And why isn't she ready?"

He wasn't going to breach Harper's confidence, so he said, "She's got a lot going on and she's not keen on dating at the moment."

"So what?" Serena threw her hands up in frustration. "Nobody has more going on than I did when Drake and I got together. I was living in *two* cities, for Pete's sake. What are you going to do about it?"

"I set her up on a blind date with a buddy of mine."

"You *what*?" She was on the move again, wearing a path in the floor. "Why would you do that? I thought you were smart, but boy, that's the dumbest thing I've ever heard. Who'd you set her up with? Justin? Dwayne? Cory? Because none of those guys are right for Harper."

He chuckled at her vehemence, although she was right about those friends. Justin and his cousin Dwayne were too aggressive for Harper, and Cory wasn't Gavin, which made him all kinds of wrong.

"Don't worry about it. I've got it covered."

She rolled her eyes. "Are you that clueless? Do I need Drake to give you a lesson in taking control?"

"Hardly."

"You're going to lose your chance, and then you'll wish you had balls enough to walk right up to her and tell her she's making a big mistake passing you up." She stopped pacing and glared at him. "You have no idea how great Harper is if you're willing to set her up with some other guy."

"I've jumped too fast and been burned before, Serena, and I'm not into repeating past mistakes. Not that I think Harper would ever be a mistake, but she's too important for me to rush into something she may not be ready for and risk ruining it. To be honest, I was completely blown away last night when I saw her. I never thought I'd see her again, and yes, she's the woman I told you about. But she doesn't need to be the center of Bayside drama or pressured into going out with me by you and the gossip girls. I know what she and I had in Virginia was special, but her well-being is more important to me than claiming her as my girlfriend. So take a deep breath, Serena. Chill out and let me do things my way."

"Wow." She sat down again. "Thanks for reminding me who you are."

He went to the couch and sat beside her. "What's *that* supposed to mean?"

"It means you and Justin are always talking smack. I forgot you're the same guy who told me how important family was to you and that you hoped to end up with a wife who understands marriage won't always be easy because the last thing you needed was a diva who had no idea what being a family really means."

He'd forgotten he'd admitted those things to her, though they were true. "So?"

"So, even though you talk a good game with Justin, you're putting Harper's well-being before your own manly urges. That means you're still one of the biggest-hearted guys I know."

"Thanks." He pushed to his feet and said, "I've got to go. And remember what I said about keeping Harp out of the Bayside drama."

"Wait!" She rushed after him as he headed out the door. "What's the plan to win her over?"

"*Good night*, Serena." He climbed into his car and rolled down the window.

"I can help!"

"No helping. No doing anything."

"But you might not get your girl!"

He winked and said, "I think you know me better than that."

HARPER SAT AT her writing desk, tapping her foot to the music streaming from her playlist while staring at her blinking cursor. She'd had a busy day of grocery shopping, unpacking, weeding her gardens, cleaning her cottage, and doing just about anything else she could think of that didn't involve going anywhere she might accidentally see one of her siblings. She'd had to do *something* to keep her mind off Gavin's threat of a blind date. When her phone rang and Chloe's number appeared on the screen, she snagged it from the desk, glad for the distraction.

"Hi, Chloe. Sorry Gavin dragged me away last night."

"Yeah, *right*," Chloe said. "I hear you and Gavin had a pretty great evening."

"From who?"

"Serena. They're business partners, remember?"

"Right, sorry." How could she have put that out of her mind? Serena could be pushy. Had Gavin told her everything? She hadn't had to worry about gossip in LA. Even with the few people she'd occasionally gone out to lunch or dinner with, she always felt like she was out of the loop.

"I have to admit, I'm a little jealous."

"You're into Gavin? I had no idea. But don't worry. It's not like that between us." Why did that leave the taste of regret in her mouth?

"No, I'm not into Gavin. I would have been if he'd showed any interest whatsoever, but nope, nothing. He's never dragged my ass down the beach."

"Sorry," Harper said, sure her nose was growing.

"Don't be. I hope it *is* like that between you two."

"Well, as I said, it's not. But if you're not into him, then why are you jealous?"

"Because you're back in town for half a minute and you've got a great guy dragging you away to be alone, and I'm over here fending off losers on dating sites and apps like Match and Tinder."

"No way!" Harper exclaimed. "Why would you do that? You're gorgeous and outgoing. When we used to hang out, guys were always hitting on you."

"According to Serena and Desiree, I'm too picky, and according to Violet, I'm too uptight."

"I don't think you're uptight."

"Then you're on Team Picky. Great. I'm probably both, too picky *and* uptight."

"No, you're not. Justin was looking at you an awful lot last night. He's hot in that bad-boy way most girls love, but I get it." She and Chloe had long ago discovered that they had similar tastes in guys, and bad boys weren't either of their types. "Most of the guys around here are either tourists who are just passing through, taken, or bad boys."

"Pretty much. But Gavin's a great guy."

Harper sighed. "I told you it's not like that. He set me up on a blind date tonight. That should tell you everything you need to know." She'd been *trying* not to think about what that really meant, but it bugged her to no end that he was willing to hand her off to a friend, even if she had turned down his offer to go out with him.

"That's what Serena said. But with *who*? He wouldn't tell Serena who it was with."

"I have no idea, and I was so flustered I forgot to ask. But it doesn't matter. He's supposed to be here any minute, and I'm *not* going."

"Oh, well, you might want to tell Gavin that. That means you can come out with us! Serena, Drake, and I are meeting Rick and Des at Undercover in about half an hour."

"My life is too much of a mess to pretend it's not, and Colton will see right through it." She winced, realizing what she'd revealed, and quickly said, "I'm still unpacking and getting used to the time difference. I hate living in chaos. I just need to get things under control."

"I hate feeling disorganized, too. Do you need help unpacking?"

Harper looked at the boxes by the door. The things she'd

shipped from LA had arrived early that morning, and they were still all packed up. "No. I'll get through it, but I appreciate the offer."

"Are you sure you're okay? You've been gone so long. It must feel weird coming back, and then being blindsided by Gavin…"

Blindsided was the perfect word for what she'd felt last night. The trouble was, she still felt off-kilter. She'd thought she'd romanticized the effect he'd had on her, but now she knew she hadn't. After their tryst in Romance, she'd thought about trying to find him. It would have been a ridiculously futile effort, since she only knew his first name and hadn't even known where he lived, but that hadn't stopped her from wanting to try *dozens* of times. And last night she'd caught herself wanting to call Chloe or Serena just to get the 411 on him. But she'd stopped herself then, too, because her life really was too much of a mess for a guy like him right now.

Maybe one day…

"Hello? Harper?"

"Sorry. I'm here, and I'm okay. Thanks for asking."

They talked for another few minutes, and after they ended the call, Harper's phone vibrated with a text from a number she didn't recognize. She read the message—*My buddy is psyched about your date. Have fun tonight!* Her pulse quickened as she typed a response. *Gavin? How did you get my number?*

His reply was immediate. *You're not the only one with fancy connections, LA girl.* A minute later another message popped up. *Did you forget you put your number in my suitcase?*

She loved that he'd gone searching for it and typed, *I'm not going on the date. I don't even know his name!* The phone vibrated a second later with his text. *Gale.*

"Gale?" She typed, *Sounds girlie*, adding a laughing emoticon.

Another text rolled in. *Hardly. GALE as in gale-force wind. The guy's going to blow you away. Trust me, beautiful.*

She rolled her eyes, trying to think up a response, but she wasn't fast enough. The phone vibrated again, and she read his text. *Remember, it's a FIRST date. You should probably keep that sunflower tat to yourself...*

Heat rushed through her as memories assaulted her. Gavin's strong hands stripping off her panties, his soft lips kissing the sunflower tattoo on her hip, his warm, wet tongue tracing the stem and each of the petals. She could still feel the sharp, scintillating points of his teeth as he tasted his way lower...

Her entire body shuddered, and she tossed her phone on the desk like she'd been burned. She was turned on and annoyed at herself for getting so carried away by mere thoughts of him.

Glaring at the phone as if it were a villain, she snapped, "I'm *not* going!" and stormed into her bedroom. "Who do you think you are anyway, setting me up with some other guy?"

She grabbed an old, ragged sweatshirt from the closet and tugged it over her cami. Then she tugged a pair of baggy sweatpants over her shorts. She turned her head upside down, shaking out her hair. *The messier the better.* She twisted it into a messy bun, securing the bun in place with a hair tie, and pulled a handful of strands free just for good measure. She went into the bathroom and pulled out her makeup, artfully smearing a little eyeliner beneath her eyes so it looked like she hadn't slept in weeks, which wasn't far from reality. She took one last look at her disheveled self in the mirror.

Perfect.

She stalked into the kitchen and grabbed the pepper shaker.

A knock sounded at her door, and as she went to answer it, she shook pepper into her hand and inhaled it. Her eyes watered and her nose burned. *How's this for beautiful? Maybe next time you'll listen when I say I'm not ready to go out.*

Chapter Four

HARPER COULDN'T STOP sneezing, but even through watery eyes and between brain-rattling sneezes, she made out Gavin standing on her porch looking insanely handsome and shaking his head. She dropped the pepper shaker as she covered her nose to keep from sneezing on *him*, but that only made things worse, because her hand was still covered with pepper.

He picked up the pepper shaker and arched a brow. "Really? This was the best you could come up with? Faking sick?"

She cough-laughed as she stepped outside, hoping the fresh air would clear her nostrils. As she tried to regain control, she glanced around, expecting to see his friend. While she was at it, she took in Gavin's sculpted bronze arms. Her gaze slid down the blue T-shirt molded to his hard chest. Her pulse quickened as she continued her visual exploration to what she knew were thick, muscular thighs beneath his cargo shorts. Her gaze drifted up along the same delicious path to his full, *smirking* lips.

God...

Annoyed with herself yet again, she wiped her peppered hand on her sweats and said, "What gives, Gavin? Where's Gale? Did he stand me up?"

"There's not a chance he'd stand you up."

She peered down the road. "Then where is he?"

"You're looking at him."

"I don't…" As understanding sank in, she said, "You *lied?*"

He dragged his narrowing eyes down her sweats, and then he eyed the pepper shaker in his hand. "Actually, I'd say you're the fibber." He motioned with his hand at himself, like he was presenting a prize, and said, "Gavin Gale Wheeler at your service. And if you think a little pepper is going to get you out of our date, you're wrong."

"You set me up on a blind date with *yourself?*" *Oh boy.* He was definitely a smooth talker.

"I'm the best there is. Let's go, beautiful. Get your keys or purse or whatever you need. We've got plans to work through the hitches in your life, and I'm an organized guy. I'd like to stick to those plans."

She'd poured her heart out last night, and it was all kinds of romantic that he hadn't forgotten. That made her even more attracted to him, which made her even more nervous. She crossed her arms and said, "I told you I'm not ready to date."

"And I told you this isn't a date. We're greasing your wheels before we take the ultimate ride." He waggled his brows.

She inhaled a shaky breath, knowing just how *ultimate* that ride was.

He rolled his shoulders back and said, "It's important that you're fully in control of every aspect of your life before you let the one and only man who matters into it."

How could he be so confident about them? She looked down at her shabby clothes and said, "I can't go like this."

"Why? You look beautiful. *Stunning*, really." He held her gaze, the honesty in his eyes urging her to just go with it. "I love the extra effort you put into your eye makeup. Were you going for the smoky look? It's all the rage this summer. Come on, time to get your keys. Or Mace," he said teasingly as he took her hand and stepped into her cottage.

His gaze swept over the hardwood floors in the cozy living room. Her writing desk sat against the wall to their left, with a vase full of flowers from her gardens. Beside the desk, an armoire housed her television and space for her notebooks, printing paper, and other necessities. A sofa sat against the wall to the right, and there were three stools at the counter that separated the kitchen from the living room.

Gavin whistled. "I bet you get lost in here, huh?"

"Ha ha. What can I say? I don't make much money, and this was all I could afford. But the truth is, I love it. I don't need much space." Her one-bedroom cottage was only three hundred and fifty square feet. It used to be part of the vacation cottage community next door. The owner had parceled off the five cottages on this side of the road and sold them as individual homes.

Gavin snagged her phone from the desk and handed it to her. "It was a joke. This place is adorable. Wait until you see my place. It's not big or glamorous, and I *do* make a lot of money." He winked and glanced into her bedroom. "King bed. *Nice.*"

"Stop." She elbowed him. "You're not getting into that bed."

He stepped closer, and when he reached for her face, she struggled to ignore the rising temperature between them. He brushed his thumb over her cheek and beneath her nose with a thoughtful expression and said, "*Pepper.* You went to a lot of trouble to get out of this date."

"Not really."

His eyes drifted over her shoulder to the built-in bookshelves surrounding the front door. "Whoa! Be still my heart. Those are awesome."

"Right? I *love* them."

"Looks like we have more in common than just being incredible in bed."

She choked out a surprised sound.

"You know it's true." He motioned toward the flowers on her desk and said, "But I clearly need to up my game. You obviously met some dude between last night and this morning, and he brought you flowers."

The tease in his eyes made her smile. "Yeah, well, you know. Word got around that I was home and single guys are *flocking*."

"Let them flock. After tonight, none of them will measure up." He took her hand and said, "Where are your sneakers?"

"I never wear sneakers."

He picked up the sandals by the door and plunked them down by her feet. "Slip your feet in, princess."

"Gavin…"

"Don't bother trying to dissuade me." He knelt and slipped her feet into the sandals. Then he stood and looked around the room. "We're friends, remember? Friends don't let friends hide out."

"I think that's supposed to be *drive drunk*."

"I wouldn't let you do that, either. Where are your house keys?"

She pointed to a bowl on the counter. Holding tightly to her hand, he dragged her to the counter, retrieved the keys, and said, "Purse?"

"If you want to take out the ratty-looking girl, then this *is* a date, and you're paying, right? I shouldn't need my wallet."

He chuckled and headed out the door. "You don't need my

help at all, do you? Last night was just a ploy to get me to take you out."

He closed and locked the door without releasing her hand, and then he hauled her against him, and holy cow, he felt *good*.

His expression turned serious and he said, "Let's get one thing straight, Harp. I know you've gone through some shit, but I'd like to think we're friends, and one thing you'll learn, if you haven't already, is that I'll never lie to you. Do you believe me?"

"I think so." She wanted to, and she truly thought she did, but she didn't trust her judgment enough to say for sure.

"Okay, *that's* going on our list to work on, too." He smiled and said, "Right here, right now, I want you to promise me that you'll leave that 'take out the ratty-looking girl' nonsense behind. You're gorgeous, and no amount of messy hair or smeared makeup will ever make you look anything less than beautiful. Ugliness comes from within. That's something you should have learned from the time you were a kid. Don't all parents teach their kids beauty starts from the inside?"

"Yes, but—"

"No *buts*, okay? If you were an ugly person you wouldn't have friends who care so deeply about you. And by *ugly* I mean *inside*, because you could be caught in a fire tomorrow and your looks could change, but that still wouldn't make you ugly." He paused for a long time, his words sinking in. Then he said, with no less vehemence, "I value honesty, integrity, and kindness, so I sure as hell wouldn't have been with you in Virginia, much less thought about you after that first night, if you didn't embody all those things."

"Gavin, that was..." She didn't have the words to explain how that made her feel, but it was *big*, and it was *real*.

"Promise?"

She'd almost forgotten what that promise was supposed to be. *Promise me that you'll leave that 'take out the ratty-looking girl' nonsense behind.* She nodded. "I'll try."

He cupped her face with his warm, strong hand and brushed his thumb over her cheek again. "That's all I can ask. Let's do this, friend. Let's go kick some troubled ass."

His touch felt like a promise to keep her safe during this *trouble intervention.*

As they walked to his car, doubt crept in. She tried to push it aside. *Stop being so hard on yourself and just enjoy the evening. Like when we were in Romance.* Her body warmed, and she reminded herself to *also* be cautious. *There will be no sunflower kissing tonight.*

He opened the door of his car for her, smiling like she'd given him the best gift ever by agreeing to go out with him. "Your chariot awaits."

Maybe just one kiss…

AS THEY DROVE into the town of Brewster, butterflies took flight in Harper's stomach. She fidgeted with her sweatshirt and asked, "Where are we going?"

"My place." He glanced at her and said, "For a lesson in confidence building."

Her nerves flamed at what that might mean. "I *am* confident, and for your information, we are not ending up in *your* bed, either."

"For a girl who doesn't generally do hookups, you're pretty focused on sex."

"I'm only like that with you, because you…" *Make me want to do things I shouldn't.* She could *not* say that. "Give off a sexual vibe, and it gets my brain going in that direction."

He laughed as he turned off the main road. "Do I?"

"Don't act surprised. You know what you're doing." She remembered what Chloe had said about him not showing any interest in her. Those butterflies swarmed again as she added, "At least with me."

He turned down a wooded lane. A minute later a sly smile worked its way across his tempting lips as he turned down another tree-lined street. "Seems to me you're pretty good at picking up cues from men."

"It's easy to pick up on sexy cues. It's the hidden ones, the ones guys don't want me to know, that cause me trouble. Like with the guy who was engaged. I should have realized there was a reason he took off by ten o'clock every night and why he'd cancel our dates with excuses of work a little too often. But I wasn't raised to distrust people. I wasn't looking for hints of a hidden life. But that doesn't mean I'm not confident. I just know where my weaknesses lie."

He pulled down a long driveway. Cape Cod towns blurred together to outsiders, but Harper had grown up on the Cape, and she knew the differences. Much of the property in Wellfleet and Truro was within the boundaries of the Cape Cod National Seashore and off-limits to development, which meant there were fewer homes, less commercialization, and higher real estate prices than in Eastham and Brewster. She found it interesting that Gavin had chosen to live in a less expensive area after his comment about making a lot of money.

He parked in front of a cute, though unremarkable, cedar-sided rambler with a wide front porch that ran between a bump out on either side. Mature trees shaded a good part of the property, and long grasses sprouted up, unkempt and sparse as a balding man's bedhead. There was no defined parking area, just a smattering of grass and sandy dirt, which was common on the Cape. But Gavin beautified spaces for a living. Harper was surprised his lawn wasn't manicured with overflowing gardens, although the natural beauty of the land brought an unexpected sense of serenity.

Gavin opened her door and took her hand as she stepped from the car, leading her down a stone path toward the side of the house. "Listen, Harp, I didn't mean you weren't a confident person. Your confidence is one of the things that I was—I *am*— very attracted to. You're the wordsmith. I'm obviously better with interior design than words. What I meant was that you let a few bad experiences undermine your confidence about your abilities to read people, and tonight I hope to help you let that go."

"That's true, I guess. But good luck. I've tried to let it go," she said as one of the large kettle ponds the Cape was known for came into view. Moonlight danced along the surface. At the end of the stone path, which forked off and ran along the back of the house, was a wooden dock with a ladder at the end and a rowboat tied to a piling.

"Wow, Gavin. This is gorgeous."

"Thanks. I wanted a place that reminded me of home. I grew up fishing with my dad and my brother, Beckett, and having parties at the creek with our friends. Kind of like the bonfires we have here, only with about five times as many people. I hadn't realized how much I missed being around the water until I left Boston."

"Like when I was in California. I don't think there's any

place quite like home. Where in Virginia are you from?"

"Oak Falls. I know it's stupid, but I'm glad you didn't forget where I was from."

"I remember everything about that night," she said softly.

"Me too," he said, holding her gaze.

The air between them heated despite the cool breeze. Harper struggled against the desire to move closer, to *be* closer. Close enough to kiss when the feeling hit.

In the next breath, Gavin cleared his throat and looked out over the water, as if he was struggling with the same raw emotions.

"You probably know Des and Emery grew up there, too." Emery Andrews was Desiree's best friend. A year after Desiree moved to the Cape, Emery followed and began teaching yoga at the inn. She'd fallen in love with Dean Masters, and they'd eloped last winter. "Violet lived there for a few years when she was little, though I didn't know her then. I had heard that Des and Emery moved to the Cape, but I didn't know where. It was a nice surprise to see everyone again."

"Were you guys good friends?"

"Oak Falls is really small. You pretty much hang out with everyone who's close to your age."

"It's crazy that you guys grew up together and all ended up here."

"I think it's fate. You know, six degrees of separation and all that."

"Maybe," she said absently. "I've been gone for so long, I feel out of touch. I missed engagements, weddings, and from what Chloe and Serena told me last night, Violet introduced them to a whole new group of friends who hang out at a coffee shop in Harwich."

"Common Grounds. Justin and I hang out there, too. I'll take you there sometime." He took her hand and headed down the dock.

"I like to write in coffee shops and cafés, and sometimes at the Wellfleet Pier."

"Really? I think you'll like the atmosphere at Common Grounds. It's very eclectic, and the people who hang out there are interesting, from all walks of life. It might give you inspiration for your writing, which by the way, I want to hear all about."

She looked out over the water, listening to the sounds of the rowboat tapping the dock and the leaves rustling in the breeze, and said, "I'm afraid there's not much to tell these days."

"We'll see about that." He motioned toward the rowboat. "Ready for Regaining Confidence 101? I hope you like to fish."

"I've always been more of a sit-in-the-grass-and-make-flower-crowns type of girl." She glanced in the boat and saw life jackets, blankets, a tackle box, and fishing rods. He either kept his boat ready, or he'd gone to some trouble for her. That thought made her feel good all over.

"Ah, that explains it."

"Explains what?"

"How a few bad experiences can make you feel capsized." He stepped into the boat and reached for her hand. "Come on."

"I figured you as more of a wine-and-dine type of guy."

"I have to wine and dine clients. Why would I want to do that with you? I think we just uncovered part of the problem."

"What part?"

"Your expectations are that guys treat you as they'd treat anyone else. When a guy really likes a woman, he should make the effort to show her she's *unlike* anyone else and do new things." He wiggled his fingers and said, "Come on, beautiful. Don't tell me you're afraid to fish."

No, but I might be afraid of how wise you are in the ways of men and women.

"I'm not afraid, just surprised. You're different than I thought you'd be." She shimmied out of her sweatpants.

He whistled. "Who knew fishing would make you strip?"

"I don't want to get my pants wet." She folded her sweatpants and said, "Should I just leave them here?"

"Yes, cutoffs too, if you'd like."

She rolled her eyes.

He chuckled. "How about the sweatshirt?"

"No. It's too cold." She took his hand, and the boat rocked as she stepped in.

"I've got you." He put his arms around her, gathering her against him and adjusting his feet to balance the boat.

Heat spread through her like wildfire. His body was hard, his arms safe and strong, bringing rise to memories of what it had been like to be naked in them. Before their night in Romance, she hadn't realized one night could create so many enticingly vivid memories. Then again, she'd never experienced a night like the one they'd shared. Gavin had broken down her defenses with nothing more than conversation, laughter, and dancing at the festival. From the very moment they'd met there was an instant connection, sexually and emotionally. When they'd walked into town, they'd meandered through shops hand in hand like they'd been together forever. They made wishes in the fountain and had eaten at a cute pizzeria on the main drag. By the time they'd finally kissed, *she'd* been the one to make the move and *take* it.

She'd forgotten that until just now. He was looking at her

the same way he had that night, with wonder, attraction, and something much deeper that she forced herself not to even try to define. She'd thought she'd imagined that look, but it was as real as the man himself.

GAVIN TRIED TO keep his emotions in check, but the desire in Harper's eyes made him want to kiss her and protect her at once, just like it had when they'd first met. "Don't worry, sweetheart," he said, his emotions as blatant in his voice as they were in his heart. "I'll keep you warm."

"Yes," she whispered. Surprise flashed in her eyes, and she went rigid in his arms. In a cooler tone she said, "I know just how good you are at making me *warm*, but I'm not sure how that will help with my ability to read guys."

"*Right.* I lost my head for a minute there."

He helped her sit on the bench, and as he untied the boat and pushed away from the dock, he said, "Fresh air helps clear your head, and everyone knows you need a clear head to read guys, because we can be a tricky species." He sat across from her and began rowing. "I have a feeling you've been so focused on your bad experiences, it's been a while since you've taken the time to clear the chaos from your mind."

"You can say that again. I have a tendency to pick things apart until they're nothing but bones."

He could see that, and he had a cure for it. He reached for her hand. "Come here." He guided her down beside him and said, "Have you ever rowed a boat?"

She shook her head.

"Time to learn." He moved off the bench and crouched

behind her. Then he shifted her to the middle of the bench. He wrapped her fingers around the oars, covering them with his own, and said, "You want to hold the ends, with your thumb on the tip." Memories of her delicate hands wrapped around his cock flooded him, though it had been her tongue on the tip that had teased and taunted him until he'd been ready to explode. He cleared his throat to try to clear the lust from his brain, but with his chest pressed to her back, he felt her heart beating just as hard and fast as his. Knowing she was just as affected as he was made him want to continue down a dark, sensual path, but that wouldn't help her with her troubles, and in the long run, that was more important than satisfying the desire he'd harbored for months.

He forced himself to focus on helping her clear her head, which was torture, because getting her hot and bothered was so damn enticing. "Make sure the blades of the oars dip just beneath the surface of the water. Be careful not to bury them too deep."

Fuck. He'd like to be buried deep…

He moved her hands in a rowing motion. "This might feel awkward, and that's okay."

There had been no awkwardness when they'd tumbled into bed together the first time, or when they'd made love the second, third, or fourth times either.

"Mm-hm. Isn't it more romantic if *you* row?" She crushed against his chest with every backward row.

"I don't know, sweetheart, but I'm liking my position right now."

She laughed softly, glancing at him over her shoulder. Moonlight reflected in her eyes, and for a beat they simply looked at each other. So many women had to try too hard with revealing clothing, too much makeup, and desperation oozing from their pores. She was naturally beautiful in a girl-next-door-only-better way that spoke to parts of him that he hadn't thought about in a very long time.

One oar dipped too low, and she lost her grip. "Shoot!"

The oar shot up, and he realized his hands had slipped from the oars to around her waist. He grabbed the oar and said, "It's okay. We've got it." He reached around her, placing the oar in her hand and wrapping his hands around hers again. "Take it slow and steady."

"Do you do this with all your dates?" she asked, rowing again.

"You have to ask? What did I tell you about expecting guys to go the extra mile with you?"

"But this was supposed to be a *friend* date," she pointed out sassily.

"The best relationships start as friends. Just ask Serena and Drake." He sat back, letting her row alone and thinking about how true that statement was. He knew if he kissed her, she wouldn't stop them there. Once they let go, the heat between them would be too strong, just as it had been the night they'd spent together. But he wanted to earn her trust. Even more strongly, he wanted her to trust herself before they took their relationship to the next level because the only woman he wanted was finally right there within his reach, and once they took that step, he knew he'd never want it to end.

"You look hot taking control of the boat like that," he said, and she smiled over her shoulder.

"This isn't so hard."

He could make so many dirty retorts right then, but he kept them under wraps, and when they reached the middle of the pond, he shifted closer again. "This is far enough."

He wrapped his hands over hers and showed her how to lift the oars and rest them inside the boat.

"That was fun," she said. She gripped the sides of the boat as he moved to the bench across from her. "Do you do this a lot? By yourself, I mean."

"A couple times a week. I like to get my mind out of the trenches." He opened the tackle box and withdrew a bottle of peach tea. "For you, madam."

"You remembered…"

He winked and withdrew a plastic container with an array of cheese and crackers, setting it on the bench beside her. "In case you get hungry, since we're catching our dinner."

"We are?" Her eyes widened.

"Please tell me you like to eat fish."

"I love it." She unscrewed the top of her drink and took a sip. Her gaze rolled over his face as she screwed the top back on and set it on the floor of the boat. "And I like doing this, being here on the water with you. It's *different*."

"So are you, sweetheart." He pulled the other tackle box out from beneath the bench. "I don't suppose you've ever baited a line?"

"Ew." Her nose wrinkled adorably.

He chuckled. "I'll tell you what. I'll bait the lines; you can be in charge of feeding me."

"You're pretty good at this dating thing, aren't you? You have lots of ways to get a woman to do intimate things, like helping with rowing and feeding you, without coming across as too pushy. I like it."

Good to know. As he baited their fishing lines, he said, "Tell me something, Harp. You said you pick things apart. Are bad

58

experiences with guys a pattern for you?"

"No." She put a piece of cheese on a cracker and lifted it to his lips. As he bit into it, she said, "I mean, I've had some bad dates, but not like the things that happened in LA."

"What about long-term relationships? Have you had many?"

"A few months here and there, but there's never been one great love of my life that I lost, if that's what you're getting at. What about you?"

"I'll let you in on a secret, but if you ruin my rep, I'll have to kill you."

"Now you *have* to tell me." She bit into a cracker.

He chuckled. "Nothing long-term since my first year of college. I date, and I've been with my share of women, but I'm not the player Chloe thinks I am. I come from a traditional family, and I want that someday. If anything, I'm careful. I think it takes a bigger man to pass up a one-night stand than it does to take advantage of it."

She stared at him as she took a drink of her tea. As she re-capped the bottle, she said, "We had a one-night stand."

"Technically that's not true. You're here now."

"Oh, Mr. Wheeler," she said as she fed him another bite, "you have all the answers."

"No, I don't. How many guys would you guess you've gone out with over the past decade? Not slept with, just accepted a date from?"

"I don't know. Maybe eight or ten?"

"And how many of those were bad?"

"Other than the ones in LA? None, really. They just weren't particularly good."

"Fair enough. Who decided *who* you'd go out with for all those years? Jana? Serena? Another friend? Who decided when you were ready to break things off?"

"Me, of course. Why?"

"Because it sounds to me like you've got a history of trusting your own instincts and they've never steered you wrong. That's a pretty solid foundation, and yet you're letting *two* bad experiences undermine it." He cast a line into the water and handed Harper the fishing rod. "Two unusual or bad experiences, Harp, not ten or even five, but *two*." He set a thoughtful gaze on her and said, "That seems a bit out of proportion and unfair to *you*."

Chapter Five

GAVIN CAST ANOTHER line and said, "You dated a cheater, who we'll call the asshole, and a guy who happened to prefer the sampler platter to the steak or seafood. Those things could have happened to anyone. Hell, I've been cheated on, and these days threesomes are commonplace."

She nearly choked on that. "Commonplace? Have you had a threesome?"

"No. I told you, I'm more of a traditional guy. Nothing intrigues me about sharing someone I'm intimate with, but that's not a hard limit for lots of people." He reached over and reeled in her line a little. "If you have too much slack in the line, you won't feel the fish when it bites. You know what? Fishing is a lot like dating. You throw more back than you keep."

"That's the truth. Do you want another cracker?"

"No, thanks. Some sugar would be good." He winked, and her cheeks pinked up. He reached into the tackle box again, withdrawing two red lollipops. "Your favorite."

"You really did remember everything."

When they were in Romance, they'd wandered into a candy store. The retailer was out of red lollipops, and Gavin had insisted on walking several blocks to the grocery store, where he'd bought a bag of lollipops just to give her the red ones. It had touched her then as much as his thoughtfulness touched her now.

He took the wrapper off the lollipops and handed her one.

"Basically, you're saying I'm being too hard on myself?" she asked.

"Exactly. You're a smart woman. You followed your heart and made a career doing what you love. I don't think it's your instincts that are giving you trouble. You said your show was canceled?"

"After months of rewrites, casting, more rewrites based on the cast, and finally filming, the show wasn't picked up. It really gutted me."

"I can only imagine," he said empathetically. "I'm so sorry you went through that, but you had nothing to do with the show not being picked up, Harp. I understand why it dragged you down. You worked your ass off to get there. You left your home with high hopes of becoming something bigger and better, or...?"

"Just becoming *something*," she confessed.

"But it sounds like you had already achieved what most screenwriters pray for and never do. You wrote a cable show a few years ago. I looked it up, and it was funny and sexy, and it ran for two seasons."

"Then it was dropped."

"But that's the world you *chose* to play in. If it were easy, everyone would do it. Do you realize how amazing it is that your *first* cable show ran for *two* seasons? I did some research, and only about twenty percent of sitcoms are renewed for a second season."

"You researched it?"

"I did, and I looked into the show you were working on that didn't get picked up. From what I read, it had to do with Hollywood politics, not the writing itself."

"Yeah, I know. That's what everyone said. I can't believe you researched it."

He shrugged one shoulder, like it wasn't a big deal, when it felt huge to her.

"I wanted to know if you had a reason to worry about your career or not."

"I *do*," she said. "It's not easy to sell a show, and I haven't written anything but garbage since it all went down. I had to take a job writing current event articles for the newspaper just for a paycheck. Talk about going backward."

There was a tug on his fishing line, and he reeled it in a little, pulled back on the rod, then reeled it again. "That's not going backward. That's finding your footing until your next muse comes along."

"Whatever. It is what it is. Do you have a fish on the line?" she asked excitedly.

"Feels like it. Give me your rod. You can reel mine in." He took her rod and handed her his.

"No! I can't. I've never done it before."

He put her hand on the rod and said, "You *can*."

"What if I drop it?" she asked nervously, clutching the rod like a lifeline.

"You won't." He set her rod on the floor of the boat. "Just let the fish guide you. When it tugs, you pull back a little and reel it in slowly."

Her heart raced as she concentrated, pulling and reeling as he'd described.

"That's it. Keep going."

His encouragement, and the way he was watching her, like he was as excited as she was, made it even more fun. "I hope I don't lose it. What if I do?"

"Then we'll starve," he teased. "You're doing great. You're going to reel that fish in, and I bet your writing isn't as horrible as you think, either. I have some work to do this weekend. How about we hit the coffee shop tomorrow with our laptops for a working date and see if we can stir up some inspiration?"

She was having such a good time, it was hard to remember why she hadn't wanted to accept his offer for a date in the first place. "I have to unpack the rest of my things and get organized this weekend or I'm going to lose my mind. I have a meeting with my boss at the newspaper on Monday and some other things to take care of Tuesday and Wednesday. But I'd really like to fit it in at some point."

"Then we'll find the time." He reached over and felt her line. "Good job, Harp. Reel it in all the way. You've got this."

She did as he said, squealing with delight as a big flapping fish broke the surface. "I did it! I got one! What do I do now?"

He grabbed the line and said, "I think you mean what do *I* do, unless you want to get the hook out of its mouth?"

"Ew!"

"I've got it. But first..." He dug his phone out of his pocket and took a picture of her holding the line with the fish dangling from it. He put his phone in the tackle box. As he removed the hook he said, "It's a small-mouthed bass, about sixteen inches. Nice job, Harp."

"It was your fish. I just reeled it in."

"You reeled it in all right..."

He held her gaze, and her pulse sprinted at the innuendo in his eyes. Maybe he was right and she *was* giving too much weight to the combination of the bad dates and the show being canceled. Maybe she *should* trust her instincts.

Lord knew she wanted to.

They continued fishing and talking, and after catching two more, Gavin said, "Ready to go clean the fish and cook them for dinner?"

"Sure. This has been so much fun. Thank you for not letting me hide away in my cottage."

"If I have it my way," he said as they reeled in their lines, "you'll never want to hide away again."

He looked casual with a pole in his hand and the breeze lifting his hair. But his gaze wasn't casual at all, the way it bored into her soul, imploring her to hear the meaningful words he said.

Her pole bent, snapping her from her Gavin-induced trance. "I've got one!" The front of her rod bent so far over she was afraid it would snap. She stood up to get a better grip and said, "I need help. Take it. It's really strong."

"Not a chance, sweetheart. This is your big catch. You've got it."

"I don't know about that," she said, leaning back as she reeled it in.

"Trust yourself. That's the theme of tonight, right?"

She looked at him at the same moment her line pitched forward. She lost her footing and screamed as she tumbled over the edge of the boat and into the frigid, black water. She couldn't see a thing as she swam toward what she hoped was the surface, clinging to the rod with one hand. She felt a *whoosh* beside her and struggled to hold the air in her lungs as an arm circled her belly, dragging her in the opposite direction.

She broke the surface and gulped for air.

"I've got you, Harp," Gavin panted out. He had one arm belted around her middle, using his legs and his other arm to tread water. "It's okay. You're okay, babe. I've got you."

She was clinging to him with one arm around his neck and her legs around his waist and realized she was crying. For some reason that made her laugh, which made him laugh.

"You okay?" he said.

"Yes. Scared, embarrassed, but…" She lifted the rod from the water, proud to have never let go, and they both laughed.

"My little fisherwoman." He tossed the fishing rod into the boat with one hand, still holding onto her.

His eyes found hers again, and she became aware of his muscles moving hard and insistent to keep them both afloat, the seriousness of his gaze, the feel of his strong hand on her skin, and the romantic moonlight raining down on them.

"How can you doubt yourself about *anything*, Harper? Those guys don't know what they missed by screwing you over. If you were mine, I'd never make that mistake."

She didn't think, didn't hesitate, as she crushed her lips to his warm, soft mouth. Even with his legs pumping and water splashing their faces, kissing Gavin was just as sensual and thrilling as she remembered. He held her tighter, deepening the kiss as they bobbed in the water, and *sweet Lord*, how she'd missed *him*.

When their lips parted, her head was spinning. "Sorry. *No.* I'm not sorry. I liked it. But—"

His deep laughter stopped her ramblings.

"You trusted your instincts, Harp. That's a good thing."

"Uh-huh," she said. "But my life is still a mess. I can't be with you like that until I have my own head on straight. I like you, Gavin. I *really* like you, and I don't want to mess this up, but I'm sure to if my life is in a state of chaos."

"I get it. You're not ready. We'll chalk that kiss up to how irresistible I am. But just so you know, you can trust your instincts with me anytime you'd like."

God, he was so cocky and cute, she wanted to kiss him again!

"Come on, you're shivering. Let's get back to my place and warm you up." He helped her into the boat, and as he climbed in after her, he said, "Who knows, you might have *other* instincts you want to follow."

She wrapped her arms around herself, shivering despite the way her insides were still vibrating from that incredible kiss.

His eyes flamed, and he said, "I'm always available. Lips, hands, and other body parts, too…"

She reached over the side and splashed him, but it was she who needed the dose of cold water, because she was already fantasizing about those other body parts…

BY THE TIME they climbed out of the boat, Harper's teeth were chattering. Gavin lent her a sweatshirt to wear with her sweatpants and suggested she take a hot shower while he rinsed off and then prepared dinner. Trying not to think about her naked in his guest bathroom while he rinsed off was impossible. He had visions of that sexy sunflower—and what kissing it did to her. He forced himself to think about algebra, an instant boner killer, and rushed through his shower to start dinner.

With the fish and vegetables on the grill, he made a fire in the fire pit and went inside to grab a few blankets. He found Harper holding her wet clothes and looking at the pictures of his family and friends on the wall by the master bedroom. Her hair was twisted up in a bun, and the sleeves of his favorite college sweatshirt were rolled up above her wrists. Even in baggy sweatpants and the oversized sweatshirt, she was the sexiest woman alive. Her face tipped up as she stepped closer to get a better look at the pictures, and he took a better look at her. She made his house feel warmer, happier, and she looked comfortable. A far cry from the sick act she'd put on earlier. He had no idea how or why, but he had the overwhelming sensation that she belonged there.

She turned, catching him admiring her, and blushed. "Thanks for letting me shower. Sorry I fell in."

"I'm not," he said, coming to her side.

She inhaled sharply and then turned her attention to the pictures on the wall. "Is this your brother? The dark-haired guy?" She pointed to a picture of Gavin and Beckett sitting on their parents' deck, taken right before he left for college.

"Yeah, that's Beckett."

"Is he the one you went to the festival with? He's handsome."

"He's not my type, but yeah, I guess." Gavin had never had any jealousy issues, but he couldn't ignore the pang in his gut her comment caused. They'd been so into each other at the festival, she'd never had a chance to meet Beckett. Now he wished she had, because for the first time in years, he was with someone he wanted a relationship with. "I only have one brother. I went home that weekend, and Beckett dragged me to the festival. It was the best thing he's ever done."

She held his gaze and licked her lips, leaving them wet, and *man*, he wanted to kiss her again.

Desperately.

But he'd promised himself he'd give her the space she need-ed to heal and find her footing, so he shoved that urge down deep.

"I'm glad he did," she said. "He looks nice. Do you miss him?"

"From time to time, I guess. We text and talk pretty often, mostly to give each other shit about our sports teams or just to shoot the breeze. He keeps me up to date on what's going on back home and with our parents."

"Are these them?" She pointed to a picture of his parents standing by a tree in their front yard.

"That's them. Mark and Marjorie Wheeler."

"Your mom looks just like that actress Rene Russo."

"Everyone says that," he said.

"What do your parents do?"

"My father runs Wheeler Industries, a farm-equipment manufacturer. My mom didn't work when we were growing up, but now she does, part-time at a gift shop. She doesn't need the money, but I think she gets lonely when my father is at work. I try to call her pretty often."

"Aw, that's sweet. I bet she appreciates it."

"I think she does. What about your parents?"

"They live in Hyannis. They're very old-school. My dad's a businessman, and my mom seems happy being a homemaker, doing crossword puzzles, making meals for my father. He's so appreciative, he never takes her for granted. I know they're happy."

"You said you weren't worried about how your family would react to your show being canceled. What's holding you back from telling them?"

"My parents believe in nine-to-five jobs and traditional roles in relationships. According to them, we all should have been married with two kids by the time we were twenty-five. Jana and I should have husbands who are suit-wearing businessmen, and Brock and Colton should have wives who volunteer and go to PTA meetings." She laughed softly. "We all veered so far from their hopes, it's like we rebelled, but really, we just followed our hearts. I don't think they're disappointed in us, but I do think they worry, you know? They never really understood Brock's and Jana's desire to box, Colton's sexuality, or my desire to have my own career. They accept us and support our decisions, but there's a generational gap, and we all feel it."

"Which leaves each of you trying to prove your worth to them?"

"I don't know about my brothers or sister, but maybe in some ways, for me. Although they've never made any of us feel like we're *less than* anything, so it's probably all in my head. They're proud of me, and I hope they always will be."

He wanted to sit down with her parents and tell them how amazing the daughter they'd raised was. She hadn't just hit a bump in the road. Her road had opened up beneath her. It could have swallowed her whole, but here she was, striving not to let it. If that wasn't the sign of a remarkable woman, he didn't know what was.

"Despite all that, some of their values definitely wore off on me. I've always been a white-picket-fence kind of girl. I just want my career, too." She looked at the picture again and said, "You look like both of your parents. I just look like my mom."

He knew she was trying to change the subject, so he didn't push for more information about her family. "Then your mother must be beautiful." He took her wet clothes from her hands. "Why don't I toss these in the washer while we eat?"

"You don't have to do that." She followed him into his laundry room.

"It's okay. I'm washing mine anyway. And don't worry," he said teasingly, "I'll keep my hands off your lingerie." She blushed, and he couldn't resist adding, "*Skin* is better than silk any day."

"Are you always like this?"

"Nice?" he said as he started the washer.

"Flirty and cocky."

He wrapped his arms around her waist and gazed into her smiling eyes. "Maybe."

"That's not an answer."

Loving the heat in her eyes, he said, "I'm a nice guy who can be flirty and cocky, and when you're ready, I promise you'll get all the *best* parts of me."

"Gavin."

His name sounded soft and alluring rolling off her tongue. The urge to kiss her was so strong, he had to joke his way out of it before he took her places she wasn't ready to go.

"Stop looking at me like I'm a piece of meat. Your dinner is on the grill." He kissed the tip of her nose and took her hand, leading her into the living room.

"I can see you're not going to make this easy."

"Make what easy?" He knew exactly *what*. He shouldn't be sending flirtatious messages when she wasn't ready, but he loved seeing desire and restraint warring in her eyes.

"Nothing. I like your house," she said in an obvious, and adorable, attempt to change the subject again. "It's very rustic, not at all what I pictured."

Open ceilings with exposed rafters, paneled walls, and marred hardwood floors gave his house more of a cabin feel.

Built-in bookshelves filled to the hilt took up three-quarters of one wall. Gavin had disappeared into books as much as he'd lost himself in work over the years. A wide stone fireplace anchored the far side of the room between the entrances to each of the two guest bedrooms. Large windows spanned the back wall, offering stunning views of the water.

"You mean you didn't expect an interior designer to live in a house with knotty-pine paneling, cheap furniture, and an archaic kitchen?" Gavin was a private guy, and he rarely had people over to his house. Serena and Drake had come over a time or two, and Justin stopped by sometimes. Other than hanging up pictures of his friends and family, he hadn't put any effort into decorating, much to his friends' dismay. Justin was always on his case to do something with his yard.

"Something like that," she said with a smile.

"I think a home should be someplace you can kick back and enjoy yourself, not worry about whether you'll ruin the furniture."

"I have no problem with any of that," she said. "It's just curious that you haven't given your house your own touch, that's all." She made a beeline for his grandfather's vintage wooden stereo cabinet. "Is this what I think it is? Does it have a record player?"

"Yes. It was my grandfather's. Are you into vinyl?"

"Not really, but we had one of these when I was growing up." She ran her hand over the top. "It's gorgeous."

"I restored it. I love listening to vinyl."

She opened the empty cabinet and looked around the room. "Where are your records?"

He pointed to the closed double doors on the far side of the room. "In the sunroom."

"You have a sunroom?"

"Yeah. I'm surprised you didn't notice it from the dock. It has great views of the water." He placed his hand on Harper's lower back, wanting the connection as he guided her to the sunroom. He pushed open the doors, and moonlight spilled in through the nearly floor-to-ceiling windows, casting shadows of pitch pine trees over the boxes on one side of the room.

"Why is this gorgeous room empty?" She walked in and looked out the windows.

"I was going to make it into my office, but I haven't gotten around to it. I don't work from home as often as I used to, so I don't really need it. My records are in those boxes." He noticed smoke coming off the grill and said, "We should check on dinner. I hope you're hungry. The fish we caught should taste amazing."

"I'm always hungry," she said as they went out to the patio.

He waggled his brows.

She rolled her eyes. "You're impossible."

"You didn't feel me struggling when you attacked me in the water, did you? I'm obviously very possible."

She blushed, and it made her look even sexier.

He transferred the fish and vegetables to their plates and said, "I'm glad you're not one of those women who pretends not to eat, then goes home and scarfs down a gallon of ice cream."

"I never said I don't scarf down ice cream."

THEY ATE DINNER on the patio. The fish was delicious, and conversation came easily, as if they'd known each other for years rather than days. They laughed a lot, talking about their friends and reliving Harper's tumble into the water. Harper told him about her life in LA, which was more work than play, as he'd expected, and he caught her up on all the happenings around Bayside over the winter.

After dinner, he told her how much he enjoyed working with Serena.

"We clicked from the start, and our career aspirations and visions were in line, as were our ethics. We're a great team."

"Well, everyone here sure loves you."

"As I do them," he said as they carried their dishes inside. "I had friends when I lived in Boston, but I was so focused on work, I never connected with them the way I did with friends back home. Coming here and meeting all of Serena's friends was a refreshing change, and just what I needed."

"I'm glad you did, or we probably never would have seen each other again."

He transferred their clothes into the dryer, grabbed a blanket for Harper, and they went back outside and sat on lounge chairs by the fire.

"I think that's another thing that dragged me down in LA," Harper said. "I made friends, but I felt like I could be anyone."

"*Replaceable*," he suggested, knowing exactly how she felt. "I know how it feels to be lonely in a city of millions."

"Exactly. It's not that I think I'm special, or need special treatment, but I know with my friends here, we mean something to each other. In any case, I'm glad to be home."

"I think you're pretty special, Harp."

She pulled the blanket around her shoulders, her brows knitted. "I've never been with a guy where things were this easy. What are you hiding? There has to be something, some skeleton in the closet? A fetish that'll repulse me?"

He laughed. "No weird fetishes to speak of, although I'm open to anything you want to try."

She pulled her legs up to her chest and wrapped her arms around them. "We've already tried a lot."

They sure had. They'd explored each other's bodies all night long at the bed-and-breakfast, playing and pushing each other's boundaries. They'd even made good use of the tie he'd worn on the flight from Boston. Hell, they'd made good use of the dresser, the table, and the bathtub, too.

A breeze swept over the patio, and she shivered.

"Are you too cold? Do you want to go inside?"

"I'm a little chilly, but I don't want to go in. I like being out here with you."

He shifted on the lounge chair and reached for her hand. "Come over here. I'll keep you warm." She hesitated, and he said, "Fully dressed."

She moved beside him, and he covered her with the blanket. He put his arm around her, and she fit perfectly, like his matching puzzle piece.

"You're warm," she said, and turned toward him, resting her head on his chest. She stretched her arm over his stomach, snuggling closer. "This doesn't mean I want to get naked. Is that unfair? I don't want you to think I'm a tease."

"Believe it or not, Harp, I'm not looking to get laid. I like you too much to rush into anything before we're ready. Friendship is important, and I'm enjoying getting to know you better. How we get along when we're fully dressed is just as important as how we connect when we're naked."

"I've never met anyone like you. I can't decide if you're really this nice, or if it's all part of some big plan."

He kissed her forehead and said, "You can worry all you want, but with me, what you see is what you get. Tell me about this job you've got, writing about current events. When do you start?"

"This week. My first assignment is covering a pre-season concert the Chatham Band is putting on Wednesday night."

"Great. I'll bring dinner."

She tipped her face up. "You want to go with me? Don't you have anything better to do on a Wednesday night?"

"This chick I'm really into just got back into town, and I hear she'll be there."

She rested her cheek on his chest again and hugged him. "Thank you. It's not really Chloe's scene, and most of my other friends are taken. I was dreading going alone. You know it'll be packed, right? With lots of families and loud kids."

"I love kids," he said. "Why? Are you a kid hater?"

"Of course not."

"Some people think kids should be seen and not heard. I've never understood that. In Oak Falls we have Friday-night jam sessions every few weeks at my friends' barn. People of any age can get up onstage and play an instrument. Sometimes there are twenty people up there, and it sounds *terrible*. But it's fun. Kids are running around, spilling sodas and eating cookies, and people dance and sing. Everyone brings food. My mom usually makes her famous tuna-noodle casserole, which sounds really gross, but man, it's the best. She makes it with buttery biscuits that melt in your mouth. And Nana's everything cookies. *Man*, I miss those."

"Nana? Is that your grandmother?"

"No, my friend's grandmother. Everyone calls her Nana. Some of my best childhood memories are of those jam sessions.

And as a teenager." He whistled. "You don't want to know."

"Why? Did you sneak into the hayloft with your girl-friends?"

"Nah. Usually down to the creek. What about you? Where'd you sneak off to?" He wanted to know everything about her.

"I never really snuck off anywhere with boys. That was more Jana's and Colton's style. I hung around at home or at the beach with my girlfriends."

"Aw, come on. You've got to give me something. How about your first-kiss story?"

"With tongue or without?"

He squeezed her tight. "You naughty thing. Let's go innocent. The first kiss without tongue, because quite honestly, I'd like to pretend only my tongue has ever had the pleasure of dancing with yours."

She blinked up at him and said, "There haven't been many, I can tell you that."

"Harper Garner, you have no idea what knowing that does to me, so even if you're lying, please keep lying to me."

"It's the truth, but let me tell you about Charlie, my first lips-only kiss. We were in sixth grade, and we used to walk home from school together. One day when we got to my house, he was acting nervous, and he looked me in the eye and said, 'I need to kiss you.' I was about as clueless as a girl could be, so I asked why, and he said because he really liked me and his older brother told him if he didn't kiss me, someone else would. So I puckered up and got my first kiss. I thought it was a pretty perfect first kiss, because I liked him, too. Unfortunately, Brock had stayed home from school that day and saw it. He stormed outside, looming over the poor kid, and proceeded to give him hell. Charlie never walked me home again."

"Were you mad at Brock?"

"Heck yes I was mad at him. He was a bully."

"He was protective. There's a difference. I like knowing that about him."

"Well, then you'd better watch your back, because not much has changed. Although, he does have a girlfriend now, so maybe he's got less time to *loom* than he used to." She giggled and rested her cheek on his chest again. "How about your first kiss?"

"I was twelve, she was thirteen, and I thought I was hot shit. Her name was Twyla, and it was at one of the jam sessions. We smashed teeth and I cut her lip. I wasn't very suave back then."

They both laughed.

"I'm glad to report you're much better at it now." She pressed a kiss to his ribs through his shirt. "You probably shouldn't mention that to Chloe. You might never live it down. Hey, Gavin?"

"Yeah?"

"Thanks for tonight. It helped. I think I'm going to try to swing by my parents' house this weekend and get in touch with my brothers and sister, let them know I'm home and try to see them, too."

"I'm glad to hear it. At the end of the day, family is all that matters."

"Mm-hm," she said softly.

They fell into comfortable silence. If Gavin listened carefully, he could hear past the swishing leaves to the soft, peaceful sounds of Harper's breathing, which had slowed to the sounds of slumber. Maybe she was jet-lagged, or maybe she was trusting her instincts again with him. Either way, he wouldn't let her down. He tucked the blanket around her and closed his eyes, thanking the stars above for whatever magic had to have happened to bring her back into his life.

When it dawned on him that it wasn't magic that had brought her back, but the cancelation of her show, guilt sliced through him, strengthening his resolve to help her find her next muse.

Chapter Six

A COOL BREEZE brushed over Harper's cheek. She slowly became aware of Gavin's heart beating against her chest, something hard against her belly, and a very large hand down the back of her sweatpants, holding her bare ass. Her eyes flew open, and his grip on her ass tightened. She was lying on *top* of him on the lounge chair.

He made a sad moaning sound, and the arm that was draped across her back pressed firmer, holding her in place. "Don't move. You feel good."

He felt amazing, too. He was warm and firm. *Hard. Oh God!*

"Gavin…"

"What? Nothing happened. You trusted your instincts and fell asleep. It was nice being close to you."

"Your hand is on my ass," she pointed out.

He pressed his warm lips to her forehead and squeezed her butt. "Commando. Nice." He opened his eyes, and he groaned in the darkness. "It's not even morning yet."

"If the phrase 'morning wood' means anything, then your body disagrees despite the color of the sky."

"That's your fault, beautiful." He shifted them onto their

sides and put one thick leg over both of hers, trapping her against him.

She couldn't suppress a smile. "Sorry I fell asleep on you."

"I'm not." He pressed his lips to hers, like it was the most natural thing in the world. The strange thing was, it felt that way to her, too, and even more so when he said, "Morning, beautiful. Want to watch the sunrise?"

"I would love that, but you'll have to move your hand."

"I thought you'd never ask." He moved it lower, his fingers grazing very close to her privates.

"Gavin!"

She pulled his hand from her pants, and he rolled on top of her. His sexy, *happy* green eyes coasted over her face. His hair was spiky, and his scruff was thick, like his arousal. Heat darted through her. She quickly shifted her eyes away.

"What just happened?" he asked with a serious tone.

"Nothing," she said, trying to stop an unstoppable smile.

"You're an awful liar. You're even more stunning when you wake up in my arms."

"And you're full of cheesy lines in the morning. You should move."

He pressed his hips forward.

"Gavin!" She laughed. "I meant *off* me."

"Sorry, I misunderstood." He kissed her again, just a quick brush of his lips. "For a writer, you're not very clear with your requests."

She pulled the blanket around her as they sat up. "I'll try to remember that. I can't believe I fell asleep on you. I haven't slept that well in weeks."

"You should sleep with me more often, because you were out like a light. Did you know you snore?"

"I do not!" *Holy cow. Do I?*

He chuckled and pulled her up to her feet. "It's this quiet, girlie snore, like this." He made a soft snoring sound.

Harper covered her face. "Oh my gosh! I'm such a mess."

He gathered her in his arms, grinning like he'd never been happier, and said, "Your hair is a tangled mess, you snore, and at one point I woke up with your hand cupping my package."

"*Ohmygosh.*" She covered her face again.

He lowered her hands and said, "You're *real*, Harp. It was one of the things I first noticed about you when we met, and you've proved it every minute we've been together since. Real can be messy, and I always believed that meant it wasn't always pretty." He lifted the ends of her hair, which had come undone from her bun and fell in tangles around her shoulders. "I didn't realize I was wrong until this morning. Apparently *messy* can also be *beautiful.*"

"Wow," she said a little breathily. "How are you still single?"

He stretched, and the hem of his shirt lifted, revealing a path of toned, tanned abs and a tease of the treasure trail she remembered so well.

"It's a *choice.*" He patted her butt and said, "Let's go."

He headed for the house, and she hurried to keep up. "I thought we were watching the sunrise."

"We are, but I have to pee like a racehorse, and unless you want me to whip it out right here…" He put his hand on the button of his shorts.

"Bathroom," she said.

After using the facilities, finger combing her hair, and finger brushing her teeth with Gavin's toothpaste, she snuggled with him beneath a blanket on the dock. The sun eased into the sky, pushing shades of orange and yellow into the blue-gray dawn, until a bright new color appeared. Harper glanced at Gavin and realized he was pushing the clouds of the last few months away, allowing her to find her way to a bright new day, too. And here she was, thinking those months had formed an impenetrable wall.

"I'm glad you slept," he said, breaking through her thoughts. "You sure you can't hang out today and hit the coffee shop?"

"I think I'm going to swing by my parents' house this afternoon, and I need to start unpacking. But we're still on for the concert Wednesday, right?"

"Absolutely. Want help unpacking?"

She didn't want their time together to end and wondered if he was serious. "Don't you have better things to do?"

"Probably, but I like spending time with you. Besides, who knows what secrets I can uncover by helping you unpack."

"You'll be sorely disappointed. But you know what? As much as I want to see you today, I'm not sure what my parents' plans are or when I'll be back from visiting them. Can we do it tomorrow in case they want me to stay for the day, or have dinner? I've been gone so long, I don't want to rush them."

"Of course. That sounds great." He pulled out his phone. "Let me just send Justin a text and let him know I won't be riding tomorrow."

"Riding?"

"Yeah. I got a motorcycle license a few months ago. When the weather's nice I try to ride with Justin and the guys."

She'd never expected to find a guy on a motorcycle sexy, but she imagined Gavin in a black leather jacket, straddling a motorcycle. And then she took that thought one step further, picturing herself sitting behind him, her arms wrapped around him as they cruised down the road, and holy cow. That was *scorching* hot.

"I'm guessing whatever *didn't* happen earlier when you blushed isn't happening again?" he teased with a shock of heat in his eyes.

She swatted him, and he chuckled.

They settled back into companionable silence, and after a while Harper said, "Do you ever bring your computer and work out here?" She loved her house and gardens, but there was definitely something more inspiring about being on the water.

"I thought I might when I first bought the place, but I never have. I spend all day being 'on,' pitching, working with clients, finessing distributors. This has become more of a place where I come to relax and center my mind."

"I understand that. Writing is the opposite. It's a very quiet job, since I'm always in my own head. I think that's why I like working at cafés or at the pier. I get inspired by the things around me. But this is inspiring in a different way. The colors, the water, the trees. It's serene." There were a few houses in the distance, but they were far enough away that it felt like they were all alone.

"I guess it would be good inspiration for creating settings?"

"That, yes, but I meant the *energy* is different. I feel different energy when I write while sitting by my gardens or at my desk in my cottage than I do when I write in a café or on the pier, with people milling about and lives going in every which direction. This is totally different from any of that. It's like I can hear myself think in a different way than I can in those places, which makes me wonder if that might play out in my writing."

"You're welcome to write here anytime, Harp."

"I didn't say that to try to weasel my way into your yard."

He hugged her against his side and said, "You weaseled your way into my mind months ago; you might as well weasel your way into the rest of my life."

IF GAVIN HAD his way, he'd have kept Harper at his house all day, relaxing by the water, talking, writing, or whatever else she wanted to do. He enjoyed being with her. She wasn't just finding her way into his life. She was tiptoeing into his heart. He hadn't let a woman in for so long, he hadn't recognized just how big his feelings for her were. Although he should have, given that she'd been on his mind for almost a year. He wondered what she was working on now and why she thought it sucked. What was her *plan* to get out of her writing slump? She was definitely a planner. He could spot one a mile away, and she'd had a to-do list on her desk by her computer with a note to call her parents at the very top. She might have been putting off seeing them, but her family was very much on her mind, which he considered the mark of a solid, grounded person.

He glanced at her sitting in the passenger seat of his car in her shorts and his Boston College sweatshirt. Under that bulky sweatshirt she wore a sexy light-pink spaghetti-strap top with a built-in bra that left *nothing* to his imagination. He'd hardly had time to admire her in it before she'd put his sweatshirt over it and announced that she was keeping it. That confidence to take what she wanted was just one more thing he fucking loved about her. She might not trust all her instincts, but she was getting there.

She fidgeted with the ends of her hair and said, "What?"

"Everything." He reached for her hand. He might not have been waiting for her, because he hadn't known he'd see her again, but as he held her hand, he realized his heart hadn't been fully functioning until she'd shown up and jolted it back to life.

She eyed their joined hands, but she didn't pull away. At thirty-plus years old, that shouldn't make him feel like he'd won the lottery, but after months of wondering if he'd imagined her, it sure as hell did. He was bubbling over with happiness, and he wanted to share it with their friends, to let them know that this incredible woman lit him up, even if she wasn't his quite yet.

"We didn't eat breakfast. Are you hungry?"

"A little," she said. "I can grab something at home."

"I have a better idea." Maybe it was a dick move, but he didn't care. Life owed him a few dick moves. He drove directly to Summer House Inn to have breakfast with their friends.

He pulled up the driveway, passing Devi's Discoveries, the art gallery where Desiree and Violet sold their mother's and Desiree's paintings and Violet's pottery and batiks. There was an adult-toy shop in the back of the gallery. Gavin imagined how red Harper would turn if he suggested they check it out.

He drove past Violet and Andre's cottage, where they lived when they weren't traveling overseas setting up medical clinics for Andre's company, Operation SHINE, and parked in front of the Victorian inn overlooking the bay, beside Chloe's car.

Serena and Emery came out the side door of the inn carrying plates and joined Chloe and Daphne at the table where they gathered for breakfast. Daphne ran the offices of Bayside Resort and lived on site, like Serena, Drake, Emery, and Dean. She bounced her almost-two-year-old daughter, Hadley, on her lap. Even from the parking lot Gavin could see Chloe's mouth moving a mile a minute. It was a familiar scene. He didn't join them every day, but he tried to catch up once or twice a week, when he'd go running with the guys.

"I'm so glad everyone still gets together for breakfast," Harper said as they climbed from the car.

He was like a teenager who just got his first kiss, all foolish grins and cocky swagger as he draped an arm around her neck.

Harper looked curiously up at him. "Are you *trying* to raise eyebrows?"

"You need to know you can handle anything, right?"

The girls noticed them approaching and waved.

As he waved, he said, "No time like the present to regain that confidence."

"Troublemaker," Harper said under her breath as they approached the gate to the side yard.

"Look who arrived in the *same* vehicle," Emery teased as Violet came out of the house carrying a plate of pastries. Emery wore yoga pants, a sports bra, and a smart-ass smirk as she said, "Either Gavin's running a car service or…"

"He got right on the fuckery bandwagon to welcome Harper home." Violet set the plate down as Gavin opened the gate and Cosmos, Desiree's scrappy little dog, ran circles around their feet and barked.

"*No*, he did not," Harper said, pinked cheeked, glowering at Gavin.

"That blush says otherwise," Chloe said with a waggle of her brows.

Harper rolled her eyes. Gavin debated clearing things up, but a little more teasing would solidify them as a couple in their friends' minds, so he let it go.

"When did this happen? What have I missed?" Daphne eyed Harper and Gavin.

Violet glanced at them with amusement. She was a tough, tattooed biker, although she'd softened a tad since getting together with Andre. Gavin still never knew what to expect from her. She was as dark, brash, and fearless as her half sister, Desiree, was blond, proper, and careful.

"Apparently Gavin and Harper hooked up last summer in Virginia," Violet explained. "And they liked it so much, they're enjoying repeat performances."

Gavin had forgotten how quickly gossip traveled among his friends. The crassness of Violet's statement rubbed him the wrong way, and he said, "Christ, Vi. We're not *hooking up*."

"Harper! Welcome back," Desiree exclaimed as she came outside carrying a pot of coffee. She and Rick lived at the inn. She set down the pot and hugged Harper. "I've missed you *so* much."

"Me too," Harper said. "I missed everyone. It's good to be back." She bent down, smiling at Hadley as she tickled her chin. "Hello, sweetie. I bet you don't remember me."

Hadley stared stoically at her, her little lips pursed like she didn't have time for this nonsense.

"Still no luck getting her to smile, or is it just me?" Harper asked as she sat beside Daphne.

"It's not you. She still won't smile for anyone except Drake and Andre," Daphne said apologetically, brushing her hand over Hadley's fine brown hair.

"Sometimes she smiles for *me*," Gavin said proudly.

"Apparently so does Harper," Violet said, earning a round of giggles.

"Where'd you get that sweatshirt, Harper?" Chloe asked, looking knowingly at Serena. "You spent the night with Gavin, didn't you? That's *his* sweatshirt."

"You needed a *sweatshirt* to tell you that?" Violet scoffed, glancing at Harper. "That is well-fucked hair if I've ever seen it."

"We did *not* sleep together!" Harper exclaimed, shooting visual daggers at Gavin. "We were *fishing!*"

"We were. She's telling the truth," Gavin said.

"Is fishing code for sex?" Desiree blinked innocently around the table. "I can't keep up with your code talk."

Gavin chuckled. "No, Des. It's not. We were literally fishing. Harper fell in. She was jet-lagged, and she fell asleep at my place."

"*Nothing* happened," Harper clarified.

Gavin sat in the chair beside her and draped an arm around her shoulder, whispering, "Well, a little more than nothing,"

Harper scowled. "Are you *trying* to egg them on?"

He tugged on the shoulder of her sweatshirt and said, "You are wearing my sweatshirt when you have a perfectly good one in the car. That's got to mean something."

"Yes, but I didn't know we were coming *here*." Harper's brows slanted, and she nibbled on her lower lip.

"Why are you so embarrassed, Harper?" Chloe asked. "Gavin's a great guy. It's not like you're slumming it. And you look cute in his sweatshirt."

Harper threw up her hands. "Fine, *geez*! We kissed, okay?"

"O-*kay* then. Now that *that's* straightened out..." Violet grabbed a pastry and took a big bite.

"God, you guys. We're taking things day by day, *okay*? We're friends, and yes, maybe we'll be more one day, but we're not sleeping together," Harper said emphatically.

"*Yet*," Emery said. "Dean and I were just friends, too."

Chloe said, "Technically, you *slept* together last night."

Gavin chuckled.

"Drake and I were just friends, too," Serena chimed in, grinning with her secret knowledge.

"Wait, I'm confused," Daphne said. "I know what's happening now, but did you two hook up in Virginia like Vi said? Or is that just a rumor?"

Emery, Serena, and Chloe all said, "They did," at the same time.

"Ugh!" Harper looked up at the sky and said, "I do *not* want my sex life on display."

"Okay, you guys," Gavin said, pleased to have himself linked to Harper in the minds of their friends. "You've all had your fun. From now on, my relationship with Harper is off-limits. And for the record, we're not hooking up." The girls mumbled their disbelief, and an approving smile curved Harper's lips, which made him wish he'd stopped them sooner. "I'm helping Harper with a few things, and we're close, so you'll probably see us arriving and leaving places together a lot from now on."

Harper's gaze softened.

He pulled her closer and whispered, "One day you'll be proud to call me yours."

"You're doing it again," she said quietly.

"What's that?"

"Making me forget why I'm fighting what's between us."

His heart filled up, and the urge to seal her words with a kiss were so strong, he leaned in to do just that.

"If you don't want the Real Housewives of Bayside talking about you," Violet said loudly, "you might want to cut that shit out."

Gavin ground his teeth together, a breath away from kissing

Harper. Laughter rang out around them.

"Maybe you should recruit Harper into your book club," Violet suggested. She bit into her pastry, holding Gavin's stare.

"Yes! We should," Daphne agreed. "We have the best book club!"

"I love book clubs," Harper said. "What kind of books do you read?"

Violet winked at Gavin and said, "You can thank me later. The vultures just need something to cling to."

He mouthed, *Thank you.*

"Erotic romance," Chloe said. "This month we're reading *Turn Away*, by L. A. Ward." She fanned her face.

"I *love* erotic romance," Harper said. "How dirty are we talking?"

Gavin's ears perked up, listening to the girls discussing the dark and dirty books they read, which they claimed had as much humor and heart as they did erotic scenes. Harper seemed extremely well versed in the genre. He thought about the night of the festival, when he'd tested both their boundaries, doing things he'd never wanted to do with any other woman. She'd said she'd always wanted to explore her sexuality in ways she'd only read about. Now he understood even more clearly. She'd trusted him enough to live out her erotic fantasies with him, just as he'd taken the leap and trusted her.

"WE CHAT ONLINE all the time because we have members all over the country," Daphne explained. "But every few months we choose a physical place to meet, and whoever can make it joins us. The only rule is that the place has to have a beach."

"We're meeting Friday at Red River Beach in Harwich for a barbecue and book chat. We won't always stay local for the get-togethers, though, since it's not fair to other members. But this month it was Steph's turn to choose the book and she chose the place," Chloe said.

"Who's Steph?" Harper asked.

"Violet introduced us to her," Chloe said. "She's one of her friends from Common Grounds. She's really cool."

Harper glanced at Violet, who was gazing out at the dunes, where Drake, Rick, and Dean were jogging toward them with a man Harper didn't recognize. The way Violet was practically drooling over the unfamiliar sandy-haired guy, Harper assumed he was Andre, Violet's new boyfriend Serena had told her about. "I've never seen Vi googly-eyed over a guy."

"Look at that man, Harper." Violet's voice was full of lust. "I'm not just googly-eyed, I'm fucking hot just thinking about what that sweaty body will feel like."

"Wow, *okay*..." Harper blushed and said, "Back to the book club..."

Harper was as excited to join the book club as she was to see so many of her good friends married and partnered off. Emery met Dean at the gate, while Drake and Rick headed straight to Serena and Desiree. Violet went to Andre with a loving expression. It was strange and wonderful to see this softer side of Violet as Andre pulled her into his arms. He whispered something that made Violet blush, a sight Harper would have bet money she'd never see.

Drake patted Hadley on the head, then leaned down to kiss Serena. "Hey there, Supergirl." Serena pulled him down to the chair beside her and climbed into his lap.

"How was your run?" Desiree asked Rick after receiving a

tender kiss on her lips.

Rick raked a hand through his dark hair and said, "Great, but the best part is always coming home to you."

"Does anyone else ever wish you could push fast-forward through all this lovey-dovey stuff?" Chloe teased.

"Uh-huh," Daphne said. "It makes me remember what I don't have."

"Never give up." Gavin squeezed Harper's shoulder.

Rick came toward Harper and said, "Our resident celebrity has returned! It's great to see you. Get up here and give us a hug."

She smiled as she pushed to her feet. "It's good to be back."

"The girls thought you'd left them for good," Dean's deep voice boomed as he came up behind her.

The guys were all athletic, but Dean was massive, like Harper's brother Brock. All powerful, hard edges. She didn't know Dean quite as well as she knew the others, but in the short time she'd spent with him, she'd learned that beneath his bearded, brick exterior, like Brock, he was kind, careful, and patient.

Dean and Rick crushed Harper between them in a sweaty hug that made everyone laugh and Harper groan.

"Bet you missed us," Rick said as he took a seat beside Desiree.

Harper sat beside Gavin and said, "You, yes. Your sweat? Not so much."

"Careful, you two," Violet said. "She's with Gavin now, and I doubt he likes the idea of a Harper *manwich*."

"The girls said you two left together the other night," Dean said.

Gavin grinned, and Harper didn't know how to respond, because it was true. They *had* left together.

"Andre, this is our friend Harper," Violet said. "The one I told you about who's been on the West Coast getting famous."

Harper's stomach sank at the thought of letting down her friends, but she knew Gavin was right when he'd reminded her they'd always been there for her and they loved her no matter what her career status was.

"Ah, the elusive Harper exists after all." Andre flashed a friendly grin. "How did you like LA?"

Gavin nodded encouragingly, and she said, "Actually, despite what I told some of you the other night, it wasn't all that great. I was embarrassed to tell you the truth, but my show was canceled. After months of rewrites and hard work, it didn't get picked up, my agent dumped me, *and* I had some *awful* dating experiences."

"Oh, no," Desiree said. "I'm so sorry."

"Why were you embarrassed?" Serena asked. "It's not like it's your fault."

"It felt like it was my fault. If the writing were better, maybe it would have gotten picked up."

Emery pointed her fork at Harper and said, "That's crap. My brothers work in the entertainment industry. That kind of thing happens all the time, and it usually has nothing to do with the writer. But think of it this way: Now you have more experience. You've been there. You *made* it! Even if the show wasn't picked up, you sold the pilot! That's a really big deal. But the best news is, now we've got you back." She blew Harper a kiss.

Relief swept through Harper. Harper had met Emery's three brothers when they'd visited a few summers ago. She wasn't sure what her brother Austin did for a living, but she knew Ethan ran one of the most successful television movie channels and

Alec ran an entertainment magazine.

"I'm sorry your show wasn't picked up," Violet said. "But you also mentioned something about bad dating experiences. Does someone need his LA ass kicked? Because Andre and I are here for the summer. We can take a quick trip out West to put a guy or two in their places if need be."

Andre draped an arm over Violet's shoulder and said, "Have I told you lately how much I adore when your claws come out to protect your friends?"

"Nobody needs to be beat up," Harper said, and she was pretty sure if they did, Gavin would be happy to do it. "Although the guy I sat next to on the plane might disagree. The poor guy was just trying to be nice, and it was like I'd taken bitch pills that morning. I was so angry and anxious, I chewed him out. It was pretty ugly."

"He's a guy. You probably made his day," Serena said.

"He did give me his number," Harper said, noticing a slightly jealous look in Gavin's eyes. "He said if I ever decide to write, to give him a call."

"Maybe he likes bitchy women. What are you going to do now?" Chloe asked.

"For now I'll be writing articles for the newspaper and trying to find my next muse." Harper looked at Gavin and mouthed, *Thank you.* He was good at pushing her in ways she never thought she needed. He did it casually, with a slight nod and a satisfied look in his eyes, as he was now.

Violet eyed the two of them and said, "Looks like you might have already found him."

Yeah, I think I might have.

"I'm sure you'll find your groove again," Serena said. "For what it's worth, I'm really glad you're back and that you and

Gavin are hanging out together."

"Oh my gosh, you guys!" Emery set her phone on the table and said, "I just got a text from my brother Ethan. He invited us out on his yacht to watch the fireworks for the Fourth. No pressure or anything, but if you want to go, he'll be at the Provincetown Pier and the yacht leaves at six o'clock."

"The Fourth is weeks away, but we'll go, right, Drake?" Serena said.

Drake nodded. "Sounds good to me."

"I still can't believe my brother owns a yacht," Emery said as she snagged a piece of Dean's pastry.

"That's what happens when you're Showtime's biggest competitor," Gavin said. "The guy's come a long way from our little hometown. I think it sounds great. What do you say, Harp?"

"Sounds fun. I'm slated to write an article about the Provincetown parade for the newspaper, so I'll already be there."

As the girls made plans for the holiday, Gavin leaned closer to Harper and said, "Then so will I."

Chapter Seven

GAVIN SHOWED UP Sunday on a shiny black motorcycle, wearing jeans, black boots, and a look that said he'd missed Harper almost as much as the scorching-hot kiss he'd given her did. It wasn't even a French kiss, just a firm press of his lips as he held her in the circle of his arms. Before they'd met, she hadn't known it was possible for a kiss or an embrace to send tingles from her head to her toes, but ever since they'd agreed to take things slowly, the intensity of her desires had magnified.

From the moment he'd arrived, Gavin had made himself at home, flipping through her notebooks, reading old scripts she'd taken to LA in case the inspiration to finish them hit while she was there. He'd read some of them aloud, which was embarrassing, but it had been an excellent lesson in revision practices. Hearing someone else read her work made it easier for her to spot the flaws. He'd joked about some of her lines, and at one point they had tears in their eyes from laughter. It wasn't just her sexual desires that were intensifying. Her emotions toward Gavin as a trusted, admired friend were deepening. She was even feeling different about herself. Now, after hours of unpacking, as they tossed cardboard boxes into the recycle bins at the other end of her development, she was thinking about that hello kiss, wanting so much more.

"Did you ever think unpacking would be so much fun?" Gavin asked.

He took her hand and they headed back toward her cottage, the gravel crunching beneath their feet. The first thing he'd asked her when he'd arrived, after the kiss and before letting her out of his arms, was how her visit with her parents had gone. He'd held her until she'd answered, like he'd wanted to make sure he was there for her in case it had gone badly. She told him that her visit had gone well, and his relief had shown in his eyes. He was genuine in his affections. Everything he did helped her let down her guard. She was pretty sure that with Gavin she didn't need to be guarded at all.

"What I think," she said as they passed her neighbor's cottage, "is that you make everything better."

He put his arm around her and kissed her temple. "Glad to hear it's mutual. I like your community, by the way. It's cute."

"I like it, too." She even liked living a hop, skip, and a beat from transient renters. There were always new people to chat with and kids playing in the yards, as they were now. She hadn't realized how much she'd missed the casualness of her lifestyle when she'd been in LA. There, her days had been rushed and stressed. Gavin made her forget her worries about what might come next or where her career was headed enough to remember how much she enjoyed life.

She looked up at his handsome face and said, "Every time I'm with you we laugh."

"See, Harp? You wasted all that time in LA trying to fit in with people who weren't your *tribe*, when you could have been here getting to know the newest member."

"You were wrong about yourself, Mr. Wheeler. You *are*

quite a wordsmith." And she really liked the way he used those words. He pushed just enough to make her *want* to be closer. She looked down at her side pressed against his and realized it'd already become natural for him to hold her.

"Think of all the time we have to make up for," he said as they came to her yard.

His gaze moved to the gardens she'd cultivated over the years. "You have quite a green thumb."

"I've always loved gardening, and flowers make me happy." She walked over to his shiny black motorcycle and ran her hand along the seat. "Probably like this makes you happy. Can I sit on it?"

He put his hands on her waist, pulling her closer, his eyes darkening seductively as he said, "You want to *straddle* my *hog*?"

Her heart raced. "That's a loaded question if I ever heard one."

He didn't say a word as his grip tightened around her waist, and he lifted her off her feet like she was light as a feather.

"Gavin!" she squealed, grabbing his shoulders as he moved her over the center of the bike, her long skirt waving around her feet.

"Spread 'em, sweetheart." He lowered her to the seat with a look of sheer satisfaction. "You're officially the first woman to sit on my bike."

That made it even more thrilling. She grabbed the handlebars, feeling strangely powerful. "It feels even bigger than it looks."

He climbed onto the bike, wrapping his arms around her middle, and kissed the side of her neck, sending goose bumps skittering over her flesh.

"You might want to be careful what you say, or I'm liable to slip up and say something you're not ready for." He pressed a titillating kiss to her neck and then spoke in a gravelly voice directly into her ear. "Like, how about I carry you into the bedroom and refresh your memory about something that feels every bit as big as it looks."

Yes, yes, yes!

Her fingers fell from the handlebars to her thighs, and she told herself to calm down. He covered her hands with his and said, "We wouldn't want to make you uncomfortable, would we?"

His voice slithered beneath her skin, burrowing into her core. She tried to swallow, but her mouth was bone dry.

He squeezed her thighs, and in the next breath he said, "So, how about we take her for a ride?" He leaned back, putting space between them, as if he, too, needed to break the spell he'd put them both under.

"A ride, yes, that sounds good," she said shakily. *But first I need to change my underwear...*

He helped her climb awkwardly off the bike and said, "I love this sexy skirt, but you should change into jeans for the ride. Gotta keep my girl safe."

My girl...

Her swooning heart sent her eyes to the ground for fear he'd see how much she wanted him. Even the press of his hand on her back as they went into her cottage made her needier for his touch.

Her mind raced, but she couldn't hang on to any one thought as she went to change. She stood in the middle of her bedroom, wanting to barrel into the living room, tear off his clothes, and drag his fine ass into her bedroom to do all the naughty things they'd done in Virginia. She was desperate to feel him buried deep inside her and to see his gorgeous green eyes silently saying everything they hadn't been brave enough to give voice to that night. She wanted to hide away in the cottage for days, rediscovering each other's bodies like the outside world didn't exist.

Stop, stop, stop! She turned away from the door and grabbed a pair of jeans and tossed a pair of socks on the bed. She pulled on her jeans, and then she exhaled a long breath and sank down to the edge of the bed, clutching the bedspread in her fists as she tried to regain control of her runaway emotions. She closed her eyes, but she could still feel his lips on her skin, his warm breath heating her up as his words sent flames to her core.

"What is going on with me?" she mumbled as she put on her socks and shoved her feet into a pair of boots. This was ridiculous. So what if they got along like they'd known each other forever and he understood her like no one else ever had? Just because the sight of him made her entire body flame didn't mean she had to jump his bones.

Right?

She hadn't wanted to jump anyone's bones since the night of the festival. And that night, she couldn't have helped herself if her life had depended on it.

Was this crazy, or could it be fate? Is that why she'd never stopped thinking about him?

Are we meant to be together?

She stared at the bedroom door, hope rising inside her. With her heart in her throat, she pulled it open. Gavin stood a few feet away, looking at a picture of her and Brock he must have taken from the bookshelf. His eyes met hers, sweeping slowly over her face, her body, and then their eyes collided again, and her heart tumbled inside her chest.

"Hello, beautiful," he said. "Ready?"

She huffed out a breath and strode across the room. "Almost."

She grabbed his face between her hands and kissed him *hard*. He crushed her to him, feasting on her mouth, making her greedy for more. Her emotions reeled, skidding and soaring, making her a little dizzy. Somewhere in the back of her mind she knew this was unfair to both of them, but if she didn't get the neediness out, she'd never make it through the day. When his hand slipped to her butt, she forced herself to break their kiss. She was panting, her skin was on fire, and he was looking at her like a starving lion who'd just zeroed in on his prey. And holy cow, she wanted to be his next meal. But she made herself step back. She smoothed her shaky hand down the front of her tank top, feeling her erratic heartbeat against her palm, and tried to think past the rush of blood in her ears.

"Now that that's out of the way," she said more confidently than she felt, "I'm ready to go." She grabbed her keys and headed straight out the front door.

TORTURE WASN'T A strong enough word to describe the feeling of holding back with Harper any better than *scorching* described the heat coursing through Gavin's body as they rode his motorcycle toward Provincetown. *Exquisite agony* was a much better description for both. Harper's soft body was pressed against his back, her hands clutching his stomach. Thank God for the cool air whipping over his skin, or he might have caught fire. He'd brought two helmets, knowing he wanted to take her for a ride after the way she'd reacted to hearing he drove a motorcycle, but he hadn't thought to bring a second vented jacket, so he'd given her his.

They parked at the pier, and he helped her take off her helmet. Her silky blond hair tumbled over her shoulders. She shook it out, grinning from ear to ear.

"That was amazing!" she exclaimed. "I'm going to write a biker into my next script."

She was so damn hot and happy, he had to kiss her, but he was careful to make it a chaste one for fear of walking around aroused for the rest of the day.

"Just don't name him Gavin," he said as she peeled off his jacket. "The last thing I need is more fangirls." He put the jacket in the compartment and locked the helmets to the bike.

Over the past several months he'd wished he'd had a picture of Parker aka Harper. He pulled out his phone as he draped an arm around her to take a selfie.

"Smile pretty so you can say you knew me when…"

She smiled brightly. He took a picture, then kissed her cheek and took another. He pocketed his phone and reached for her hand, heading for Commercial Street, the main drag through Provincetown. "Let's see what fun awaits us."

The artsy community was home to galleries, restaurants, nightclubs, and eclectic shops, attracting thousands of tourists over the summers. Flags hung above the crowded sidewalks and streets, proudly displaying the LGBTQ rainbow. They passed an artist painting a caricature of a man and his Great Dane. A group of people watched a pantomime outside a bakery. Street performers and musicians were standard fare on street corners and the lawns of the library and the town hall.

"I love it here," Harper said as they made their way down the busy sidewalk. "Do you have any place like this back home?"

"No. Oak Falls is very rural, known for horse farms mostly. I bet you can gain a lot of inspiration for your stories here. Do you ever come here to write?"

"I have, but it's more fun to people watch and not have to worry about work."

"Thanks for letting me read your scripts today. They were funny and interesting. What do you consider them? Drama?"

"Not really. When I think of drama, I think of *This Is Us*, seriously heavy stuff, which is about *all* I've been able to write lately. That's *not* my normal voice, so while I love *This Is Us* and dramas in general, my writing feels crappy because it's too heavy for my voice."

"Oh, come on. I read several pages of your work, and they were all great."

"Well, this one isn't. Trust me."

"If I trusted you with certain evaluations, we'd never have had the last couple of days together."

"I think I know when my writing stinks. I'll show you." She pulled her phone from her pocket, tapping at the screen. "I've got my current script on Dropbox." She handed him the phone and crossed her arms, watching him expectantly. "I'm telling you, it's garbage."

He began reading. The tone was unremarkable and slow, so different from what he'd read earlier. It didn't even seem like it was written by the same person. He handed her back the phone and said, "You're right. It's crap."

"*Geez.*" She shoved her phone in her pocket. "Don't feel the need to cushion the blow or anything."

He gathered her in his arms, meeting her sad eyes. "I'm sorry. I don't mean to hurt your feelings, but whatever that was, it wasn't written by you. It was written by some heartbroken, *dimmed* version of you."

Her shoulders slumped. "I told you it was bad. My forte has always been more *Sex and the City* meets *Friends*. Romantic comedies. I would give my left foot to be able to find my way back to comedic stories, but every time I sit down to write, a poorly written version of *This Is Us* comes out."

"Because you let what happened in LA suck that voice out of you," he said as they stopped to listen to a couple of long-haired guys play guitars in front of the town hall. "You should write about those experiences, find the humor in them."

"And *relive* them? No, thank you."

"Think about it, Harp. I bet lots of women can relate to what you've gone through. You could even bring in a male main character. Believe it or not, guys have bad experiences, too. I once dated a twin, only I had no idea she was a twin. Don't lose your mind trying to figure this one out, but she didn't like me."

She feigned a gasp. "No."

"I know. Hard to believe, right? Listen to what this chick did. Instead of breaking up with me, she swapped places with her sister, who was totally into me. It took me almost three weeks to realize what they'd done."

"They were *that* similar?"

"In all fairness, it was when I was in high school, and I wasn't exactly the most attentive guy back then. That didn't come until a few years later, after I'd had enough bad experiences to I realize I was *letting* them happen to me. I finally took control of my life. But what I'm getting at is that I learned from those bad experiences, and I changed. If you don't want to continue down the *This Is Us* road forever, writing stories that will rip people's hearts out, then maybe you need to start seeing your experiences through new eyes. Use what happened as a *slingshot* to propel your career instead of ties that bind it in a bad place. It might be just the thing you need to write the best romantic comedy ever."

"You make it sound doable, but I'm not even sure I want to pitch to Hollywood ever again. I don't fit in there."

"One wrong person in our lives can throw every aspect of it into turmoil. You can fit in anywhere you want to, as long as you're with the right people." As he said the words, memories of a past he'd spent years trying to forget came rushing forward, hitting him with an impact that momentarily left him numb. He'd buried the horrible experience so deep, he'd nearly forgotten about it. But this wasn't about him or the heartache he'd suffered, or the unplanned pregnancy that had set his world spinning. Now wasn't the time to reveal those things. He pushed those memories aside and focused on helping Harper find her stable ground, just as he had so long ago.

"You went through a tough time, Harp. Your world was pulled out from beneath your feet. It's time to rebuild it on your terms. You don't need Hollywood. Or maybe you do in the long run if you want that type of status career. For now, how about concentrating on healing Harper and writing something for yourself or a local theater?"

Her eyes brightened. "The WHAT Theater in Wellfleet is where my love of the arts started. My parents used to take us all the time, and I worked there throughout high school, learning all about the behind-the-scenes aspects of productions. Jana acted there for years, too."

"Then it sounds like we have a solid direction." He laced his fingers with hers and pressed a kiss to the back of her hand as they walked down the sidewalk. "And once you write the scene where your main character meets her handsome one-night stand turned boyfriend, every woman on earth will want to be her."

"I have no idea how you can be that cocky without coming across as arrogant."

"It's a gift," he said with a wink.

She laughed and said, "Think we can go into Adam's Pharmacy?"

"Sure, but I've got condoms if you're thinking of thanking me for the idea," he teased.

"Get *over* yourself," she said, swatting his chest. She tugged him across the street to the pharmacy. "I want to get a notebook and a pen."

After Gavin bought a notebook, pen, and a box of condoms—just to make Harper blush—he and Harper explored the shops, stopping into almost every one of them. They found funky hats and took pictures wearing them, which Harper posted on her Instagram account. They shared gelato from the Purple Feather and checked out the funky clothes at Shop Therapy and other cool stores. They spent a long time in the bookstores and learned that they both had an affinity for memoirs. Harper did a happy dance after finding the book the girls were reading in the book club. Gavin thumbed through it, telling her they'd have to act out every sexual scene to make sure she was ready for the meeting. That earned him another playful smack, but the heated look in her eyes told him she wasn't completely against the idea. He added two more erotic romances to the pile before paying. In an effort to earn another adorable blush, Gavin told the clerk they liked to read them aloud to each other. Not only did Harper blush, but she snuggled closer, hiding her face in his chest. He made a mental note to embarrass her more often.

As the afternoon turned to evening, they meandered through galleries and more cool shops. Harper began leaning into him, taking his hand whenever the urge hit.

They had dinner at the Governor Bradford, sharing fries and steamy kisses. When the sun set, they found themselves sitting on the beach by the pier. Seagulls pecked at the wet sand along the shore. Couples walked hand in hand, and the din of the town hung in the evening air. Harper sat cross-legged in her jeans and tank top, her hair lifting in the bay breeze as she jotted down notes and told him about the ideas he'd inspired for a story. She looked radiant as she chatted animatedly, her voice rising with excitement, her pen moving quicker across the page. He was glad to see she'd shaken off more of the clouds that had followed her home from LA, allowing the effervescent, confident woman he'd met all those months ago to shine through.

"You're happiest when you're writing, aren't you?" he asked.

She looked at him and said, "I always thought I was. But lately I'd say writing and spending time with you are neck and neck." She leaned closer and whispered, "But you're edging ahead in the race."

He kissed her then, slow and sweet, and said, "Welcome back, Harper."

By the time they drove back to her cottage, Gavin was utterly and completely intoxicated by her. He unlocked her door, and when he put the keys in her hand, he drew her into his arms. He felt a difference in her, as if a great weight had been lifted from her shoulders.

When he gazed into her eyes, she fidgeted nervously with her keys and said, "Do you want to come in?"

"More than anything in this world," he said honestly.

They'd had such a good day, there was only one way he

wanted it to end. But Harper had laid herself bare to him, exposing her vulnerable underbelly, and she deserved the same. Making love to her before he admitted what he'd hidden from almost everyone else in his life would cast darkness on those lights in her eyes, and he couldn't bear to be the cause of that.

Not tonight.

Instead he said, "This was the best day I've had since the day I met you. But if I walk into your house with the way I'm feeling about you right now, I won't walk back out until tomorrow."

"*Oh*...um..." Desire and restraint swam in her eyes.

He lowered his forehead to hers, knowing he had to be strong enough for both of them. Their kisses told him they were on the same page, but he knew that even though Harper was coming back into her own, *she* might still feel like she was on tenuous ground in her own mind. There were enough obstacles for her to second-guess right now. He didn't want to do anything that would cause her to second-guess *them*, so he did one of the hardest things he'd ever had to do.

He kissed her good night and headed home for a cold shower.

Chapter Eight

AFTER SPENDING THE weekend with Harper, transparency became the focus of Gavin's thoughts. He needed—*wanted*—to tell Harper what he'd gone through in college. Talking about it might bring back the trust issues he'd spent years overcoming, and he didn't want to risk that with her, but he knew he had to. He'd never imagined how good sharing his space could feel, but Harper had taken him up on his offer to work from his dock, and when he'd found her, looking beautiful and immersed in her writing, down by the water Monday evening, it had made his day. Knowing she might be there made him look forward to coming home to the house he loved but had never quite made into a *home*. They'd gone to Common Grounds for dinner, and as he'd thought she might, she loved the people and the atmosphere. When he'd taken her home last night, he'd tried to tell her what had happened his first year of college, but she'd looked at him like he was everything she'd ever wanted, and he'd let it go. He was meeting Justin and a few of their buddies for a drink tonight, but tomorrow he and Harper were going to the Chatham Band concert, and come hell or high water, he was going to tell her.

Gavin turned his thoughts back to Mia Stone, who was

leaning over the conference table at the Ocean Edge Resort. They'd spent the last two hours going over design elements for the new boutique. Photographs of artwork, catalogs for furniture and lighting, swatches of fabric, and other proposed design elements were spread over the table.

Mia's dark hair curtained her face as she picked up the blood-orange paint sample he'd brought. "I have to admit, based on our initial meeting I thought you'd come back with pale blues and buttercup yellow, which seem to be the standard colors for coastal boutiques. I adore your bold, unexpected take on things, and I think Josh and Riley will, too."

"Excellent. Mixing the bolder colors and textures with the lighter furniture gives the eclectic, more energetic feel you're trying to achieve."

"I agree," she said as she sat down in a chair.

"Then I'll get started on scheduling our team." He began gathering his things and said, "Are you enjoying your time on the Cape?"

Mia crossed her legs and sat back with a relaxed smile Gavin saw a lot more often from clients since moving out of the city. "I love it here. It's a world away from New York in terms of pace. I love New York, but this is a nice change. The people are definitely easier to work with. You don't have any single men who like the city lying around, do you?" She leaned forward with a glimmer in her eyes. "Please tell me that you and Serena run a matchmaking business on the side."

Mia was a beautiful woman who zipped around in skinny jeans, low-cut blouses, and sky-high heels as if they were running shoes. They had worked together over the phone for a few weeks before she'd come out to the Cape. She was professional and friendly, with a sharp sense of humor.

"I doubt you have trouble in that department," Gavin said as he put a handful of catalogs in his briefcase.

"Getting dates isn't a problem. Guys hit on me a lot. By the way, I appreciate that you never have. Some businessmen forget we have professional boundaries."

Mrs. Cachelle came to mind, and he said, "We all have clients like that. I'd never cross those lines. I also have someone special in my life, and I'd never embarrass her like that."

"That says a lot about you. I'm going to have to start hiring a PI to check out my dates before accepting. Everyone seems to have a hidden agenda."

"I hear ya on that front." *Loud and clear*, he thought with a bite of guilt. He didn't have a hidden agenda, but he believed in honesty, and it was definitely time to show his hand to Harper.

He closed his briefcase, turning his thoughts back to Mia, and said, "Serena's husband knows a good PI. Reggie Steele. Let me know if you want his number."

Amusement shone in her eyes. "I know Reggie. We've worked with him. Gosh, I haven't seen him in years, but maybe I should give him a call…"

They joked about Mia hiring Reggie to *prequalify* her dates and then circled back to discussing the boutique. Gavin promised to be in touch the following week to firm up schedules.

After he left, he received a text from Harper with a picture of her tanned, toned legs dangling off the edge of the dock, her toes skimming the water. *I had a great writing day! I love working here. Thank you! How did your meeting go? Have fun with the guys tonight.*

He climbed into his car and called her as he drove out of the parking lot. "Hey, beautiful."

"Hi. I hope I'm not cramping your style by monopolizing your dock."

He heard the smile in her voice and wished he were there to see it. "You are my style, sweetheart. Nothing you do can cramp it."

"How did the meeting go? Did you dazzle Mia with your ideas?"

"She was almost as dazzled as I am by your smile."

"Would you like a cracker with that cheese?"

He heard her giggle and said, "Yes, please. I can't wait to see you tomorrow. Send me a selfie to tide me over until the concert."

"Gavin Wheeler, you could charm the panties off a nun."

Forget the nun, he wanted Harper.

They talked for a few more minutes, and then Harper said, "I'm heading home. Have fun with the guys. I'll see you tomorrow."

Tomorrow, then the next day, and if I have it my way, every day thereafter.

IF ANYONE HAD told Harper last week that she would enjoy writing articles for the newspaper, she would have balked. She'd thought newspaper articles were a thing of her past, stepping stones to bigger, better challenges. But a lot had changed since she'd come home, including her perspective, and she owed it to the deliciously sexy man sitting on a blanket a few feet away. It was Wednesday night, and they were at Kate Gould Park in Chatham. Balloons waved in the breeze, tied to long strings attached to children's wrists and the backs of chairs. Families and groups of friends and lovers picnicked on the lawn, chatting, dancing, and taking pictures of the forty-piece band. Gavin looked handsome and relaxed, watching a young father dance with his two adorable, pigtailed little girls by the bandstand. He'd been so patient while Harper interviewed families. She was finally holding her last interview of the night with Edna and Frank Boema, an elderly couple who had been attending the concerts for more than thirty years.

Edna, a pleasantly plump woman with frizzy gray hair and serious dark eyes, had just finished telling Harper that she'd celebrated her eightieth birthday last weekend. Now she was rattling off pieces of history about the band. "Did you know the band was started by just twelve members in 1931?"

"Yes, I did, actually," Harper said. "I grew up coming to these concerts, and my father made sure my siblings and I knew the history of how it all began. It's hard to believe so little has changed since then." The band still wore white pants and white shoes with colorful blazers, though they'd switched from blue to red. Some things never changed. *Like Gavin.* He was the same person she'd met almost a year ago, a thoughtful, deep thinker. His patience, support, sense of humor, and his dedication to his clients made him even more attractive. Not to mention those steamy kisses…

"The concerts didn't start here, you know," Frank said, drawing Harper from her thoughts. Frank was an affable, balding man who wore his dress pants belted just below his chest, a short-sleeve dress shirt, and a tie. His skin was marred with age spots and mapped with wrinkles.

"Oh?" Harper knew the original bandstand had been in the parking lot next to the town offices, but she let Frank take the stage.

After a long history lesson, Frank said, "Eddie and I had our first date here."

"I'd love to hear about that." Harper took copious notes as they shared details of the date that led to their long, happy marriage. Edna told her about how, on the advice of her older sisters, she'd played hard to get and had turned down his first three offers for dates. The fourth time he'd asked, he'd told her it would be his last request—and she'd told him she wanted to accept the first time he'd asked and that she hoped she was the last woman he'd ever ask out. After the concert they'd gotten pizza and taken it to the beach, where according to Frank, they fell in love beneath the stars.

Their story was just the foundation she needed to create a tale of moonlit family traditions for the article. When she finished the interview, she made her way back to Gavin.

Her heart skipped as he stood up to his full height, reaching for her hand. She tossed her notebook on the blanket and took his hand.

He pulled her closer, his arm circling her waist. "How's it going, Lois Lane?"

"I think I finally have enough for the article. Sorry it took so long."

He pressed his lips to hers and said, "You're creating magic for millions of readers. No need to be sorry. But see those women over there?" He nodded toward a group of older women wearing fancy bright red hats. "They've been eyeing me like I'm a container of Bengay. I think you'd better dance with me before they come over and start stripping down and rubbing their bodies all over me."

One of the women wiggled her fingers in a flirty wave and another winked.

"Wow, I'm *right here*," she said. "Those cougars have got some nerve."

He chuckled and waved to the woman. Then he began swaying to the music. "Do you blame them? I'm a hot commodity."

"Yes, you are," she said.

"Not quite as hot as you are," he said.

They danced to "Moon River" and the next song and the next, never missing a word. Gavin danced like he'd been born with rhythm in his blood and sang like he was born with lyrics on his tongue.

"How do you know all the words?"

"Middle school choir," he said as he dipped her over his arm.

"You were in *choir*? That must have been so cute. Did you have a pencil protector, too?"

He nipped at her lower lip. "Small town. *Everyone* was in choir."

The band started playing "Sweet Caroline." Gavin twirled her around, making her laugh, which earned one of his glorious smiles.

"My father used to dance like this with me when I was little," she said.

"No wonder you're such a good dancer." He pulled her in close, swaying to the beat. When the song changed to a slower one, he said, "I'll have to thank your father one day."

"Trying to meet my family, are you?" She was meeting with her brothers and sister Saturday for breakfast. She thought about inviting Gavin, but he didn't need to be bored with hearing the same stories he'd already suffered through about LA while she brought them up to speed on her life.

"When you're ready," he said. "I enjoyed watching you interview families tonight."

"You watched me?" That made her feel good all over.

"Mm-hm." He kissed her softly as they danced. "You're good with people, Harp. It's no wonder each interview took a while. I thought, or maybe *hoped*, it was just me you enchanted, but I saw it in the eyes of everyone you spoke with. They were enamored with the personable beauty taking an interest in them. That wasn't faked either, was it? You really enjoyed talking with them."

"I did. I had forgotten how fun it was to interview people. That last couple I spoke to has been coming here for more than thirty years. They brought their children when they were younger. Their kids no longer live on the Cape, but when they visit they bring their grandchildren to the concerts."

"I love that," he said.

"Me too, and I love dancing with you."

"Me too, sweetheart," he said, holding her tighter. "You mentioned being a white-picket-fence girl before you went to LA. Are you still?"

"I am. Maybe I'm crazy, but ever since I was a little girl, I had visions of a white wedding, a picket fence, and nights like this with my children falling asleep on the way home in the car."

"You've got a romantic heart." He pressed his lips to hers, and then he said, "I like that about you, Harper. I'm glad you didn't let those bad experiences steal those dreams." His gaze turned serious and he said, "I once let someone steal that dream from me, and it took a long time to get it back."

"One of the twins?"

"No. They were just playing around. My first year of college

I had a pretty serious relationship with a girl named Corinne. She's the first and last girl I took home to meet my family. They thought she was totally wrong for me, and she *really* disliked them. Their reactions should have tipped me off that I was missing something big, but I was blinded by youth and stupidity. Corinne thought they were too small town, and she rubbed them the wrong way. My father is pretty well off, but he's a self-made man and he came up from nothing. He's careful with his money and you'd never know he was well off because he doesn't flaunt it. He's very down-to-earth. I've never heard my parents say a negative thing about a person, which is another reason I should have listened when they said she was a gold digger. But I thought she was just misunderstood and that I could help her to be understood."

"Do you mean you thought you could *fix* her?" She felt a little sick at the thought that he was one of those guys who was attracted to what she called broken birds—women with issues. Did he feel that way about her?

"No, and please don't ever think that what I had with her was anything like what we have. I'm not trying to *fix* you, Harper. You're not broken. You were hurt, and for good reason. There's a difference. Anyone who cared about you could have helped you see past the grief over losing your show and a couple of bad relationships."

"Maybe my friends would, but most guys would wash their hands of a woman who was that down on things. I could have easily gotten such thick skin I didn't let anyone in."

"You *do* have thick skin, sweetheart. How could you not? But even thick skin on you is soft and loving, not harsh or cold. The reason I say I wasn't trying to *fix* Corinne is because I didn't think she was broken. She said her parents were overbearing and had tried to control every aspect of her life. She told me that her family had disowned her and that she was paying for school with loans and scholarships. I had never met her family. If I had, I would have realized how wrong I was. To make a long story short, she got pregnant, and in the end she wasn't who I thought she was."

Harper's stomach clenched. "You have a child?"

"No. I thought I was going to, but once I told her I would quit college and we could raise the baby in Oak Falls, where I could get a job at my father's company and we would have family support, I guess it threw a monkey wrench into her plans. A week later she aborted the baby and broke up with me—in that order. She told me the baby wasn't mine anyway. I had wondered how it happened since we always used condoms, but you know, they're only ninety-nine percent effective. I figured we were just unlucky. But then I found out she'd been seeing some other guy almost the whole time. She told me it was my baby because she thought I was a cash wagon and that my father's money was family money I'd have access to. I found out later that her family *hadn't* disowned her. *She'd* snubbed *them* because they wouldn't cater to her expensive demands, but they were paying for her schooling, books, and housing. Apparently all that wasn't enough for her. And honestly, who knows if she was ever really pregnant?"

"Gavin, that's *awful*."

"It pretty much broke me for a while. I had trouble trusting women, and trusting *myself*, for a long time. But the truth is, I didn't love her. I was young and away from my family for the first time. I think I needed her affection to fill a gap, which is embarrassing to admit. You see, other people have one-night stands, but I'm not wired that way. I had a relationship that seemed good enough at the time, and when she got pregnant I wanted to do the right thing."

He shook his head with a pinched expression, and she realized they were still swaying, though the music had become white noise to the pain in her heart for Gavin.

"I was incredibly young and unfathomably stupid," he said. "But it was what it was, and it was just one more reason I hadn't been home in so long when I met Serena. Corinne drove a wedge between me and my family, and I let it happen. I took her side from the get-go instead of listening to the people who had known me my whole life and who were only looking out for me. Afterward, I was ashamed of taking her side, so I stayed away from home. Things are better with my family now, but it was a long, hard road."

"No wonder you pushed me to be honest with my family." She was heartbroken for him, but she couldn't ignore the question gnawing at her. "I'm sorry, but I have to ask if you're one of those guys who needs broken women."

"God no. I wouldn't call her *broken*, Harper. She knew exactly what she was doing. She was manipulative and conniving, not broken. I later talked to her family and found out I wasn't the first guy she'd done that to. I never understood why I was put through such a horrible time, thinking I was having a kid, then realizing I was being played. But now I'm glad I went through it."

"Why? It must have been so awful without close friends or family to help you."

"It was, but when you appeared on the beach after nearly a year, my heart stopped, Harper. I was beginning to think I'd conjured our night together, and then you were there, like an angel from above, only the light in your eyes had dimmed. But that experience helped me understand what you were facing. It helped me understand what it was like to have your world pulled out from under you. I think fate brought us together again, Harp, and had I not gone through that, I wouldn't have known how to relate to what you'd been through, much less help you move past it."

Harper couldn't imagine how Gavin thought what he'd gone through was similar to her experiences. His was so much bigger, more heartbreaking. But now she understood why he was so patient and looked at things through a different lens than she had. He'd been drowning and had found his way back up to the surface. He was even stronger than she thought.

The song ended, and everyone clapped as the bandleader conferred with another band member. Gavin held Harper tighter, continuing to dance to their own private beat. She rested her head on his shoulder, his heartbeat steady and sure against her cheek. In those quiet moments, the impact of how much of himself he'd shared hit her, along with the realization that he'd taken what sounded like the worst time in his life and turned it positive for her.

She gazed up at the man who had taken hold of her heart almost a year ago and cradled it in his hands for all this time. She had already been falling for him, and this just tipped the scales.

When the band started playing "My Girl," Gavin held her gaze, singing every word to her. He'd had his heart ripped out, and somehow this incredible man was still able to trust, to give himself over without hesitation. She wanted to do that, too.

He twirled her, then held her close again, and she melted against him. As the song ended, he lowered his lips to hers, kissing her deeply.

Applause and cheers rang out, and she felt him smiling into their kisses. When she drew back, the women with the red hats hooted, cheering louder and waving their hats. Harper realized most of the audience was looking at her and Gavin.

"What's going on?" Harper asked.

With stars in his eyes Gavin said, "The women in the red hats are the wives of some of the band members. They did me a favor and got the band to play that song for us."

Harper swore the earth moved, lifting her higher. She put her arm around his neck, pulling his mouth toward hers, and said, "Then let's give them something to cheer about."

LATER THAT EVENING they stumbled into Harper's cottage in a fit of kisses and laughter, reliving the end of the concert. She hoped Gavin wasn't going to take off right away, as he had the other night. In all the time they'd spent together this week, they hadn't done anything more than kissing, but tonight she wanted to.

"When that red-hat woman grabbed you for the next dance, I thought I'd never get you back," Harper said as she set her bag on the desk.

"She wasn't bad, but the woman who grabbed me after her? She pinched my cheeks. And I don't mean the ones on my face." Gavin hauled her against him, grabbing her butt with both hands, and her body flamed. "You don't have to worry about not getting me back, Harp. I am so into you…"

"Good," she said a little breathlessly, "because I'd hate to have to call Jana and have her kick some old lady's ass." He smelled like man and desire wrapped up in one strong, sexy package.

"Finally learning I'm worth fighting for, huh?"

Her heart was racing, and his hungry eyes told her he was right there with her, longing for more.

"I've never been a fighter." She ran her fingers over his biceps, trying to sound seductive as she said, "But I think it's time to learn."

"Sweetheart," he whispered softly, and his mouth came coaxingly down over hers.

Months of fantasies and days of heady anticipation came rushing out in eager gropes and penetrating kisses. Harper could barely think past the inferno blazing inside her as they tumbled down to the couch. His arousal pressed firmly against her center, thrusting with each ravenous plunge of his tongue. She pushed her hands beneath his shirt, loving the way his muscles flexed with his every move as he kissed her roughly but touched her tenderly. The conflicting sensations stole her breath. His lips slipped to her cheek in a series of feathery kisses.

"God, what you do to me," he whispered against her skin. "I'm going to make you feel so good you'll never want to leave my side."

Oh, yes! The desire in his voice had her arching beneath him, pulling his mouth back to hers for more. He kissed her so slow and deep, reminding her of the way he made love, powerful and sensual at once. His kisses consumed her, and her ability to think drifted away. He intensified his efforts, and she lost herself in the hot strokes of his tongue, the feel of his hand moving up her bare thigh. Her skirt bunched around her bottom. She rocked up, and he guided her legs around his waist. His powerful body flexed as he angled his hips, pressing exquisitely against her center. Even through the thick denim of his jeans she felt his girth, remembered the feel of him pushing into her.

He slicked his tongue along her lower lip, then trapped it between his teeth, tugging gently, sending jolts of electricity arcing through her. She moaned, bowing up beneath him as he kissed her jaw, and his hot, wet mouth trailed kisses down her neck.

"*Don't stop….*" The needy plea came without warning, but the next came with vehemence. "Touch me, Gavin."

He made a raw, masculine sound and reclaimed her mouth as his hand pushed beneath her blousy top. He cupped her breast, his thumb brushing over her nipple until it throbbed for more. Spikes of desire darted through her as he kissed his way down her neck again, lifting and repositioning himself lower on the couch to kiss her belly. The first touch of his lips on her stomach pulled a greedy moan from her lungs. She buried her hands in his hair, holding tight to the man who felt incredible *and* familiar, like no time had passed since he'd last devoured her body.

He took his time, loving every inch of her stomach and waist. He brushed his lips over her hip. He kissed her tattoo, then traced it with his tongue. "God, I missed this sunflower."

His rough voice made her even more combustible.

He kissed his way up her belly and ribs, rolling her shirt up over her breasts, and trailed openmouthed kisses along the skin just below her bra. When he unhooked the front clasp, gently pushing the cups to the side, she bit her lower lip to keep from whimpering. He teased her nipples in languid mind-numbing circles, and those whimpers broke free despite her resistance. He nipped at her sensitive flesh until her body felt like a tangle of live wires. She writhed and arched beneath him, openly begging for more.

His mouth covered her breast with the same torturous restraint, painfully slow and expertly maddening. He flattened his tongue over the taut peak, dragging it in long, leisurely strokes, each one making her gasp and tremble. He shifted his body, lying half on her, half beside. His cock pressed temptingly against her leg, and his big, hot hand traveled down her belly. His fingers moved light and teasingly around her belly button, beneath her skirt, and along the lace at the top of her panties. He teased her there while they kissed, their tongues dancing deliciously. His hand moved lower, along the lace edge above her thigh. Her breathing was so erratic, she wasn't sure she was really breathing at all. He gripped her thigh tight, driving flashes of heat and ice into her core. When he finally stroked her through the thin material of her damp panties, the air rushed from her lungs. His appreciative groan and hard thrust of his hips made her even wetter. His thick fingers pushed beneath her panties, and they both groaned in desperation. He sucked her breast harder, *ravenously*, as his fingers entered her. Her hips shot off the cushion, and she gasped with his every suck, every touch, every stroke over that magical, secret spot. Her skin tingled and burned. Blood throbbed in her veins, rushed through her ears, and when his thumb came into play, teasing the sensitive nub at the apex of her sex at the same moment he bit down, she shattered into a million electrified pieces.

"Gavin! *Oh, Gav—*"

Her hips bucked as the climax tore through her, unchaining all of her pent-up emotions. She undulated, emitting a string of indiscernible pleasure-soaked sounds. He stayed with her, taking her impossibly higher, until her world tilted and she careened into another explosive orgasm.

She was going to die.

She just knew it.

This immense pleasure had to be deadly.

Gavin didn't stop there. He continued his masterful ministrations, lavishing her other breast with the same loving attention and taking her right up to the edge of ecstasy so many times, when he finally moved over her, still fully clothed, she lay panting and spent. His mouth covered hers with renewed vigor, his hard length pressing rhythmically against her center as he made love to her mouth, reigniting her oversensitive body and sending her soaring again.

When she finally drifted down from the clouds, she was shaking all over. Her limbs felt like lead. Even holding on to Gavin was too much effort. Her arms fell limply to the cushions.

Her entire body was tingling and numb at once. His kisses became softer, like secrets. She wasn't even sure she was still kissing him back. She was completely and utterly drunk on him.

"I think you put me in an orgasm coma," she managed just above a whisper. "I want to reciprocate, but I'm not sure I can move."

He smiled appreciatively and said, "Don't move, sweetheart. Get some rest."

Her eyes opened, and the love in his drew a dreamy sigh from her lungs. "But that's not fair to you."

He kissed her lips, her cheek, then her lips again, and said, "What we have isn't about fair, sweetheart. Neither of us is the type to rush into sex. We've known that from the start. In Virginia, we thought we had only that one night together, but now we can take our time. When we finally come together, I want you to be sure, Harper. Sure it's what you want. Sure of *us*. Because we both know how good we are together, and once we're there again, I'll never want to let you go."

He was cradling her heart again, knowing exactly what she needed and making sure she got it.

"I love making you feel good," he whispered. His warm lips touched hers again in a kiss so sweet, she wanted to disappear into it. "Get some rest, Sleeping Beauty. I'll text you tomorrow."

Chapter Nine

HARPER AWOKE TO a knock on her door Thursday morning before dawn. She reached blindly for her phone as she sat up and saw she'd missed a call from Gavin. Goose bumps rose on her flesh as she bolted to her feet. She'd thought about him all night! How could he possibly have known?

Gavin's sweatshirt tumbled down her thighs as she ran to the door and pulled it open. A rush of brisk air stung her skin, but the sight of Gavin standing on the porch, looking gorgeous in a dark hoodie and jeans, soothed the sting.

"Good morning, beautiful."

"Hi." She couldn't stop smiling and she didn't even know why he was there. It was *that* good to see him. His gaze moved slowly down her body, heating her up from the inside out.

"I couldn't go to work knowing I left you in an orgasm coma last night." He stepped closer, blocking the cool air as he pressed his warm lips to hers. "I have the perfect remedy. Breakfast on the beach as we watch the sunrise. I've got everything we need in the car."

Her heart skipped a beat. "I might need to have an orgasm coma every night."

"That can be arranged."

Her nipples pebbled at the thought. "Come in. I just need to get dressed."

She brushed her teeth and hair as quickly as she could, shimmied into her jeans, and slipped on a pair of sandals. She found Gavin leafing through the book she was reading for the book club.

"Seems pretty dirty," he said flirtatiously.

"Incredibly. I love it, and I have to finish reading it by tomorrow night for the meeting. Hey, would you mind if I read on your dock? It's quieter than going to the beach or the pier." Her heart raced as she searched for her keys.

"Not at all. My dock is your dock. What are you looking for?"

"My keys. I thought I left them on my desk."

He swept his arm around her waist, drawing her into his arms. "I already grabbed your keys, sweetheart. What else do you need?"

"Just a proper 'good morning.'" She went up on her toes and pressed her lips to his. He deepened the kiss, sending rivers of heat washing through her. She sighed as their lips parted. "Best morning *ever*."

They drove to Newcomb Hollow Beach and left their shoes in the car. Harper's feet sank into the cold sand as they carried blankets and breakfast down the long path from the dunes to the beach. They laid out a blanket and settled in to watch the sunrise with to-go cups of coffee Gavin had bought on his way over. He opened the bag from Dunkin' Donuts and handed her a banana-chocolate muffin.

"I hope they're still your favorite," he said as he unwrapped his muffin.

"You really do remember everything."

He pressed his lips to hers and said, "Every kiss, every touch, every 'Oh, Gavin, *yes!*'"

She buried her face in his chest, laughing. When she lifted her face, he kissed her again and said, "Best memory *ever*."

They ate their muffins, listening to the ebb and flow of the tide. There was nothing quite as beautiful as the dawn of a new day on Cape Cod. The brisk morning air kissed her cheeks, but Harper was warm tucked against Gavin's side as rolling waves crashed into the shore.

"Hear that?" Gavin said, holding her tighter against him as they sipped their coffee. "The waves remind me of you, calmly building momentum, waiting for the right moment before you give it your all."

"Does that mean I'm a tease?"

He kissed her temple, a small smile on his lips. "No, sweetheart. The ocean doesn't tease. It's one of Mother Nature's powerful gifts. Stronger than almost anything can resist and gentle enough to radiate beauty and give a sense of calm. It deserves respect and admiration."

"That's a really nice thing to say."

"It's true. If you think about how you were on that plane ride home, feeling like your world was out of control."

"I think the guy who sat next to me would attest to the fact that I was more like a wicked hurricane."

"You weren't the hurricane, Harp. You were the thrashing waves caused by the violent winds of the hurricane. Once the storm cleared and you could see past the dark clouds, you settled back into the sweet, focused woman you've always been."

The sun crept over the horizon like fire easing into the sky. Harper felt like she was experiencing it for the first time, and she knew it was because she was sharing it with Gavin.

"If I'm the sea, what are you?"

He picked up a piece of his muffin and offered it to her as he said, "You tell me."

She opened her mouth, and after he put the treat on her tongue, she kissed his fingertips, thinking about his analogy. "I think you're the wind."

"The cause of the storm? I'm not sure that's good."

"It is, because the wind calms and enlivens the sea. It pushes it in different directions, reaching outside its normal comfort zones, urging it to take over new ground and then easing. Leaving it to find its own way."

"And *that* is why you're the writer. How's your writing coming along?"

"Incredibly well. I'm excited with the new direction. Looking at my experiences from a different perspective has changed the way I write. I feel reborn in a way. I didn't expect it, but I think it's funnier. You were right to suggest that I take the hopes of Hollywood off the table and just focus on writing something good. Thank you for that."

"Sometimes it takes a fresh outlook to change a stifling situation."

As they finished eating, her thoughts returned to last night and all that Gavin had told her about his experience with Corinne. She dug her toes in the sand by the edge of the blanket and said, "You mentioned that what you went through with Corinne had stolen your dreams for a long time but that you got them back. What dreams are you working on now?"

His eyes warmed, moving slowly from her eyes to her mouth. His hand brushed along her cheek to the base of her neck, drawing her closer. His lips grazed hers ever so lightly as he said, "Do you want to hear my dreams or my *fantasies*?"

The hard press of his lips brought her arms around his neck, and as she leaned into him, he lowered her to the blanket, deepening the kiss. The sounds of the ocean coalesced with the lust rushing through her veins, and she pushed her hands into his hair, holding his mouth to hers. He made her want and need. He made her crave things she'd only ever wanted with him. His hand moved down her side and he gripped her hip, holding tight. His efforts went from rough and demanding to soft and alluring, like the tide, making her head swim and her heart soar.

When he drew back, kissing the edges of her lips, her cheeks, and then her lips again, she said, "I want to hear your dreams."

He gazed down at her and said, "Finding my forever."

Her heart fluttered, and she gathered the courage to say, "And your fantasies?"

His eyes heated even more, turning her flutters into a frenzy. He covered her mouth with his in the same dizzying rhythm as before. She rose when he eased his efforts, trying to take more of him, landing hard beneath the press of his chest when he gave her what she wanted. She felt weightless, the world felt timeless, and when their lips parted, he left her breathless.

"You're my fantasy, sweetheart," he said in a voice laden with emotions. "You have been since the day I met you."

Chapter Ten

HARPER WAS NO longer tiptoeing into his heart. She'd *invaded* it. The night of the band concert had opened some sort of sexual and emotional vortex. When Harper had given more of herself to him yesterday morning at the beach, he'd been right there with her, falling harder, wanting to be a bigger part of her world. They'd become ravenous for each other, but he'd handed Harper the reins, letting her set their sexual pace as best he could. It was killing him to hold back, and he couldn't stop thinking about her. Even as he watched his buddies shoot pool at Common Grounds, his mind kept drifting back to Harper. She'd texted earlier and said her boss was so impressed with the article she'd written he'd assigned her three more. She was on fire, professionally and emotionally.

"Gavin, are you riding with us tomorrow?" Dwayne asked.

Justin's cousin Dwayne was a stocky ex-Marine and a member of the Dark Knights. He gave off an I-don't-give-a-shit attitude, but his eyes told a different story, revealing the grief he carried from the loss of his younger sister to suicide several years earlier.

"Probably not," Gavin said. He leaned against the wall, watching Cory take his shot.

"Pussy whipped?" Dwayne glanced at Justin, who shrugged. "You missed last weekend, too."

"Sorry, dude. My girl is way hotter than you guys." Gavin smirked.

"True that," Justin said as he walked around the pool table assessing his next shot.

Gavin pushed from the wall and patted Dwayne's shoulder. "This weekend is *all* hers."

"He's just jealous," Cory said. "Dwayne's going through a dry spell."

Dwayne scoffed. "Dry spell my ass. I get more action than you could ever dream of."

As the guys gave each other hell, Gavin's mind reeled back to the prior afternoon, when he'd arrived home from work and found Harper swimming in the pond. The book she was reading for the book club lay on the dock beside her clothes, laptop, and a towel. She'd climbed up the ladder wearing a skimpy aqua bikini and a wanton look in her eyes. His sweet Harper had strutted determinedly toward him, hips swaying seductively, taut nipples pressing against the thin material of her bikini top. She'd crushed her mouth to his, devouring him like she'd been waiting all day to do it. She'd mumbled something about him reminding her of the hero in the book she was reading as she made quick work of opening his slacks. She'd dropped to her knees right there on the dock and taken his cock in her hands. Her gorgeous baby blues locked on his face as she teased the head of his shaft with her tongue. When she'd taken him to the back of her throat, the erotic sight of her loving him had nearly made him come. But he'd held out, enjoying every magnificent stroke, suck, and slick of her tongue. When she cupped his balls, giving them one perfect *tug*, he'd finally let go, and she'd swallowed everything he had to give. He'd swept her into his arms and carried her up to a lounge chair on the patio, where he'd stripped off her sexy little bikini bottoms and feasted on her until she'd come so many times, she'd fallen asleep in his arms.

Cory nudged Gavin. "Dude, Justin asked you a question."

Gavin shook his head to try to clear his thoughts and said, "Shit, sorry, man. I must have zoned out." His cock was at half-mast. He took a swig of his drink, forcing himself to think about algebra.

"I said, I picked up that client you referred me to. The Cachelles? They hired me to do the stonework for their guesthouse." Justin's lips curved up. "You didn't tell me the woman was horny as a dog in heat."

"Married?" Dwayne asked.

Justin nodded. "And hot."

"Let me guess, you gave her what she wanted," Cory said as he leaned over the pool table, lining up his shot. With a quick flick of his chin, his shaggy brown hair moved from in front of his eyes as he took the shot, knocking a ball into the side pocket.

"Think I'm an asshole?" Justin scoffed. "Let me rephrase that. I am an asshole, but not that big of an asshole." He looked at Gavin and said, "A little warning would have been nice."

"Hey, no one warned me," Gavin said. "Serena has a field day reliving the way that woman hit on me." The only woman he wanted to hit on him was out at Red River Beach, talking about the erotic novel he'd skimmed the other night when they were at her place. "Anyone feel like hitting Red River Beach?"

"Steph is at Red River tonight for a book club meeting," Elliott Appleton said as he picked up Gavin's and Cory's empty glasses. Elliott had longish sandy-blond hair, wore wire-framed glasses, and knew every customer by name. He also had Down syndrome. He pushed his glasses up to the bridge of his nose and said, "They read *dirty* books. Steph and Gabe blush when they read them." Elliott's older sister, Gabe, a vivacious, curvy redhead, owned Common Grounds.

They all laughed.

"Is Gabe in the book club?" Justin lifted his pool cue to line up his shot.

"No. She says she works too much," Elliott said. "Are you in the book club, Gavin?"

"No. I think it's only for chicks," Gavin said.

Elliott said, "Then why do you want to go there? It's too dark to swim."

"Because his woman is there," Dwayne explained.

Elliott nodded. "If I had a woman I'd go where she was instead of hanging out with these slackers, too." He walked away chuckling.

Justin squinted as he took his shot and said, "Is Chloe in the book club?"

Gavin nodded. "Chloe, Daphne, Steph…"

"I'm in," Dwayne said.

"I'm game," Justin said with a devious grin.

"We're in the middle of a game," Cory complained.

"You can stay here and play with your balls," Justin said. "We've got better things to do."

"Stay here my ass." Cory set his pool cue in the holder.

"Hey," Gabe said as they plowed toward the front door. "Where are you guys hurrying off to?"

"Red River Beach," Gavin said. "Crashing the book club meeting."

"That's very brave of you fools. Good luck with that," she called after them.

THE BOOK CLUB meeting was even more fun than Harper had imagined. Harper sat on a blanket with Chloe, Daphne, and her new friend, Steph, a brown-eyed poet and herbal shop owner with red and purple streaks in her long dark hair. They'd cooked burgers on a portable grill and had eaten dinner as their long-distance members introduced themselves over Skype. Dixie, a gorgeous tattooed redhead, and her friend Izzy, a sassy brunette, from Maryland, and Paige, a pretty brunette with a sweet demeanor, from Upstate New York. Harper was surprised to find out that the club had hundreds of members across the United States, but many of them preferred the club's online forums to in-person or video meetings.

They'd been chatting for quite a while, discussing the book and their lives in equal measure. Harper pulled her sweater tighter around her as a breeze swept up the beach.

"I'd love to know why you chose this book," Paige said. "I *hot pinked* nearly half the book."

"*Hot pinked?*" Daphne looked around the group. "Is that a sex term I don't know about?"

Paige laughed. "No. I highlight typos and grammatical errors in hot pink on my ereader app."

"What are you, the grammar police?" Dixie asked.

"I am. It's a curse," Paige said.

"It did have a lot of typos," Steph agreed. "I should have paid more attention to the sample before choosing it. But it had more than seven hundred reviews the first week of release and

I'd never even heard of the author. I figured it had to be good."

Paige said, "I hadn't heard of the author either. The author must have an amazing marketing team to get that many reviews that fast. Personally, I thought the hero was a little *too* demanding. He's not my type of five-star hero."

"Really? I loved that side of him," Chloe said. "I wasn't sure at first, because he was a bit of an asshole, but then I warmed to his ways. Did anyone else dislike him?"

Harper listened as the girls shared their thoughts, holding hers close to her chest. She liked when Gavin got demanding, but he did it in a much more gentlemanly way than the hero in the book had. Gavin's demands came out charming and laden with desire, whereas the hero in the book was crass. But the pleasure he took when he allowed his heroine to take control? That was *hot*.

"And I have no issue with some types of bondage," Dixie said, "but if any man ever asked me to strip down and then left me there for twenty minutes while he took a phone call, I'd be done with him right then and there."

Izzy nodded, her straight dark hair brushing her shoulders. "I agree. Get your ass in here and fuck me or I'll walk out that door."

"I don't know," Daphne said. "I'm on the fence about him. I read chapter seventeen, about his past and what he was thinking four times, and I still can't decide if he's a jerk or just misunderstood. The phone call thing might piss me off, and he had some weird habits, but something about his raw emotions after everything he'd been through spoke to me."

Harper agreed. "I'm with you. He *was* overly demanding—not just sexually, but he was also possessive, in good ways and bad. I hated that he needed to know where she was all the time and who she was calling. That would drive me insane. But there's something romantic about how in love with the heroine he was, right? Or am I crazy?"

Everyone talked at once, agreeing about the romantic side of the hero. Harper didn't think a fictional hero could ever come close to her and Gavin's first date or the afternoon they'd spent in Provincetown. She smiled inwardly thinking about his offering up an *orgasm-coma remedy*. That was about the cutest, most romantic thing she'd ever experienced.

"Would you ever date someone like that?" Steph asked.

"No," Harper and Daphne said in unison.

"With all the action I'm *not* getting these days, if he has a heartbeat and looks hot, I'll date him." Chloe laughed.

"I hear ya," Steph said.

"I would date a guy like that. He's got an edge to him, and I love that—*but* he'd have to play by *my* rules!" Izzy said.

"The guy threatened to kill his own brother, Iz," Dixie pointed out. "I'm not sure he'd play by anyone else's rules. By the way, I totally want to read his brother's book. He was hot."

"Me too," Chloe and Steph agreed.

"Well, I could never date a guy like that." Paige shook her head. "My brothers Knox and Landon wouldn't let a guy like that near me. Besides, I don't think I could give up control and let a man tie me up. I like to read about it, but actually doing it would scare me."

Harper pressed her lips together in an effort to remain straight-faced. She had let Gavin bind her wrists in Virginia, which she'd never imagined letting anyone do before meeting him. Then again, he'd let her bind his, too, and she'd never imagined enjoying doing that. But the control it had given her had been beyond thrilling.

"Not even if you loved him?" Dixie asked.

Paige shrugged, discomfort written all over her face. "I've never been in love, but my gut says no."

"Well, you'd be missing out. Not that I'm into BDSM or anything," Izzy said. "But I can definitely get into a little silk-tie action. I think it can bring you closer."

"Speaking of closer," Harper said, needing to change the subject before she accidentally revealed something she shouldn't. "How hot was chapter twenty?"

She fanned her face as the girls chimed in about the erotic scene in which the heroine marched into her hero's office, locked his door, and proceeded to give him the best blow job of his life. She'd been so turned on by the idea of taking control like that and making Gavin moan with appreciation, she'd had to dive into the pond to try to cool down. It hadn't worked. When Gavin had appeared on the dock, looking like sex on legs in his dress pants and button-down shirt, she'd thrown caution to the wind and taken *exactly* what she'd wanted. She hadn't even had an excuse for her inner hussy coming out other than imagining Gavin as the hero in the scene in the book, and she didn't care. She'd gone for it, just as eagerly as she had in Virginia.

And she frigging loved it!

Her pulse quickened just thinking about how Gavin had *growled* and *hissed* with appreciation and tangled his hands in her hair. She could still feel his thick shaft thrusting in and out of her mouth—

"Oh my God, *seriously?*" Chloe said loudly, jerking Harper from her thoughts.

She took a big drink of her iced tea, following Chloe's gaze to the four men strutting down the beach carrying motorcycle helmets. She'd recognize Gavin's sexy stride anywhere. Lust swirled inside her as he came into focus, his eyes riveted on her.

"Ladies," Justin said as he flopped down beside Chloe. His friends sat between Daphne and Steph.

"What are you doing here?" Chloe demanded.

Gavin sat behind Harper, his long legs stretched out on either side of her as he pulled her back against his chest, kissed her cheek, and said, "Hello, beautiful."

Her stomach flip-flopped. "Hi."

"Checking out the hot-chick book club." Justin waved toward the iPad and said, "Hey, cuz."

Dixie rolled her eyes.

"You're cousins?" Paige asked.

"Yup," Justin said. "My mom is Dixie's father's sister."

Harper was happy to see Gavin even though she knew he shouldn't have crashed their meeting. She hoped the other girls weren't too annoyed. She pointed to the two guys she didn't recognize and said, "Who are those guys?"

"Dwayne is Justin's cousin. He's the one with the short hair. The longer-haired guy is Cory. I met them through Violet last fall. I see you met Steph. She's known these guys forever." He kissed her cheek and said, "Miss me?"

Miss you? Well, let's see...I was just fantasizing about doing dirty things to you with my mouth. Does that count? She leaned back, snuggling closer, and said, "More than you can imagine."

"I have a pretty vivid imagination," he said in a husky voice.

"Hey, Harper!" Izzy hollered. "Don't get too cozy over there." She looked at Justin and said, "Sorry, hot tattooed cousin of Dixie's, but y'all need to take your sexy asses away from here."

Justin scoffed. "Why? Maybe we read the book."

"Do you even know *how* to read?" Chloe asked.

"Want to find out just how much I know about erotic romance?" Justin asked with a sly grin. "I bet I could put that book to shame."

As Chloe and Justin tried to one-up each other, Dixie and Izzy joined in. Paige and Daphne remained completely silent.

"You shouldn't have come," Steph said to Dwayne. "Why are you always causing trouble?"

"A little trouble can be a whole lot of fun," Cory said, making Daphne blush.

"I'd like to get into trouble with you," Gavin whispered in Harper's ear.

He pressed a kiss beside her ear, and Harper closed her eyes, reveling in him.

Dwayne leaned closer to Steph and said, "Just because you've known me since I was a kid doesn't mean you can boss me around."

Steph narrowed her eyes. "Wanna bet?"

Gavin pressed his lips to Harper's cheek again, drawing her attention. "Are you having a good time with the girls?"

"Yes. It's really fun."

He slipped his hand beneath her shirt and sweater, brushing his thumb over her flesh. "It's crazy, but I miss you already. Are we still on for a date to the flea market tomorrow after you have breakfast with your family?"

"Mm-hm." She glanced over her shoulder and said, "Will you be home?"

He kissed her neck. "Waiting for you."

"Daph, where's my favorite little girl tonight?" Justin asked.

"Hadley? She's freaking adorable," Cory said. "Then again, she's Daph's daughter, so..."

Daphne blushed again. "Hadley's with my sister. Mama needed a girls' night out."

"I think she's coming around to me. I almost got a smile out of her when I ran into you guys at PJ's." Justin looked at Chloe and said, "Ladies of all ages love me."

"I hear ya, cuz." Dwayne and Justin bumped fists.

Chloe rolled her eyes. "More like *some* ladies love you. Some of us think you're full of yourself."

"Is that jealousy I hear?" Justin cocked a brow. "You could be full of me, too. All you have to do is say the word."

"I can tell he's your cousin, Dix," Izzy said. "He's as cocky as your brothers."

Chloe glowered at Justin. "Isn't it time for y'all to go back to whatever it is you do on Friday nights? How would you like it if we crashed one of your Dark Knight meetings?"

"Christ, you're a buzzkill." Justin pushed to his feet. "Let's blow this hen party."

Cory and Dwayne stood up.

Gavin hugged Harper from behind. "I'd better go." He pushed to his feet, then crouched beside her and brought her hand to his lips, kissing the back of it. "Until tomorrow, sweetheart."

He leaned in and kissed her.

"Maybe you two should get a room," Justin said.

Gavin paid him no attention and continued holding Harper's hand as he rose to his feet. He slid his hand along her palm to the very tips of her fingers. Then he blew her a kiss and mouthed, *Tomorrow*, before heading off with the guys.

Harper's insides hummed with happiness as she watched him walk away. He glanced over his shoulder, and she wondered how it was possible to miss him thirty seconds after he'd left her.

When the guys were out of earshot, Paige said, "You've been holding out on us, Harper. Who was that gorgeous man?"

"That's Gavin Wheeler," Chloe said before she could respond. "Harper hooked up with him last summer at a music festival and apparently she snagged his heart, because he's been gaga over her since she came back. Can you tell I'm jealous?"

Harper felt her cheeks burn.

"What music fest was *that*?" Izzy asked. "I might need to take a road trip."

"It was the annual summer music festival in Romance, Virginia, and it was insane. People camped out for two days, and it rained on and off, so there was mud everywhere. I went with my brother Colton as my last hurrah before heading out to LA. But Colton has the hots for the lead singer for Inferno, and he was there, so he took off."

"Axsel's *hot*," Daphne exclaimed.

"I'd like to show him just how good women can be," Izzy said.

"Sexuality doesn't work like that," Paige said. "But he is really cute."

"I know, but it'd be fun to try." Izzy waggled her brows, and they all cracked up. "So, Harper, Colton left you alone and Gavin *found* you?"

"Yes, actually. I was trying to figure out how to get to town, and I guess I looked lost, because he came up to me and said, 'You're looking in the wrong place, sweetheart. I'm right here.' It was a cheesy line, but something in the way he said it didn't feel cheesy. And you *saw* him. He was handsome, and funny, and he had this twinkle in his eyes."

"It's called being horny," Dixie said.

"I'm sure it was," she admitted. "But I think it was more than that. He wasn't like the other guys who had made cheesy comments to me. Gavin was smart, and he didn't talk about nonsense. We had such a great time together. Yes, he flirted, and yes, we ended up together for the night—"

"Oh, hot tent sex. I love that!" Izzy exclaimed.

Dixie looked at Izzy like she'd lost her mind. "When have you *ever* been camping?"

"I haven't. I want to, though," Izzy said. "And when I do, it's definitely going to include hot tent sex."

"Well, there was probably a lot of hot tent sex going on, but we went into town and stayed at the cutest B and B. The night was just as beautiful as he is." Harper sighed with the memory of Gavin sweeping her into his arms and carrying her over the threshold of their room. *Welcome to Heaven, Parker*, he'd said as he lowered his mouth to hers. And then he'd proceeded to take her to paradise and back into the wee hours of the morning.

"That's so romantic," Paige said.

"Is he as *good* as he is handsome?" Izzy asked.

"Oh gosh." Harper shifted her eyes away from the girls, who were looking at her expectantly. She had never been the type of person to share intimate details. She hadn't even had sex with him again yet, but she wanted to. *Oh*, how she wanted to. Every day was a lesson in restraint. Gavin was waiting for her to open that door, and she wasn't even sure why she was holding back anymore. She finally said, "Let's just say there are certain benefits from being with Gavin. He leads with his heart, not his *you know*."

"You are so lucky," Daphne said. "I hope I find that someday, but the only romance I have time for is fictional. Thank God for book boyfriends."

A gust of wind blew over the beach, and everyone made *brr* noises. Chloe zipped up her sweatshirt and said, "Well, *Bob* might not be romantic, but he's loyal, and he doesn't say stupid shit that makes me wonder why I like him."

"I thought you weren't having any luck with Match," Harper said.

"You're on Match?" Izzy asked. "*Why?*"

"Because good men are *not* a dime a dozen in this tourist town." Amusement rose in Chloe's eyes. "*Bob* isn't from Match. He's my battery-operated boyfriend."

"There are many benefits to a boyfriend with an on/off button," Dixie said.

They all laughed, but Harper noticed that Daphne and Paige were just as pink cheeked as she felt. Jana had always been verbal about her active and *interesting* sex life, which had left Harper feeling alone in the relatively vanilla sex life she'd had before she met Gavin. Until they'd come together, she'd never been with a man she wanted to get on her knees for, much less explore tying each other up or lying practically naked on a lounge chair while he did dirty things to her.

She was glad to see she probably wasn't alone in waiting for the right man to come along. But even if she was, being alone on the journey that had led her to Gavin was worth every vanilla second, because Gavin was like the biggest, best mixed-flavored sundae with all the toppings.

Chapter Eleven

"IT'S ABOUT TIME I got a hug from you," Brock said as he crushed Harper in his arms Saturday morning. At six foot four, he towered over Harper. "I've missed you, sis."

"I missed you *all* so much," Harper said, hugging Brock's girlfriend, Cree Redmond.

At first glance Cree looked like the complete opposite of Harper's clean-cut, rule-following brother, with her raven hair, head-to-toe black attire, colorful tattoos, and military-style boots. Cree was a tattoo artist and an incredible singer, as was Brock. In addition to being a champion boxer and owning a boxing club, Brock also sang in an a capella group with two of his friends. According to Brock, who had told Harper all about Cree while she was in LA, Cree's sunny disposition and her love of singing were just two things they had in common, as evident by the adoration in Brock's eyes.

Harper was passed from Jana's embrace to Hunter's, and finally, to Colton's, before they settled in around a table at PB Boulangerie, a French bakery and bistro.

"Harper, can you believe Mr. Picky has finally handed over his heart?" Jana looked gorgeous in a pretty colorful sundress and strappy leather sandals, an outfit similar to the one Harper was wearing. Her gaze moved between Brock and Cree.

"There's nothing wrong with picky," Cree said.

Brock put his arm around her, pulling her into a kiss. He was a tough, serious guy, and it was nice to see this softer side of him.

"It only took you a few *years* of lusting after Cree to *finally* make your move." Hunter put his arm around Jana and said, "I should have given you lessons in instant gratification."

Hunter and Jana's relationship had started with hookups, until they'd realized they were only hooking up with each other. It had taken Jana a while to admit she was in love with him, while Hunter was quicker to the admission. Harper had been floored when Jana and Hunter finally admitted to being a couple. She'd never imagined her rebellious younger sister would settle down before her. But she was happy for them then and even more so now that their relationship had stood the test of time.

"Brock and Harper were cut from different fabric than me and Jana were," Colton teased. It was a running joke in their family. Brock and Harper were the careful ones, while there was very little Colton and Jana were afraid of.

Harper looked at Colton with his bleached-blond hair and blue tattoos on his arm, and she wondered if he'd ever end up with just one special guy, or if he'd always play the field.

"In my defense," Brock said, "I thought Cree was taken, and I'm not an asshole."

"The good thing about how long it took us to finally come together is that by the time we did, we knew we were *it* for each other." Cree put her hand on Brock's leg and said, "I think our timing was perfect."

Brock leaned in for another kiss, and Harper's heart

squeezed. As excited as she was to be with her family, she missed Gavin. They'd texted last night until she could no longer keep her eyes open, only to have him appear in her dreams. Her naughtily scrumptious dreams.

"I sent you the video of Brock and Cree singing together the night they fell in love onstage, didn't I, Harper?" Jana asked, pulling Harper from her thoughts. She had taken the video during an open-mic night at Colton's bar, Undercover, when Brock had dragged Cree onstage for the very first time. Cree's voice was raspy and eclectic, like a mix of Janis Joplin and Grace VanderWaal.

"Yes, and I loved it." Harper paused as the waitress approached.

After the waitress took their orders and left to fill them, Harper said, "I wish I could have been there."

"We have customers asking for Cree all the time." Colton took a drink of water and said, "But she's on her way to being a huge star."

"Hardly," Cree said shyly.

Brock squeezed Cree's shoulder and said, "She's being modest. Drake hooked us up with Boone Stryker, who passed along a demo of Cree's songs to his agent. His agent is working his magic to get her a music deal." Boone was a major rock star whom Serena had arranged to have perform at the grand opening of one of Drake's music stores.

"Are you kidding? That's awesome!" Harper gushed. She thought Cree's news might bring a pang of jealousy, since her big chance at stardom had fallen through the cracks. But she was in too good a place with Gavin and her writing to feel anything but joy for her. Gavin had been right to push her toward using her experiences for inspiration. Her writing was stronger than it had ever been.

"Don't get too excited yet. It might not happen," Cree said. "But your brother convinced me to put some of my music up online, and people seem to like it."

Jana rolled her eyes. "*Seem to like it* is an understatement. She has *thirty thousand* followers on Instagram, most of which were added after she started publicizing her music."

"And she's had a few hundred thousand downloads of her music," Brock bragged. "I'm so proud of her."

Cree curled into Brock's side and kissed his chin. "I owe it all to you."

"We don't *owe*. We help each other shine." Brock touched his lips to hers.

Harper wished Gavin were there to share in the excitement.

"Damn, bro," Colton said. "You're so *mushy* right now, we're going to need a mop to get you off the floor."

Brock grinned and said, "Well, get the mop ready, because you'll need it over the holidays." He lifted Cree's left hand from his leg, revealing a sparkling diamond ring on her finger. "We're getting married!"

Jana and Harper squealed and jumped up to hug them.

"Congratulations!" Harper said as she hugged Brock.

"I want to be a bridesmaid!" Jana exclaimed, hugging Cree.

"Definitely. I need help planning the wedding, though," Cree said as Harper hugged her and Jana hugged Brock.

Hunter lifted his glass and said, "Congratulations. To another happy marriage."

The waitress brought their food. Harper was anxious to tell everyone about Gavin, but she didn't want to overshadow Brock and Cree's excitement as they talked about their wedding plans.

"We're thinking about having the wedding at Bayside Resort or maybe Summer House Inn," Cree said. "We want to invite all our friends from the Seaside community, too."

"That's going to be a big wedding," Hunter said. His brother and his wife owned a cottage at Seaside, as did many of their friends.

"I know, but how can we not invite all of our closest friends?" Cree said.

"You definitely have to invite everyone from Seaside. If it wasn't for them, you never would have met Brock. They were instrumental in bringing me and Hunter together, too," Jana said, happily eyeing Hunter. "It looks like there will be *two* reasons to celebrate over the holidays. We're pregnant! I'm due the week before Christmas!"

Harper gasped and hugged Jana as everyone else talked over each other, and the guys bumped fists. "A *baby*! I'm so happy for you guys."

"Will you help me set up the nursery?" Jana asked.

"I wouldn't miss it!" Harper said.

Jana looked at Cree, who was talking a million miles an hour about how much she loved babies, and said, "Will you help, too?"

"Absolutely!" Cree said.

After talking giddily about Cree's and Jana's news, Harper was about ready to burst with her own exciting news. She waited until there was a pause in the conversation, when she was sure she wouldn't be stealing anyone else's thunder, and said, "I have news, too."

She told them about her show being canceled, and then she said, "I was embarrassed to tell you guys. I'm sorry I lied about what it was really like while I was away."

Brock reached across the table and covered her hand with his. "Harper, you never have to keep anything from us."

"I know. I wasn't in a good place. I wasn't thinking straight, because there was more going on." She told them about her awful dates, and she even shared the embarrassing story of yelling at the poor guy sitting next to her on the plane.

Brock looked like he wanted to kill someone. "I would have flown out there and taught that cheater a lesson."

"Which is just one reason I didn't tell you about it when it happened," Harper said.

"Damn, Harps, you have better luck with guys than I do," Colton said, breaking the tension.

"I actually owe you a huge thank-you, Colton. Remember when you ditched me at the music festival?"

"You went to a music festival with Colton?" Jana asked.

Brock was watching her intently.

Harper hadn't told Brock or Jana about the festival, and she wasn't surprised Colton hadn't either. He'd always been a good secret keeper, and he knew how far outside her comfort zone she'd stepped.

"The annual music fest in Romance, Virginia," Colton explained.

"It was right before I left for LA. I figured since I was starting over, I might as well jump in with both feet and try something else. It wasn't like I was having any luck with guys the old-fashioned way, and moving across the country was already way out of my comfort zone. So I took a page from your playbook, Jana, and tried a one-night stand. Look how good it turned out for you and Hunter."

"Christ." Brock scrubbed a hand down his face. "And you decided to do that in another *state*, without me there to make sure you were okay?"

"Hey, I was there," Colton argued.

Brock glowered. "You *ditched* her. Was this the festival with that musician you're into?"

An arrogant grin appeared on Colton's face, and he said, "Oh yeah. I was in *deep*, too."

Harper slapped Colton's arm. "Pig."

Colton chuckled.

"Brock, I'm not a kid. I knew what I was getting into." Harper thought about that and added, "Sort of, anyway. It turns out I suck at one-night stands. I met this great guy and we had an amazing night, but then I couldn't stop thinking about him afterward."

Jana's eyes filled with concern. "I can't wrap my head around you having a one-night stand. I'm not sure if I should be proud of you, or feel guilty that you did it, because it's obviously my fault. I wish you had come to me for guidance first."

"Colton gave me advice."

Brock glowered at him.

"Here's the thing," Harper said. "It wasn't just like a quick...*you know*...and then it was over. We spent the whole day together, and that night, and then I put my number in the pocket of his suitcase before sneaking out while he was asleep."

"Oh no, Harper." Jana shook her head. "I feel sick at the thought of you doing that, and I'm the one who was always pushing you to loosen up."

"Well, I'm *glad* I did it. I really connected with the guy, and when I got back to the Cape, I saw him again. I've seen him almost every day since. His name is Gavin Wheeler."

"Gavin?" Jana said. "Serena Mallery's business partner? He's hot."

Hunter's eyes narrowed. "Babe…?"

"What? He's not as hot as *you*," Jana clarified.

"We know Gavin," Brock said. "He's a good guy, Harper, but anything could have happened to you out there."

"But it *didn't*," Colton reminded him.

"Can you two stop? Something *did* happen," Harper said adamantly. "That's the point I'm trying to make. I met a guy who's a great listener, he's family oriented, and he has encouraged me in all the best ways. I was nervous about telling you guys, or my friends, that my show was canceled, and I didn't trust my own instincts with men because of what happened. I couldn't even *write*. Can you imagine that?"

"No, because writing to you has always been like boxing is to me," Brock said with concern in his voice. "I'm sorry you went through such a hard time, and I'm glad you had someone who helped you, but, Harper, *we're* your family. You should have come to us."

"I know, and I'm sorry. But my whole life felt upside down, and honestly, I felt stuck. I needed to be pushed, even if I didn't realize it. Gavin did. He wouldn't let me just wallow in that awful headspace where everything felt negative. He urged me to write about my experiences in LA, to see them differently, and it's like he opened a dam to my creativity. And he didn't just help with that aspect of my life. We talk about everything. He understands who I am and what I need. He knew how far outside my comfort zone I've been over the past several months, and he knew that night in Virginia, too. I am one hundred percent certain that if I had tried to hook up with any other man that night, I wouldn't have gone through with it."

She looked at Brock, knowing how much he loved and cared about her and how much pressure he'd put on himself to keep them all safe throughout the years. "Brock, there are some things a woman has to figure out without the protection of her family. It's different working through things with him than it would be with you or Jana or Colton. I'm sure it's the same way for you and Cree, and Jana and Hunter. I can't explain it, but I trust my instincts."

Oh my God, I really do.

The realization took her by surprise, bolstering her confidence and her courage.

"I know I did the right thing. And I wish Gavin were here right now, because seeing you guys so in love makes me miss him like crazy." She'd been holding part of herself back from Gavin, waiting to make love with him until she was sure about where they were heading, but now all she wanted was to be in his arms. She couldn't know for sure where they were heading. But as long as they were together, she knew they were moving in the right direction.

"I've never seen you like this." Jana studied Harper's face. "Are you *falling* for him?"

"I don't know. Maybe?" she confessed, her heart hammering against her ribs as *yes* floated in her heart. "This morning I thought I was losing my mind because I've never thought about a man every minute like I do with him. I didn't think it could possibly be normal, much less reciprocated."

"I think about Brock nonstop," Cree said. "Sometimes he's just in the other room and I miss him."

Brock pressed a kiss to her temple. "Me too."

"That's how I feel," Harper said.

"You *know* how often I think of Hunter," Jana said. "But, Harper, why would you ever think it wouldn't be reciprocated? You're an amazing woman, and any guy would be lucky to be with you."

"You've always had guys after you at Undercover," Colton said.

"Yeah, the *wrong* guys."

"Harper," Brock said, "when you meet the person you can't live without, it's only natural to think about them all the time. And when you finally come together with them, those thoughts only get stronger."

"When they're bummed, you're bummed," Hunter added. "When they're happy, you want to do everything within your power to keep them that way. That's *love*, Harper. You might not be there yet, but if you feel those things, it's definitely worth holding on to while you figure it out."

"Oh, I'm holding on," she said. "But I've also been holding back, because I've never experienced so many emotions all at once. Let me finish telling you about this morning. There I was, trying to convince myself I was crazy, and when I walked out my front door to come here, I found the sweetest note on my porch from Gavin, along with a handful of red lollipops tied together with a pink ribbon and a matchbook from the Wysteria Inn where we'd stayed in Virginia."

She thought of the note, feeling good all over. *Good morning, beautiful. Have fun with your family. Remember, you achieved greatness before you ever went to LA. Your family knows how special you are. The only thing that's changed is that now you've got more inspiration for your writing and a great boyfriend! Can't wait to hold you in my arms again.*

"That's pretty sweet," Colton said.

"Pretty sweet? Are you kidding? That's super romantic," Cree added.

Jana raised her brows and said, "If you told him about your

red lollipop fetish you must *really* like him, because you hate how red lollipops make your tongue and the inside of your lips red. You always said you'd never eat one in front of a guy."

"I know! And until Gavin, I never have." Harper laughed. "I thought about that when we were in the candy store in Virginia, but I *wanted* Gavin to know my secret. I'm telling you, *everything* is different with him. Do you know what he did when I told him that I wouldn't eat a red lollipop in front of him even though it was my favorite? He went in search of red lollipops. He said I should never be embarrassed to do anything I enjoy."

"Oh, Harper," Jana said. "He sounds like he's really for you."

"He is." He'd pushed her then with the same gentleness he encouraged her now. But he hadn't pushed her to do the one thing she knew he wanted as badly as she did. Her pulse sped up with that realization. She didn't want to hold back anymore.

Not even for another second.

Harper pushed to her feet and dug through her purse for her wallet and keys.

"What are you doing?" Jana asked.

"I'm sorry. I have to go." She threw money on the table and said, "I love you guys. I'll be in touch, but there's something I need to do right now." As she ran for the door she remembered her siblings' news and called across the restaurant, "Congratulations! I love you!"

She ran through the parking lot to her car, and then she sped the whole way to Gavin's house. By the time she arrived she was out of breath.

She flew out of her car and ran up his walk, pounding on the door like a madwoman.

She was *mad* all right.
Mad about Gavin.

"BASICALLY, WHAT I'M hearing is that you owe me big-time for dragging your ass to that music festival."

Gavin stepped off the dock, speaking through his AirPods to Beckett. "Yeah, I do. Everything is different with Harper in my life. I can't even explain it, but *man*, Beck, I want to do things I haven't *ever* wanted to do, like finally making my house more of a home. I can't wait for you to meet her."

"*Whoa.* Does that mean you're actually bringing her home? Dude, this *is* serious. Are you sure? You remember what went down the last time you did that."

His jaw clenched. "Harper's not anything like Corinne. You'll love her as much as I do." He looked out over the water and said, "It's crazy, Beck, but she'll be here in about an hour and I'm counting down the minutes like a lovesick teenager." He headed for the house. "I'm thinking about bringing her home with me for Thanksgiving."

"No shit? You think you'll still be together?"

"Hell yes. Have you listened to anything I've just said?" Gavin opened the patio door, and as he stepped inside he heard someone banging on the front door. "Hold on. I have to answer the door."

He strode through the house and opened the front door. Harper launched herself into his arms, wrapping her arms and legs around him like a second skin and crushing her mouth to his.

"I missed you," she panted out between frantic kisses. "I

don't want to hold back anymore. I want it all with you, Gavin. Take me to your bedroom."

"Man she sounds hot." Beckett's voice jarred Gavin from his reverie.

"End the call, Beckett," he growled against Harper's lips.

She drew back, confusion in her eyes. "*Beckett?*"

Holding Harper with one arm, he tore his AirPods from his ears and threw them to the floor. "Forget him."

He grabbed the back of her head, bringing her mouth to his, their tongues tangling in a passionate dance as he carried her toward the bedroom. He wanted to know what changed, why she suddenly wanted more of him. But she was in his arms, kissing him like she needed him to survive, and in that moment that was all that mattered. He lowered them both to the bed, their tongues thrusting, tasting, memorizing the feel of each other's mouths. He ran his hands along her thighs, barely able to think past the need to be inside her. He broke their kiss long enough to reach behind him with one hand and tug his shirt over his head.

Her hands played over his chest, her lips curving up in appreciation. "God, I love your body."

The need in her voice made his cock throb. She was gorgeous, her golden hair spilling over his sheets, the creamy halter top of her dress resting against her tanned skin, the skirt bunched around her waist, and her pretty lace panties begging to be removed.

"Not half as much as I love yours," he said, taking her in another fierce kiss.

One tug on the strings around her neck freed her breasts. He kissed a path down her neck, over her breastbone, and then he teased her breasts the way he'd learned she loved. She arched and moaned, every sexy sound making him harder, *hungrier*. He stripped away her dress, and his heart nearly stopped at the sight of her naked, save for the peach panties he was about to tear off with his teeth. And that tattoo. He'd seen it in his most erotic fantasies. The mark of the woman he'd never forget.

She reached for him, but he was on a mission to make her feel better than she ever had. As his hands slid down her ribs to the dip at the swell of her hips, he kissed and sucked, licked and teased every soft, supple inch of her.

She buried her hands in his hair, his tongue sliding in and out of her belly button. She arched and whimpered as his mouth moved lower, teasing along her hips. He slicked his tongue along her inner thigh, inhaling her sweet scent. Then he breathed over the wet trail he'd left, and goose bumps traveled up her flesh. He gave her other thigh the same attention, clutching her hips as he teased her. He licked her through her damp panties, earning a loud, greedy moan. He grabbed the thin material between his teeth, looped his fingers beneath the lace covering her hips, and dragged her panties down her legs. He tossed them aside and loved his way up her legs, kissing and caressing all the way up to the apex of her thighs. He kissed the tender skin around her glistening sex until she rocked and begged for more. The need in her voice was the most erotic sound he'd ever heard. He splayed his hands on her inner thighs and dragged his tongue along her wetness.

"Oh *Lord*," she said in one long breath.

"So *sweet*, baby."

He did it again, one long, slow stroke over her swollen sex.

"*Gavin, Gavin, Gavin...*" she whispered.

He loved teasing her. Knowing she trusted him with her whole self in the light of day, body and soul, made their lovemaking that much more intense and special. He palmed her breast as he teased her again, squeezing her nipple. She panted, whimpering and writhing against him with every slick of his tongue. He knew what she needed, and covered her sex with his mouth, fucking her with his tongue, teasing her with his fingers, taking her right up to the edge of ecstasy—and holding her there. When she was breathless and flushed, he focused on the place she needed it most, sending her soaring. Her hips bucked and her sex pulsed as he feasted on her.

As she came down from the clouds, he sent her right back up and over the edge again, her essence exploding over his tongue. Her nails dug into his shoulders. He'd never felt so alive, so enraptured by pleasuring a woman. He moved off the bed long enough to strip naked. Her eyes fluttered open as he reached into his nightstand and grabbed a condom. He tore it open with his teeth as her gaze hit his cock. The raw passion in her eyes made him impossibly harder.

"I'm on the pill," she said shakily.

"You've had enough bumps in your road lately, sweetheart. I'm not taking any chances with you. No accidental pregnancies to upend your life."

"Or yours," she said sweetly as he sheathed his hard length.

He came down over her and cradled her face between his hands. He wanted to tell her that she could upend his life any day of the week, that what he felt for her was so much bigger than anything he'd ever felt before. But he didn't want to scare her off, so he kissed her softly and said, "I want nothing more than to feel *everything* when our bodies come together. We'll know when we're ready to risk it."

He kissed her as their bodies aligned, deepening the kiss as they became one, and the rest of the world fell away. He reveled in the feel of her breasts against his chest, her soft thighs beneath his, her tight body swallowing every inch of him. She felt even more incredible and they fit even more perfectly than he remembered. He cradled her body against his, fighting a war inside him, wanting to stay right there as desperately as he wanted to unleash his every emotion and love her hard.

He buried his face in her hair and neck and said, "This is where you belong, Harp. With me, in my bed, in my arms."

"Yes," she said with so much emotion, he had to see her face, had to see the love in her eyes. "Love me, Gavin."

Their mouths came together as they began to move, and they quickly found their rhythm, just as they had all those months ago. She wrapped her feet around the backs of his legs, angling her hips so he could drive in deeper. Never in his life had he felt so connected, so in sync with another human being. Being this close, having her body wrapped around him in every sense, made him feel whole in ways he never had.

Harper's fingernails dug into his flesh, and he pumped faster, pushed harder. He nearly lost his mind as her orgasm took hold, squeezing his cock so tight he saw stars. A rush of heat consumed him, and he fought against the mounting pressure, wanting to send her soaring again. When she fell back to the mattress, panting, eyes closed, he pushed his hands beneath her, holding her ass as he pounded into her. He guided her legs higher, around his waist. She curled up beneath him, licking and kissing his shoulder. *Christ.* She must have remembered how that had driven him right up to the brink of madness last time. He remembered what she loved, too, and he moved his hands over her ass, teasing her other entrance.

She breathed, "Yes," against his shoulder.

"Come for me again, baby," he coaxed.

She panted against his cheek, pleading, "*Dontstopdontstop.*"

He moved his fingers through her wetness and returned

them to the spot she wanted. Slick with her arousal, he pushed one finger into her bottom. She bit down on his shoulder as she came, rocking and moaning, squeezing his shaft so tight, pressure spiked down his spine, catapulting him over the edge with such intensity, he feared his powerful thrusts would hurt her as he ground out her name through gritted teeth. She was right there with him, clawing at his skin, gasping for breaths.

His head fell beside hers, and he tried to remember how to breathe. "Did I hurt you?" he panted out.

"No. You're perfect. We're perfect together."

Thank God. After the last aftershock rumbled through him, he rolled onto his side, removed and tied off the condom, and tossed it in the trash, not wanting to move away from her just yet. He gathered her in his arms, sealing their love with a kiss.

They lay tangled together, their hearts beating frantically as sunlight streamed in through the windows, warming their naked bodies, and still Gavin ached for more. He'd been insatiable the first time they'd made love, too. He ran his hand down her back and cupped her ass. She made a sensual sound, and just like that, he was hard again.

"Gavin," she whispered.

He saw so many emotions swimming in her eyes, his chest constricted. Could she possibly feel as much for him as he felt for her? "Yes, love?"

She pressed her softness against his arousal and said, "Can we do it again?"

He kissed her deeply. "Again." He reached for another condom and said, "And again."

He kissed her long and slow, and then he rose onto his knees to sheathe himself.

She reached out to help, her eyes alive with pleasure as she said, *"And again..."*

Chapter Twelve

LATER THAT MORNING, Harper lay in Gavin's arms on his couch watching the end of a movie. After almost a year of living on worried breaths, thinking about the man she never expected to see again, she could finally fill her lungs to capacity. They'd lain in bed talking and dozing off for a long time after making love until Harper's stomach growled too loudly to ignore. Then they'd forced themselves out of bed long enough to eat a snack, only to fall back into bed for *dessert*. They'd showered together, which was another first for her. They'd taken their time washing and caressing each other, kissing and loving without actually making love. It was the most sensual experience she'd ever had. Then again, everything was starting to feel sensual with Gavin. Even lying wordlessly in his arms was physically and emotionally gratifying.

She remembered their first night together, when she was preparing to embark on a scary journey to the other side of the country. She'd been living on the same unsteady breaths then. Spending time with Gavin had centered her then, too. Everything had felt so right, she'd wanted to explore and do all the sexy things she'd read about with him. She *hadn't* done it all, though she probably would have if he'd asked. But the things they had done had felt natural, not taboo. The same way it had when she'd thrown caution to the wind and taken control and when she'd begged for more when he was already buried deep inside her. Was it possible she'd met her soul mate in the most unlikely way?

She cuddled closer to him, thankful that this time she didn't have to catch a plane or wonder if he'd call.

As the credits rolled across the screen, she turned to face him, and he kissed her softly.

"Do you have any writing you need to get done today?" Gavin asked.

"No. I printed out my work the other day and I've been reading and revising it. I need a break." She pressed her lips to his. "Am I keeping you from working?"

"When I lived in Boston I worked every weekend. Now I try not to."

"What did you do? Go through Workaholics Anonymous?"

"Nah. I wasn't always a workaholic. But the bad experience in college that I told you about changed everything. Going against my family's wishes and continuing to see Corinne had created a rift between us, as I said, and for a while I drank too much, played around too much. Eventually I failed a test and realized I needed to pull myself together."

"One test did that for you? God, you sound like me. If Jana heard that, she'd say we were made for each other."

"We are, babe. Hell, I thought we were when we first met." He kissed her and said, "After I tanked that test, I threw myself into schoolwork. I wasn't ready to see my family again, so I got an internship for the summer with a design firm in Boston. The summer bled into the next school year, and the following summer I got offered a great summer job in Boston. Before I knew it, I had graduated and was working full time at KHB, where I eventually met Serena. I spent years working day and night, through the weekends, trying to climb that corporate ladder and only going home for quick trips over the holidays. Somewhere along the way I'd let go of the anger and hurt that caused me to become a workaholic in the first place, but my personal life had become nonexistent. When Serena started working at KHB, I had an incredible job offer from a competitor. But I'd lived in Boston for years and I didn't like who I had become. I had no close friends, and I hadn't been home in ages. I hadn't even made time to call and really talk to my parents. Beckett and I texted a lot, but even that relationship was strained."

"Wow, it sounds like you went from that bad relationship straight into workaholic mode and stayed there."

"I did. And when I saw how much Serena missed everyone here, it reminded me of everything I had lost. I finally called my parents and had a long talk with my father. We hadn't done that in ages, and it felt so good. I knew I had to fix things back home. That weekend I went home, and Beckett dragged me to the festival, where I met you. Meeting you changed *everything* for me."

"I'm sure you met lots of women over the years, Gavin. Why would I, of all people, change anything?"

He ran his fingers through her hair, his gaze serious. "You really don't know how special you are, do you? Harp, when I say things to you, I need you to know, to really believe in your heart, that they're true."

"I do, Gavin. I just meant that you're a good-looking guy with a huge heart and a great career. You could have any woman you want."

"Maybe, but I could turn that around, and it's probably the only way you'll understand what I mean. You're a gorgeous woman, with a huge heart, and a great career, even if it has taken a new path lately. You could have any man you want."

"Most guys are not what they claim to be. And now I have you, the only man I want."

"Then you understand when I say that you woke me up from years of pushing through a life I wasn't really living. Suddenly there was this beautiful, smart woman who, like me, was feeling a little lost and did something out of the ordinary for herself. You had what most other women don't. I've said this before, and it's the best way I can describe how I felt when we met. You might have been trying to be something you weren't with the one-night stand, but so was I. You were—you are—the realest person I know, Harper. *Real* is rare, or at least that's how it feels to me. You told me when you thought I was full of it, and we were so alike, with our normally careful natures and our sense of humor. I felt alive for the first time in years."

"I did, too," she confessed. "That might be why I felt so sidelined by the other guys I went out with, because they weren't real."

"Harper, this will seem unbelievable, but you were the catalyst to my partnering with Serena. I had the world at my fingertips with that job offer in Boston, but after connecting with you on a level I never imagined possible in the space of *hours*, not *years*, I realized that wasn't the world I wanted. I wasn't raised to be the guy who lived to work and put family aside. I had lost my way, and after meeting you, I decided to partner with Serena. I may not have known the exact path I needed to follow, but I knew I was heading in the right direction."

"I'm glad you did, or we might never have reconnected."

"Me too, sweetheart. And I'm not ashamed to admit that I was completely gutted when I woke up and found you were gone."

She lowered her eyes. "I'm sorry. I hated leaving you, but I already felt attached, and saying goodbye would have made it that much harder to leave."

"That feeling of loss was just another thing that drove me to make changes in my life. I never let go of the hope that I'd see you again, and I'm pretty sure I drove Justin crazy talking about *Parker*. He tells everyone I'm the best wingman because he's a great guy and the type of friend who builds you up in front of others. But I sucked. I wasn't interested in the women we met. It got to the point where I'd leave bars early, alone, and he'd just shake his head. He told me he was going to put out an APB for a blonde named Parker."

She laughed, and he kissed her again. "It's true, sweetheart. You can ask him if you'd like." He brushed his fingers over the nape of her neck and said, "Stay…"

"Hm?" She was still processing all he'd said, tucking away every word so she could revisit them later.

"I spent almost a year wishing we'd had time like this. Stay with me tonight. Stay for the weekend. For the *week*. I don't want our time together to end. You love working by the water, and this way you won't have to drive back and forth to your place."

There was no place she'd rather be than right there with him every free minute they had, sleeping in his arms, waking to his kisses, sharing breakfasts and dinners. She trusted her instincts about Gavin, but as much as she wanted to be with him, she was still a little nervous about moving too quickly.

"How about if I stay for the rest of the weekend and then we play it by ear?"

"That sounds great, my careful girl," he said, and kissed her hard, grinning like he'd gotten the gift of a lifetime, and she sure felt like she had.

"But I have to go home and get clean clothes, toiletries, my work stuff. I have events to cover this week, and I should review my notes at some point. Do you still want to go to the flea market today? I'd love to pick up some of my friend Leanna's jam."

"Ah, the famous Luscious Leanna's Sweet Treats jam."

"You know Leanna Remington?"

"I met Leanna and her husband, Kurt, through Drake and Serena. I wish I was into thrillers, because from what I hear, Kurt's an amazing author. We'll swing by your place to pick up your stuff and hit the flea market while we're out."

As they sat up, he took her hand and said, "I know this feels fast, Harp, but how many guys can say they wished at a fountain and their wish actually came true? I'm starting to believe in fate, and I don't want to waste a second of our time together." He must have seen the surprise in her eyes, because he said, "When we tossed our pennies into the fountain, I wished we could be more than a one-night stand."

Her heart turned over in her chest, because she'd wished for almost the same thing. She'd wished he'd call. Little did she know she'd inadvertently *hidden* her phone number from him. They'd made their wishes in the fountain before they'd even slept together. For a guy who had thought he was getting a one-night stand to want more before they'd even had *that* made her believe in fate, too.

"You knew I was going away and you still wished for more?"

He pulled her to her feet and gathered her in his arms, gazing deeply into her eyes. "Yes, because what I had with you in just a few hours was more than anything I'd ever had before." He brushed his lips over hers and said, "I knew one night couldn't be it for us, so I wished that it was only the beginning of our story."

WHEN THEY ARRIVED at Harper's cottage, Gavin wrapped his arms around her from behind as she unlocked the door and said, "Would you mind if we cut a few flowers from your garden to bring to my place? My girlfriend loves flowers."

"Great idea," she said, turning to kiss him before pushing the door open. "Excuse the mess. I always print out my work when I'm reading through it the first time."

There were papers spread out over her desk, coffee table, counters, and even on the couch cushions. Nearly every page was marked up in red ink, with notes scribbled in the margins.

"So this is what you do when you're not at my place."

"Not always," she said as she gathered the papers. "This is what I do after most of the first draft is done. Your brilliant idea of using my experiences in LA for inspiration was just what I needed to get my creative juices flowing."

"Which is awesome, but how do you work like this? Where do you sit?"

She shrugged. "Wherever. I'm used to it, and I can't do this outside because, as you can imagine, a breeze would create havoc with my organization."

"This is *organized*?" He raised his brow.

"If I had more space, I might set up tables or something, but this works for me."

She was so selfless in her pursuit of her dreams, it made him want to give everything he had to help her achieve them. "I can't wait to read what you've written."

He reached for a piece of paper, and she grabbed his hand, stopping him.

"Uh-uh. You can't read it until I tweak it."

He pulled her in close and said, "Maybe I can entice you into sharing sooner."

His lips came down over hers, and she returned his efforts eagerly, going up on her toes for more. His hands slid down to her backside as he deepened the kiss, and she melted against him. Man, he loved the way she reacted to him with all the same emotions he felt.

She pressed her hands to his chest, abruptly breaking their connection. "You might be able to charm my panties off, but you're not going to read this until it's a bit more polished."

"Hold on to the *charming your panties off* thought for a second. That means your writing is good, right? Because when you thought your writing wasn't your best, you let me read it."

"I hope it's good, but I don't know for sure."

He kissed her neck. "I could help you decide."

"I can see this is going to take nerves of steel." She stepped back, her cheeks flushed. She held her hand up like a barrier as she placed the papers she was holding on the desk. "It's not fair to use that wicked mouth of yours to coerce me like that."

He hauled her against him, loving the heat in her eyes and the giggle that slipped out. "How would you like me to use it? Like this?" He sealed his mouth over her neck, sucking hard, and she gasped a sharp breath. "Or maybe you prefer this?" He dragged his tongue down the center of her chest and tugged her top down so he could lick the swell of her breast.

"Gavin," she said breathily. "We're going to end up in the bedroom again."

"And that's bad because...?" He swore he saw her mind churning, like she was digging deep to come up with a reason.

"You're right." She grabbed his hand and dragged him toward the bedroom. "There are worse addictions than having sex with my boyfriend."

His chest constricted at how easily the endearment sailed from her lips.

As they tumbled down to the mattress in a tangle of gropes and hungry kisses, he intended to show her just how much more than an addiction he hoped to become.

AFTER MAKING GOOD use of the condoms they'd bought at the pharmacy in Provincetown, they showered *again*, packed up enough of Harper's things for the next two nights, and cut flowers to take to his house. Harper put the flowers in a wide-bottomed vase that wouldn't topple over in the car, and then they made their way to the Wellfleet Flea Market.

The flea market was held in the parking lot of the drive-in theater. It was bustling, with people moving in and out of the snack building and between vendor booths. Canopies were lined up as far as the eye could see. Colorful banners flapped in the breeze, and children darted in and out of the playground. Harper set the vase beside the car in the parking lot so the flowers wouldn't die while they meandered through the market.

"Aren't you worried someone will take those?" Gavin asked as they walked toward the colorful canopies, which brightened the overcast day.

"If they do, they need them more than we do."

They strolled hand in hand through the market, checking out used books, jewelry, clothing, collectibles, and various arts and crafts. It was a balmy afternoon, the type of oppressive heat that begged the sky to open up and give relief.

"Wow, it looks like he emptied his garage over here." Harper pulled him toward a booth with boxes of old records, tools, books, and a plethora of other miscellaneous items mixed in with furniture and Oriental rugs.

An older man with thin gray hair and skin like leather said "Howdy" as they approached. He sat in a folding chair with a scruffy dog at his feet.

"Hi," Harper said as she blazed a path around boxes toward whatever she'd spotted. "Gavin, look." She pointed to two decorative wooden plaques. A rustic chain with a mason jar hung from a large fishing hook at the top of each one. "You know those string lights they sell at the Christmas Store in Orleans? You could put those in the jars, and they'd go perfectly in your bedroom or even your living room, don't you think?" Her eyes brimmed with excitement. "You know what? You could get a bunch of mason jars and use solar string lights along the path down to the dock at night."

Her reached for her and said, "Aren't I supposed to be the designer?"

"I'm sorry. Do you hate that idea? It is too cheesy?"

"No, babe. I was only teasing. I love the plaques, and I love your idea of lining the path to the dock." He put his arms around her and said, "I know I said I hadn't decorated because I wanted the house to be comfortable, and I did. But what I didn't realize until the last few weeks was that it always felt like something was missing. I think that something was you."

She went up on her toes and touched her lips to his in the sweetest kiss. "Maybe we were both missing something in our lives."

"If I have my way, you'll never miss a thing ever again."

"Careful making promises you can't keep," she said. "Let's see if we can find some cool vinyl records. What's your favorite genre?"

"Classic rock, of course."

"I can't wait to hear your collection," she said as they looked through a box of records. "We should unpack them. Are there any records you wish you could find? Maybe we'll get lucky."

"I already got lucky." He leaned in for another kiss and said, "Because you're right here by my side."

"Charmer," she said with a sexy smile.

"Only for you, Harp." Gavin paid for the plaques, and then he patted her butt and said, "Okay, girlie. Let's hunt for the impossible, a limited-edition pink-vinyl pressing of Pink Floyd's *Animals*."

"Pink vinyl? They made those?"

"Pretty cool, huh?" He took her hand and they went in search of the album.

They hit every record vendor and came up empty, except for the fun they had, which was better than any damn album anyway. They stopped along the way to leaf through paperbacks and check out crafts and clothing. They bought two jars of jam from Leanna and visited with her until she got swamped with customers. Then they went to the snack building and bought burgers, which they ate in the beer garden as the clouds rolled in.

On the way back to Gavin's house, they stopped at an antiques store. Harper found an old-fashioned fishing pole that had been repurposed. She thought it would also be perfect for his house. It had been formed into an arch with jute threaded through it instead of fishing line. Four picture frames hung from lines of jute attached to each of the tiny metal guides along the rod, and two decorative lures hung from the tip of the rod.

By the time they got home, the ominous dark sky opened up. They ran inside with their flowers and purchases, and Harper confiscated another of Gavin's sweatshirts.

As sheets of rain pummeled the patio, Harper flitted around his living room in her sexy little shorts and his sweatshirt, pointing out different places where they could hang the decorations. He was a sought-after designer with years of experience, and yet it had taken this incredible woman who thought she couldn't trust her instincts and didn't seem to mind, or notice, that she didn't have her own proper workspace to start turning his house into a home.

Chapter Thirteen

IT RAINED ALL night and into Sunday morning, which suited Harper just fine. Last night they'd opened the windows in the living room while they were eating pizza and binge-watching movies. They'd cuddled, and kissed, and when they'd finally gone to bed, they'd opened the bedroom windows, too. Harper found rainfall soothing. Not that she had any nervous energy left to soothe after the way Gavin had worshipped and loved every inch of her. They'd made love and talked into the wee hours of the morning, falling into comfortable silences broken only by the sound of the rain.

It was *perfect*.

And she was beginning to think Gavin was, too. She wasn't fooling herself into thinking he was some type of superhuman without flaws. He cursed when the remote control didn't work, he left the toothpaste uncapped, which was one of her pet peeves, and he was still nagging her about allowing him to read her script. She was sure he had plenty of other flaws she had yet to discover, but so did she. Didn't everyone? More importantly, she loved the way he listened and how openly he shared everything about himself. Last night he told her all about the clients he was working with and the projects he hoped to pitch after the summer. It was easy to see why he and Serena worked so well together. They were both meticulous and committed to ensuring their clients got the best service and the best designs, while protecting their bottom line without cutting corners.

She watched him now as he moved around the kitchen making coffee. His hair was still damp from their shower, and his jeans hung low around his hips, molding to his perfect rear end. In the shower she'd noticed that she'd left nail marks in the cheeks of that perfect rear end from holding on so tight. When she pointed them out, Gavin stood taller, wearing them proudly, as if they were medals.

He turned with a steaming mug in his hand and a sexy smile on his lips. She wished it would rain for weeks and flood the roads. Then they'd have an excuse to stay hidden away and she wouldn't have to think about whether they were moving too fast. They could just *be*.

"You look deep in thought. What's going on in that brilliant mind of yours?" Gavin set the mug down in front of her.

"Just thinking about how much I like being with you." *And how I want more of it.*

"That's a good thing since you already agreed to stay here tonight, and in my world, there are no takebacks." He leaned across the counter and kissed her. "Want to go get a week's worth of clothes from your place and promise me more nights you can't take back?"

"How can you charm and push at the same time?" *And why is it so devastatingly appealing?*

Probably because he'd read her mind and said exactly what she wanted to do.

He came around the counter and put his hands on her thighs. The heated look in his eyes made her stomach flutter.

"You're wearing my favorite T-shirt and red lace panties beneath these skimpy shorts. I think it's *you* who is using her charms and silently pushing all of my buttons. You know what it does to me when you look at me with that dreamy expression and the sweet smile that reeled me in the very first time I saw it."

He pulled her to the edge of the stool and against him in one swift move. His lips swooped down, claiming hers. His tongue swept over hers, intoxicatingly slowly, lulling her deeper into him. He made a low, greedy sound, and she answered it with one of her own.

"I like seeing you in my house," he said against her lips.

"I like being here."

He pressed his palm to her cheek, brushing his thumb over her skin. She leaned into his touch as he said, "I love having you in my bed." His eyes turned serious, and the corner of his mouth tipped up. "And if I don't step away from you to make you breakfast, I'm going to get even pushier."

"You make me want you to be *pushy*."

He gave her a chaste kiss. "Want and need are two different things, sweetheart. We've got nothing but time. At least that's what I'm telling myself to keep from locking you in my bedroom twenty-four-seven." He walked back into the kitchen. "What's on your article agenda this week?"

"Lots of fun stuff," she said, thinking of the email she'd received earlier from her boss. "Wednesday afternoon I have a children's play to review. I'm thinking of asking Jana to go with me since it's at a time when she's not teaching dance. I'm covering a book signing in Brewster Thursday, and next week there's a Humane Society event I'm excited about. Who doesn't love puppies and kitties?"

"So I shouldn't be surprised if you come home with a new pet?"

"I don't have space for a pet. Can you imagine a puppy creating havoc with my papers spread all over?"

He sipped his coffee. "Sounds like you're enjoying going back to your roots after all."

"I'm actually having a lot of fun with it, and I have you to thank. If I hadn't found my groove with the new script, I probably wouldn't enjoy writing the articles so much."

"All I did was make a suggestion. The rest is all you, babe." He walked over to the pantry and said, "Ready for your very first Wheeler Special?"

"I thought I had my first Wheeler Special in Virginia," she teased, knowing he was referring to his father's famous spinach omelets with a special sauce and homemade croissants.

He chuckled and began setting ingredients on the counter. "Smart-ass. This breakfast will blow you away."

She didn't need breakfast for that. He'd already blown her away with his encouragement, his humor, and the way he made her feel sexy, feminine, and adored, bedhead and all.

"It's going to take me a little time to cook breakfast, so make yourself at home while the *master chef* takes control."

"If you're as good in the kitchen as you are in the bedroom, I might be in trouble."

She blew him a kiss and wandered over to the bookshelves to check out the titles. Among the books she found a small framed picture of Gavin standing next to his father. Gavin was all elbows and knees. He couldn't have been older than eight or nine. He wore shorts and no shirt. His shaggy hair hung over his eyes, and he was beaming at the camera, holding a fishing pole with a fish dangling off a hook. His father was smiling proudly, one arm around Gavin. His father had darker hair than Gavin, but he had the same smile, the same cut of his jaw.

Her heart hurt thinking about the years he and his family had lost because of a girl. She was glad they'd recovered from the rift, but she wished she could have been around then to help him find his way back to his family sooner, the same way he'd helped her see past her own issues.

She grabbed her messenger bag and the blanket they'd used last night from the couch and headed for the sunroom to get some work done. She set her bag on the floor, once again hit by the beauty of the spacious room. She spread the blanket out in the middle of the floor, and then she retrieved the vase of flowers from her garden and put it on the floor by the blanket. She opened all the windows to let the sound of the rain trickle in, and then she began laying out her papers and turned on her laptop. But the room still felt empty.

She went back to the bookcase for the picture of Gavin and his father, placed it by the flowers in the sunroom, and happily settled into her work.

WHEN GAVIN FINISHED cooking breakfast, he found Harper sitting cross-legged on a blanket in the middle of the sunroom with a stack of papers in her lap and a red pen tucked behind her ear, engrossed in reading over her work. She'd twisted her hair into a knot on the top of her head. A few sexy tendrils framed her face. Papers were strewn out across the floor, as they had been in her cottage, and the flowers they'd picked brightened the room in a vase beside her laptop. He glanced over his shoulder at the fishing-rod frames they'd hung over the fireplace. He still needed to figure out what pictures to put in them, but even without them, it added a homey touch to the room. They'd hung the mason jar plaques in the bedroom on either side of the bed. Even those small touches made his house feel more like a home. And now here she was, enjoying the room he'd spent almost a year ignoring. He took a moment to admire the woman who had made every aspect of his life better. In the span of a couple weeks, she'd woken parts of him that had been asleep for far too long.

He touched Harper's shoulder, startling her. "Sorry, babe. I didn't mean to startle you, but that's a good sign. If you're that into your writing, it has to be good."

"I think it *is*," she said confidently.

"That's great. Does that mean I can read it?"

She looked down at the papers in her lap, her fingers curling possessively over the edges. "They're not as rough as I thought they were. You can read it if you promise to be honest."

He chuckled. "As I recall, last time I was *too* honest."

"Maybe cushion it this time if it's really bad, or soften the blow with a kiss. I need you to be too honest. It's hard to tell if I think it's good because my last story was so bad, or because it's really good writing."

"Okay." He made an *X* over his heart. "One hundred percent honesty coming up, softened with a kiss if need be. But first, breakfast is ready. How about if I bring it in here? I like what you've done to the space, by the way."

She wrinkled her nose and said, "Are you sure you don't mind? I didn't mean to take over. I just love this room."

"And I love seeing you in it."

He gave her a quick kiss and went to get breakfast. When he returned with a tray of food, she'd cleared a space for him beside her.

"Mm. It looks and smells delicious. Who do I have to thank for your mad cooking skills? Mom or Dad?"

He handed her a plate and said, "Both." As he sat down, he noticed a picture of him and his father near the flowers. He set his plate beside the blanket and picked up the picture, warmed by the memory of when it was taken. "Now you're confiscating my pictures as well as my clothes?"

"Didn't I tell you I was a kleptomaniac?" She laughed softly. "It felt empty in here, and I was lonely, so I brought you and your dad in to keep me company."

He loved the way she made herself at home, but what he liked even more was the way she was looking at him, with the same confidence she'd had when they'd first met.

"I remember when this picture was taken," he said. "It was a great fishing trip, and Beckett missed it. I tried to wake him up to come with us at sunrise, but he sleeps like the dead. I couldn't get him out of bed. When we got home that evening, Beckett snubbed me for hours."

"Jana used to hate it when I'd get to do something she didn't. But she wasn't a snubber. She'd holler and stomp around, letting everyone in a ten-mile radius know she was pissed." She took a bite of her omelet. "*Mm*, Gavin. You are definitely as good in the kitchen as you are in the bedroom."

"You should see me in the sunroom," he said flirtatiously.

She bumped him with her shoulder. "I can't wait to find out. But first I need to eat this insanely good food my boyfriend slaved over."

"And *I* need to read your story. Where do I start?"

She set down her plate and went around the room gathering papers. "I really think this was the right direction for me, using my bad dates and losing the show. You'll see that my heroine is basically me, a woman who moved across the country to follow her dream, and then her life falls apart." She handed him a stack of papers.

"What about the part where she meets the handsome, awesome guy who she can't live without?"

"I'm not at that point in the story yet. I'm not sure it's going to be that easy for her," Harper said as she sat beside him. "I think this is perfect for a long series. I want to talk to Chloe and some of the other girls about their bad dating experiences and try to use them in the story. Maybe she meets the guy and thinks it could be right, but then things keep happening that make them go back and forth between friends and lovers."

"I don't like that idea in real life, sweetheart."

"Because *we're* not a romantic comedy. The *last* thing I want is to go through a hundred more bad dates, or find you kissing some other woman and have to castrate you." She popped another bite of egg into her mouth.

"Ouch!"

"You know what I mean. Who has time for that kind of heartache?" Her eyes narrowed. "You don't have another woman in the wings, do you?"

"Nope. I'm not an asshole. And I'm glad you're not looking for more dates."

"I just found you. Do you really think I'm dumb enough to take out the hook and toss you back in the water?" She pushed to her feet and said, "Now I'm full of nervous energy. I'm going to get some jam for the croissants. Do you want anything?"

"No, thanks."

She left the room with a bounce in her step, similar to the quickening beat of his heart.

He turned his attention to the story as he ate.

When Harper returned, she fidgeted nervously, stealing glances at him as he read. After they finished eating, she told him to keep reading and went to wash the dishes.

She never came back.

When he was done, he found her pacing the living room, biting her nails.

She stopped cold at the sight of him. "Well? Does it suck? Is it okay? I know I have scenes to flesh out, and—"

Her words were lost in the press of his lips. "Remember what I said about writing for the WHAT Theater?"

"Yes."

"Forget it."

Her shoulders slumped. "It's that bad?"

"No, babe. It's that good. The local theater is too small for this. You need to finish it and get it out to whoever got you your last deal, because it's fucking hilarious. I mean, I feel horrible for the girl, but women are going to eat this up."

She squealed and threw her arms around his neck. "I'm so happy!" She pushed away, and her smile morphed into a worried frown. "What about guys? Marketability has to be there for the widest audience possible."

"You know *way* too much about how guys think. How could you have ever thought your instincts were off? The lines in the bar scene are spot-on, babe. And I loved the way you handled the scene when she found out the guy she was dating wanted a threesome. But please tell me that's not how it really happened."

In the scene, the heroine was contemplating finally sleeping with her boyfriend, and she received a package before their date. The gift was a pair of leather pants and a corset. She thought it was strange, but she played along because they had a fun, quirky relationship. She wore the outfit to his house for dinner despite being uncomfortable, having a wedgie, and almost tripping in her heels because the pants were too tight. The guy answered the door dressed in a suit. When he opened the door wider, she noticed he was holding a leash that was attached to a leather collar with spikes around another man's neck. When the woman finally picked her jaw up off the floor, she casually mentioned needing to retrieve her whip from the car and then hightailed it out of there.

"Of course not!" Harper exclaimed. "But I figured the more outlandish the better. Relationships start with *swipes* these days. You never know what to expect."

He pulled her into his arms and said, "It's brilliant, Harp. Absolutely *genius.*"

"Really?"

"Really!" He spun her around as they kissed. When he set her down, she was smiling so big it had to hurt. "You should ask Emery if Ethan can help you get it out there."

She shook her head, pacing again. "No. I'm not going to use any contacts like that. I have to earn this on my own or I'll always wonder if my writing is good enough or if Emery just called in a favor. I have contacts. And I met that guy on the plane, remember? What if he does work somewhere big? For all I know, he could work with Netflix."

"The guy you chewed out?"

"Mm-hm. But I'm getting way ahead of myself. I can't think about any of that until it's done and the writing is perfect."

"Then let's get started." He headed into the bedroom to grab a sketch pad from a drawer.

"What are you doing?"

He came out of the room waving the drawing pad. "You're not the only one who's found their muse."

"Did you get more ideas for Ocean Edge?"

He reached for her hand and said, "I think it's time I start doing a little decorating around here. But first, let's push the couch into the sunroom."

Her eyes lit up. "The couch? What a great idea! We'll be even more productive and comfortable."

"Especially when we try to help each other through those mental blocks we're sure to encounter." His hands slid down to her butt.

"Mr. Wheeler, are you trying to distract me from writing?"

"No way. I fully support this endeavor and plan to give you lots of *inspiration*. Just tell me one thing: If I send you a leather outfit, what are the chances you'll wear it for me?"

"That depends. Does it come with a whip?"

"You are a dirty girl." He nipped at her lip, chuckling.

"Only for you…"

Chapter Fourteen

THE CAPE CHILDREN'S Amphitheater was located down a wooded road on the outskirts of Brewster, on the personal property of an eccentric retired actor, Harvey Fine, whom Harper would be interviewing after the show. Harvey's father, who was also an actor prior to his passing, had built the amphitheater for his personal use. Sometime after inheriting the theater, Harvey began allowing local performing arts groups to hold performances there. Harper had fond memories of watching Jana onstage there when they were younger. She looked at her beautiful blond sister, sitting on the edge of her seat beside her in a flowing sundress and cute colorful sandals, watching children perform *The Wizard of Oz.* Jana's hand rested on her belly. She was glad Jana had agreed to join her. It was Wednesday afternoon, and they'd lucked out with a warm, sunny day.

When had her rebellious little sister grown into such a mature mama-to-be? She wondered what would have become of their friendship if she'd stayed in LA. Would Harper have inevitably changed to fit in with the people there? Would she have become a workaholic like Gavin had when he was away from his friends and family? Luckily, she'd never have to find out.

"They're magnificent," Jana whispered. "I was never this good at their age."

"You were better." She used to be jealous of Jana's ability to flawlessly mold herself into any role, while Harper could only be herself. She was no longer jealous of that ability, as she had her own qualities of which she was proud. She was capable of writing great stories, and sure, she'd lost sight of that for a while and some of her stories were crap, but that was all part of finding her voice.

My muse.

Her mind drifted back to her weekend with Gavin. Her thoughts never strayed far from him. They'd ordered Chinese food Sunday evening and eaten it in the sunroom while they worked. Gavin had begun sketching designs for his house, pointing out color schemes and textures online and asking for Harper's opinion as much as she'd asked for his when she'd read him excerpts from her story. She'd never imagined feeling so *partnered* with anyone. She loved sharing all parts of her life with him.

"We should have done something like this," Jana said softly, eyes on the stage.

"You did *exactly* this."

Jana looked at Harper and said, "No, I mean *you and me.* You write, I act and dance. We should have done our *own* theater."

"Like the plays we used to put on for Mom and Dad in the living room?"

"No, for *real.* We should have done it *years* ago."

Harper was sure her sister had lost her mind. "Years ago we were two broke blondes, and I'm not too far from that now."

"We could have made it work. The guy who built this place always did."

"He was a *billionaire*." Harper glanced at the back of Mr. Fine's balding head. He was in his late eighties, with failing health, but he still managed to watch nearly every performance, sometimes from the window of his library. Today he was perched in a wheelchair in the front row. An umbrella shaded him from the sun.

"Shh," the woman beside Jana said with a discerning look.

"Sorry," Jana and Harper mumbled.

Jana turned so the woman couldn't see her smirk and shrugged at Harper like she used to when they were little, as if to say, *Oops*. A minute later she leaned closer and said, "I bet her kid has the lead." She was quiet for only a moment before whispering, "I still think we could have done it. You and me in business together? We'd have had so much fun."

The woman glared at them again.

About five minutes later Jana leaned closer and said, "By the way, your one-word responses to my texts about the other morning sucked. I want the lowdown on what happened after you ran off from breakfast to meet Gavin."

Harper *and* the woman on the other side of Jana both shushed her.

Jana mouthed, *Sorry*. She managed not to whisper for *most* of the remaining show.

After the show and two long rounds of applause, Jana joined the audience and the actors in the food tent for a buffet lunch next to the most spectacular gardens Harper had ever seen. They were overflowing with flowers and greenery, untamed and bushy, which she loved, although each garden was well defined by a large mulch bed.

Harper hurried across the lawn, notebook in hand, and fell into step with Mr. Fine's faithful assistant of the last decade, Jack Steele, who was younger than she imagined and looked to be in his early thirties. He was sharply dressed and strikingly handsome—tall and dark, with an air of mystery like a Hollywood movie star.

"Hi, Mr. Steele? Mr. Fine? I'm Harper Garner with the *Cape Cod Times*."

"Jack, please," Mr. Steele said in a dignified voice that caused Harper to stand up straighter. He stopped pushing the wheelchair to unhurriedly, yet firmly, shake her hand. His hand was warm and soft, the kind of hand caregivers should have. "It's a pleasure to meet you."

"It's a pleasure to meet you, too." Harper shifted her gaze to Harvey Fine, also sharply dressed in a gray cardigan over a white button-down. His legs were covered with a plaid blanket. He had a slightly long face, and the hair on the sides of his head and the few strands on top were winter white and looked downy soft. His hands and face were speckled with age spots, and his skin was translucent. An oxygen tube snaked from beneath his nose, over his ears, to the oxygen tank attached to the back of his wheelchair.

"Thank you for taking the time to chat with me, Mr. Fine," she said. "My sister used to act on your stage, and I've enjoyed many performances here."

He lifted bushy brows over friendly gray eyes and said, "I don't have much time left, so I hope you're a fast talker. And please, call me Harvey, and call him *Jock*."

Jack rolled his eyes.

When Harper raised her brow, Harvey said, "Don't look at him like he has a choice in the matter. His name's been *Jock* for a decade. Just look at the handsome creature, for goodness' sake."

"Okay, Harvey and Jock it is," she said. "Don't worry. I can be as quick as you'd like."

Harvey's thin lips curved up and he glanced at Jock to say, "How many times have you said that to a woman?"

Harper felt her eyes widen. She stifled a laugh.

"Not as many times as you'd think," Jock said with a drone of boredom, as if he'd heard it a million times, although there was no missing the affectionate glimmer of amusement in his eyes.

Harvey lifted his frail hand, pointing one birdlike finger at Jock. "Ah, but how many times did they believe you?"

Harper laughed.

"I knew I could make you laugh," Harvey said as they headed for the house. "A pretty young woman like you should be laughing all the time. There's not enough laughter in the world anymore. Everyone's worried about making their mark or what the big guys in positions of power are doing. What happened to the days when kids were the focus? When laughter was more important than the daily news? That's what the world needs more of." He waved his hand dismissively as Jock pushed his wheelchair up the ramp beside the front steps of the house. "Have I rambled enough yet?"

Jock pushed a button beside the door, and the two front doors opened. "You surpassed *enough* about ten years ago."

"Smart-ass," Harvey said with a rough laugh, which led to a raspy, hacking cough as they entered the house.

Once inside, Jock crouched beside the wheelchair with one hand on Harvey's shoulder, his eyes laden with concern, as he handed Harvey a monogrammed handkerchief. Harvey held it in front of his mouth as he slowly regained control. Jock took another handkerchief from his pocket and dabbed wetness from around Harvey's eyes.

"Are you okay?" Harper asked.

"Yes, I believe so." Harvey winked at her. "Aging gracefully is not easy, but you should have seen how charming I was as a younger man." He started coughing again, and when it finally subsided, he was wheezing.

"I can do this another time if you'd like," Harper offered.

"He's okay," Jock reassured her, giving Harvey's shoulder a squeeze. "This is just the universe's way of telling him to stop flirting with younger women."

Harvey cough-laughed. "Probably right, son." He tipped his face up to Harper and said, "Unless, of course, you'd like me to flirt with you?"

And so began one of the most intriguing interviews Harper had ever experienced.

ON THE WAY back to Jana's house, Harper told Jana about the interview. "Every article I've ever read about the amphitheater has focused on the property, which is why I focused on Harvey. Jana, Harvey is such an impressive and kind man. He worked on Broadway, and he didn't want to live on the Cape. He *reluctantly* took over here—his word, not mine. Nobody has ever published anything negative about his father. Apparently he was a real prick, and horrible to Harvey. When Harvey came here from New York, he intended to sell the property, but then he met Adele, who later became his wife. He called her his *goddess of sweetness.*" Her throat thickened thinking of the love she'd seen in Harvey's eyes when he spoke of her. "She lost both her legs in a car accident on their seventh date."

"Oh *no*." Jana's face crumpled. "I performed there many times, and I never even knew he was married."

"That's not surprising. He lost her to cancer just eight years after they were married. Her ashes were spread over the gardens, and he stayed in the area to be closer to her. When I was leaving, Jock told me that Harvey has never talked about Adele to anyone. I felt funny about putting any of that in the article, but Jock said Harvey knows his days are numbered and that by telling me about Adele, it means Harvey trusts me to give his love for Adele a voice for the world to hear."

"That's tragically beautiful."

"I know. My heart hurt during the whole interview, even when he made me laugh. Harvey said it was a good thing he'd fallen in love with Adele the very moment he'd met her, because after the accident she was in so much grief over the loss of her legs, she could barely stand being around *herself*." Harper's eyes teared up just as they had during the interview, and she blinked them dry. "He said it was during her recovery that he learned how important laughter was. From then on, he made it his goal to help Adele see the humor in life, and since losing her, he said he laughs to remember her. That's why he opens the amphitheater only for children's plays and why he hosts buffets afterward, so the children can be with their friends and run around. He and Adele never had children. He said he surrounds himself with the people who laugh the most."

Jana rubbed her belly. "Kids."

"Exactly. You should have seen him with Jock, and the way Harvey's face brightened when he talked about his great-niece, Tegan, who he hopes will one day take over the property. Can you imagine facing all of that loss and coming out with an outlook like he has?" As she said it, she knew she would do the same thing if something were to happen to Gavin.

Jana nodded. "I can, actually."

"Me too…"

Jana studied her face like she had at lunch. "You feel that way about Gavin, don't you?"

Harper felt herself smiling.

"I *knew* it! It's about time you fessed up. Did you really think you'd get away with telling me everything was *fine* or *good* when you took off after breakfast last weekend? When you ran off, I told everyone I'd never seen you like that. You're glowing, Harper, and you're not even pregnant." Her eyes widened. "Are you?"

"No!" Harper laughed. "I'm happy, but I'm also a lit-tle…something. Confused? Hesitant? I don't know."

"Okay, let me help with that. It's all good if you do it with someone you love. Ties are for wrists; ball gags are for—"

"Stop! I know all that." Harper felt her cheeks burn.

"Oh, does my prim-and-proper sister have a naughty side?"

Yes. "No!"

"Poor Gavin," Jana said with a pouty face.

"I'm naughty enough. Can you please focus for a second?"

When the Brewster Scoop came into view, Jana yelled, "Stop! Ice cream. I *need* it."

"I can see focusing is even harder when you're preggers." She pulled into the parking lot.

"I will focus like a laser beam once I have some sugar."

They got ice cream cones, and Jana suggested they walk down to Breakwater Beach, which was around the corner. "I promised myself I'd work off any extra calories I ate, and I'm eating a *lot*. I never stop. I swear I'm going to be eight hundred pounds after I have this baby."

"And you'll still be gorgeous," Harper said as they walked past the Brewster General Store and turned down Breakwater Road, a residential street lined with pretty cottages.

"Hunter seems to think so." Jana licked her ice cream and said, "So, give me the lowdown on you and Gavin."

Harper sighed dreamily. "Remember how you and Hunter toyed with each other for a long time before you finally realized you both wanted the same thing?"

"You mean *tortured*, don't you?" Jana said. "We were stubborn. Neither of us would admit what we really wanted. But *you* knew. You're the one who told me to lay it all on the line and confront him."

"Yeah. You were always crazy about him, but you got off on the whole oil and water thing that defined your relationship. Gavin and I are the opposite of you and Hunter. There are no games, no pretending or posturing. Or at least *mostly*."

"Mostly? What does that mean? He better not be fucking with your head or—"

"Calm down." Harper licked her ice cream. "I love that you're so protective of me, but you don't have to be with him. It's not him. It's *me*. He wants more togetherness, and I do too, Jana, more than you can imagine. We spent the whole weekend together, every single minute of it."

"This sounds promising. In bed or out?"

"Both," Harper admitted, and for the first time in her life she wanted to share something intimate, because being with Gavin was too good to hold in. "We made love a *lot*. Being with Gavin is heavenly. I never knew it could be like this, but he's loving and sometimes demanding in a really wonderful way.

He's rough and sweet at once, and…" She snapped her mouth shut, realizing how much she'd revealed.

"About damn time I get to hear you say that. Harper, this is fantastic! I always worried you'd end up with some guy with a pocket protector or something."

"*Ohmygod*, really?"

Jana laughed. "I don't know. You were always so strait-laced."

"That's just it. I *was*. I just…It's him, Jana. I think I'm like Harvey. He fell in love with his wife the first time he saw her. And the first time I saw Gavin, the first time I talked to him, I knew he was different. He's amazing. But it's not just that— we're so alike. He's a hard worker, but he doesn't get lost in it, although he said he used to and that really messed with him." She told Jana about Corinne and the pregnancy scare and how Gavin had become a workaholic, not finding his way back to his family and having a life until years later.

"It's amazing he trusts women at all after that."

"I know," Harper said. "And because of what he's gone through, he understands me and what I went through. He makes enjoying life, being with friends, and reaching out to his family more of a priority now. Oh, and you'll love this. How many guys do you know who actually make their bed every morning?"

"Oh no. He does *not*."

"He does!"

Jana bumped Harper with her shoulder. "You have *definitely* met your soul mate. Hunter and I are too busy messing ours up for either of us to ever bother making it."

"I'm sure you are. You know why this weekend was so wonderful? We were just living our lives, and it was like we'd always been together. We went out and had fun, but we also spent hours working on our separate projects and helping each other with ideas. He's incredibly supportive of my writing. And he doesn't hold anything back. He tells me when it's bad, which most people wouldn't do, and I appreciate that."

"You're so weird about that. If my dancing weren't up to par, Hunter better lie to me about it. I don't want him to hurt my feelings."

"Well, it stings to be criticized, but trust is all about honesty for me, and knowing he could be that honest? That's like the best gift ever. Now that I have found my voice, and my writing doesn't suck, he's encouraging me to start submitting my work again. I didn't tell you this, but after my show was canceled, I basically wrote off the idea of ever getting anything sold again. He's inspiring me in so many ways, bringing parts of me to life that I never knew existed."

"Those sexy parts." Jana waggled her brows. "He's a keeper. Good sex is like ice cream. You can never have too much."

"I'm learning that," Harper said with a good dose of embarrassment. "I've never felt like I could share *all* of myself with anyone until Gavin."

"Okay, I understand what you're saying. You're talking about your naughty side, right?"

Harper rolled her eyes. "It's not all about sex."

"I know, but physical attraction usually comes first, and since you were looking for a hookup at that festival *you didn't tell me about*"—she gave Harper a disapproving look—"it was probably a purely physical attraction at first. You know, like you saw him and thought, *He's hot. I'd do him.* That's not a bad thing. Look at me and Hunter. We were all about each other's hot bods and having great sex a long time before we were in love."

"Okay, fine, *yes*, at first glance I thought he was hot, and we have a great sexual connection. Better than I have ever had with any other guy. If they gave out prizes for amazing orgasms, he'd win. *Every time.* But we have so much more than that."

"Then what's the problem?"

"The problem is, I think I'm scared and I know I shouldn't be. He wanted me to stay all *week* with him. I've been working on his dock lately, and we love being together."

"He has a dock?"

"Mm-hm. He lives on a kettle pond in Brewster."

"*Sweet.* You love writing by the water."

"He taught me to fish." She smiled with the memory of that wonderful, romantic night.

"Dad will never believe that. I can't even picture you fishing, which means Gavin really has you hooked. So, let me get this straight. I'm not hearing anything to be scared of. Did you stay over this week?"

"I wanted to stay with him more than anything in the world. But I forced myself to go home Monday night, despite Gavin giving me dozens of delicious reasons to stay. And then last night we went out to dinner and for a walk on the beach. Then he took me back to his place to show me the mason jar lights he'd put along the path to the dock, which I'd suggested the other day."

"He sounds perfect for you, Harper. He's clearly a good listener, and if he's making changes at home, he clearly cares about your happiness. We both know you wouldn't be with a guy who wasn't a good man. You're too particular. So what *aren't* you telling me?"

The cool, salty sea air reached them before the water appeared just beyond the trees. It felt good to be home.

"That's just it," Harper said. "I was with a guy who wasn't a good man and I didn't know it. Remember the guy who was engaged? What if I'm missing something? That's why I went home again last night instead of staying at his place. I was scared to trust myself and lay my heart on the line, and then I spent all night berating myself for doing that, because whether I like it or not, my heart is already on the line. And I trust him, Jana. I trust who he is, the man he'll be in the future. I just *know*. So why did I go home?"

"Oh, Harper. Because you're *you*, and you believe in learning from your mistakes, which is usually a good thing. But sometimes you just have to say *fuck the mistakes* and put yourself out there."

"You make it sound easy, and it wasn't easy for you. You denied it even when Hunter wanted more of a commitment."

"I had commitment issues. You never have, and that's a good thing, Harper. You're much better at relationships than I ever was," Jana said as they crossed the parking lot toward the beach.

Colorful umbrellas flapped in the breeze as children played in the sand and by the water's edge. There were a handful of people in the water, including a group of twentysomethings tossing a football and dunking one another. Jana and Harper kicked off their sandals and walked down to the water.

"I get that you're scared," Jana said as they strolled along the shore. "But do you *want* to be all in with him? Or is there some reason you think you need to pull away besides worrying that the other shoe is going to fall?"

Harper's pulse quickened. "Honestly?"

"No, Harper. Lie to me," Jana said sarcastically. "Yes. I'm

your sister. I love you and I want you to be happy." She laced her fingers with Harper's and said, "And sometimes you stand in your own way."

"I know. The truth is, I started falling for Gavin that night in Virginia, and then I spent months thinking about him, *wishing* I could see him and thinking he wasn't interested in me because of the whole note-in-the-suitcase thing I told you about. Anyway, I convinced myself that I'd built him up to some unachievable fantasy. And then we reconnected, and he's ten times the man I met that night. It's like I've fallen off the side of a cliff and all I want is to land in his arms—and I know he'd catch me, Jana. It's the scariest and most magnificent thing I've ever felt." She shivered with emotion. "I have goose bumps all over just from admitting that to you."

"I'm so happy for you!" Jana gave her a one-armed hug, trying to keep her hair from blowing into their ice cream cones. "Love *is* scary. There's not much that's scarier, except maybe this." She rubbed her belly. "But it's a different type of fear. I think you should forget about that other shoe that might drop and let yourself be happy. Think of it this way. You have spent your life being careful and doing the right thing. You had to have a few bad experiences to know how wonderful this one is, to appreciate Gavin for all he is and all you are together. I think you should stay at his house if that's what your heart wants, or bring him to yours. Just don't spend your time punishing yourself, or him, because you dated a jerk."

"That makes sense," Harper said. "When did you get so smart about relationships?"

"I had a great mentor. It just took me a while to slow down and hear all the things she said over the years."

They walked along the wet sand, each lost in her own

thoughts as the waves crashed over their feet.

"Thank you for listening. I appreciate it." Harper finished her ice cream and said, "You're scared about the baby? Do you want to talk about it?"

"I just want to be a good mom. What if I screw up our baby? I know what type of trouble kids can get into. What if I'm too overprotective or too lenient? Hunter is great with kids, and he thinks I am, too, but I worry, you know?"

"I think that's natural, don't you? Mom was overprotective."

"And I rebelled. If we have a girl, I don't want her to be afraid of commitment, or to need a thousand things going on at once to make her happy like I did. I made so many mistakes over the years."

"Oh, Jana. You know what I think? The fact that you're worrying will make you the *best* mother. You care. You'll make mistakes—everyone does. But you could never screw up your child. You're too loving, and I've seen you with kids. You're patient and you're a great listener. What was it you said to me about not waiting for that other shoe to fall?"

Jana looked out over the water and reached for Harper's hand. "You'll be there if I need you?"

Tears stung Harper's eyes, and she noticed Jana's were glassy, too. "Always. But I know you'll be fine."

"Thank you." Jana sighed and said, "On another note, are you going to take a chance and submit your pages?"

"Yes—when they're done. I'll have to see if my agent will take me back, or I might try to get another agent. I know a few people who had friends and managers pitch for them. I have to figure that out. I'm working on writing the second episode, and then I have to read, revise, polish. You know the drill."

"I'm so glad. Are you going to submit to the guy you chewed out on the plane?"

Harper had almost forgotten she'd told her about him. "Only if I get desperate and everyone else turns me down. The last thing I need is to be reminded of that day. God, I was such a bitch to the poor guy. You know what? He might have lied. Maybe he's not even in the business. In any case, please don't mention that I'm going to submit to anyone yet. I haven't even told Gavin I'm definitely going to do it yet. I don't want to jinx it, and I don't want to disappoint him if I get turned down. You don't think that counts as lying, do you?"

Jana shook her head. "Definitely not. Wait until you get good news to celebrate."

"And if I get bad news?"

"Then you tell Gavin, cry on his shoulder, and get great cheer-up sex."

Harper laughed. "You have it all figured out."

As they headed back the way they came, Harper realized she was getting ready to take a leap of faith with her script, and that felt right, even if it was scary. Maybe it was time to take one with Gavin, too.

Chapter Fifteen

SUNDAY MORNING HARPER lay on Gavin's bed in her underwear, reading on her phone and listening to Gavin pacing the living room. He was on the phone with his brother. Every few minutes he'd laugh or exclaim, "No way!" or "Holy shit." They'd been staying together every night since she and Jana went to the play a week and a half ago, and she *loved* their everyday life. Gavin had cleared space for her clothes in his closet and drawers, and when they'd stayed at her cottage, she'd done the same for him. Their days were busy with work, and sometimes they hung out with their friends and other times it was just the two of them, but they always fell asleep wrapped up in each other's arms. It was the best feeling in the world. She was surprised at how the blending of their lives had *eased* her worries. When they had dinner with Harper's family, Harper had confessed that to Jana, and her sister had said it was because Harper was born to be married and that maybe Gavin was, too. That had started Harper thinking about the future in a bigger way. She imagined celebrating the holidays together, attending Brock and Cree's wedding, ringing in the New Year, and maybe even toasting the success of her new script. She was getting ahead of herself, but she felt blessed to be with a man who she *wanted* a future with.

Her phone vibrated with a text from Chloe. *Are you still coming to the inn for breakfast?* Over the past few days, Chloe and the girls had told her all sorts of funny dating stories, giving her new ideas for her script.

Harper thumbed out, *Yes*, added a smiling emoji, and sent the message.

Gavin was going riding with Justin, Dwayne, and a few other guys, and Harper had plans to join all the girls for breakfast and then hang out on the beach for the morning with Steph, Chloe, and Jana. She couldn't believe she'd been in LA for *months* and had never just relaxed on the beach. Her life had been *go, go, go*, and she'd never slowed down. But between Gavin treasuring his downtime and her girlfriends' pursuit of the perfect tan, she was falling back into the laid-back lifestyle of the Cape and loving every second of it—*and* every second of this cohabitating thing they were doing. Later that afternoon, she and Gavin were going shopping for new living room furniture. He was still figuring out exactly what to do with the sunroom, or maybe he was holding off because she'd been using the floor to organize her papers, though he didn't seem to mind. Every few days he brought home flowers and refilled the vase they'd brought from her cottage. It was still in the sunroom, along with two others they'd picked up last weekend.

Gavin's laughter floated into the room, and her thoughts returned to last night, when they'd gone out on the rowboat. Gavin had wanted to do some night fishing, and she'd brought her Kindle so she could read the next novel for their book club. She'd read the sexy passages aloud to him and was surprised she hadn't been the least bit embarrassed. They had fun critiquing the scenes, and when they'd eventually gone inside, they'd acted them out. Or at least they'd started to, but they'd quickly gotten lost in each other and forgotten to think at all.

Another text from Chloe rolled in. *Serena said please ask Gavin for the Wharf folder and bring it with you.*

The Wharf was a restaurant Gavin and Serena were redesigning. Gavin had shown Harper some of the designs they'd come up with, which were gorgeous. It was fun to learn more about his job and to watch him in action. He was as passionate about finding the right products and themes for his clients as he was about everything else he did, including discussing *Harper's* work. She loved that about him. She was getting closer to submitting her script, and her articles were coming along well, though her editor had delayed the article about Harvey Fine in order to fit in other articles about events that had popped up. She was glad for the extra time. She wanted the article to be perfect, something Harvey would be proud to read, and she'd been endlessly tweaking it.

She typed, *Will do*, and sent the text to Chloe.

Gavin glanced into the bedroom as he passed. He stopped, took two steps backward, and then his big, sexy body filled the doorframe, wearing only a pair of black boxer briefs. His eyes raked hungrily over her, causing her insides to sizzle.

Harper quickly thumbed out another text, *I might be a little late*, and sent it to Chloe.

Gavin covered the mouthpiece of his cell phone and said, "I thought you were getting dressed to meet the girls."

He wasn't leaving for another hour to meet Justin, so she rolled onto her side, giving him a view of her bare breasts. "I was, but I lay down on the bed to read a chapter or two for the book club, and then Chloe texted. Serena wants me to bring the Wharf folder to breakfast."

He stepped into the room and said, "Uh-huh."

She wasn't sure if that was meant for her or Beckett, but when his eyes trailed down her body again, he got hard, and she decided to tease him a little more. She set her phone on the nightstand and rolled onto her back, stretched her arms above her head, and sighed dramatically. "I told Chloe I'd be a little late." She trailed her fingertips between her breasts and down to the edge of her panties.

His jaw tightened and he said, "Beck, I gotta go." He set his phone on the nightstand and crawled over her with a sinful look in his eyes. "You are such a tease." He lowered his lips to hers, giving her lower lip a tug between his teeth.

She slithered down the bed and hooked her fingers into his briefs, pulling them down as she said, "I'm only a tease if I don't follow through." She had never realized how much of herself she'd held back until she'd been with Gavin, and now she never held back at all.

He kicked off his briefs and she slicked her tongue along his hard length. He made one of those purely male sounds that drove her wild. When she took him in her mouth, he moaned, his hips pulsing in a slow rhythm. She gripped his hips, urging him to move faster and harder, and he willingly complied, fucking her mouth good and hard.

Just when she felt him nearing the edge, his taut muscles hard against her hands, he withdrew and growled, "I need more." He tore off her panties and lay on his back. As she moved to straddle him, he said, "We're not done feasting, sweetheart. Turn around. I need to taste you."

Lord…

Hearing him say that heightened her arousal and her senses. She straddled his shoulders, and as he brought his mouth between her legs, she lowered her mouth over his shaft, moaning around it. She tried to concentrate on finding her rhythm, but his every lick and stroke sent thrills rushing through her, and when he brought his fingers into play, one teasing her bottom, the other teasing those sensitive nerves up front, she lost all control. Her orgasm tore through her. Her limbs trembled and shook as fireworks went off inside her. It was all she could do to try to remember how to breathe. When she finally came down from the peak, she tried again to pleasure him, working him with her hand and mouth. But he was on a mission to make her lose her mind, and if she'd learned one thing about Gavin, it was that he never fell short of his desires *or* his promises.

He was relentless, and oh, how she loved it!

After the third time she came, her limbs felt like wet noodles as aftershocks jerked through her. Her head hung between her shoulders, and he slapped her bottom just hard enough to make her want more. They'd discovered her little kink by accident, and she'd been shocked at how much she'd like it. He'd teasingly slapped her bottom when they were making love one night. The sting had done something wicked to her sex, and she'd asked him to do it again. The sexy little slap while they were fooling around was *hot*, especially since Gavin loved her bottom so much. He was always patting it, touching it, kissing it.

He gave her ass another tap, then pressed a kiss there. "I need to see you, gorgeous."

He shifted her beside him and grabbed a condom from the nightstand, sheathing himself. Confidence and desire billowed off of him as he lowered himself to his back and reached for her hand, helped her straddle his hips.

When he was buried deep inside her, he pulled her face closer to his and said, "You light me up, Harper, inside and out." He touched his lips to hers and said, "It's not just the sex, baby. It's everything about you. Your sweet smiles, your playful teases, and that look in your eyes right now that says you're falling hard for me and you don't want to say it out loud."

Her heart slammed against her ribs. Could he feel it? Did he know it was trying to break free? To become one with his?

He cradled her face between his hands, gazing deeply into her eyes as he said, "Know this, sweetheart. I'm falling for you and I never want to stop."

Before she could respond, he kissed her. Their bodies moved in exquisite harmony, and as they soared toward the clouds, his confession pulled hers to the surface and she whispered, "I've already fallen."

LATER THAT AFTERNOON, after a long ride with the guys, Gavin and Harper shopped for furniture. He was still riding the high off their morning confessions.

"What about this one?" Harper plopped down on a couch and patted the cushion beside her. Her skin had the fresh glow of a new tan, and her hair fell in silky waves over the thin straps of her tank dress.

He sat down, pulled her closer, and said, "I can't really tell." They were alone in the back of the store, so he leaned over her, pressing her down to her back as they kissed.

"Is this what you think is going to happen on your new couch?" she asked with a sweet laugh.

"I don't think we're allowed to do what'll probably happen

on our couch in here, but this is a good start." He kissed her again and said, "I'm just trying to be thorough. There are a lot of things to consider when purchasing furniture." He laced their hands together, lifting hers over her head, but the couch wasn't deep enough. "This couch is a total cock blocker. If I can't hold your hands, it'll never work."

He got up, and she giggled as he pulled her up beside him. He led her to an extra-deep couch with a cuddler on one end.

"You want a sex pit," she whispered.

"What I want is a couch that is large enough and comfortable enough for me to hold you, love you, and fall asleep tangled up in you, so you'll never want to leave my arms." He sat on the oversized cushions of the cuddler and pulled her down to his lap. He put his hand beneath her hair, caressing the nape of her neck, and said, "See, beautiful? Isn't this nice?"

"I'm not sure yet." She looked around the showroom. She got up on her knees and straddled his hips. Her arms circled his neck and her eyes darkened. "Yeah. This feels right."

"God, Harper. You make it impossible not to love you."

She touched her forehead to his and whispered, "You love sex. Don't confuse that with loving me."

In one swift move he took her down to her back and pinned her hands beside her head, returning her wide grin with one of his own as he said, "I've never told a woman I love her before. Not once."

"*Gavin*," she said with love in her eyes.

"It's true. Don't ever believe I would be shallow enough to say something so important because of sex. Especially to you. I said I was falling for you because I didn't want to scare you off, but I *love* you, Harper. I love your careful nature as much as I love our hot, sexy nights. I love the way our lives have come together. I love falling asleep with you safe in my arms and waking to your sweet snoring sounds."

She laughed, and a tear slipped from her eyes.

"I told my parents about you, sweetheart. I want to bring you home to meet them at Thanksgiving."

"Oh, Gavin, I love you so much. You could never scare me off, and I'd love to meet your family."

As he lowered his lips to hers, someone cleared their throat, and Harper flew to her feet, taking Gavin up with her. A saleswoman stood beside the cuddler. She looked to be in her late forties, and her smile told Gavin she was used to catching couples in compromising positions.

"Hi. I'm Gavin Wheeler." He shook her hand and said, "This is my girlfriend, Harper. We'll take this couch."

Harper whispered, "You haven't even looked around."

"I just handed you my heart on those cushions. That couch is ours."

With a dreamy expression, Harper leaned into him and said, "You're really something, and I'm *so* glad you're mine."

"I am, too," the saleswoman said. "If you'd like to hand her your heart again on an armchair or a table, we have plenty of other pieces that match this set."

Chapter Sixteen

"THESE GUYS ARE out of their minds," Gavin said as he and Serena walked out of the Wharf Thursday afternoon. The owners had completely changed directions and decided that outfitting the restaurant in stainless steel and glass was a good idea. "Do they realize they're in a beach community? Their building is a converted cottage, for Pete's sake."

Serena set her bag on the hood of her car, glancing back at the restaurant. She looked strikingly professional in a black skirt and a royal-blue blouse. "It's that crazy branding company they've started using. I recommended three local companies, but the owner's sister's boyfriend is supposed to be some kind of branding guru. The trouble is, he's never even *been* to the East Coast. He has no idea about the difference between Province-town, Orleans, or Boston, much less how the restaurant interiors differ."

"Know what I think?"

"That we should walk away and count our blessings to be free of them? The last thing we need is to design a restaurant that is sure to fail and will reflect badly on our company."

"No. I think we need to meet with their branding guy."

"I suggested that," she reminded him. The owners had

nixed the idea.

"Maybe we shouldn't *suggest* it. We accepted this contract based on designing in the fashion we pitched, one that's consistent with the food they offer, their reputation, and the location. I think we should *demand* the meeting. Sure, we can walk away and pick up another client, but there's a piece of me that feels bad for these guys."

Serena put her hand on her hip and said, "Because they're making bad business decisions? You're such a softie."

"I can't help it. They took over the restaurant from their parents. It's not like they have fifty years of experience. When we decided to open our business together, we agreed we weren't going to be *only* financially driven. We wanted to be good at what we did, to make a difference and make a name for ourselves. Part of being good at what we do is giving our two cents in a way that we can be heard." He shrugged and said, "What have we got to lose? Even if they say no, we're in no worse shape than if we'd cut ties now. But if they agree and we build a solid enough case that their branding guy can't see past it, then we're helping them in a way that *feels* good."

Serena's lips curved up. "You're right. We have nothing to lose. Want to go back in right now?"

"Not now." He and Harper had plans to barbecue tonight. She'd been working feverishly on her script, her new assignments, and the article she'd written about Harvey. He wanted to pick up some flowers to surprise her with on the way home.

"Let's sit on it for a day and set up an appointment tomorrow. That way we can walk in with a document in hand to nullify the contract so they know we're serious."

"I knew there was a reason I liked you. You can be a hard-ass when it serves you well."

"You liked me because of the old Wheeler charm," he teased.

"Actually, it was the cookies you used to leave on my desk. Speaking of which, it's been a long time since I've seen any of those." She cocked her head to the side and said, "Although, given how lovey-dovey you and Harper were at breakfast yesterday, I guess you've got better things on your mind than cookies. I love that you two are shacking up."

He chuckled. "*Shacking up?* That sounds very nineties."

"What do you call it?"

"I don't know, but I fucking love it."

"What's *wifey* cooking for you tonight?"

"I'm the cook," he corrected her. "All she has to do is light my fire."

She rolled her eyes again. "Guys are all the same." She lowered her voice, mocking him, and said, "Light my fire, be good in the bedroom." In her normal tone, she said, "Do you think girls tell each other that all our guys have to do is…?" She giggled and quickly said, "Never mind. I take that back."

Gavin laughed. "I've seen what the girls read in that book club. None of y'all are innocent."

"I've never implied innocence." She unlocked her car door and grabbed her bag. "Hey, did you *really* buy furniture for your place? Have you done the sunroom yet?" The first few months after he'd bought the house, Serena had nagged him incessantly to *get with the program* and decorate.

"Yes to the furniture, no to the sunroom, but I have some ideas." Their new couch, coffee table, and armchair had been delivered, along with a dining set they'd found during the same shopping trip.

"Sounds like Harper is helping my little Gavin grow up,"

she teased. "See you tomorrow."

He chuckled as he climbed into his car. He was still smiling when he pulled down his street a little while later. There was no better feeling than coming home to find Harper writing on the dock, enjoying a snack at their new dining room table, or listening to one of the records from his collection, which they'd finally unpacked. Yesterday after work they'd gone to the Earth House, which sold vintage records, clothing, and various other items, and they'd picked up a couple of records. He'd forgotten what it was like to be with someone he wanted to share those parts of himself with.

As he pulled into the driveway, Justin's motorcycle came into view, and just beyond was a front yard he hardly recognized. On either side of the front steps, gorgeous, kidney-shaped flower beds overflowed with colorful blooms. Harper was perched on her knees, wearing shorts and a bikini top, her hair pinned up in a high ponytail, with a pair of flowered rubber boots on her feet. She was moving dirt around the base of unwieldy tiger lilies, talking to Justin. Justin's arms were crossed over his black Cape Stone T-shirt, and even from the side Gavin could see he wore a serious expression. His beard jumped as if his jaw was clenching.

Gavin climbed from his car with the flowers he'd bought for Harper, and they both looked over. "I must have missed the invitation to the party."

Harper pushed to her feet with a tentative smile. She was stunning in a polka-dot bikini top and her favorite cutoffs—the ones with embroidered peace signs and flowers around the pockets. "I hope it's okay. Oh my gosh, you brought me flowers! They're beautiful! Thank you!" She took the bouquet as she talked excitedly. "I didn't mean to take over the yard. I had all this extra energy and couldn't focus on writing, so I ran out to the store to pick up a few things. While I was out, I passed the Farm, with all their gorgeous flowers on display, and got inspired to garden."

He leaned in for a kiss and said, "They're almost as beautiful as you are, and you can take over anything you'd like, sweetheart. What's going on, Jus?"

"I came by to see if you guys wanted to grab a beer at Common Grounds and found Harper knee-deep in dirt, trying to save your sorry front yard. I was just telling her that I've been after you for months to do something with this place."

"I never had much inspiration before." He pulled Harper closer.

Justin scoffed. "I don't see *your* knees covered in dirt. You've got a hell of a girlfriend."

"Yeah, I do." He kissed her cheek.

"Hey, Justin, why don't you stick around and eat with us?" Harper suggested. "We're just throwing burgers on the grill, but we've got beer in the fridge."

Just when he didn't think his life could get much better, she surprised him. There was something wonderful about his best friend and his girlfriend hitting it off. "That's a great idea."

"Sounds cool to me," Justin agreed.

Harper wiped her hands on her shorts and said, "I just need to wash up. Gosh, I've been going, going, going since first thing this morning."

"Where did all this extra energy come from?" Gavin asked.

Her eyes lit up as she said, "It all started this morning when I was trying to write. I'm almost ready to grovel to my ex-agent and see if she'll pitch my script, and I'm really nervous about it. I felt like I'd downed five cups of coffee. It's like putting myself out there naked for everyone to judge."

"Babe, your work is fantastic, just like *you*."

"Is this about the new script you're writing that you've been talking about?" Justin asked.

"Yes."

"Well, you might want to wait another couple of weeks," Justin said. "Our business is slammed right now because we're trying to wrap up the work we can before the week of the Fourth. We don't even send bids for new jobs until the week after the holiday. We've found that anything submitted within two weeks of a major holiday gets buried in people's inboxes."

"Oh, good point. Geez, how could I have forgotten about the Fourth?" Harper breathed a sigh of relief.

"You're kind of bouncing off the walls," Justin said.

"I know! Thank you for reminding me. I'll wait until after the holiday. But that's not all that's going on." She shifted a wide-eyed gaze to Gavin. "I wanted to call you so badly, but I didn't want to interrupt your meetings. While I was out running errands, I got a call from the producer I worked with in LA. They have ideas for a new twist on the pilot I sold them. It's a pretty significant rewrite, and they want me to come out there to work with them on it."

"Babe, that's amazing. You probably should have *led* with that news." A pang of longing sliced through Gavin at the thought of Harper going away after they'd just found each other. He'd never hold her back, but he was worried about how it could crush her if the show were to get canceled again. "You said it was a big deal to be part of the writing team. Being asked *twice* confirms just how incredible you are. When do you leave?"

Her shoulders sank. "I don't know if I want to accept."

"Whoa, Harp," Gavin said. "This is everything you've been hoping for. This is *why* you write."

"I know, but I'm just getting settled back here and…" She reached for Gavin's hand. "We have *us*, and I'm going to put feelers out with other places for my new script."

"Sweetheart, you're not missing out on an opportunity because of me. I'll fly out to see you every weekend if you want, but don't give up a chance to make your dreams come true."

"It does sound like the opportunity of a lifetime," Justin added.

"I know," she said in a pained voice. "But for the first time in ages, I'm *really* happy with what I'm doing and who I'm spending time with. I'm in the middle of a project I believe in, and I *just* got my life back. I don't know what I'm going to do. I told him I need two weeks to think about it. And right now I need to get cleaned up, you need to change out of your work clothes, and Justin needs a cold beer. So, let's get this party started!"

"But, Harp—"

"No, *but Harps*." She grabbed Gavin's and Justin's arms and headed for the front door. "I don't want to think about it tonight. I have two weeks to decide, and I'm not going to ruin tonight by overthinking, and you're not allowed to either."

"Hey, I'm not overthinking," Justin said as he opened the front door. "A beer sounds good to me."

Gavin held Harper on the front porch as Justin went inside. He gazed into her eyes, waiting until he had her complete attention before saying, "Harper, we don't have to talk about it right now, but please know that whatever you do, it won't hurt what we have, okay? Don't ever hold yourself back because of me."

"Okay."

"I mean it. I want everything for you, and that includes being there to help you reach every star in the sky. Promise me you won't let our relationship hold you back."

She went up on her toes and pressed her lips to his. "I know. I promise." She took his hand and said, "Come on. Let's go in."

"Gavin, this place looks awesome!" Justin called out from the kitchen. "What'd you do, hire a decorator?"

"Funny," Gavin said sarcastically, noticing the delicious aroma of fresh-baked goods hanging in the air. "What smells so good?"

"Nana's everything cookies," Harper said.

Gavin stopped cold, sure he'd misheard her. "*Whose* cookies?"

Justin poked his smiling face out of the kitchen and said, "Mind if I snag a cookie?"

"Sure," Harper said, grinning. "It's *Nana's* recipe. I tracked down Beckett on Instagram to see if I could get some recent pictures for the fishing-rod frames. I didn't want to just steal his pictures, so I messaged him and told him what I was doing. We got to talking, and I asked him about the cookies."

"Dude, these are amazing." Justin handed him a cookie. "I'm going to light the grill and chill on the patio while you get the lowdown, change your clothes, and whatnot."

"Thanks." He took a bite of the cookie, and sweetness exploded over his tongue. "Oh my God, Harper. These are better than Nana's." He set the cookie on the counter and gathered her in his arms, kissing her again, overwhelmed with love for her. "I can't believe you tracked Nana down and made my favorite cookies."

"It was fun, and Beckett is hilarious. I *love* him, Gavin, and he thinks the world of you. He connected me to your mom for the cookie recipe, and we talked on the phone for half an hour. Then she gave me Nana's phone number, and Nana kept me on the phone forever. They were both so nice, and it's obvious how much they miss you. Nana said you should come home for your birthday so she can throw you a party. I didn't know your birthday was at the end of July. Why didn't you tell me?"

She must have misread the look of surprise on his face over all that she'd done, because she said, "Oh no. Did I overstep? I just wanted to get the pictures, and then one thing led to another—"

He lowered his mouth to hers, silencing her with the hard press of his lips. When he felt the tension ease from her body, he kissed her longer, wanting to make sure she knew just how much he appreciated everything she'd done.

When their lips finally parted, he looked at the amazing woman in his arms and said, "You can't overstep, Harper. I'm just surprised at how much trouble you went to for me. You're amazing, sweetheart."

"Good, because I'm so happy I got in contact with them." She grabbed a stack of pictures from the counter and handed them to him. "Look at the pictures Beckett sent me. That's why I went into town, to get them printed off my phone. I know you have great pictures of your family on the other wall, but these are more recent."

He leafed through the pictures of his family gathered around the Christmas tree at the Jerichos' barn, and the picture of him and Beckett sitting with beers in their hands on their parents' couch. There was a picture of Gavin and his parents arm in arm and one of him and his mother sitting together with sparkling holiday lights behind them. His throat thickened with emotion.

"Sweetheart…" He lifted his gaze, spotting another envelope beside her keys on the counter. "Are those more pictures?"

"Those are pictures I want to put up at my place."

"Can I see?"

She nodded, and he grabbed the envelope and leafed through the pictures they'd taken together over the past several weeks. She'd even printed the picture he'd texted to her after their first date, the one in which she was holding the fishing rod with the fish she'd caught. "I don't understand. Why don't you want to put these up here?"

"I didn't want to seem too presumptuous."

"My sweet, careful girl, you tracked down my brother, spoke to my mother, and to Nana, who I'm not even related to. You beautified my front yard, and you're worried that giving me pictures of *us* would be too presumptuous?"

She lifted one shoulder in an adorable shrug.

"I think your instincts are off after all, babe." He gathered her in his arms and said, "I want pictures of us *here*. I want you to *presume*, Harper. Presume *everything* your little heart desires, and while you're presuming, while you're thinking over the offer you have from LA, know that I'm the one thing you can take for granted, okay?"

She looked all choked up as her arms circled his neck. "I'll never take you for granted."

"Not me, just my love for you. Promise me?" he asked.

She nodded.

"That's my girl."

As their mouths came together, he vowed to make sure she kept that promise.

"Can we hurry up the *whatnot?*" Justin's voice broke through their reverie. "You haven't even changed your clothes yet? Dude, you need some lessons in hosting."

Harper blushed, and Gavin whispered, "I like the whatnot."

Justin grabbed the hamburger meat from the fridge and said, "You know what? You've waited a long time for each other. Go back to your tonsil inspections. I'll cook dinner." He snagged another cookie and headed out the patio door.

Gavin gazed into Harper's eyes and said, "You heard the man," and lowered his lips to hers.

Chapter Seventeen

HARPER'S EDITOR WAS ready to run the article about Harvey. She'd called Jock and scheduled an appointment to bring it by for Harvey to review today, Tuesday, before they sent it for publication. There were no performances this afternoon, and the lack of cars and noise, and the missing buffet tent and chairs, gave the property a little colder, and lonelier, aura. It was no wonder Harvey surrounded himself with as much life as he could.

Harper climbed the front steps and knocked on the heavy wooden door. She'd poured her heart and soul into this article and was excited to see Harvey's reaction.

A pretty blonde with either very sad or tired blue eyes answered the door wearing a pair of yoga pants and a tank top. Harper wondered if she was Jock's girlfriend.

"Hi. I'm Harper Garner with the *Cape Cod Times*. I have an appointment with Mr. Fine to go over an article I've written about him."

The woman looked over her shoulder, then stepped outside, closing the door behind her. "Hi. I'm Tegan, Harvey's great-niece."

"Oh! Harvey told me about you. It's nice to meet you."

Tegan swallowed hard, tears dampening her eyes. "My great-uncle passed away yesterday. We haven't told anyone yet. We're still making arrangements, and…." She swiped at her tears.

"Oh no, I'm so sorry." Tears fell from Harper's eyes. She tried to will them away, but there was no stopping the sadness from coming out.

"We all are." She waved at the porch step. "Have a seat, please."

"I should probably go so you can be with your family," Harper said, wiping her tears.

"No, please, sit on the steps with me. I'd like to talk, if you don't mind. Uncle Harvey mentioned you before he passed." A shaky smile appeared as she wiped her eyes. "Actually, he said, 'When Harper brings that story, you read it. I want it told.' What's the story about, exactly?"

"Harvey and Adele and their life together. He also told me about you and, of course, his friendship with Jock." She couldn't stop her tears from falling. "I'm sorry. I don't mean to…I knew he didn't have long to live, but your uncle, Harvey, he…I really enjoyed meeting him."

"Thank you. May I read the article?"

"Oh, of course." Harper handed her the envelope, and she stood to leave.

Tegan touched her hand. "Would you mind staying for a few minutes while I read it? It's just me and Jock here, and he's so upset right now. It's nice to see another friendly face."

"Sure." Harper sat and pulled herself together as Tegan read the article.

Tears streamed down Tegan's cheeks as she read. She covered her mouth when she laughed softly, and afterward, she pressed the papers to her chest and said, "You really did get to him. He would have loved what you've written."

Harper breathed a sigh of relief. "I'm so glad. I wanted readers to come away with a sense of how special Harvey was."

"You've achieved that. My uncle was a very private man. Jock said my uncle told him that you reminded him of me."

"Blond hair and blue eyes," Harper said.

Tegan shook her head. "Uncle Harvey never saw what people looked like. Except with Jock. He loved to tease him. But if Uncle Harvey said you reminded him of me, then he thought you were creative, strong-willed, and someone who could not only do his story justice, but give his love for my aunt a voice. This story will probably create relationship goals for millions of people. Just like my great uncle's stories about them did for me." She put the papers on her lap and gazed down at them.

"What will happen to the property? To Jock?"

"Jock isn't a caregiver by trade, but his loyalty to my uncle was unwavering. Uncle Harvey went through five caregivers before Jock stepped in to help out temporarily. Jock has endured more than his share of loss, but that's not my story to tell. He and my uncle needed each other. They got along so well, Jock stayed on. He's wrecked, of course, but after he grieves, he'll probably go back to writing."

"I didn't know he was a writer."

"I'm not sure he still is," Tegan said. "And as far as this place goes, I know my uncle talked about me taking over, and if he really did leave it to me in his will, then the last thing I want to do is sell it. But I don't know how to run a place like this. I make children's costumes for a princess boutique, and I'm a nip-and-tuck girl for a clothing store. I also work for my sister's photography business, editing her pictures. In those areas, I'm a pro. But this?" She shrugged.

"But you have Jock and all of your uncle's contacts and friends in the industry. Surely they can help guide you."

"From what Jock says, there are a lot of politics involved with the business. He never wanted the theater to be used by only one group. My uncle was an eccentric man who loved laughter and did what made him happy, which was allowing performers to use the amphitheater. He orchestrated luncheons, schedules, and negotiated contracts and such right up until the end. How can I fill his shoes without screwing them up? Not to mention that I have a whole life back in Peaceful Harbor—"

"Maryland?"

Tegan nodded. "You've heard of it? It's about as big as my fist."

"I just joined a book club here. It's mostly online, but there are members from all over. At the last meeting two members Skyped in from Peaceful Harbor. Dixie and Izzy, but I can't remember their last names."

"I'm in that book club! My friend Isla hooked me up."

"No way! This is crazy. Is that Isla Redmond? Because my brother Brock just got engaged to Cree Redmond, who is also from Peaceful Harbor, and her sister—"

"Is Isla!"

They both laughed.

"This is so funny. I know Dixie and Izzy really well," Tegan said. "I've only used the online forums for the book club, though."

"Well, if you end up staying here, then you can come to a meeting with me."

"That sounds fun. By the way, did you read the last book, *Turn Away*, by L. A. Ward?"

"Mm-hm." They talked about the book club, and Harper was glad it lightened the mood. "Small world, huh?"

"I'll say."

"You know, I recently had an *upheaval* in my life, and a friend showed me that sometimes all you really need to figure something out is the right person or people by your side to help. If Harvey left you this property and you decide to make a go of it, my sister, Jana, performed in local theaters for years. I don't know much about the technical side of running something like this, but I write scripts, and I have contacts all over the area because we grew up here. We'd be happy to help you find your way. Jana's really nice, and she runs her own dance company, so she's got good business sense."

"You wouldn't mind?"

"No, not at all. Actually, I think it would be fun."

"I don't even know how to pay you for something like that."

Harper thought about Gavin, Jana, and all their friends and how being around people she trusted made everything seem possible.

"You don't have to pay us. Your uncle went through so much with Adele, and he stayed here to be closer to where their life together took place. He was a very special man, and he told me he hoped you'd take over. Nobody should have to go through trying times without friends by their side. Consider our help *paying it forward*, helping to keep the laughter alive."

"Gosh, I don't know what to say. I'm a *big* pay-it-forward person. I know it sounds silly, but just hearing you say that makes me breathe a little easier."

"It's not silly. You've got a lot on your shoulders right now. If you need anything while you're here, I'm happy to help."

Tegan looked up at the sky with fresh tears in her eyes and said, "Why do I feel like we were supposed to meet?" She wiped her eyes, smiling at Harper despite her tears. "I think this is Uncle Harvey's doing. This is just the type of thing he'd orchestrate, plopping a friend down beside me."

"Well, he did have a sense of humor."

"Oh boy, did he ever." Tegan went on to talk about her uncle's shenanigans, of which there were many. "I spent a lot of time here when I was growing up, and one of his favorite things to do was to show up for dinner wearing a funny mask or dressed like a character from a show. But he'd act like nothing was out of the ordinary. He was always doing things like that. One summer I fell and needed stitches. When we got to the hospital, the doctor came in wearing a mask with a cat's mouth and nose drawn on it and a hat that had cat ears. My uncle had brought them with him to the hospital just to make me laugh while I got my stitches."

Tears tumbled down Tegan's cheeks. "I miss him so much already. He's only been gone for a day, and I keep expecting to see him."

Harper embraced her. "That means you loved him as much as he loved you."

Harper didn't know if they sat on the porch hugging for five minutes or twenty, but after, they talked for nearly two hours. They exchanged phone numbers, and by the time Harper got ready to leave, she really had made a new friend.

"How long will you be in town?"

"I don't know for sure," Tegan said. "Some of it will depend on what happens with the estate. But at least through August, until the last performance takes place. There are a lot of decisions to be made between now and then. You'll let me know when the article will run?"

"Of course. Do you want me to add information about his passing? Not anything like an obituary, but I could title the article something like *Saying Goodbye to a Fine Man* and mention his passing and how much he'll be missed?"

Tegan's eyes teared up again. "That would be really nice."

"Okay. I'll let you know when I finish those changes so you can read them before they're published. Will you please let me know when the funeral will be? I'd like to attend."

"There won't be one. Uncle Harvey didn't believe in funerals. He wants to be cremated and his ashes to be spread in the gardens, with Adele's."

That didn't surprise Harper. He was going to be with the woman he loved. When she looked at it that way, she wasn't quite so sad.

"Thank you for spending your afternoon talking to me, for making me laugh, and for writing such a nice article," Tegan said. "You know, my uncle always said love, laughter, and friendship are the only universal languages with the power to heal even the most broken of hearts. I'm sure he's with Adele, smiling down on us right now."

"Probably with a funny mask on," Harper said as she stood to leave. "Please give Jock my condolences."

"I will. I'd invite you in to say it yourself, but he'd be mortified if anyone saw him this upset. I'm sure he'll be in touch with you."

They embraced again, and Harper said, "I'm sorry we met under these circumstances, but I am glad we did."

As Harper drove away, she called Gavin and Jana to give them the sad news about Harvey and to tell Jana that she'd offered her up to help Tegan.

When she got to Gavin's house, she went down to the dock with a copy of the article, a notepad, and a pen to work on the necessary modifications. As she tried to find her voice, sadness rested heavily on her shoulders. She gazed out at the water and Harvey's voice came back to her.

Everyone's worried about making their mark or what the big guys in positions of power are doing. What happened to the days when kids were the focus? When laughter was more important than the daily news? That's what the world needs more of. She'd hardly laughed at all the entire time she'd been in LA. There had been a few moments of levity, but not true, belly-hurting laughter like she had here with Gavin and their friends. She was a million times happier here than she had been in LA. Just thinking about going back made her feel queasy. She thought of the note Gavin had left on her front porch. *Remember, you achieved greatness before you even went to LA. Your family knows how special you are.* Gavin had not only shown her the way back to who she'd once been, but he'd reminded her that her self-worth had nothing to do with her career. And then he'd encouraged her to do whatever she needed to achieve her goals. She was starting to realize her goals were changing, too.

GAVIN LEFT WORK early to make sure Harper was okay. He'd offered to come home when she'd called and told him about Harvey's passing, but she'd assured him that she was fine, and she was going to work on revising the article about him. But as the hours passed and the day trudged on, he hated the idea of her being alone when she was sad.

He wasn't surprised to see her sitting on the dock with her

feet dangling in the water. Beside her, a rock held down a notebook with a few loose papers sticking out. He admired the familiar scene from afar for a moment. It was one of his favorites. A few strands of her hair lifted in the breeze and she tucked them behind her ear. His heart squeezed. They'd talked about her offer to return to LA, and though she hadn't come to a decision yet, he had.

He walked down the path to the dock, trying to imagine what it would be like to come home to an empty house again. Whether she went to LA for a day, a week, or longer didn't matter, because he'd feel like a piece of him was missing every single second she was gone.

She turned as he stepped onto the dock. Her hair blew across her cheek, reminding him of the first night he'd seen her again at the bonfire with their friends.

"Gavin!" She tucked her hair behind her ear and popped to her feet, hurrying toward him in her long gauzy skirt and crop top. She looked full of life and happier than he expected after the news she'd received.

He loved that outfit. Hell, he loved her in anything as much as he loved her naked.

She ran into his arms and kissed him like she'd been waiting all day to do it. God, he loved her, and he loved the way she loved him.

"You're doing okay?" he asked.

"*Yes!*" she said loudly, stretching her arms out to the sides. "I've had a revelation. I thought I wasn't happy in LA because of everything that happened there, but it wasn't that. Any of that stuff could have happened when I was here. I was unhappy because I didn't *fit* there. I have bigger aspirations for my writing, but that doesn't mean I want to leave my *home* or my family and friends. And I know you don't want me to make decisions based on us, but we both know our relationship has to play into any big decisions. Otherwise what are we doing together? Don't worry. I'm not saying my decision is based on our relationship. I'm saying there's no sense in pretending I didn't weigh in the idea of being away from you for however long they want me. And my decision?" She laughed and twirled around. "It's based on *laughter*, Gavin. I want to laugh and be happy and write. And yes, I want to make my mark within the industry, but not at the expense of my happiness. Going to LA gives someone else the power to pull the rug out from under me again. I don't want that!"

He tried to keep up, but she was talking so fast he had trouble deciphering what decision she had made.

"If they want me to do rewrites, I'll do them from here. Take it or leave it. That's what I'm going to tell them. And I know I don't have anything solid here yet—but *yet* leaves lots of room for success, right? I'm almost ready to put feelers out for my current script. And maybe I screwed myself with that guy from the plane because I was too bitchy, but that's just *one* guy, *one* company. If he even runs a streaming service like he claimed. For all I know, he might have lied. But I believe in myself again, Gavin, and I believe in the project I'm working on. It's good writing and a great story. And you know what else? Tegan needs help if or when she takes over the amphitheater, and it would be fun to do that. I know we'd get along. Jana would help, too, and even though it's not a moneymaker, it would make me happy. I want to be that guiding hand like you were for me. I want to pay it forward, because that will make me happy."

"You're staying?" Damn, that got him all choked up.

She twirled back to him and pressed her hands to his chest, her eyes dazzling with excitement. "What do you think, Mr. Wheeler? Am I nuts for choosing happiness over seeing my name in lights?"

"Not even a little," he said. "Selfishly, I want you right here in my arms, and I'm happy to set up lights across the back of the house. Hell, across the sky. Big, flashy lights that spell out your name so you never feel like you've missed out on a damn thing."

She poked her finger into his chest and said, "You just got major nooky points, Mr. Wheeler."

They kissed and laughed, and between those relieved kisses, he said, "Harper, if you ever do get the LA bug, there are all sorts of options to make that area more appealing. I bet you'd enjoy LA if we were there together. I can arrange to work from afar for a week or two if need be."

"You would do that?"

"There's nothing I won't do for you. I'd have to work it out with Serena, but you're not alone in any of this anymore, sweetheart. You don't have to choose between here and there when there's a huge amount of middle ground."

"Middle ground, okay. I'll think about that, but my gut tells me not to try to find that middle ground right now. I still have a bad taste for the LA lifestyle and a delicious taste for *this*." She kissed him again, long and deep and deliciously seductively.

"Let's celebrate," he said.

"I don't have anything to celebrate yet. I haven't even told them my decision. They might turn down my offer to do rewrites from here."

"We're not celebrating your career move, sweetheart. We're celebrating the fact that you've embraced your instincts on all levels."

"In that case, kick off those shoes and take off all your clothes," she said as she stripped off her shirt and wiggled out of her skirt. She pushed off her panties and whipped off her bra, tossing it at him as she said, "Race you!" and ran off the end of the dock.

Gavin stripped naked and followed her in. He swam underwater, tickling her ribs as he broke the surface. She squealed, futilely trying to swim away, and he pulled her against him. She wrapped her arms around his neck, out of breath and panting as he treaded water for the both of them.

"I wish I had stayed in Romance, Virginia, and come back to the Cape with you," she said with droplets of water dripping down her cheeks.

"I lived in Boston then."

"Close enough, because eventually we would have landed right where we are, and we wouldn't have lost out on so much time together."

"That's the beautiful thing about time, Harp. It's on our side."

Her brow knitted. "What if we die tomorrow?"

"Then we've lived, loved, and laughed today." He lowered his face toward hers and said, "I, for one, plan on making it a hell of a good day."

Chapter Eighteen

THE FOURTH OF July arrived with sunshine and the buzz of excitement in the air. The sight of waving flags and smiling faces as Uncle Sam made his way down the main drag of Provincetown on wobbly stilts brought a rush of cherished memories. Memories of Harper's teenage years and beyond, when she had finally been able to attend events like the Provincetown parade with her siblings. The outlandish and artsy community wasn't her conservative parents' favorite place, but Harper and her siblings loved it. Harper and Gavin had arrived early enough for Harper to conduct interviews with retailers, residents, and tourists before the big event. By the time the parade started, they'd put her bag in the car and met up with Colton, Jana, and Hunter. Brock and Cree had gotten held up in traffic, and they were meeting them in front of the town hall in ten minutes. Later, they were meeting Emery and their friends at her brother Ethan's yacht.

"We should head for the town hall," Harper said to Gavin.

"What?" Gavin leaned closer to hear her over the crowd. He made a white T-shirt and khaki shorts look like a million bucks. He and Colton had gotten American flags painted on their cheeks while Harper had been interviewing. Gavin also had

Harper's name painted on his forearm.

"We need to meet Brock and Cree!" she hollered as a band marched by, playing an unfamiliar tune.

Gavin nodded and tapped Hunter on the shoulder. He pointed in the direction of the town hall. "Time to go!"

Gavin put his arm around Harper and kissed her, while Hunter grabbed Jana, who was busy stuffing a hot dog into her mouth. They fell into step with Colton, who was proudly wearing a white Styrofoam top hat with the rainbow flag on the front.

A colorful float rolled down the street, blaring music, carrying several men dressed as women in flouncy red, white, and blue dresses with fluffy boas wrapped around their necks. They were dancing and waving to the crowd.

As they neared the town hall, Gavin pointed to the families sitting on the lawn picnicking, playing, and waving at the passing parade and said, "That'll be us one day."

Harper's heart stumbled.

"Don't look so shocked," he said into her ear. "I can picture you surrounded by towheaded toddlers, sneaking frosting off their cupcakes while they're busy watching the parade."

She loved knowing she wasn't the only one dreaming of their future. "They can have their frosting as long as I get the red lollipops."

"I'll give you a lolly," he said heatedly, and pressed his lips to hers.

A group of cyclists passed dressed in colorful costumes and honking high-pitched horns, drawing their attention to the road. A fire truck rolled down the street behind them, lights flashing. Flags hung from the side of the fire truck, and people sat on top, waving and throwing candy into the applauding and whistling crowd.

Harper spotted Brock standing by the corner at the same moment Jana yelled,

"There's Brock and Cree!"

Brock's massive frame dwarfed Cree, who was tucked against his side. They were talking with Tegan and Jock. Harper was surprised to see Tegan and Jock there. Jock looked like a different person in jeans and a T-shirt.

"Jana, that's Tegan, Harvey's great-niece, the one I told you about." Harper pointed to Tegan. "She's from the same town as Cree. Come on. I want to introduce you."

"Hi, you guys," Cree said as they approached. Her black hair hung over her shoulders. She looked cute in a gray tank top and black cutoffs, with her black boots. How she managed to look sweet and not tough in that outfit was beyond Harper, but she pulled it off well. "Can you believe with all these people, we ran into Tegan and Jock?"

"It's that small-world thing again," Tegan said as she embraced Harper. "I loved the revisions to the article you sent. Thank you."

"Oh good, they're running it after the holiday." She turned to Jock and said, "I'm so sorry about Harvey. Are you doing okay?"

"Yeah. I miss him, but you know…" Jock said solemnly.

"Let me introduce Tegan and Jock to everyone before you two get to gabbing," Cree said.

As Cree made the introductions, explaining how she knew Tegan from their hometown, Brock sidled up to Gavin and nodded toward the grass a few feet away, indicating for Gavin to go with him so they could speak privately.

"Be right back, babe." Gavin stepped onto the grass.

"Brock, what are you doing?" Harper asked.

He looked at Gavin and said, "Making sure Gavin and I are on the same page."

"Seriously?" Harper complained as Brock and Gavin walked away. "We had dinner together a couple of weeks ago. Did I miss something between now and then?" Gavin had gotten along great with her brothers, although he had given Colton a hard time about abandoning her at the music festival. Colton had played it cool and reminded him that it was a good thing he had, or they'd never have met.

"Let him go or he'll think he failed you," Colton said. "He didn't get to do his big-brother thing at dinner."

Harper sighed. "What's he going to do, say *hurt my sister and I'll kill you?*"

"Nah, I've already told him that," Colton said. Then he and Hunter high-fived. He turned his attention to Jock and said, "So, you're a nurse? I hear nurses are good with their hands."

Harper choked on her breath and coughed. "Oh my gosh, Colton!"

Tegan, Jana, and Hunter laughed. Cree blushed and turned away.

"It's okay," Jock said with a smile that didn't reach his eyes. Harper could tell it was grief causing that strain and not her brother's flirtatious comment. "I'm not a nurse, but I am pretty good with my hands."

"Works for me," Colton said. "Want to grab a beer?"

"Sure, but you know I bat for the other team, right?" Jock asked.

Colton shrugged. "Can't blame a guy for trying. Let's go find a place to chill. Hunt, you want to join us?"

"Go, keep an eye on Colton," Jana urged.

Hunter leaned in to kiss Jana and said, "Love you. I'll leave my phone on."

After they walked away, Harper said, "Is Jock okay?"

"He will be. My sister, Cici, and I dragged him here to get him out of the house," Tegan explained. "My sister took her husband and kids to get their faces painted. I'm glad your brother got Jock to go for a drink. He needs it. They read the will, and my uncle's sense of humor outlived him. He left Jock an old-fashioned typewriter *and* two million dollars that he gets only if he publishes something."

Harper blinked several times. "Wow. Talk about pressure."

"Heck, I'll write something for him," Jana said. "That's a lot of money."

Tegan's concern for Jock was written in her eyes. "I asked him what he was going to do, and he said he had some things to deal with before he can even think about writing. He said he's not sure where he'll end up."

"Do you think he's upset about the contingency?" Harper asked. "He worked for Harvey for so long."

Tegan shook her head. "Jock doesn't care about money. It's the challenge that struck a chord. I just hope he comes back here, since it looks like I'll be here trying to carry on my uncle's legacy after the winter."

"We're ready to help," Harper said as Brock and Gavin joined them. She glanced at Brock, who gave her a thumbs-up as he reclaimed Cree with an arm around her waist. Harper shook her head. Brock's need to be overprotective would never change.

Gavin slung his arm over Harper's shoulder and kissed beside her ear, whispering, "You're lucky to have him looking out for you." He flashed a killer smile at Tegan and said, "Sorry I got pulled away. Tegan, right? I'm Gavin. Harper's my better half. I'm sorry about your uncle. He really made an impact on Harper. If you need anything, just let us know."

"Thank you." Tegan said. "You guys are all so nice. I have to admit, if I hadn't met Harper, I would probably still be trying to decide if I could commit to handling the theater, or if I should hand it over to someone else." She looked appreciatively at Harper. And then she pulled her phone from her pocket and read a text. "Looks like my sister and her family decided to go on a whale watch." She thumbed out a text, and as she put her phone in her pocket, she said, "I should probably find Jock."

"Why don't you join us for lunch?" Harper suggested. "I'll text Colton and have them meet us at the Patio. They have all sorts of food."

They made their way to the restaurant and met up with the others. Lunch was delicious, and conversations were light and fun. While Harper, Jana, and Tegan were discussing how they could work together to figure out the best way for Tegan to move forward, Cree suggested the idea of hosting children's singing and instrumental events in addition to plays.

"I love that idea!" Tegan exclaimed. "I feel like we need some brainstorming, but not until after I figure out how to temporarily wrap up my life in Maryland before jumping in with two feet here."

As the girls talked, the guys enjoyed their own conversations. It was nice being out with everyone and seeing her brothers get along so well with Gavin. His hand rested on her leg, and every few minutes he'd squeeze her thigh or slip his fingers into the slit on the side of her maxi dress, brushing his fingers over her skin, like he needed that extra little connection.

Gavin leaned closer and whispered, "I love you. Are you having a good time?"

He'd said those three little words dozens of times and they still sent her heart into a frenzy every time he said them. Now it was made even more special by the silent look of approval in Brock's eyes. She didn't need his, or anyone else's, approval, but it was nice to have it. She couldn't imagine letting anything come between them, and it occurred to her that what she felt was probably similar to how Gavin had felt when he'd gone against his family's wishes.

Colton set down his beer and said, "Gavin, did Harper tell you about the time she was sleepwalking and Jana found her standing over her bed talking about the squirrels stealing her lollipops?"

"No!" Harper said. "I can't believe you'd bring that up. I was *eight*."

"How about the time she and Jana decided to be hula dancers in the middle of one of our parents' dinner parties?" Brock asked. "They came downstairs wearing skirts and paper cups they'd rigged up like bras."

Everyone laughed, and Brock started to tell the story.

Harper pointed at him and said, "If you don't stop, I'll tell Cree about the time you came downstairs during Mom and Dad's Christmas party wearing nothing but your boxing gloves."

"I was five!" Brock said.

"I want to hear the story," Cree pleaded.

Embarrassment avoided, Harper told the story about Brock, and when she was done, Colton began telling the sleepwalking story.

Harper tossed her napkin at him and said, "I take back

everything I said about missing you when I was in LA."

Colton blew her a kiss.

Gavin pulled her closer and said, "I don't know about sleepwalking, but you sure are cute when you snore."

"You too?" She swatted his arm. "Is *nothing* sacred?"

Gavin lowered his voice and said, "I didn't tell them about you falling out of the boat."

"Oh, I *have* to hear this one," Jana pleaded.

Gavin arched a brow, and Harper waved her hand, giving him the floor. As he told the story, laugher erupted, and Harper was right there with them, remembering how funny it was, and the magnificent kiss that had followed. That story parlayed into another, spurring more laughter and leading to stories about others at the table. Brock told a story about Colton getting caught in a compromising position when he told their parents he and a buddy were *studying*. Harper doubled over in hysterics as Brock embellished, making it sound far worse, and funnier, than it had been.

With Gavin by her side, Tegan wiping happy tears from her eyes, and Jock's hearty laughter ringing out, Harper realized just how right Harvey had been about love, laughter, and friendship being universal languages with the power to heal.

GAVIN AND HARPER spent the rest of the day knocking around Provincetown, getting to know Jock and Tegan better, and hanging with Harper's family. It was fun to see Harper in the roles of older and younger sister. After witnessing all the hugs, inside jokes, and sibling banter, Gavin couldn't even imagine how she'd lasted for almost a year living thousands of miles away from her family. He'd known she was stronger than she'd thought, and this afternoon had confirmed it.

Now it was six o'clock. Colton had met up with his buddies two hours earlier, Tegan and Jock were long gone, and they'd just said goodbye to the rest of her family, who were joining their friends from Seaside to watch the fireworks. Gavin and Harper grabbed their backpack from the car, in which they'd packed bathing suits, Harper's sweater, and Gavin's sweatshirt. With the pack over his shoulder, Gavin clung tightly to Harper's hand as they ran down the Provincetown Pier to meet their friends at Ethan's yacht.

"How will we know his boat?" Harper ran with one hand pressed against her chest, holding the plunging neckline of her royal-blue-and-white striped spaghetti strap dress in place so her boobs didn't pop out. The skirt was slit on both sides from thigh to ankle and whipped around her legs with every step. She looked scorching hot.

"It's a *yacht*," he reminded her. "It should be easy to spot."

"You know Ethan, right?"

"Yeah. He's older than me, but you know, small town and all that. He's a good guy."

"I know. I've met him," she said, pointing to the sleek yacht at the end of the pier. "That has to be it." She slowed to a walk, trying to catch her breath.

"You okay?" He pulled her closer. "Maybe you should start jogging with me."

"I think I'll stick with yoga, which, by the way, I need to get back into now that my life is more settled." Her lips curved up and she said, "Besides, I'm going to gain ten pounds if I keep baking cookies for you."

Gavin and Harper had called his family after he'd learned

about their furtive introduction. They got along so well, his mother and Nana had kept in touch with Harper, and they were continually sending her recipes.

"Then yoga it is," he teased as they came to the yacht. He smacked her ass and said, "But if you're worried, ten pounds heavier won't change a thing."

"Harper! Gavin!" Serena waved from the deck and ran down the ramp to greet them in her bikini top and shorts. "I'm so glad you made it!" She hugged Harper and looped her arms into theirs as they walked up the ramp and boarded the yacht. "The guys are inside, and the girls are catching the last of the sun on the upper deck."

"This yacht is *insane*," Harper said. "Ethan is so laid-back. I never pictured him as a yacht guy."

"You mean he doesn't act like a billionaire?" Gavin said as they followed Serena toward the front of the yacht. "That's true, but when we were growing up, he was the guy everyone thought would make it big. He knew about everything. It didn't matter if it was sports, money, or politics."

Desiree and Emery were lying on lounge chairs in their bathing suits and sunglasses. Drinks with tiny umbrellas sat on the tables beside them.

Desiree got up as they approached, looking cute in a yellow one-piece bathing suit. "Hi, you guys."

"You're here!" Emery jumped to her feet in her green bikini and slipped her feet into flip-flops. "Did you bring bathing suits?"

"Sure did." Gavin set his backpack on the deck.

"Good. Let's get you guys drinks." Emery ushered them to the wet bar and said, "What'll it be?"

"I'll have whatever you guys are having," Harper said.

"Gavin?" Emery asked.

"A beer is cool, thanks."

Ethan came around the side of the deck, followed by Drake, Dean, and an athletic-looking brown-haired guy Gavin didn't recognize.

"*Oh my God,*" Harper said, panic-stricken and low, under her breath. She buried her face in Gavin's shirt. "That's the guy! What's *he* doing here?"

"Ethan?" Gavin asked.

"No!" She moved behind him as the girls gathered around.

"What's wrong?" Serena asked.

"That guy!" Harper whispered harshly. "He's the one I yelled at on the plane. Why is he here?"

"Trey?" Serena, Emery, and Desiree all said at once.

"Shh!" Harper said. She looked like she was going to be sick. Gavin reached for her, but she stepped back, as if she wished she could disappear.

"Ethan's new business partner?" Emery asked. "Trey?"

"That's me," the other guy said, raising both hands with a friendly grin.

Trey's gaze landed on Harper at the same moment Ethan pulled Gavin into a manly embrace and said, "Gavin! My man!"

Harper peered out from within the circle of her friends, her face sheet white. Trey stopped cold, staring at Harper, and she shrank further behind the girls.

Trey squinted, and then his eyes widened. "Holy shit!" he exclaimed with a hearty laugh. "*Heartbreak?* Is that you?"

Heartbreak? What the hell is that all about?

"Good to see you, man," Gavin said to Ethan and quickly went to Harper's side. He wanted to rescue her, to say something so she didn't have to, but he knew she needed to see she could handle *anything*, so he put his hand on her lower back, offering her his steady, silent, support.

"Plane girl." Trey shook his head. "Man, oh man. I never thought I'd see you again."

Harper swallowed hard, forcing a strained smile that made Gavin's heart hurt.

"Hi." She stood up a little straighter, looking Trey in the eyes as she said, "It's *Harper*, actually, and I'm sorry for yelling at you on the plane."

Her resilience overtook her urge to hide, and Gavin couldn't have been prouder.

"You're not the first to do that," Trey said. He glanced at Gavin, and then his amused eyes found Harper again. "Looks like you're off your man hiatus. Does that mean you're writing again, too?"

"Yes," she said more confidently. "This is my boyfriend, Gavin Wheeler. Gavin, this is the guy I chewed out on the plane."

"Trey Ryder." He extended his hand, and Gavin shook it. "You have quite a girlfriend."

"Yes, I do," he said proudly. "I hear she gave you an earful."

Trey cocked a grin. "You could say that. I figure any woman who could shut me down that fast has a lot to say."

"I can't believe you chewed out Ethan's partner," Emery exclaimed.

"Know what's funny? Trey is Drew Ryder's brother," Serena said. "Drew's an architect. Gavin and I worked with him in Boston, and their sister is Isabel—Izzy—from the book club."

Harper made a frustrated sound. "Great, I've embarrassed myself with six degrees of separation? How was I supposed to know who he was? He never said he was with Ethan's company.

He was just a guy who was unlucky enough to sit next to *me* on a really bad day."

"Harper," Ethan said with a kind tone, "the streaming arm of the company, which Trey runs, is a new endeavor. Even if he'd said he heads up Reelflix, you probably wouldn't have put it together with my Movietime channel. For what it's worth, Trey said nice things about the *feisty girl on the plane* who was *probably a damn good writer, but if writing doesn't work out, should go into acting.*"

"*God...*" Harper sighed. "I'm sorry. I'm really not a jerk in my everyday life."

Trey waved his hand like it was no big deal. "Save the apologies and tell me about what you're writing."

"She's got an amazing script, a romantic comedy," Gavin raved. "It's *golden.*"

"*Gavin,*" Harper complained, blushing again.

He hugged her against his side, turning away from the others as he said, "This is an opportunity you deserve. Own it, babe. Turn me on with your confidence."

She blinked up at him with trepidation in her eyes, and in the space of a few heart-pounding seconds, her shoulders squared, her chin lifted, and her eyes narrowed in determination. She turned toward Trey and said, "Let's sit down, and I'll tell you about the chaotic and hilarious life of my heroine."

As they walked away from the group, the girls scurried over to Gavin, whispering and giggling about Harper going off on Trey and how they hoped something good would come of it. Was Gavin the only one who realized something already had? The Harper he'd met in Romance was back in full force, and she was *magnificent.*

Chapter Nineteen

HARPER FELT SICK again, and not because Ethan's yacht was cruising out to sea. She'd given Trey her best pitch, which she'd been mulling over for the past couple of weeks. She could hardly believe that a little more than a month ago she'd sat beside this man so disappointed in herself she'd hated the world, and she'd spewed that hate like vomit in his direction. She had no idea why he hadn't told her to bug off then, or why he'd bothered listening to her pitch now. Although he hadn't cracked a smile the whole time she'd been talking. He was probably trying to figure out how to turn her down without making the crazy lady flip out.

He pulled a pair of dark sunglasses from the pocket of his expensive-looking short-sleeve navy shirt and put them on as he leaned back on the luxurious sofa and casually stretched one arm across the back of the cushion. With his brown hair blowing in the wind, he looked like he *belonged* on a yacht. She refused to let him incite doubt that would drag her down. She believed in her work, and even if he hated it, she still thought it was good.

"I'd like to read the first few pages," he said evenly.

Hope swelled inside her, even though she was pretty sure he

was still just being kind so as not to make waves and ruin everyone's evening. "Okay. I'll email them to you tomorrow."

"Why wait? I'm sure you have your work on the cloud or Dropbox. Pull it up on your phone. Let me take a read."

"Now?" She wasn't sure she wanted to be turned down *now*. It was a gorgeous evening, and she was with Gavin and all her friends. This was supposed to be a joyous occasion, not a judging game.

"Once I get back to my office I'll be bogged down trying to catch up. Go on, pull it up on your phone."

"I, um…"

He crossed his arms, his lips curving into a challenge. "Did I misread your confidence as potential? Did those experiences in LA you told me about ruin you? Because if you don't believe in your work, no one else in the industry will either."

No shit, Sherlock. Anger simmered inside her. "I *believe* in my work."

He held her gaze from behind those dark sunglasses, his expression as serious as if he were negotiating world peace, and said, "Prove it."

"I *will*. Excuse me while I get my phone." She stalked across the deck to Gavin, anger and nervousness whipping through her like a hurricane. *Be the wind, not the water. Be calm. I've got this.*

Gavin was talking to Drake, and he reached for her as she approached. "Hey, babe. How'd it go?"

"I don't know," she said sharply. "May I please have my phone? He wants to read my work *now*. I'm wondering if this is some kind of payback for how I treated him on the plane. I can't tell if he's a nice guy or a vindictive jerk."

"Oh *man*." Drake shook his head.

"Ethan wouldn't partner with an asshole." Gavin withdrew

her phone from his pocket and placed it in her hand. He curled his fingers around hers, holding her gaze with the steady support he'd given her since they first met. "Your writing is good, Harper. Don't let him make you doubt that."

She glanced at Trey, looking out at the water. Or at least he seemed to be focused on the water. She'd never know if he was laughing at her from behind those dark sunglasses. Knowing one person's opinion could stop her chances in its tracks with that company was making her sick. Putting her happiness in the hands of others *sucked*, but writing was as much a part of her as the air she breathed, and no part of her wanted to change careers. She pulled up her big-girl panties and put on her bravest face and said, "That's like saying don't be cold when I'm standing in the snow naked, but I'm trying my best not to give him that power."

"Atta girl." Gavin pulled her in for a kiss, his eyes brimming with love. "I believe in you, babe. Go get 'em."

She inhaled a shaky breath and headed back toward Trey. *It doesn't matter if he likes it or not. It's good. I'm a good writer. My work has been sold before and it will be again.*

As she closed the distance between them, anger burned through her doubt. Anger at *herself* for once again putting herself in a situation where someone else had the power to pull the rug out from under her. She wasn't about to stop doing what she loved most. She realized she was looking through clouds again, and then another realization set in. To be in control of her happiness, she had to be in complete control of her career.

She sat beside Trey, navigating to the document on her phone, and an idea began to form. The heck with the clouds. She wanted to be the sun *and* the wind. She couldn't change the industry or the structure and politics of how shows were chosen or funded, but maybe she didn't have to.

"Here you are." She handed Trey her phone, crossed her arms and legs, and sat back feeling more in control than she ever had.

"Thank you."

She watched Trey's face morphing from serious to amused to serious again, and she thought of all the things Harvey had said. What was she doing? Trying to make her mark? Was that so bad? The burning in her stomach told her it might be, but her ambition told her otherwise. But what if he *was* just being nice, as she'd assumed earlier? If that was the case, then his scrutiny was kind of demeaning. Even though she knew this was how things worked and she should be thankful to have this time with such a powerful man, it definitely *wasn't* making her happy. She was on that damn roller coaster again, and Lord help her, she was ready to jump off.

She got up and went to the railing to try to clear her head. The cold, salty air stung her face. Her hair whipped in the wind like a wild torrent. As the sun dipped from the sky, she reminded herself she shouldn't feel like her entire career was on the line based on one man's opinion. But she did care. Wouldn't anyone? The longer the battle waged on in her mind, the more determined she became to start living life on her own terms and stop putting herself in a position to have her career halted by any *one* person.

By the time Trey finished reading and joined her by the railing, she'd let go of the last shred of hope that he'd like her work and had begun clinging to the idea of a different future. A brighter future where *she* held the strings, where she didn't just write, but she brought her series to life on a stage for the community she loved. Maybe Gavin was wrong and her work *wasn't* too big for local theater. Maybe it would be the *biggest* thing to hit local theater.

Nobody performed live episodic entertainment on the Cape. It was a grand idea, but she needed help—and she knew just the person to call.

Jana.

"Thank you for letting me read your work." Trey handed her the phone and leaned his hip against the railing. He took off his sunglasses and crossed his arms, openly studying her. "Can I be blatantly honest with you?"

"Of course," she said as confidently as she could, though her insides were twisting into knots. And she hated that with a passion.

"I don't think this is series material."

Her stomach sank like lead, and just as quickly, anger trampled on the disappointment, smashing it to pieces. "Thank you for your opinion," she said as calmly as she could, while thinking about her plans. *Yes,* it would be treacherously hard. *Yes,* it had taken years before she was hired to do anything other than writing articles and short stories. But a few years ago she *had* sold a pilot, and she had continued on to be part of the team that wrote a successful cable show for two seasons, and that was something. *That was my start, and this will not be my end.*

"It's good," Trey said. "It's funny, topical, and touches on all the troubles of dating in the Internet age. But no matter how you cut it, you can only drag on that lifestyle in a series for so long before it gets old. I don't think it's a strong enough hook to carry forward more than a season or two."

"That's fair." She had to agree. She'd been asking herself

how she could take the third season in a new, exciting direction without losing the flavor that she hoped would resonate enough to hold viewers' interests through the first two seasons.

He leaned his forearms over the railing and said, "This is a tough industry, Harper, but there *is* an audience for your work."

"Thank you. I know there is." She didn't need a patronizing lecture to let her down easy, citing all the reasons she should continue writing and try again when she had something stronger.

"Have you thought about pitching it as a movie?" he asked.

Surprise gripped her, and hope fluttered in her chest, shoving her right onto the emotional roller-coaster ride she'd just convinced herself she didn't need or want. A movie would be *huge*, but she didn't write movies. She wrote pilots with hopes of writing series.

"No, I hadn't considered that."

"You should." He looked up at her with a smile so genuine, it eased her anxiety. "Romcoms are hot, and I think your work has promise."

"I don't know. Reworking it into a movie is no small task." *And it all might be for naught.*

He rose to his full height again and said, "Afraid of the challenge, Heartbreak?"

"No," she said emphatically. She had other ideas that deserved consideration. But those ideas would take capital, and having a movie under her belt would not only be an amazing achievement, but it would give her credibility and capital.

Damn this roller coaster.

"Are you submitting this elsewhere?" he asked.

"I was going to," she admitted. "But I'm tossing around an idea that would put a different spin on the presentation of the series."

He arched a brow. "Oh yeah? What's that?"

She glanced at Gavin, catching him watching them. Her heart skipped. Even from across the ship she could feel his unwavering support. She'd hoped to tell him about her idea before she told anyone else, but she had the undivided attention of one of the most powerful men in media, and she'd be a fool to pass that up. "I'm thinking about working with performers to make live episodic productions."

"Interesting. I haven't seen that done."

"Don't get any ideas about stealing my brainchild," she said, only half teasing.

He scoffed. "I have enough on my plate. Not to mention I'm not an asshole. I'm not sure this will translate well into a Broadway production. Tell me what you're thinking."

"I'm not sure of specifics yet, but I'm not thinking of Broadway. I'm thinking about doing it here. My friend just inherited an amphitheater, and there are performing arts companies all over the Cape. Tourists come by the thousands over the summers, and the local arts do very well. I'm thinking about maybe a three-episode series that's produced weekly and runs all summer. If someone is here for a week, they can watch all three episodes. Say, Monday, Wednesday, and Friday. If they're here for longer, they can watch one a week, or whenever they can fit it in. It would keep viewers coming back, and if it's well written and appeals to locals, then perhaps I could even expand it to an indoor production over the winter to keep their attention. There's never enough going on in the winter here. The audience would be smaller, so maybe the productions are limited to one week during the month. I've only just thought of the idea, so I don't have it fleshed out yet."

"That could be just north of genius." His lips quirked up. "Or it could tank."

"That's helpful," she said sarcastically.

"You didn't ask for my advice, but I like the idea. It's fresh and new, innovative. But I strongly suggest doing market research to see if it holds water."

She tried to quell the urge to do a happy dance and said, "Market research. Of course." She had no idea what kind of market research he meant, but Jana might.

"You'll need capital to pull off something like that. You should consider rewriting the script as a movie and using that money to fund your theater projects. I can't make any promises, but I'd be happy to read it when you're done."

"Thank you. I appreciate that."

"Now, what do you say we rejoin the others before your boyfriend comes to rescue you from the asshole industry rep?"

Her head was spinning, but when Gavin's eyes locked on hers, one thing became crystal clear, and she said, "Gavin isn't a rescuer. He's more of a *director*."

"Why is that?"

"He doesn't fix. He has great vision, and he doesn't take over or *fix* people's problems. He's like the wind. He nudges and guides, clearing the clouds so others don't get off track on their path to fulfillment."

LATER THAT EVENING, as Gavin grabbed Harper's sweater from the backpack, he thought about the idea she'd shared with everyone over dinner. It sounded like a huge undertaking and a great new direction. He was glad their friends had chimed in, offering to help Harper succeed. He wondered how the woman who had looked like she was going to be sick at the sight of the man she'd chewed out on the plane had found the inspiration, and confidence, to take control of her career in the way she'd described. He'd offered to ask Beckett if he'd consider investing in the idea once she figured out exactly what she was doing, but she'd turned him down. She didn't want to use familial connections if she could help it.

Once upon a time, Gavin had believed women would always disappoint him. But Harper never failed to surprise him.

Harper stood at the railing with the others as the fireworks began, her dress drifting around her legs, her hair lifting with the bay breeze. Vibrant starbursts exploded in the midnight-blue sky, raining down over the inky water. Gavin helped her put on her sweater and wrapped his arms around her from behind. She leaned back against his chest, covering his hands with hers as they watched the fireworks. She was so relaxed, so in the moment, and he was so into *her*, he wanted to stay right there forever, in a state of bliss, with their best friends, and world, celebrating around them.

"Isn't this beautiful?" she said. "It's been a great day."

He kissed her cheek. "The day's not over yet. I've been thinking about your idea. It's going to take a lot of planning, and you'll need space to do that."

"I'll figure it out. I want to talk to Jana to see if she thinks the concept will work, and to Tegan, because I think it would be fun to put shows on at her place, but they're adult shows, so I'm not sure she will be interested."

"It's a brilliant idea." He turned her in his arms and kissed her softly. She smelled like happiness and tasted like love. An enticing combination he knew he'd never get enough of. "You need an office, I need an office, and my sunroom needs some attention." He kissed her again and said, "You can't keep spreading all your papers out on the furniture and floor."

Her brow wrinkled. "You don't like my organization methods."

He kissed her again as fireworks *boomed* overhead. "I love *all* your methods." He kissed her neck. "And later, I plan on showing you just how much."

She wound her arms around his neck, furtively glancing at the others, who were entranced by the lights in the sky. "Why wait?" she said seductively, her eyes dark and alluring. "Everyone's watching the fireworks, and you always say I light you up..."

"Are you propositioning me?"

"Yes, Mr. Wheeler, I am. What are you going to do about it?" She arched her sexy brow.

Oh, he'd show her *exactly* what he was going to do about it.

He took her hand, hauling her into the cabin. He crushed her to him, kissing and groping as they stumbled down the stairs. They came to a lounge area, but Gavin wasn't taking any chances of someone walking in on them. He threw open one door after another until he found a bedroom. He backed her up against the door, fumbling with the lock as they kissed. She arched into him, and he reached into the slits of her dress, grabbed hold of her panties, and tore them down. She kicked them off, and he dropped to his knees, spreading her legs so he could feast on her.

He lifted one of her long legs over his shoulder, ravenously devouring her. She clawed at his flesh, a string of pleas flying from her lungs. "*Yes! Harder. Yourteethyourteethyourteeth!*" Her greediness sent adrenaline pounding through his veins. He grazed his teeth over her most sensitive nerves, fucked her with his tongue, fast and hard. She rose onto her toes, gasping one sharp inhalation after another. "*Yes! Don't stop!*" Her fingernails dug into his skin, and her head fell back as she cried out his name—"*Gavin!*"—and surrendered to the fierceness of her climax.

"*You*," she pleaded, pulling him up by fistfuls of his hair. "I need *you*."

He fished a condom from his wallet, stripped down his shorts, and sheathed his length. He crashed his mouth over hers as he lifted her into his arms and entered her in one hard thrust, and they both cried out. He pounded into her, and suddenly she stilled, her eyes wide.

"Listen," she said frantically. They listened to the silence. "The fireworks are over? They'll notice we're missing. Wait, they haven't done the grand finale."

"Neither have we."

He crushed his mouth to hers as the explosive sounds of fireworks rang out, giving her a finale she'd never forget.

Chapter Twenty

HARPER AND SERENA climbed onto stepstools, holding opposite ends of a shelf they were hanging above the windows in Gavin's sunroom, which they were turning into an office. It had been a week and a half since their yachting adventure, and in the days since, Harper had been feverishly revising her script to turn it into a movie, discussing her ideas for live episodic theater with Jana and Tegan, and falling deeper in love with Gavin. Gavin had been equally busy putting the final touches on the boutique at Ocean Edge, working on the Wharf restaurant redesigns with Serena, and romancing Harper every chance he got. His thoughtfulness knew no bounds. Last weekend he'd set up a rolling typing stand and chair with an attached umbrella on the dock for her to write more comfortably by the water.

"Does this look straight?" Serena asked as Drake and Gavin came into the sunroom carrying the two sawhorses Gavin and Harper had painted white last weekend. They were going to be used as the base of a large worktable.

"If by straight you mean a straight angle, then yes." Gavin set down the sawhorse, looking strikingly handsome in running shorts and a dark tank top. He and Drake had gone running with the guys before meeting Harper and Serena at the inn for breakfast with their friends.

Drake grabbed the level and set it on the shelf. "When in doubt, use the tools."

"We want the room to look shabby chic." Harper motioned with her chin toward the distressed wooden desk by the back windows. "It doesn't have to be perfect."

Gavin chuckled as he and Drake hoisted the wooden tabletop and set it on the sawhorses. "I always use a level, babe. Lift the left side of the shelf a little."

Serena lifted her side of the shelf, and after a few adjustments the shelf was up, and they climbed down from their stools. Harper admired the tables the guys were setting up along the walls, which would be perfect for her to spread out her papers when she was editing. They'd also bought a seafoam-green sofa, an ottoman, and two desks. Gavin had the best vision. With the sunlight streaming through the windows, the room was warm, inviting, and inspiring.

Gavin smacked her butt as he headed for the door and said, "Be right back, beautiful. Let's go, Drake."

She watched him leave the room. He glanced over his shoulder as if he could feel her eyes on him, then winked.

"Stop ogling your man," Serena teased.

"If you insist."

"I insist. I want to get this done so we have time to go to Common Grounds for dinner. Drake's going to play his guitar for me at the open mic. I can't wait to go all fangirl on him."

Harper laughed. "You're so cute."

"Just wicked in love with my man. But you know the feeling. I see the way you get all dreamy-eyed over Gavin."

Serena picked up the picture of the dock at sunset that Harper had taken. The rowboat was tied to the end of the dock, and the rolling typing stand sat a few feet away. In the distance, the sun cast golden rays across the treetops, spreading ribbons of oranges and yellows across the blue-gray evening sky.

"This is the perfect representation of you and Gavin," Serena said. "Where do you want to hang it?"

She couldn't agree more. It gave a sense of privacy, and it reminded Harper of their first date and made her think of how far they'd come. "I was thinking about the wall by the door." She grabbed the hardware and a hammer.

As Harper hammered in the picture hanger, Serena said, "When you first met Gavin, did you ever think you'd be practically living with him a year later?"

"No, but you know I hoped I'd see him again. I told you about the whole number-in-the-zipper-pocket debacle."

She hung the picture, and they both stepped back to look at it.

"Gavin told me about the LA offer falling through. Are you okay?"

She'd gotten the call two days ago. It had been a blow to her ego, but she knew she'd made the right decision. "Yes, I'm fine. They want the person who does the rewrites to be on set during production, and that's the last place I want to be. My career aspirations have changed so much, it would have hindered moving forward in a new direction. I need all the time I can get to rework my script for Trey. Plus, I need to write something new for the theater. I know it's a long shot, but if he options the script, I can't use it for the theater. And I really need him to option it so I can use that capital to fund my new endeavor."

"If anyone can do it, you can. You've always been driven, and you've got me and the girls to help with romantic comedy ideas. I'm so excited about what you're doing. I think live episodes will be fun to watch. You said Tegan is all for it, right? Oh, by the way, the article you wrote about her uncle made me cry. It was really good, Harper."

"Thank you. I was happy with it, and so were Tegan and Jock. As far as my new project goes, Tegan thinks she's interested. But she's only here through August, and then she's going home until the spring. I think she's a little overwhelmed at the moment and needs to process everything that has landed in her lap. She's still grieving, too. We'll see how it all shakes out. I hope it works, but if she decides not to host the shows at her amphitheater, there are other places I can do it. Jana's talking with her contacts to see what types of research they have, if any. But to be honest, I feel like this is one of those know-it-in-my-gut projects that needs to happen."

"Like mine and Gavin's partnership," Serena said as the guys carried in a desk.

"What about our partnership?" Gavin asked as he and Drake set the desk beside the other one, facing the back windows.

"We knew it was right, so we did it," Serena answered.

Drake set down his end of the desk and said, "Like our marriage."

"Exactly." Serena put her arms around him and kissed him.

Gavin pulled Harper into his arms and said, "How's this, babe?"

"I love it, almost as much as I love you."

"I think my cheesy lines wore off on you." He kissed her and said, "And I love that, almost as much as I love you."

He and Drake chuckled as they left the room to get the sofa.

"With so many projects on your plate, I can't believe you

found time to shop with Gavin." Serena waved to the furniture. "Can I just say, *wow*? I'm a little jealous of this space. I might just have to come here to work sometimes."

"That sounds good to me," Harper said. "There's definitely enough space for *two* incredible designers. Oh, speaking of designing, I got approval to do an article about the grand opening of the boutique at Ocean Edge. Gavin said Mia was pleased with how it turned out." The grand opening was next weekend, and they were attending it together.

"That's an understatement. She's *thrilled*," Serena said as the guys carried in the sofa. "You should be proud of Gavin."

"I'm always proud of Gavin," Harper said honestly, earning a sexy smile as he and Drake set the sofa down. "He cares about everyone—his clients, his friends, his family." She thought about how she was getting to know his family. Gavin's mother had called Harper to see if she had any ideas about what Gavin might want for his birthday, and they'd had a nice chat. And last week when Beckett called, Gavin put him on speakerphone and they'd all joked around.

She reached for Gavin's hand and said, "And look what he's done for me. I don't even live here, and he's created this beautiful space for me to share with him."

He gathered her in his arms with a coy expression and said, "About that little technicality. Isn't it time we make it official? We've been making this house into a home for weeks. Move in with me for *real*, Harper. We can rent out your cottage, or sell it if you want. I don't want to *play* house anymore, Harp. I want this house to be *our* home."

Excitement bubbled up inside Harper, and her heart lodged in her throat.

Before she could find her voice, Serena squealed. "*Ohmygo-*

dohmygodohmygod! I knew it!" She hugged Harper, making everyone laugh.

"You didn't give me time to accept!" Harper pried herself from Serena, and Gavin hauled her into his arms. Her heart was beating so fast, she could barely breathe.

"What do you say, sweetheart?"

"Yes, of course! I say *yes!*"

Gavin lifted her off her feet as he kissed her, his smile pressing against her lips.

When he set her toes on the floor, she said, "We can rent out my cottage, but are you sure? This is a huge step."

"Oh my gosh, shut up and kiss him again!" Serena urged.

Harper did just that, and then she gazed up at him and said, "We're really doing this?"

"We're really doing this." He pressed his lips to hers again.

"Congratulations!" Drake clapped Gavin on the back. "Now we have three things to celebrate. Your new living arrangements, which I think means I'll be doing more heavy lifting soon, Harper's new ventures, and Gavin's birthday. This calls for a night at Undercover."

"Yes!" Serena agreed. "That gives me two weeks to get the word out. Harper, maybe you can get Colton to have an open-mic night. I'm dying to hear Cree and Brock sing again."

Harper and Gavin were still gazing into each other's eyes. She never wanted to forget this moment, the look in his eyes, and the excitement sparking around them.

"*Haaarper.*" Serena nudged her.

"Yes," Harper finally said. "Great idea. Would you guys mind if I invited Tegan and Jock? Tegan's coming to our July book club meeting. It would be a great way for the girls to meet her, and Jock is so nice. He really enjoyed meeting everyone on the Fourth." She looked at Gavin and said, "I'd love to include them, unless you'd rather we didn't?"

Gavin laced his fingers with hers and said, "Actually, I think it's a great idea, but I was thinking we'd invite our friends here for my birthday, grill some food, have a few beers. Nothing big."

"Here?" Harper asked, knowing how much Gavin cherished his privacy.

"Yes, *here*." Gavin's brows knitted. "Unless you'd rather not?"

"No, I'd rather. *Definitely*. I love the idea of having people over to your house."

"*Our* house," he reminded her.

"Sorry, my head is still in the clouds. *Our* house."

"I need to sit down." Serena sat on the sofa. "I can't believe my ears. Gavin Wheeler wants to host a get-together."

"I think this qualifies as a current event," Drake said as he sat down beside Serena and pulled her closer. "Harper should write an article about it since it might be a once-in-a-lifetime event."

"Gavin, are you sure?" Harper asked.

"Sweetheart, I've been certain of only a few things in my life. Telling you I love you and asking you to move in are at the top of the list. My house never felt like a home until you came into it, and a *home* is even better with friends in it."

Chapter Twenty-One

THE TWO WEEKS before Gavin's birthday passed in a blur. With the help of their friends, they'd moved Harper out of her cottage, and next week they were listing it for rent with an agent. They'd had to buy more bookshelves, but Harper's bedroom furniture was perfect in their second guest room, making their home even more complete. Gavin had picked up a new client, and Harper continued to work like a fiend. In addition to her own projects, she'd managed to write three articles. She'd covered the grand opening of the boutique, which had gone spectacularly well, and a gallery opening, which Gavin had attended with her. They'd also gone to a comedy show in Provincetown with their friends, after which Harper interviewed the comedians. It was a blast.

Gavin grabbed his motorcycle helmet and headed for the sunroom, where Harper was working on revisions. "Hey, babe."

She glanced over her shoulder. Her hair was piled on top of her head in a messy bun. "Hi. Are you leaving?"

She rose to her feet, and her long salmon halter dress tumbled to the tops of her feet. Her pretty red toenails peeked out from beneath the hem. She and the girls had gotten together last night for their book club meeting. She'd come home with painted nails, ready to rip his clothes off. Apparently book club meetings weren't all about books, and they were also quite arousing.

He really liked book club nights.

He pulled her close and kissed her. "Yeah, the guys are waiting. Are you sure you don't want to take a break and ride with us?"

"I wish I could. I want to get some editing done before everyone gets here." They'd invited all their friends for a *celebration of their lives* rather than a birthday party. "I'll come with you next weekend. I promise."

"Good. I'll miss you." He kissed her tenderly, but as usual, they quickly caught fire. When Harper pushed her hands up his neck and into his hair, holding tight, heat seared beneath his skin. "*God*, babe," he said between kisses. "I hate leaving you."

She pushed away, grinning like she'd meant to get him hard as stone. "Now you'll think of me while you're gone."

"I always think of you." He hauled her in for another kiss. "Nobody's coming until six tonight, right?"

"Mm-hm," she said, kissing along his jaw.

"Good. I'll be home around three." He grabbed her ass and said, "That gives me plenty of time to tie you up and have my way with you."

Her eyes darkened as she rubbed against him like a cat in heat. "I'll be waiting."

"Riding with a hard-on. This should be interesting." He kissed her again and headed for the door. "Love you. Good luck on your revisions."

He paused on the front porch, admiring the gardens. They'd gotten into a water fight with the hose the other night and ended up rolling around in the front yard covered in mud.

Harper had breathed new life into him, filling gaps he hadn't realized existed. His phone vibrated, and he read Justin's text. *Hurry your ass up.*

He shoved his phone into his pocket and headed over to Justin's.

Justin, Dwayne, and Zander, one of Justin's younger brothers and also a Dark Knight, were waiting out front when he arrived. Dwayne looked up from his phone briefly as Gavin cut the engine and climbed off his bike. Then he went back to whatever he was looking at on his phone.

"Hard time cutting that ball and chain?" Zander flashed an arrogant smile and raked a hand through his thick brown hair. "I've got metal cutters to set you free."

"The only shackles in my house are the ones we're both into, asshole." Gavin chuckled and shook his hand. "Good to see you, man. We're having a get-together tonight. You should swing by and meet Harper." He'd invited Dwayne and Justin the other night, when he and Harper had seen them at Common Grounds.

"Thanks, man," Zander said. "Justin said your old lady's pretty sweet, but that comment just kicked her up to the *fucking hot* category."

"That she is." Gavin glanced at Justin, who shrugged. He knew Zander was just talking shit, but his protective urges surged and he said, "Keep yourself in check around her, because if you step out of line, I will fuck you up."

"*Shit,*" Zander said sarcastically.

"Watch yourself, Zan," Justin said. "Gavin may look like a gentleman, but he's an animal." He bumped fists with Gavin and said, "Harper didn't want to ride today?"

Harper had gone riding with them twice, and she'd loved it.

"She's still hammering out those movie revisions. She'll come next weekend."

"Cool."

Dwayne shoved his phone in his pocket and said, "You ladies want to do your hair next, or can we take this party on the road?"

"Chill, dude." Zander grabbed his helmet and glanced at Gavin. "Are there going to be any single chicks at your place tonight?"

"Sure, Chloe, Steph, Daphne, and Harper's friend Tegan."

Dwayne looked over and said, "Go near Steph and I'll break your fingers, Z-man."

Zander scoffed.

"Same goes for Chloe," Justin said with a menacing stare. "She's a lady. She doesn't need you sniffing around."

Zander straddled his bike and said, "I know what the ladies like." He made an obscene gesture with his tongue.

Justin stepped forward and Gavin grabbed his arm, stopping him. "He's *trying* to piss you off. It's what brothers do, man. Ignore it or make her yours."

Justin wrenched his arm free, glowering at Zander as he said, "Don't be a dick, Zan. Chicks hate dicks."

"Then you're doing something wrong, because chicks love my dick." Zander put on his helmet, ending the conversation.

Gavin chuckled as they climbed on their bikes and started them up.

Justin rode by Zander, and Zander flicked him off.

All three of Justin's brothers were good guys, but they loved to give each other shit. Hell, didn't all brothers? Beckett had called Gavin at the ass-crack of dawn to wish him a happy birthday, like he did every year. He'd been out with their friends riding horses since four in the morning, and Gavin got to say hello to all of them. It was awesome. He was looking forward to introducing all of his friends to Harper over Thanksgiving, when they were heading to Oak Falls.

Justin sped down the driveway, and as Gavin fell into line between Zander and Dwayne, his thoughts returned to Harper, the way they always did. Some people had a happy place or the thing they did that brought them the most joy. He knew their long motorcycle rides filled both those spots for his buddies, but while Gavin loved his guy time, *Harper* had become his happiest place and his biggest thrill.

Three o'clock couldn't come soon enough.

AFTER HIS RIDE, Gavin blew through his front door feeling invigorated, his body still vibrating from the hours he'd spent straddling his bike. He put his helmet and keys on the table by the door, shrugged off his coat, and hollered in the direction of the sunroom as he headed for the bedroom, "Babe, I just need to shower off and then the birthday boy wants to *play*. Meet me in the bedroom." He tugged off his shirt, and as he threw open the bedroom door, he called over his shoulder, "Naked!"

"Surprise!"

"Holy fu—" His parents' smiling faces came into focus among a sea of helium balloons. Beckett stood a few feet away, doubled over in laughter. It took a minute for Gavin to make sense of seeing them there. "Mom? Dad?" He felt Harper's hand on his back and turned to meet her beautiful blushing face, and his heart filled to near bursting. "Baby, you did this?"

"We couldn't celebrate your birthday without your family,"

she said. "When Nana told me it was your birthday, I called your mom back and asked if they could manage a weekend trip."

"Aw, babe." He pulled her into his arms, pressing a kiss to her temple as he tried to reel in his emotions. "You've been planning it all this time?"

She nodded. "I picked them up at the Provincetown Airport two hours ago. I'm sorry my parents are out of town, but they promised to have dinner with us after they get back."

"I'd love that."

"Harper is a doll, Gavin," his mother said, smiling warmly at Harper. Her dirty-blond hair brushed her shoulders. It had grown longer since he'd last seen her. "She's been the perfect hostess. No wonder you've sounded like a different person this summer. Happy birthday, sweetheart."

His mother hugged him tight. She smelled familiar, eliciting all his best childhood memories, causing his chest to constrict. She lowered her voice and said, "And don't worry about the *naked* comment. We understand young love."

Christ. He looked over her shoulder at Beckett, who was smirking, and said, "You could have warned me, Beck. I talked to you at four thirty this morning."

"And ruin the surprise?" Beckett said. "I'd never disappoint Harper like that."

Smart-ass.

"We swore him to secrecy," his father said.

The sleeves of his father's light-blue button-down were rolled up to his forearms, revealing a scar he'd gotten when Gavin was seven. Memories of that fateful afternoon rolled in. They'd been fishing, and his father had given a fishing knife to Gavin to cut a line. Beckett had called Gavin's name, and Gavin had turned, accidentally slicing open his father's arm. Gavin would never forget the terrifying sight of blood gushing from his father's arm or how his father had calmly taken his sobbing son by the shoulders, seemingly oblivious to his own pain, and forced Gavin to look him in the eyes as he said, *I'm fine, buddy. This is nothing. Accidents happen, but this is why you need to always focus on what you're doing and not on the nonsense around you. Let me wrap my arm, and we'll try again.* As he'd tied his T-shirt around the wound, he'd lectured Gavin and Beckett about safety for what felt like the millionth—and the *first*—time. That time, Gavin had listened. Always the teacher, his father had patiently helped Gavin cut the line, and then he'd taken them home and had gone alone to the hospital, where he'd received seven stitches.

"How are you, son?" his father asked. His thick dark hair had flecks of gray around the temples. He embraced Gavin, holding him a beat longer than his mother had, and said, "I've missed you."

Damn, now he was choked up even more.

"I've missed you, too, Dad. How long can you stay?"

"Just for the weekend," his father said. "You'll be sick of us by the time we leave Sunday night."

"Hardly," Gavin said.

"Good to see your ugly mug." Beckett tugged him into a manly embrace. "I've got to say, I was pretty disappointed to find out the hot blonde messaging me on Instagram was your girlfriend."

Gavin scoffed. "I bet you were." He glanced at Harper, gathering balloons with his parents and taking them out of the bedroom. The brightness in his parents' eyes brought a rush of unpleasant memories of when they'd met Corinne. What a beautiful difference this was.

As he and Beckett grabbed handfuls of balloons and carried them into the living room, Gavin thought about last summer, when he'd reached out to his family to try to mend the distance that his brief, once-a-year visits had created. They had welcomed him with open arms, and they hadn't made him feel guilty or held it against him in any way.

He'd never make that mistake again.

He looked at Harper, helping his father hang a birthday banner over the fireplace, and he knew she'd never put him in a position where he felt like he had to.

Chapter Twenty-Two

OVER THE COURSE of the afternoon, with the help of his mother, Harper cooked all Gavin's favorite dishes and treats, while the guys pestered them for tastes—and Gavin stole kisses from his beautiful, thoughtful girlfriend. The friendship between his family and Harper was so real, he knew it was seeping into the very walls of their home. When Serena, Chloe, and Jana showed up, they helped Harper and his mother transform the inside of their home into a celebration of colors and lights, while Gavin, Beckett, and their father decorated the patio and the path to the dock. They hung paper lanterns from tree limbs, strung streamers with bright nylon tassels over the patio, lined the path to the dock with mason jars, and decorated the dock with strings of blue lights. They set up long tables for the food, and the girls decorated them with candles and flowers.

Hours later, their yard was bustling with the din of good friends and family. Gavin sipped his beer, chuckling to himself as Rick made silly faces at Hadley, trying to coax a smile from Daphne's little girl. Hadley's stoic expression remained firmly in place even as Andre and Drake dropped to their knees and joined the effort.

Hadley pushed to her feet in her pretty pink dress and toddled toward Jock, who was chatting with Tegan, Harper, and Jana. Hadley wrapped her little arms around Jock's leg, and his jaw went tight. He looked uncomfortably at Tegan, who reached for the little girl. But Hadley clung tighter to Jock's leg, her cheeks puffed out in anger as she leaned away from Tegan's touch. When Tegan stepped back, Hadley looked up at Jock, and a wide, toothy grin appeared on her sweet face.

There was a collective "Aww."

"I can't believe it," Daphne said, glancing shyly at Jock. "You must be a pretty special man to win my little girl over."

Jock glanced at Daphne and said, "Her radar's off."

"Come on, dude. What's your secret?" Rick asked. "We've been trying to get her to smile forever."

Jock shrugged, looking a little bewildered as the guys joked about Hadley being into the strong, silent type.

Harper must have noticed Jock's discomfort because she crouched beside Hadley. She'd changed into a sexy floral wraparound dress, tied at the waist. It was shorter in front than in the back, and in her crouched position, it showed off her thighs. She said something to Hadley and held her arms out. Hadley toddled into them, and Harper shifted her on her hip as she stood up. Gavin's heart did a double take, imagining Harper with *their* baby as she spoke to the little cherub-cheeked girl, earning the cutest smile of the night.

Gavin's father sidled up to him with Justin and Beckett and said, "That look on your face tells a story, son."

"Yeah? What story is that?"

His father slung an arm over his shoulder and said, "The one that ends in happily ever after and grandbabies for me and your mother."

"No pressure or anything," Beckett teased.

They both laughed.

"No pressure necessary," their father said. "Gavin will know when it's right. You have quite a tight-knit group of friends here, Gavin. It's nice to meet them and to know you've found your way back."

Gavin met his father's gaze, knowing exactly what he meant. Not back to these same friends, but back to being *Gavin Wheeler*, the man who not only let people into his life but into the very heart of who he was. It'd been a long time. "I'm sorry I ever let anyone or anything come between us. I got lost for a while, Dad, but I am back, and I'm here to stay."

"That's water under the bridge, son," his father said. "Don't give it another thought. We sure don't."

"Besides, we have more important things to worry about, like is Steph dating Dwayne, or is she fair game?" Beckett motioned toward Steph, who was talking with Violet, Dwayne, and Zander. Dwayne had one arm around Violet and the other around Steph. Zander's eyes were trained on Tegan.

"We're leaving tomorrow afternoon," their father reminded him. "Do you really want to start something you can't finish?"

A cocky grin slid across Beckett's face. "Oh, I'll finish, all right, Dad. Several times, in fact."

"That's my cue to go find your mother."

As their father walked away, Beckett said, "No wonder you haven't invited me out here to hang with you. You were afraid of the competition."

Gavin scoffed. "Hardly, bro. The only woman I've been interested in for the past year is the gorgeous blonde in that sexy dress over there."

"Good, then tell me about Steph. I love those streaks in her hair."

"Really? You're usually Mr. Conservative."

"Shows how well you really know me. I wear ties for a reason, dude, and it has nothing to do with appearances."

Then we have that in common.

"Steph and Dwayne grew up together—they're not a couple. But don't leave me with a mess—or a broken heart—to clean up."

"Shit, bro. When have I ever done that?" Beckett took a swig of his beer and headed in Steph's direction.

"And so it starts," Gavin said to Justin.

Justin didn't respond, and Gavin realized Justin was chewing on nails, glowering at Chloe and the tall, dark, and a little-too-nerdy date she'd brought with her. According to Serena, Chloe had met him on a dating site and this was their third date. He nudged Justin.

"Hm?"

"If you like her, you should ask her out before she finds someone worthwhile on Match or Tinder."

"She better not be on fucking Tinder." Justin shifted his eyes away from Chloe. "I just want to make sure she's safe."

"He looks harmless. He's dressed nice, clean-cut, seems attentive toward her."

"Don't let looks deceive you, man. Assholes come in all shapes and sizes. Some just clean up better than others."

"Then go talk to him and feel him out," he said, catching sight of Harper standing with his mother at the top of the path that led to the dock. Moonlight spilled over her bare shoulders as she hugged his mother. His mother walked away, and Harper gazed out at the water.

Justin didn't move.

"Excuse me, buddy. There's a gorgeous blonde in a wraparound dress waiting to be kissed that I have to attend to." Gavin crossed the yard to Harper and wrapped his arms around her waist from behind. He kissed her neck and said, "Do you know how much I love you?"

"More than fishing?" She leaned back, her soft hands moving over his arms.

"Hm. I don't know. That's a tough call." He kissed her cheek and she sighed. "What are you doing over here all by yourself?"

"Remembering our first night in the rowboat and thinking about how much I like your family. Your parents are so warm and loving. They adore you, Gavin. Your mom told me stories of when you were younger and how you and Beckett used to sneak out. She said as teenagers you'd ride horses with your friends before dawn and that your father used to follow you guys there without you knowing just in case there was an emergency."

He was quiet for a moment, processing what she'd said. "I never knew that."

She tipped her face up toward his and kissed his chin. "I want to be that type of parent. The kind that lets their kids do a few rebellious things but makes sure they're safe. I wasn't ever rebellious, and maybe I missed out."

"I'll be rebellious with you. We'll sneak out after my parents go to sleep and go skinny-dipping."

She laughed, and the sweet sound warmed him all over.

He turned her in her arms, and his insides turned to liquid heat at the love in her eyes. "God, you're gorgeous, Harper. How did I get lucky enough that you chose me to share your heart with?"

"You gave good lollipops," she said with a sexy smile.

"Oh, baby, I love when you talk dirty." He lowered his lips to hers, pouring all of himself into their connection, leaving them both breathless. "Thank you for the most amazing birthday of my life." As he brushed his lips over her cheek, a phone rang in his pocket. "Who isn't *here?*"

He pulled their phones from his pockets and realized it was Harper's that was ringing. Trey's name flashed on the screen as he handed it to her.

"Oh my gosh," she said nervously. "I wonder what he wants. I haven't had time to rewrite the whole script."

"Take your time, babe. I'll go make sure Justin doesn't kill Chloe's date." He gave her a quick peck on the cheek and left her alone to take the call.

Justin was with Zander and Dwayne, and thankfully he was no longer looking at Chloe's date like he wanted to tear him apart. Gavin grabbed one of his mother's buttery biscuits from the table, watching Harper pace as she spoke to Trey.

His mother came to his side and said, "Everything okay?"

"We'll see. She's talking to Trey Ryder, the guy who asked her to rewrite her script into a movie."

"Oh? She told us all about him. She's darling, Gavin. And she seems to really understand *life.*"

Yeah, she does.

"Is that a blush I see on my boy's cheeks?" She brushed her fingers down his face. "Love is a funny thing, isn't it? When we're young, we're like birds and the world holds all sorts of promises of growing up and becoming more than we are. We spread our wings, and we see *love* like the sky, full of unreachable stars, but we can't keep ourselves from trying to reach them. We have wings after all. But as we get older, life takes nibbles out of us. Some people bleed out from those little nips. But for the lucky ones, for every nibble it takes, it gives us a lesson that makes us smarter, allows us to see clearer. And one day all those beautiful stars shower down on us, and instead of occluding our vision, we realize we never needed our wings at all, because when love is right, it finds us no matter where we are."

"Yeah," he said, too choked up to form a more coherent response.

Harper ended her call and lifted a radiant smile in their direction. She ran toward them, looking like she was going to burst.

"I think we have good news." His mother took the uneaten biscuit from his hand and said, "I'll just take care of this for you."

"GAVIN!" HARPER'S HEART was beating so fast she thought she might pass out. She grabbed Gavin's arm and hung on tight. "I can't believe it! Trey's interested! He wants in!"

"On the movie?" Gavin asked. "But you haven't finished the rewrites."

"No! On my idea! The live episodes!" She hadn't meant to yell, but she was too excited to calm down. She was still trying to wrap her head around the phone call.

Gavin hugged her. "That's fantastic!"

"Marvelous," his mother said. "Although I'm not really sure what it all means, you look happy."

Serena and Emery were heading their way.

"What's going on?" Serena called out.

"Trey wants to be part of my project!" Harper hollered, holding tightly to Gavin's hand. "Let's tell everyone at once!"

MELISSA FOSTER

They went to the patio with their friends and family, and she said, "Trey just called. He did a bunch of research, and he thinks my idea is a winner. He wants to live stream the performances on their Movietime channel. He said another channel just started doing it, and he thinks it's the next big thing!"

Everyone talked at once, congratulating her and asking questions so fast, she had a hard time keeping up.

"What does that mean for you?" Gavin's father asked.

"I don't know. He talked about partnership percentages, and they'd handle the capital, and a bunch of other things. I couldn't process it all at once."

"I'm so happy! You could be in business with Ethan!" Emery squealed.

"You need an entertainment attorney," Beckett added.

"Does that mean TV crews would be at the shows?" Tegan asked.

"I guess so," Harper said, slowing down enough to think about the offer more carefully. "He's thinking *big*, and you're right, there'd have to be film crew. I didn't think about that. I'm not sure that's what we want. That would be distracting, don't you think? Maybe they don't have to do it at every performance." She needed to slow down and center her thoughts.

"Babe, who would hold the majority ownership percentage?" Gavin asked.

"You might not retain the rights to make those types of decisions, Harper," Beckett said.

She knew Beckett was an investor, and he had a good point. "That would be awful. I'd be right where I was before all of this."

"No," Serena corrected her. "You'd be much richer."

"Rich and unhappy is no way to go through life," Harper said. "I need to think this through. Oh no, you guys, what if it turns out not to be the best idea, and I turn him down, and then he says no to a movie option? Oh God, I feel a little dizzy."

Gavin gathered her in his arms and said, "Just breathe, babe. It's okay."

She concentrated on the air filling her lungs. Gavin's loving embrace calmed her enough that she was able to take a step back from the brass rings flashing before her eyes long enough to see it more clearly.

"Are you okay, honey?" his mother asked.

She nodded and stepped from Gavin's arms. "Yes, sorry. It's a little overwhelming. I know how big a deal this is, and it could make me—*us*," she said, looking from Gavin to Tegan and Jana, "a lot of money. But the thing is, it *is* a very big deal, and big deals aren't always what they're cracked up to be." She paced, unable to believe she was about to say what she felt and needing to just the same. "I know I don't have all the details of his offer yet, but would you all think I'm crazy if I'm considering turning it down anyway? At least for now? I know I need capital, but what's appealing to me about this project is not just bringing my stories to life in a new way, but also having creative control. The minute I take someone else's money and divvy up percentages, it's *really* divvying up control. And not only that." She went to Tegan, who looked as unsure as Harper felt, and said, "If we do this at your amphitheater, bringing in a camera crew would turn Harvey's vision into a circus. I don't want that. Do you?"

Tegan shook her head, relief washing over her face. "I'm worried about how I'll keep up anyway. It sounds exciting, though, and it could mean great things for you, so if you want to check out other venues, you should do it."

"I don't think I want to. I like the idea of doing this with friends." She looked at Jana and said, "I guess we should talk about it. You might want this, Jana, and you're the one who first mentioned that you and I should have gone into business together a long time ago. I don't want to sound ungrateful."

"Ungrateful?" Jana strode over to her with a determined look in her eyes. She put her hands on her hips and said, "You have never been ungrateful a day in your life. I'm just along for the ride on this, sis. All I did was make an off-the-cuff comment. This idea is all yours, and you have to do what makes you happy."

Gavin took Harper's hand and said, "If you choose not to do this, it's not being ungrateful, Harper. It's taking care of *yourself*, protecting your vision as an artist. Trusting your instincts." He paused, and the importance of those words sank in. "I love that you're thinking in those terms. Whatever you decide, I'll support you."

"We all will," Brock said, coming forward. "It feels good to hold the cards, doesn't it, Harper? You have a media mogul coming to *you*, and I think that's worth a toast."

"Toast time!" Desiree said. She and Serena began handing out glasses.

Violet and Andre each picked up a bottle of wine. Violet said, "Hold up your glasses, party animals. Let's get this party started."

They filled everyone's glasses, and then Brock said, "To Harper!"

"To Harper!" Everyone cheered and clinked glasses.

Harper was floating on cloud nine as they toasted her opportunity. She gazed into Gavin's eyes, his love and support smiling back at her. She took his hand and held up her glass. "To Gavin. Not only is it his birthday, but without him I would probably still be writing crap and hating men. Happy birthday, my love, and thank you."

Everyone cheered. "To Gavin!"

"*Happy birthday to you*," Beckett began singing, and everyone else joined in to finish the song.

They feasted on too much cake and lots of laughter. Gavin's parents shared funny stories about Gavin's childhood birthday parties, which led to everyone else sharing their own funny stories.

It was a perfect evening, and after saying goodbye to their guests, Harper and Gavin sat with Beckett and their parents on the patio, chatting about how much his family liked their friends and Harper's siblings. She never had anything like this with her parents. They didn't like large gatherings or loud parties. She wished they'd been in town to meet Gavin's parents, but she knew at some point they'd visit again, and then she would plan a nice, quiet dinner with all of them.

Gavin's mother yawned and said, "I'm afraid I'm beat, my lovelies. It's been a long day."

"I can't believe it's ten already," his father said.

"Let's get this stuff put away and give the kids some time without us old folks bothering them." His mother pushed to her feet, and they all followed suit.

"You're not a bother. I'm so glad you were able to come and meet everyone," Harper said as they started clearing the table.

Gavin's father snagged a cookie from the tray and said, "I can't believe Gavin found a woman who can make everything cookies better than Nana." He took a bite of the cookie.

"I can't believe he found a woman at all," Beckett said with a smirk.

Gavin lunged toward him, and Beckett took off running with Gavin on his heels.

Harper laughed. "I guess boys will be boys."

"They've always been close," his mother said as they carried dishes into the house.

"There's nothing quite like brothers," his father said. "You seem close with your siblings."

"We are. Do you think it would be a mistake to pass up an opportunity like Trey is offering? Whatever Ethan touches turns to gold, and I'm sure he wouldn't have partnered with Trey if he wasn't the same way. It could mean a *lot* of money."

Gavin's father nodded. "It sure could, but Beckett is right. Investors usually hold the strings, so you're smart to think it through carefully."

She set the dishes she was carrying in the sink, and Gavin's mother did the same.

"There was a time I thought Beckett and Gavin might go into business together," his father said. "But Gavin veered toward his creative outlets, and Beckett embraced finance."

"Jackass!" Gavin's voice floated in through the open patio doors, followed by a loud *oomph*.

"Someone got tackled," his mother said as her husband came to her side.

"Remember when they were little and they'd race through the house like wild banshees?" His father's expression warmed.

"This might seem like a funny thing to say, but thank you for raising Gavin to be such a gentleman. He's kind and smart, and he's a really good man. He told me about the rift that Corinne caused and how embarrassed he was to have stuck by her side when you guys clearly saw something he didn't. As strange as this might seem, because ignoring your family's advice is probably not the best thing to do, I think it says a lot about him that he stuck with her. And that says something about the way you raised him. I know he feels guilty about all the years he wasn't there. But I also know how much he loves you, and I want you to know I'd never try to drive a wedge between him and his family."

His mother got teary-eyed and embraced her. "Oh, honey. We know you won't, and thank you. We're very proud of the two men we raised."

"And it's awfully quiet out there," his father said. "I think we'd better get out there and make sure they didn't kill each other."

They went outside, and she spotted Gavin helping Beckett to his feet in the yard, both of them laughing. They were facing away from Harper, but it was easy to imagine their smiling faces. Harper began gathering more dishes.

"You're a lucky bastard," Beckett said. "Harper's a million times better than your crazy ex-wife."

Harper spun around with her heart in her throat and said, "*What?*" at the same time Gavin and his parents did.

Gavin turned around just as Beckett said, "Corinne."

Gavin's face blanched.

Harper dropped the dish she was holding, spilling its contents onto the table.

Beckett spun around, his face a mask of sorrow and regret as he said, "Oh, shit."

"Ex-*wife?*" Harper. Couldn't. Breathe. "You mean *ex-girlfriend*, right?"

His mother took Harper's hand and squeezed it. "Honey, he

doesn't mean that. You were kidding, right, Beckett? Tell her, honey."

The mixture of shock and grief in Gavin's eyes told Harper this wasn't a joke. Bile rose in her throat, tears welled in her eyes, and she couldn't find her voice. *Married? He was married?* Beckett and Gavin looked as awful as she felt.

Beckett took a step toward her and said, "I was kidding—"

"Don't lie," Gavin said angrily. "We don't lie to each other."

"You *married* her?" his mother said as she sat in a chair at the table.

Gavin was staring at Harper, looking lost and angry and so damn sad, it made her even more confused. Her thoughts fragmented. She was rooted in place, trying to understand what was going on.

"I haven't thought about it in more than a decade," Gavin said. "It's like it never happened."

"Boys, sit. *Now.*" His father pointed to two chairs.

Beckett stumbled over to the table and lowered himself into a chair beside his father.

Gavin went to Harper, but she shrugged him off and held up her hand. "I don't understand. You were *married?*"

"For, like, a day, Harper. I told you about the baby—"

"*Baby?*" his mother cried. "You have a *baby?*"

"No!" Gavin and Beckett said at once.

"Gavin, *what* is going on?" his father asked. "We need answers."

Beckett pushed to his feet again, pacing nervously. "It's my fault. I told Gavin not to tell you when it happened. That we should act like it never happened."

"It's *my* fault," Gavin said, eyes still locked on Harper.

"Harper, I'm sorry. I didn't mean to keep it from you."

"You didn't mean to keep the fact that you were *married* from me? How about from your parents? They don't know about the pregnancy?" Tears fell hot and constant down her cheeks. She was trembling, drowning, struggling to tread water. She feared she might pass out and grabbed the back of the chair to keep from crumpling to the floor.

Chapter Twenty-Three

WHAT A FUCKING mess. The heartbreak in Harper's eyes obliterated everything else for Gavin. He felt sliced open, eviscerated. And the worst part was, he knew Harper and his parents probably felt the same way, all because he was such a fucking idiot, he'd buried that part of his past deep enough to literally forget it.

"*Who* is pregnant?" his mother pleaded.

"I should go and let you deal with your family." Harper headed for the front yard.

Gavin stepped in front of her, blocking her from leaving. "Don't go, baby. *Please* don't leave. I love you, and I would never intentionally lie to you. I honestly don't even think of it as a marriage. It was a mistake. A fucking nightmare. I thought I was doing the right thing—"

"When has lying ever been the right thing to do?" his father hollered.

"Go talk to them," Harper said miserably.

"No. I made the biggest mistake of my life back then. I'm a completely different person now. I know what love is, Harper, and I fucking love you too much to let you leave without hearing me out. Please, babe. Just give me ten minutes."

She nodded almost imperceptibly, and the air rushed from his lungs in relief.

Harper wiped her tears and walked shakily back to the patio. She sat in a chair at the end of the table, which he knew was purposeful, to keep her distance from him.

That killed him, even though he totally understood why she was so upset. He sat down beside Beckett, across from his parents, and tried to figure out where to start.

"I'm sorry, man," Beckett said regretfully.

"It's fine. I'm not mad at you. I'm pissed at myself." He looked at Harper, sitting pin straight, gripping the arms of the chair so hard her knuckles were white. He felt like he'd swallowed shards of glass as he said, "It happened my first year of college." He looked at his parents. "You'd met Corinne, and you'd tried to warn me about her."

His mother reached for his father's hand and held on tight. "That girl got her claws into you and you disappeared."

His throat clogged with emotions. "I know, and I'm sorry. There's no excuse for what I let happen between us. I was young and stupid, and I didn't see her for what she was. A few months after you met her, she got pregnant. There was already such a rift between me and you guys because I had stopped calling or coming home. I had already messed up my relationships with you..."

"Not me," Beckett said. "Never me, bro."

Gavin nodded. "Thanks. But it was such a mess. You guys didn't like Corrine, and she didn't like you. I took her side and I was ashamed of myself for the distance I'd created between us, and I was even more embarrassed because I didn't love her and she was having my child. I thought marrying her was doing the right thing, that it would make me a stand-up guy and somehow I'd be able to fix everything. We went to the courthouse and got married. A few days later I thought I'd figured out how to fix things between all of us. I told her I'd quit school and we could move to Oak Falls. I thought I would work for you, Dad, or get a job in town, and that once you heard about the baby, and once she got to know you, things would be better."

He looked at Harper. She was no longer crying, but she shifted her eyes away, refusing to meet his gaze. He wanted to go to her, to kneel at her feet and beg her to believe him, but that would only embarrass her. He struggled against the guilt and sadness tearing through him and forced himself to finish the story.

"A week later she said she aborted the baby and broke up with me. We were kids, living in separate dorms. We didn't even have wedding rings. She said the baby wasn't mine anyway and that she had no interest in living in a shitty little town. I don't even know if she was ever really pregnant or if it was part of her bigger scheme. I didn't love her, but she did *break* me, for a long damn time. I trusted her, and my head was all messed up. One week I thought I was having a child, and the next she said it was all a lie. I didn't know what to believe or where to turn. I had let everyone down." He shifted his eyes away to try to regain control.

He heard his mother crying, and he looked across the table as his father held her.

"Son..." his father said with a strained voice.

"I'm sorry, Dad, Mom." He looked at Harper and said, "Harper, I'm so sorry."

Tears ran like rivers down her cheeks. She didn't even try to wipe them away. She crossed her arms over her stomach, but she didn't look away this time. He had no idea what that meant.

"It makes me sick to think of you going through that alone," his mother said through her tears. "We're your parents, honey. We love you, regardless of what choices you make. How could you not know that?"

"I wasn't thinking straight, Mom. I was embarrassed and hurt. I'd been played in the worst way. What kind of a man gets played? Dad would never let that happen to him. I was a mess. I was angry and sad and flat-out mortified. I wasn't going to come back home with my tail between my legs. I started the annulment process, and then I drank like a fish." He told them what he'd already explained to Harper about how he fell into the bottle and then climbed back out, only to throw himself into his schoolwork and, eventually, his jobs.

"By the time I came out the other side of it, I was working at KHB and on the fast track to moving up the corporate ladder. I thought if I could make a name for myself, something to make you proud, it would compensate for all the lost time and the pain I'd caused. But I got so lost trying to bury those mistakes, I forgot who I was. I forgot how families worked, how to have meaningful friendships. At that point, my past was buried so deep, I *never* thought about it." He looked at Harper and said, "Maybe it was self-protection, a way to put my grief and shame under lock and key. I don't know. What I do know is that when I met Serena, I remembered what it was like to have friends, to care about people. That was last summer when I called you, Dad. When I came to town and Beckett dragged me to the music festival." He met Harper's gaze and said, "That's when I met Harper."

Harper cleared her throat. "Excuse me." She pushed to her feet, and Gavin stood up. "I'm sorry. I just need some space to think."

He followed her into the house, and when she grabbed her keys and phone, he touched her hand, drawing her sad eyes to his, driving the knife in his heart deeper. "Harper, please don't leave."

"I have to, Gavin. I need time to think."

He curled his hand around hers and she didn't pull away. *Thank fucking God.*

"I screwed up, Harper, but I didn't mean to. I didn't hide the baby from you, and I know I sound like a liar, saying I haven't thought about that day at the courthouse in the last decade, but it's true. I swear it on the lives of everyone I love."

"Gavin, *don't*," she said wistfully. "I can't do this now."

"Please, just hear me out. I was in survival mode. I don't know if I blocked it out, *chose* not to think about it, or what I did, but it wasn't anywhere on my radar. The *pain* of what she did was there. That was real to me, but marrying her? It's like it never happened. I don't know how else to explain it. When I think of that time in my life, the courthouse was a blip. It's not like I was in love and my marriage of twenty years broke up. We were two kids in a courthouse making things legal so I could raise a child I had no idea wasn't mine. We didn't even go back to the same dorm room afterward, Harper. Please, try to understand what it was like."

"I trusted you," she said just above a whisper. "I'm so *hurt...*"

"I know, sweetheart, and I'm sorry. I can't change how I handled it, and I'll regret it for the rest of my life. Do you think I wanted to hurt you? To hurt my parents? I *love* you more than I've ever loved anyone or anything. If I could go back to the day I told you about that time of my life and the shit show that I became afterward and *find* that awful memory so I could tell you about it, I would. God, I'd do it in a heartbeat, because while I survived losing a baby I thought was mine, I'm not sure I could ever come back from losing you."

"I have to go." Fresh tears spilled from her eyes.

He followed her outside, wanting to grab her by the shoulders and beg her to stay, but he was the hurricane and she was the sea. The harder he pushed, the farther she'd run. Watching her climb into her car nearly brought him to his knees.

"Harper!"

She stilled at his desperate plea.

"Are you coming back?"

She looked directly into his eyes, tears sliding down her cheeks, and said, "I hope so."

AS HARPER DROVE away, sobs burst from her lungs. She didn't know where to go or who to talk to. She'd just driven away from the only person she wanted to talk to. But with Gavin's mother in tears, his father looking like he'd aged ten years in the space of an hour, and Gavin...

Her strong, sensible boyfriend, the man who had helped her find her way to honesty from day one, had looked guilt-stricken and sick, like it had taken all of his strength to push words from his lungs.

How was she supposed to process her own feelings when the man she loved looked just as devastated as she was?

She thought about calling Jana. But she was the one who had convinced Harper to stop waiting for the other shoe to drop. *The frigging shoe not only dropped, it landed on my flipping head.* She wiped her eyes, driving aimlessly as she debated what to do and where to go. The thought of telling anyone what was going on was too much to bear. She drove to her cottage, but as she stepped onto the porch, she remembered Gavin's note, the lollipops he'd left, and how he'd helped her unpack her life and put it back together.

She inhaled a ragged breath and pushed the door open. As she stepped inside and looked at the stark little cottage, the place she'd once called home, it felt stifling and cold at once. She closed the door and paced, but her legs were weak. She collapsed on the sofa and cried into her hands. Thoughts *whirled* in her head, snippets of the things Gavin had said, images of the hurt in his eyes, and sounds. *God, the sounds.* His mother's soft sobs, his father's strained voice, Beckett's apologies, and Gavin's voice turning thin as a frayed thread as he told the story of his suffering.

Her head fell back against the cushion and she stared up at the ceiling, remembering how she'd faked being sick to get out of her blind date. She laughed softly, thinking of how persistent, yet careful, Gavin had been with her. He always knew just what she needed.

But he'd kept his marriage from her.

Maybe that was what *he* needed.

She pushed to her feet again, feeling like a stranger in her own house. She wasn't the same person she'd been when she got home from LA. She was better, stronger, more confident in what she wanted.

I want Gavin.

Heartache pressed in on her.

She walked to the bedroom. Even though they'd replaced the furniture so they could rent it fully furnished, images of them making love slammed into her. She turned on her heel and walked out the door.

Through the blur of tears, she climbed back into her car and drove away.

Her go-to thinking spot had become Gavin's dock. *Our dock.* More sobs bubbled out. *Pull yourself together and think.* Her mind was too cluttered with pain and love and so much confusion she was lucky she didn't drive off the road. She drove as if on autopilot, weaving through the dark streets of Wellfleet, passing galleries and restaurants, heading toward the pier, her old thinking spot. Maybe the sea air would help her make sense of her careening emotions.

She was glad to see only a handful of cars in the parking lot. Mac's Seafood and the Pearl were closed, as was the WHAT Theater and shops, leaving only the draw of the harbor. She got out of her car, wishing she'd brought a sweater, and filled her lungs with the cool night air. A group of teenagers was skateboarding at the other end of the parking lot, their voices carrying in the air. The wind picked up as she stepped onto the worn wooden slats of the pier. She passed a young couple snuggling on a blanket in the sand below. A pang of longing sliced through her.

When she reached the end of the pier, she held on to one of the splintery wooden pilings, listening to the sounds of the water splashing against the pilings, the creak of fishing boats, and tinny *clanks* of their hardware rattling in the wind. Potent, fishy scents permeated the salty air. Harper wrapped her arms around her middle, hoping the cold air would cleanse the hurt from her heart. Goose bumps rose on her flesh as her dress whipped around her legs. Cold air wasn't strong enough to do the trick. Her pain was bone deep. The problem was, she wasn't alone in her pain, and she couldn't separate Gavin's from her own. They were too entangled, and she didn't have the faintest idea how to separate them.

She lowered herself to the edge of the pier. It was so different by the bay than it was on the pond. Here the cold wind whipped, indifferent to the chaos in her mind, whereas on the pond the breeze was gentle, caressing, and soothing. *Like Gavin.* He wasn't a gale-force wind, as he'd claimed on their first date. He was a constant, stabilizing breeze that lifted and calmed. That thought sent a pang of longing and pain through her. She wished she could be angrier, flat-out pissed. It would be so much easier than being hurt and sad.

She closed her eyes, letting the cold air chill her to the bone. Maybe she could freeze the hurt out. She sat shivering against the wind for a long time, remembering how she used to come there to write. Being near the water had always helped her creativity flow, but she'd needed more than that when she'd come home from LA.

She'd needed Gavin.

He hadn't just helped her find her way back to her passion. He'd *become* one of her passions. Her biggest passion.

My best passion.

She tried to push that thought away, but it was like trying to tear off a piece of herself.

She didn't know how long she sat in the cold, but it was long enough for her toes to go numb. She heard the sound of feet shuffling on the pier and the whispering cadence of a couple in love. Her stomach clenched as their footfalls neared.

"Harper?" Violet put a hand on Harper's shoulder and crouched beside her. Her hair was as black as her leather jacket and boots. "Are you okay? You must be freezing."

Andre's concerned face came into view, and Harper's emotions plummeted. Was it really just a little while ago that they were celebrating together?

"I'm okay." She tried to mask her heartache, but there was no escaping the sadness in her voice.

"Then you won't mind if we sit with you." Violet plunked herself down beside Harper.

Andre shrugged off his zip-up sweatshirt and draped it around Harper's shoulders. He sat on Harper's other side, buffering her from the wind with his thick body.

"Thank you." She pulled the sweatshirt around herself.

They didn't say anything for a few minutes, though she knew they wanted to.

"You know, Gavin always seemed a little unsettled to me," Violet said casually. "But tonight he looked like a man who finally knew he was exactly where he belonged. Want to tell me why you're here instead of giving him a birthday celebration he'll never forget?"

"Not really," Harper mumbled.

"Okay, that's cool. He must have done something pretty bad." Violet cracked her knuckles and said, "Want me to take him out for you? Bury the body in the middle of the ocean?"

Harper shook her head. "No."

"Did you guys have a fight?" Andre asked.

Harper shrugged, tearing up again. "It wasn't a *fight*." She didn't know what to call it. A mass heartbreak, maybe?

"Well, whatever it was, I doubt it's worse than waking up in Ghana to find the person you just said *I love you* to gone without so much as a goodbye, or even a note, and then spending two years not knowing if she was alive or dead," Andre said.

Harper looked at Violet. "You did that to him?"

"Yeah. I suck," Violet said.

"Oh my gosh, I can't imagine…" That was worse than not knowing about Gavin's ex-wife.

"No, she doesn't suck," Andre said. "She was protecting herself from being hurt, and we're both in better places for it. The girls didn't tell you about everything that happened last summer?"

Harper shook her head. "Just that you guys were together before and that you showed up with Vi's mom for Des's wedding. I also heard that Vi sort of had a secret life none of us knew about."

"Yup. All true, and it was a shitty thing to do. All of it." Violet lifted apologetic eyes to Andre, who reached across Harper's lap and touched Violet's hand. "I won't go into all the gory details, but three years ago we were both in Ghana for different reasons, and we fell in love. It scared the hell out of me, which we can blame on my crazy-ass mother. Andre poured his heart out to me right after I got the message from Lizza telling me Desiree needed me here at the Cape. Remember that?"

"Yes, but you never said anything about a guy, much less being in *love*."

"Because I couldn't think about Andre without falling apart," Violet said. "The pain cut too deep, so I pretended he didn't exist and none of it ever happened. I couldn't afford to lose my shit when I was just getting to know the sister I had been separated from for so long. But trust me, I was a fucking mess."

"I could never pretend not to love Gavin. I can't even comprehend that idea, but for what it's worth, you never seemed like a mess."

Violet looked down at the water. "I was."

"Violet's messes look different from other people's messes," Andre explained.

"The worst part was that I didn't realize how lying to myself affected everyone else," Violet said with regret in her eyes. "I didn't consider hiding that part of my life—or the *new* parts of my life, my new friends, my jobs—as lying. But it was. I hurt Desiree, Serena, Emery...I unknowingly hurt everyone who trusted and loved me. The mind is a tricky thing, Harper. In leaving my past behind, I convinced everyone, including myself, that I wasn't hiding anything at all."

Just like Gavin. "How did you guys get past that? Andre, weren't you angry? Hurt?"

"It was the hardest thing I've ever gone through," Andre said. "It would have been easier if I'd hated her, but that's the thing about love. You don't have a choice in the matter, and its impact on everyone is different. The feelings that terrified Violet were the same things that made me feel whole. I was devastated when she left, and I was angry when I found her again. But our love for each other hadn't changed, and once I stepped back enough to understand *why* she left the way she did..." He shrugged. "How could I be mad at the woman I loved with every ounce of myself, when she was only trying to survive?"

Wasn't that all Gavin was doing? Her mind sailed back to when she'd heard Beckett say, *Harper's a million times better than your crazy ex-wife.* Gavin had said, "*What?*" at the same time she and his parents had. He'd sounded just as shocked and baffled by what Beckett had said as the rest of them had. That wasn't the reaction of someone who had an ex-wife on his mind.

Harper's pulse raced as she relived those first few seconds.

Gavin's face had drained of all its color. When he'd realized what he'd done, he'd looked shocked and grief-stricken, utterly devastated.

"I got lucky that Andre loved me enough to deal with my baggage." Tears glistened in Violet's eyes.

Knowing what Violet had done to Andre didn't make Harper want to stop being her friend any more than Gavin shutting himself off from his past made her want to stop being with him.

"We all have baggage," Harper said.

That's exactly what Gavin's ex-wife is. She was a lead weight that had sucked the trust and life out of him, pulled him under so deep he'd nearly drowned. Harper had baggage, too, but Gavin had saved her from making a huge mistake and hiding the truth from the people she loved for too long.

A harsh worry trickled in. What if he was hiding other things? After seeing how devastated he was after he realized what he'd done, she didn't think he was hiding anything else. In her heart, in her *soul*, she didn't think he was. But was she giving him too much credit by trusting her instincts? What if she was wrong? What then?

She remembered what Hunter had told her about love. *When they're bummed, you're bummed. When they're happy, you want to do everything within your power to keep them that way. That's love, Harper. You might not be there yet, but if you feel those things, it's definitely worth holding on to while you figure it out.*

He'd told her about the baby. Wasn't that a harder admission than the marriage?

"I want to hold on," she said, unbidden.

"What?" Violet asked.

Gavin's pained explanation slammed into her. *I was embarrassed and hurt. I'd been played in the worst way. What kind of a man gets played? Dad would never let that happen to him.* Her breathing hitched with the memory.

"You said the mind was a tricky thing!" Harper pushed to her feet, breathing hard. "That in leaving your past behind, you convinced everyone, including yourself, that you weren't hiding anything at all."

"That's right. It's true," Violet said.

She threw her arms around Violet. Andre's sweatshirt slipped off Harper's shoulders, and he caught it.

"Whoa, what was that for?" Violet asked.

"For driving the truth home. I have to go!" Harper said, clutching her keys in her hand.

"Are you okay?" Andre asked.

"I will be!" she called over her shoulder as she ran toward her car.

Chapter Twenty-Four

GAVIN SAT ON the couch beside Beckett, trying not to lose his mind. After Harper left, he'd told his parents he was going after her, but his father had convinced him to give her the space she'd asked for. Gavin agreed to give her two hours. That was *almost* two hours ago, and every passing second felt like it added another nail in his coffin.

"I can't sit here anymore. I'm going to find her." Gavin grabbed his keys and pushed to his feet.

Beckett yanked him back down. "You heard what Dad said before they went to bed. You just turned Harper's whole fucking world upside down. Give her space, man. Jesus, you'll look desperate."

Gavin glowered at him. "I *am* desperate, asshole. I love Harper. I'd take a fucking beating from Satan if it would take away the pain I've caused her. How am I ever going to win her back?"

"Gavin, you're the best man I know. Harper's smart and she loves you. She knows who you really are, just like Mom and Dad do."

He wasn't so sure. He'd had a long heart-to-heart with his parents, laying his guilt and shame on the table. His parents had made it clear that they weren't happy learning about the marriage or the baby so long after the facts, but they also reiterated that they loved him unconditionally. Burying his past had nothing to do with his parents' love toward him and everything to do with his own disappointment in himself.

"How screwed up do I have to be to have buried that shit so deep that I literally forgot we got married?"

"About as screwed up as I was before I realized the mistakes I'd made with Morgyn. They say hindsight is twenty-twenty, but really the saying should be, hindsight is an ass kicker."

Beckett had briefly dated their friend Morgyn Montgomery. He hadn't been in love with her, but he'd loved her as a friend, and when she'd come to him for business advice, he'd been too shortsighted to see her full potential and had inadvertently given her bad advice. It wasn't until after they'd broken up that he'd come to realize the mistakes he'd made.

Gavin glanced at the timer counting down on his phone. *Eleven more minutes.*

He might explode sooner than that.

"I really am sorry, man," Beckett said for the hundredth time.

"This is all on me. I just don't get it. I never bury shit like that."

"It's not like either of us had experience with this. It was a bad judgment call and, dude, you were really messed up. If you'd let that shit ride the surface, you never would have moved on."

Gavin curled his fingers around the keys, struggling to resist the urge to go after her. "Maybe you can explain that to Harper. I can't lose her, Beck. She's everything to me."

The front door opened, and Gavin jumped to his feet as

Harper walked tentatively into the room.

"You came back." With his heart in his throat, he went to her, searching her face for clues to whether she was going to end things or forgive him.

She blinked several times, her eyes moving between him and Beckett, who was on his feet, too, looking like he'd swallowed a frog. "I'm sorry I left."

"It's okay," he said, feeling like he'd just run a marathon. "Are you ready to talk?"

She nodded.

"I'm sorry for causing this mess, Harper," Beckett said. "For what it's worth, Gavin's the most honest guy I know, and he loves you with everything he has."

She nodded again, wordlessly forgiving him with a softer, glassy gaze.

Beckett nudged Gavin's shoulder and said, "I'm going out for a drive to give you guys some privacy. Can I borrow your keys?"

"Sure." When Beckett didn't move, Gavin shot him a *get the hell out of here* look.

"You're still holding your keys." Beckett pointed to Gavin's clenched fist.

He handed him the keys. He'd forgotten he was holding them.

Beckett held his gaze and said, "Love you, man."

His silent *you've got this* came through loud and clear, even if Gavin wasn't so sure he did.

After Beckett left, Harper fidgeted nervously with her keys and said, "Are your parents still up? I'd like to apologize to them for leaving."

"They went to bed an hour ago but, Harper, there's no need

to apologize. They understand why you left. They think the world of you. Can we sit down and talk?"

He started to put his hand on her lower back to guide her to the couch, but pulled back, unsure of just where she stood. For the first time since they'd met, things were awkward between them. He hated it, and he didn't have the faintest clue how to fix it or even where to start.

She sat down, still fidgeting with her keys. Her hair curtained her face, making it hard to read her expression. The clinking of her keys amplified in the silence.

The alarm on Gavin's phone went off, and Harper jumped. He grabbed the phone off the coffee table and turned it off. He took the keys from her hand and put them on the table with his phone. Then he covered her trembling fingers with his hand, and she curled her fingers around his. His emotions consumed him at that small touch.

"What was that alarm for?" she asked softly.

"You asked for space. I promised myself, and my father, I'd give you two hours before I went after you."

She leaned into him a little, and it gave him hope.

"I hate that I caused this awkwardness between us, and I know saying I'm sorry isn't enough to make up for the hurt I've caused you," he said. "I know it'll take time for you to trust me again, but if you'll give me another chance—"

"Stop," she whispered. "I think I understand why you kept it from everyone, including yourself."

"You do?" *Aw hell.* He got all choked up again.

She nodded. "When I thought my life was ruined, I had a friend who helped me see how wrong I was. You didn't have a friend like that back then. Someone to explain that Corinne's actions weren't your fault, or that you shouldn't let one bad experience rock your foundation. That same friend probably would have reminded you that you achieved greatness in the eyes of your parents the day you were born, before you became anything other than their son. And that Beckett knows how incredible you are. That friend would explain that it wouldn't matter if you chose a girl over your family for a day, a month, or even if you married her. They would always love you just the same."

His chest constricted.

"You didn't have a friend who would tell you that it's important to be honest with the people who love you." She held his hand tighter. "I'd hate to think about what I'd be like right now if I hadn't had a friend to help me move past my bad experiences."

He swallowed hard. "Harper…?"

She blinked away the dampness in her eyes and said, "You hurt me, Gavin, and that kind of hurt doesn't just go away."

"I know, and it kills me that I hurt you. I will spend the rest of my life making it up to you."

"You don't have to do that. We all handle love and grief differently. I'm hurt, but I love you for the man you are *now*. I just need to know if there's anything else you think you might be hiding."

"No. Other than that crazy shit that happened with Corinne, I'm a pretty boring guy."

A relieved laugh came out soft and lovely, like music to his ears, as tears slipped from her eyes. "You're far from boring."

"Oh, baby," he said as he pulled her into his arms. He buried his face in her neck and hair, breathing her in. "I'm so sorry, and I'm so glad you came back. I thought I'd lost you."

"You probably should thank Violet and Andre, by the way."

"Violet and Andre?"

She nodded. "I didn't tell them anything. Don't worry."

He wiped the tears from his eyes and said, "I'll tell them. I don't want secrets, sweetheart. Not from you, and not hiding in our closet to bite us in the ass. I thought I'd dealt with all that stuff with Corinne a long time ago, but I guess I just swept it under the rug."

A small smile curved her lips and she said, "It's a good thing I'm fairly capable with a broom." She took his face between her soft hands, her beautiful blue eyes imploring him to love her wholly and completely. "Please don't hurt me again, Gavin. It's too hard."

"Never again, sweetheart."

She pressed her lips to his, kissing him lightly, again and again. Every touch healed another broken piece of his heart. He wanted to steal away with her, to love her until she couldn't remember ever being hurt.

HARPER GAZED INTO Gavin's eyes, seeing relief and so much love it was inescapable. She knew he saw the same emotions in her eyes, because she loved him with every cell of her being. She kissed him again, loving the greedy way he kissed her back. She pressed her lips to his cheek and then she bit his earlobe. He hissed and turned his face so he could kiss her lips. She knew he would feel the need to be careful with her tonight, but she didn't want *careful*. She wanted affirmation of their love. She wanted to give him that, because as much as she'd gone through tonight, he'd gone through even more. He'd relived the anguish and shame he'd fought to move past for so long.

She slipped off her sandals, rose to her feet, and reached for his hand, pulling him up beside her. She touched his face, drawing it closer to hers again. She slicked her tongue along his lower lip, loving the way his eyes darkened, and she whispered, "Let's love our hurt away."

"Thank you, sweetheart," he said, his voice full of emotion.

He lifted her into his arms, and she wrapped her legs around his waist, want and need vibrating through her. Their mouths came together as he carried her into the bedroom, closing the door with one hand without breaking their hungry kisses. He lowered himself to the edge of the bed with her on his lap and they continued feasting on each other's mouths. He nipped at her lower lip, kissed her jaw, her neck, and dragged the strap of her dress down her shoulder with his teeth. *Oh*, what that did to her! His gaze locked on the lace trim of her salmon demi bra with sparking gold embellishments in the lace. He inhaled sharply, growing harder beneath her. She'd bought the lingerie set special for his birthday.

She slid the other strap down her shoulder and untied the bow at her waist, opening her wraparound dress, revealing her matching panties. His eyes flamed as she slipped off his lap and her dress fell away, puddling at her feet. She turned around, giving him an eyeful of the cheeky heart-shaped cutout across her bottom. She looked over her shoulder, and her heart pounded at the heat in his eyes.

"Happy birthday, Gavin."

He was on his feet in two seconds flat, stripping off his clothes, and then his glorious naked body pressed against her back, his hands taking their fill up front.

"Sweet Jesus, Harper."

He bit down on her shoulder, and she pressed her ass against his hard length, gyrating slowly. His cock was hard and hot on her cheeks through the cutout in her panties. She pressed her palms flat against the wall, knowing how much he loved her ass. His mouth blazed a path down her spine, slowing to kiss the dip at the base. His hands moved rough and possessive along her torso, up her stomach, and—*good Lord*—between her legs. He pushed his finger beneath her panties, stroking over her wetness and making the guttural, manly noises that always made her lose her mind. He traced his tongue along the cutout of the heart, tickling her skin as he teased her into a wet, needy frenzy. The sensations collided, making her moan and thrust, and when he dipped his fingers inside her, she clawed at the wall.

"Gavin," she panted out.

He stripped off her panties, and his thumb landed on her clit, rubbing in a mind-numbing pace as his fingers dipped inside her and worked their magic, taking her up on her toes. His tongue slipped lower, taunting alongside his fingers, sending lust and love ricocheting through her. He quickened his pace, fucking her faster with his fingers, and sealed his mouth over her inner thigh, sucking *hard*. She clamped her mouth shut to keep from crying out as she spiraled over the edge. Her hips bucked wildly, her inner muscles pulsing tight and fast. He didn't stop there. Oh no, Gavin knew just how to drive her to the brink of madness. He rose to his full height, pressing his hard chest against her back as he slid his thick cock between her legs, brushing against her swollen sex. He flattened his hands over hers, pinning her in place against the wall.

"Close your legs, baby. Squeeze me tight, like I'm inside you. I want you to come all over my cock."

Her legs weakened with his dirty talk, but she managed to

squeeze her legs together.

"That's it. Tight, baby."

She squeezed her thighs as tight as she could as he thrust his hips, sliding deliciously against her sex without entering her. She pressed back against him, wanting more, but she knew he wouldn't give it to her until she came, and sweet heaven, she adored that.

He released one of her hands and gripped her chin, turning her face so he could claim her mouth in a ravenous kiss. His tongue thrust hard and insistent to the same rhythm as his hips. When his hand pushed down her belly and his fingers found the spot that sent fire through her loins, her head fell back against his chest.

"Oh *God*," came out in one long, hot breath.

He sealed his mouth over the base of her neck, sucking and stroking with his tongue. Adrenaline coursed through her veins, making her dizzy with desire. He moved his thumb to the spot where his fingers were and put his fingers under his cock, holding it tight against her sex, putting more pressure in all the right places. She curled her fingers around his, trying her hardest not to let out the sounds exploding inside her as he took her up, up, *up*, until she was hanging on to her sanity by a thread.

"I need you on the bed, baby," he ground out as he removed her bra, lowering her shaky arms to slide it off.

"No condom," she said. "I want to feel *you*."

He turned her in his arms, his eyes so dark and lustful, her legs weakened even more. "I want to feel you, too, baby. But I'm going to marry you one day, and there's no way I'm going to take a chance that you get pregnant and think I'm marrying you for any reason other than my undying love for you."

Her heart soared as his mouth came down over hers, and they tumbled onto the bed. He gave her several quick kisses as he stretched across the bed to open the nightstand drawer, like he couldn't bear the thought of being apart from her. And after what happened earlier, she was right there with him.

He tossed a few condoms on the mattress, and she said, "Get the ties." The relief in his eyes tugged at her heart. "I trust you, Gavin. I want it all, like our first night together."

He pulled a black silk tie from the drawer and lowered himself over her, kissing her deeply. He rose up on his knees with a predatory look in his eyes, straddling her legs. His thick cock bobbed against him. Her pulse skyrocketed. She loved when they played. He dragged the soft silk teasingly around her breasts, over her nipples, and down the center of her body.

"I want you blindfolded, so every touch is heightened," he said in a low voice so rich with desire she could practically taste it.

"*Yes*, do it."

As he gently tied the silk over her eyes, she remembered the first time he'd blindfolded her. She'd been as scared as she was aroused. He'd seen her fear, and he'd told her everything he was going to do before doing it. Her fear had quickly slipped away. He'd done the same thing after they'd come back together on the Cape, and now there was no fear left to work around.

She lay on the bed with her eyes covered, his body heat soaking into her skin as his chest grazed her breasts. Her nipples pebbled as he slithered lower, teasing one sensitive peak with his tongue. His hand covered her other breast, teasing the peak as he sucked the other into his mouth. He groaned, and the guttural, sexy sound brought a rush of heat to her core. He shifted again, and his hand moved between her legs.

"*Yes*," she said breathily. When he lowered his mouth to her breast, she said, "Suck it *hard*."

He sucked so hard she felt it between her legs. His fingers entered her in one fast push, sending electric shocks pinging through her. She clamped her mouth closed to keep from crying out. He sucked and fucked and sent her spiraling over the edge. When she started to come down from the peak, he did it again, sending her right back up to the clouds. She fisted her hands in the mattress, and then he slithered down her body, taking and tasting. He spread her legs roughly, holding them apart. She held her breath, bracing herself for his ravenous feast, but his tongue breezed over her sex light as a feather. The breath rushed from her lungs. He did it again, and she tried to stifle her moan.

"That's it, baby. Don't wake my parents."

Oh God! That would be embarrassing!

He tickled her clit with his tongue, then circled back for another feathery tease, and so became the torturous rhythm. She held her breath with every swipe of his tongue, panting as he applied pressure where she needed it most, until she was so turned on, she could no longer decipher the difference. Every touch ignited inside her.

"So sweet, baby," he said without missing a beat.

She dug her heels into the mattress, hanging on to her sanity by a thread. When his thick fingers passed over her wetness and touched her bottom, she moaned, spreading her legs wider.

"Do it," she pleaded. "I can't take the anticipation. I can't think. I can barely breathe."

"You can breathe, baby, and you don't need to think. You know I'll take care of you."

Need stacked up inside her as he licked and sucked. His finger pushed into her bottom as he fucked her with his tongue, and the world spun away.

When she collapsed to the mattress, he shifted again. Cooler air brought rise to goose bumps, and then his body heat warmed her as he came down over her and took her in a rough, impassioned kiss. He tasted of her, but she didn't care. It made her want him even more. She felt his thick cock resting on her skin. The weight of his body was exquisite. He threaded his fingers into her hair, holding tight, as he deepened the kiss.

He untied the blindfold and brushed his nose tenderly over hers. "I love your mouth," he whispered hungrily, and then he recaptured her mouth, kissing her so thoroughly, heat seared between her legs and she almost came again.

She reached between them, and he lifted up enough for her to wrap her hand around his shaft. He groaned and thrust his hips, fucking her hand.

"I need your mouth." His mouth came down over hers, and his tongue thrust to the same rhythm as his hips.

She loved when he got like this, so overcome with desire he had to have all of her. He continued his luxurious devouring, until her entire body was throbbing, begging to be fucked.

He reached for a condom.

"Hurry," she said as he went up on his knees and sheathed himself.

He came down over her with that sexy grin she loved and a wicked look in his eyes. "You want me to hurry, huh?" He aligned their bodies and slid just the tip of his cock in, hissing at the tight fit.

"*Gavin*," she pleaded, pushing down on his hips while rising up beneath him.

He pulsed his hips, taking her an inch at a time, then withdrawing painfully slowly and going in deeper. She pulled his mouth to hers, sucking hard, and dug her fingernails into the back of his neck the way she knew drove him mad. His hips pistoned hard, burying him to the hilt.

"*Fuuck*," he growled.

She grinned up at him and slapped his ass. "You've had your fun driving me crazy. Now it's my turn…"

Chapter Twenty-Five

THE NEXT MORNING Harper cuddled closer to Gavin beneath the blanket on the lounge chair as the sun rose higher into the sky. They'd woken up before everyone else and had come outside to watch the sunrise. Harper had fallen asleep within minutes of coming outside, and it reminded him of the night of their first date.

He heard the front door close and kissed Harper's cheek. "I think my parents are up. That's probably my dad grabbing the newspaper."

"Mm." She wrapped her arms around his neck, snuggling against him. "I really like your parents. I'll be sad when they leave."

"Me too. Thank you for arranging their trip and the party. And, sweetheart, thank you for coming back, for trusting me. I'm sorry for hurting you."

She pressed her lips to his, silencing his heartache, and then her lips curved up. "That's in the past, and I'm looking forward to our future."

"Me too," he said. "Everyone's going out on Rick and Drake's boat today."

"I know. Desiree told me. Do you want to go?"

"If you do. I think my parents would enjoy it."

"Let me think about that. Spend the day lying in the sun with my girlfriends while my boyfriend and his wonderful family enjoy themselves? Or…"

He nuzzled against her cheek. "Or?"

"There is no *or*. There's only *us*. It sounds perfect."

The patio door opened, and his mother peered out. "*Oh*," she said with surprise. "Good morning. I didn't know you two were up. I was just going to let some fresh air in."

Harper and Gavin climbed from the lounger, the scent of bacon making him hungry.

"It's okay, Mom. We were just about to head inside." He draped the blanket around Harper, who looked adorable in cute cotton sleeping shorts and one of his sweatshirts.

"Your father is scouring the paper for Harper's latest article." She looked thoughtfully at them and said, "I'm glad you two talked things out."

As they went inside, Harper said, "I'm sorry for leaving last night. That was rude, and I wasn't thinking clearly."

"No need to apologize, honey," his mother said.

His father manned the stove in a pair of jeans and a button-down, watching over bacon, eggs, and pancakes as they cooked, which brought fond memories of his dad cooking breakfasts on the weekends when he was a kid.

"Last night was quite a blow for all of us, Gavin included. But Lord knows life isn't always easy." His mother reached for his father's hand and said, "I know a little something about needing space from a Wheeler man."

"That goes both ways, darlin'," his father said as he transferred a pile of bacon to a plate. "My mother always said marriages that float away with water as it passes under the bridge are marriages that were never meant to be. People aren't perfect, and true love takes strong, forgiving hearts." He looked at Harper and Gavin and said, "Sometimes you have to swim against the tide to make it to calmer waters. But it's those tougher times that make relationships stronger. Now, who's brave enough to wake Beckett?"

"Not me," his mother said. "That boy's a grump in the morning."

Gavin held his hands up in surrender and said, "Count me out."

His father arched a brow in Harper's direction. "Feeling brave?"

"No, she's not." Gavin pulled Harper into his arms. "Dad, Beckett sleeps *commando.*"

His father snickered.

Beckett's bedroom door opened, and he shuffled out wearing only a pair of jeans. His hair was sticking up all over. He stretched and said, "I smell bacon."

They all laughed.

Beckett put a hand on his father's shoulder as he stole a piece of bacon.

His father shook his head. "Take the plate to the table, son, and try to leave some for the rest of us."

Harper folded the blanket and set it on the couch, and they all helped bring breakfast to the table and settled in to eat.

"Now that Mom showed Harper how to cook your favorite dinner, you can keep her barefoot and pregnant in the kitchen," Beckett teased.

"I have a much better room for Harper to excel in." Gavin squeezed Harper's leg.

"Gavin!" she chided him as Beckett laughed loudly.

"I meant the *office*," Gavin said with a wink and a chuckle. "Although I would have said the *bedroom* if we weren't in the company of my parents."

Harper covered her face. "Ohmygod!"

Beckett snickered again.

"It's okay, honey," his mother said. "We know that everything Gavin says comes from his heart."

"You keep believing that, Mom," Beckett said under his breath.

Gavin punched him in the arm.

His father pointed his fork at Beckett and said, "If you ever slow down long enough to hear your heart, you'll lead with yours, too. It's who you are, Beckett. Don't fool yourself into thinking all that other nonsense is anything more than a distraction. A precursor to the real thing."

"We can always hope," his mother said.

"Dude, trust me on this," Gavin said. "When that particular organ speaks, you won't be able to ignore it." He hugged Harper against his side and kissed her temple. "True love is the most powerful thing on earth."

Harper mouthed, *I love you.*

Beckett scoffed, grumbling as he grabbed the last of the bacon. "I'm pretty sure my stomach and my"—he glanced at his parents—"other hungry body part are loud enough to drown out anything else."

They talked and joked, finishing breakfast in great moods. Gavin counted himself lucky to have such a wonderful family, and even luckier to have found a woman who seemed to enjoy them as much as he did.

As they cleared the table, Gavin said, "Rick and Drake are taking their boat out to do some fishing today with a bunch of our friends. What do you think? Want to join them?"

"Better ask your mother," his father said. "Fishing sounds great, and we really enjoyed getting to know your friends, but we don't want to miss our flight."

"We've got plenty of time," Beckett said. "Right, Mom?"

"We do," she said. "We don't leave until six."

"Then we'd better get this stuff cleaned up and head out so we don't miss them." Gavin started collecting dishes.

Harper touched his hand and said, "First I'd like to give you your birthday present."

He leaned down and whispered, "I thought you gave it to me last night."

Crimson spread over her cheeks.

"Whatever you just said was potent, dude," Beckett said as Harper buried her face in Gavin's chest.

Harper tipped her chin up and said, "That wasn't your present. That was just *love*."

She sauntered over to the record player, and a few seconds later the sounds of "Use Somebody" by Kings of Leon filled the air. It was the song Inferno had been playing when they'd danced their first dance together at the festival. She lip-synched as she took his hand and twirled into his arms.

"Do you remember dancing to this?" Harper asked.

He gazed into her beautiful eyes and said, "I remember every single thing about the day I met the love of my life."

His mother's hand covered her heart. His father drew his wife into his arms and began dancing. Beckett glided into the room singing at the top of his lungs and dancing horrendously.

With his soul mate in his arms, surrounded by the people he loved most, Gavin fell head over heels in love with Harper all over again.

Epilogue

AS GAVIN AND Harper pushed through the doors of the cute pizzeria where they'd just finished dinner, the blustery evening air stung their cheeks. They were in Romance, Virginia, and despite the unusually frigid temperatures, the charming small town was even more romantic the second time around. They'd enjoyed a pre-Thanksgiving dinner with Harper's family, and then they'd gone to Oak Falls to spend Thanksgiving with Gavin's family. During their visit, Harper had met Nana and all of Gavin's friends. They'd even attended one of the Jerichos' famous jam sessions, which was just as fabulous as Gavin had described. They'd had a wonderful visit, and Harper was eager to come back and see everyone again. She and Gavin had planned to return to the Cape yesterday, but Gavin had surprised her with a weekend at the Wysteria Inn, the quaint bed-and-breakfast where they'd first come together. He'd even arranged for them to stay in the same room.

It was the perfect end to a fantastic week.

Harper turned into Gavin's warm body and grabbed the lapels of his heavy winter coat. He wanted to make wishes in the fountain like they had last summer, and so did she, except the temperature had dropped ten degrees since the sun had gone down, and Harper was *freezing*.

She gazed up at the romantic man she adored, her teeth chattering, and said, "Are you sure you wouldn't rather cozy up in our bedroom at the inn and make our wishes in the light of day, when it's a little warmer? There won't even be water in the fountain."

"The last time I made a wish in the fountain it came true. I'm not missing out on my next wish coming true."

He put his arm around her waist as they headed for the crosswalk, passing cute old-fashioned shops with faded awnings and big picture windows lining the main road. Gone were the flower boxes and planters of summer, replaced with holiday lights and decorations. The dogwoods' bare branches stretched over the sidewalks and street like tentacles, adorned with tiny white lights. The streetlights boasted wreaths with red ribbons, and the front windows and doors of the grand old inn were outlined in sparkling colored lights.

Harper sighed. "It's every bit as beautiful in the winter as it is in the summer."

Gavin pressed his lips to hers and said, "So are you." He guided her across the street toward the fountain.

"You know what? I love your cheesy lines." She pressed her body tighter against him, stealing his warmth.

The moon shone brightly against the winter-gray sky, illuminating the town square. A statue of a man and a woman dancing stood sentinel in the middle of the fountain. The woman was sculpted midtwirl, her dress lifting at the hem, and the man was gazing happily into her eyes. Someone had wrapped red and green scarves around their necks and put matching hats and mittens on them. Against the backdrop of brick and stone buildings with elaborate decorative elements carved into the stone, the square looked like it belonged in a Norman Rockwell painting.

"The statue reminds me of us. The day we met we were dancing at the festival, and now here we are again, all bundled up for winter, just like the statue."

"It's a sign." Gavin pressed a kiss to her temple and said, "We should come back every season and make new wishes."

"I'd love that. Can we see your parents each time? And stop in to see Nana?" Nana was the most beloved, energetic grandmother in Oak Falls, and Harper had loved meeting her and her family. "We probably have to come more than four times a year, though, because I promised your mom we'd come for all your family's birthdays. And Beckett will never forgive you if you skip next year's Turkey Trot 5K run." They'd feigned exhaustion and stayed in their room, being *very* thankful for each other—in honor of Thanksgiving, of course—while everyone else went to the festivities.

Gavin hugged her tight. "You have no idea how happy I am that you like my hometown and my friends."

"Oak Falls is charming. It's not gray and gloomy like the Cape can be in the winter, and your friends are down-to-earth and easygoing. What's not to like?"

"They're real, babe, just like you, only not nearly as sexy." He kissed her and said, "Or as delicious." He rubbed his nose over hers and added, "Let's make our wishes before you turn into an icicle."

Harper stepped into the fountain and began twirling around, her breath fogging in the air. She struck a dancing pose and said, "What do you think? Would I make a good statue?"

He laughed and helped her out of the fountain. "You'd make a good *anything*. Take your gloves off, babe. It's wish time."

They pulled off their gloves and shoved them in their pockets. Cold or not, Harper was excited to be there.

Gavin handed her a quarter, keeping one for himself. "Do you know what you're going to wish for?"

"Of course!" she said, even though she was still trying to figure it out.

Wishing for more felt gluttonous because she had so many things to be thankful for. Gavin was at the top of that list, followed by their families and friends, and her new endeavors. She'd submitted the movie script to Trey and had received an option agreement last month. The money from that would fund her theatrical endeavor. They'd agreed to table his partnership offer and visit it sometime down the line. Harper was midway through the third episode of her newest script for the theater. Tegan had called last week and said she definitely wanted to move forward and work together. Jana was also on board, and Jock had even offered to consult and help guide them as best as he was able while traveling. They'd already begun making plans. Harper was still enjoying writing for the newspaper and thought she might even continue in the spring. She already had more than she ever imagined. What else could she possibly want besides the obvious—forever with Gavin?

"Do you know what you're going to wish for?" she asked.

"Oh yeah," he said coyly. "I've been thinking about it for a long time."

"If it's that Pink Floyd album, Drake and I looked everywhere before your birthday, and we couldn't find it."

He shrugged one shoulder. "That's okay. I have a backup wish that's just as good. You sure you're ready?"

"Yes!" She fisted her hand around the quarter.

He gazed into her eyes with a serious expression. "My God you're beautiful."

Her stomach tumbled. She'd never tire of the intensity of his love. "You say that like you're just seeing me for the first time."

He slipped one hand to the nape of her neck, drawing her closer, and said, "That's because you get more beautiful every time I see you." He kissed her tenderly, warming her from the inside out. "I love you, sweetheart. Wish well."

She faced the fountain with the quarter in one hand. Gavin took her other hand and said, "Okay, beautiful, close your eyes."

GAVIN WATCHED HARPER close her eyes, just as he had the first time they'd cast their wishes into the fountain. She was smiling hard, her cheeks and the tip of her nose red with cold. He loved watching her throw her hopes out for the universe to hold dear, and he'd never tire of trying to catch those hopes and make all of her dreams come true.

He made a quick wish and tossed his quarter into the fountain at the same time she did.

She squealed when their quarters clinked against the concrete and turned gleefully toward him, bouncing on her toes in her fur-lined boots. "Did you make a wish?"

"I sure did."

"Do you think it'll come true again?"

"We'll know soon enough." He dropped to one knee, his heart thundering as he met her surprised eyes.

"*Gavin?* What are you doing?"

"Hoping my wish comes true." He took her hand and said, "Harper, my love, from the very moment we met, I knew my life would never be the same. We both took a chance that night, and I didn't think anything could beat those hours we spent together. But the past several months have shown me that not only do we belong together, we get *better*, *closer*, and fall deeper in love with every passing day. You are my best friend, my lover, and you are the magic in my dreams."

Tears streaked her cheek. "*Gavin…*" she said breathlessly.

"I love you, Harp, and I want to be the man who makes you laugh, who loves you so completely, you never feel second best. I will be there for you to lean on, and I will be your biggest fan, celebrating your successes and helping you if you lose your way."

He took the engagement ring he'd had made out of his pocket, holding it up for her to see it sparking in the moonlight. The pear-shaped pink diamond was set on a diamond-encrusted band, surrounded by tiny white diamonds.

Harper gasped, and her hand flew to her heart. She mouthed his name.

He rose to his feet, gazing deeply into her loving eyes as he said, "Harper, I want to spend forever being the man you deserve and creating the family we both want. Will you marry me, sweetheart?"

"Yes!" she said tearfully.

She threw her arms around his neck and he spun her around, sealing their promises with steamy kisses. He set her feet on the ground just as it started snowing, wetting their smiling faces as he slid the ring on her finger.

"Oh, Gavin! I love you," she said through her tears as they embraced. "I can't believe it. We're getting married!"

"Believe it, baby. I've waited a long time to do this."

"You have? How long?"

"If I had asked you the first time I wanted to, when we were right here in this exact spot last summer, you would have thought I was crazy. If I had done it the second time I had the urge, the first morning you woke up in my arms on my deck, you would have laughed in my face. I could say I've waited since last summer, but the truth is, I've been waiting for you my whole life."

Ready for more Bayside? Plus series news!

Not only are Tegan, Daphne, and Jock all going to get their own happily ever after, starting with BAYSIDE FANTASIES, but Justin Wicked, his siblings, and all of his cousins, are also getting their own love stories in The Wickeds: Dark Knights at Bayside, a series of standalone novels. You can read more about Beckett Wheeler in the Bradens & Montgomerys series. Beckett will also be finding his forever love soon, though he refuses to tell me in which series he'll settle down.

A chance encounter brings Tegan Fine and Jett Masters together, and their chemistry is off the charts—even if their ideals, and their lives, are worlds apart. But Tegan is embarking on the biggest endeavor of her life on Cape Cod, and Jett has no interest in slowing down, much less putting down roots in the place he fled to escape painful family memories. Becoming friends with benefits seems like the perfect solution. But when they are trapped by torrential weather, they work side by side in the aftermath, and every passionate kiss brings them closer together. Secrets are shared, trust is built, and no promises dare be made. As their lives move on, lines begin to blur, hearts get hurt, and their true selves come into focus. Tegan and Jett are left wondering if they make the perfect storm, or if they've reached the end of their bayside fantasy.

Fall in love with Justin Wicked

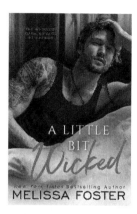

Set on the sandy shores of Cape Cod, the Wickeds feature fiercely protective heroes, strong heroines, and unbreakable family bonds. They're so fun, sexy, and emotional, you'll want to climb between the pages and join them!

What do a cocky biker and a businesswoman who has sworn off dating bad boys have in common? According to Chloe Mallery, not much. But Justin Wicked has had his eye on her for a long time, and he is sure the inescapable heat between them runs far deeper than just physical attraction. Could their difficult pasts be drawing them together, or will his protective nature be too much for her independent heart to accept? Find out, and fall in love, in *A Little Bit Wicked*, a fun, sexy standalone romance.

READY TO BINGE READ?

If you would like to read more about Harper's family, you can find Jana's and Brock's love stories in the Seaside Summers series, along with the love stories of many of their fun, sexy, and emotional friends who gather each summer at their Cape Cod cottages. They're funny, flawed, and so hot you'll be begging to enter their circle of friends.

Start reading *FREE with SEASIDE DREAMS!
(*Free in digital format at the time of this publication. Price subject to change without notice.)

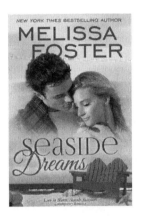

Bella Abbascia has returned to Seaside Cottages in Wellfleet, Massachusetts, as she does every summer. Only this year Bella has more on her mind than sunbathing and skinny-dipping with her girlfriends. She's quit her job, put her house on the market, and sworn off relationships while she builds a new life in her favorite place on earth. That is, until good-time Bella's prank takes a bad turn and a sinfully sexy police officer appears on the scene.

Single father and police officer Caden Grant left Boston with his fourteen-year-old son, Evan, after his partner was killed in the line of duty. He hopes to find a safer life in the small resort town of Wellfleet, and when he meets Bella during a night patrol, he realizes he's found the one thing he'd never allowed himself to hope for—or even realized he was missing.

After fourteen years of focusing solely on his son, Caden cannot resist the intense attraction he feels toward beautiful Bella, and Bella is powerless to fight the heat of their budding romance. But starting over proves more difficult than either of them imagined, and when Evan gets mixed up with the wrong kids, Caden's loyalty is put to the test. Will he give up everything to protect his son—even Bella?

Have you met Tru Blue & the Whiskeys?

If you think you know everything about bearded, tattooed men, get ready to be surprised—and to fall hard for Truman Gritt.

There's nothing Truman Gritt won't do to protect his family—including spending years in prison for a crime he didn't commit. When he's finally released, the life he knew is turned upside down by his mother's overdose, and Truman steps in to raise the children she's left behind. Truman's hard, he's secretive, and he's trying to save a brother who's even more broken than he is. He's never needed help in his life, and when beautiful Gemma Wright tries to step in, he's less than accepting. But Gemma has a way of slithering into people's lives, and eventually she pierces through his ironclad heart. When Truman's dark past collides with his future, his loyalties will be tested and he'll be faced with his toughest decision yet.

Fall in love with the fun, feisty Montgomerys!

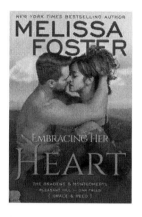

In EMBRACING HER HEART...

Leaving New York City and returning to her hometown to teach a screenplay writing class seems like just the break Grace Montgomery needs. Until her sisters wake her at four thirty in the morning to watch the hottest guys in town train wild horses and she realizes that escaping her sisters' drama-filled lives was a lot easier from hundreds of miles away. To make matters worse, she spots the one man she never wanted to see again—ruggedly handsome Reed Cross.

Reed was one of Michigan's leading historical preservation experts, but on the heels of catching his girlfriend in bed with his business partner, his uncle suffers a heart attack. Reed cuts all ties and returns home to Oak Falls to run his uncle's business. A chance encounter with Grace, his first love, brings back memories he's spent years trying to escape.

Grace is bound and determined not to fall under Reed's spell again—and Reed wants more than another taste of the woman he's never forgotten. When a midnight party brings them together, passion ignites and old wounds are reopened. Grace sets down the ground rules for the next three weeks. No touching, no kissing, and if she has it her way, no breathing, because every breath he takes steals her ability to think. But Reed has other ideas...

Love in Bloom FREE Reader Goodies

If you loved this story, be sure to check out the rest of the Love in Bloom big-family romance collection and download your free reader goodies, including publication schedules, series checklists, family trees, and more!
www.MelissaFoster.com/RG

Remember to check my sales and freebies page for periodic first-in-series free and other great offers!
www.MelissaFoster.com/LIBFree

More Books By Melissa Foster

LOVE IN BLOOM SERIES

SNOW SISTERS
Sisters in Love
Sisters in Bloom
Sisters in White

THE BRADENS at Weston
Lovers at Heart, Reimagined
Destined for Love
Friendship on Fire
Sea of Love
Bursting with Love
Hearts at Play

THE BRADENS at Trusty
Taken by Love
Fated for Love
Romancing My Love
Flirting with Love
Dreaming of Love
Crashing into Love

THE BRADENS at Peaceful Harbor
Healed by Love
Surrender My Love
River of Love
Crushing on Love
Whisper of Love
Thrill of Love

BAYSIDE SUMMERS

Bayside Desires
Bayside Passions
Bayside Heat
Bayside Escape
Bayside Romance
Bayside Fantasies

THE RYDERS

Seized by Love
Claimed by Love
Chased by Love
Rescued by Love
Swept Into Love

THE WHISKEYS: DARK KNIGHTS AT PEACEFUL HARBOR

Tru Blue
Truly, Madly, Whiskey
Driving Whiskey Wild
Wicked Whiskey Love
Mad About Moon
Taming My Whiskey

SUGAR LAKE

The Real Thing
Only for You
Love Like Ours
Finding My Girl

HARMONY POINTE

Call Her Mine
This is Love
She Loves Me

WILD BOYS AFTER DARK (Billionaires After Dark)
Logan
Heath
Jackson
Cooper

BAD BOYS AFTER DARK (Billionaires After Dark)
Mick
Dylan
Carson
Brett

<u>HARBORSIDE NIGHTS SERIES</u>
Includes characters from the Love in Bloom series
Catching Cassidy
Discovering Delilah
Tempting Tristan

More Books by Melissa
Chasing Amanda (mystery/suspense)
Come Back to Me (mystery/suspense)
Have No Shame (historical fiction/romance)
Love, Lies & Mystery (3-book bundle)
Megan's Way (literary fiction)
Traces of Kara (psychological thriller)
Where Petals Fall (suspense)

Acknowledgments

I had a blast writing about Gavin and Harper, and I hope you enjoyed their journey to forever love. I'm looking forward to writing about all of our Bayside friends, including those we've met in the coffeehouse. Many readers have asked about Rowan and his daughter, Joni, who were introduced in Bayside Escape. While they were not in this story, rest assured their happily ever after is coming.

Nothing excites me more than hearing from my fans and knowing you love my stories as much as I enjoy writing them. If you haven't joined my fan club, you can find it on Facebook. We have loads of fun, chat about books, and members get special sneak peeks of upcoming publications. facebook.com/groups/MelissaFosterFans

Heaps of gratitude go out to my meticulous and talented editorial team. Thank you, Kristen, Penina, Juliette, Marlene, Lynn, Justinn, and Elaini for all you do for me and for our readers. And as always, I am forever grateful to my family and to my own hunky hero, Les, who allows me the time to create our wonderful worlds.

Meet Melissa

www.MelissaFoster.com

Melissa Foster is a *New York Times* and *USA Today* bestselling and award-winning author. Her books have been recommended by *USA Today*'s book blog, *Hagerstown* magazine, *The Patriot*, and several other print venues. Melissa has painted and donated several murals to the Hospital for Sick Children in Washington, DC.

Visit Melissa on her website or chat with her on social media. Melissa enjoys discussing her books with book clubs and reader groups and welcomes an invitation to your event. Melissa's books are available through most online retailers in paperback, digital, and audio formats.

Made in the USA
Middletown, DE
18 September 2019